Amercian Short Stories: A Collection

O. Henry, M. Twain and others

American Short Stories: A Collection
Copyright 2015 © Jiahu Books
First Published in Great Britain in 2015 by Jiahu Books – part of
Richardson-Prachai Solutions Ltd, Egerton Gate, Milton Keynes, MK5
7HH
ISBN: 978-1-78435-130-4
A CIP catalogue record for this book is available from the British
Library.
Visit us at: jiahubooks.co.uk

O. Henry

THE GIFT OF THE MAGI

One dollar and eighty-seven cents. That was all. And sixty cents of it was in pennies. Pennies saved one and two at a time by bulldozing the grocer and the vegetable man and the butcher until one's cheeks burned with the silent imputation of parsimony that such close dealing implied. Three times Della counted it. One dollar and eighty-seven cents. And the next day would be Christmas.

There was clearly nothing left to do but flop down on the shabby little couch and howl. So Della did it. Which instigates the moral reflection that life is made up of sobs, sniffles, and smiles, with sniffles predominating.

While the mistress of the home is gradually subsiding from the first stage to the second, take a look at the home. A furnished flat at $8 per week. It did not exactly beggar description, but it certainly had that word on the look-out for the mendicancy squad.

In the vestibule below was a letter-box into which no letter would go, and an electric button from which no mortal finger could coax a ring. Also appertaining thereunto was a card bearing the name "Mr. James Dillingham Young."

The "Dillingham" had been flung to the breeze during a former period of prosperity when its possessor was being paid $30 per week. Now, when the income was shrunk to $20, the letters of "Dillingham" looked blurred, as though they were thinking seriously of contracting to a modest and unassuming D. But whenever Mr. James Dillingham Young came home and reached his flat above he was called "Jim" and greatly hugged by Mrs. James Dillingham Young, already introduced to you as Della. Which is all very good.

Della finished her cry and attended to her cheeks with the powder rag. She stood by the window and looked out dully at a grey cat walking a grey fence in a grey backyard. To-morrow would be Christmas Day, and she had only $1.87 with which to buy Jim a present. She had been saving every penny she could for months, with this result. Twenty dollars a week doesn't go far. Expenses had been greater than she had calculated. They always are. Only $1.87 to buy a present for Jim. Her Jim. Many a happy hour she had spent planning for something nice for him. Something fine and rare and sterling--something just a little bit near to being worthy of the honour of being owned by Jim.

There was a pier-glass between the windows of the room. Perhaps you have seen a pier-glass in an $8 Bat. A very thin and very agile person may, by observing his reflection in a rapid sequence of longitudinal strips, obtain a fairly accurate conception of his looks. Della, being slender, had mastered the art.

Suddenly she whirled from the window and stood before the glass. Her eyes were shining brilliantly, but her face had lost its colour within twenty seconds. Rapidly she pulled down her hair and let it fall to its full length.

Now, there were two possessions of the James Dillingham Youngs in which they both took a mighty pride. One was Jim's gold watch that had been his father's and his grandfather's. The other was Della's hair. Had the Queen of Sheba lived in the flat across the airshaft, Della would have let her hair hang out of the window some day to dry just to depreciate Her Majesty's jewels and gifts. Had King Solomon been the janitor, with all his treasures piled up in the basement, Jim would have pulled out his watch every time he passed, just to see him pluck at his beard from envy.

So now Della's beautiful hair fell about her, rippling and shining like a cascade of brown waters. It reached below her knee and made itself almost a garment for her. And then she did it up again nervously and quickly. Once she faltered for a minute and stood still while a tear or two splashed on the worn red carpet.

On went her old brown jacket; on went her old brown hat. With a whirl of skirts and with the brilliant sparkle still in her eyes, she cluttered out of the door and down the stairs to the street.

Where she stopped the sign read: "Mme Sofronie. Hair Goods of All Kinds." One Eight up Della ran, and collected herself, panting. Madame, large, too white, chilly, hardly looked the "Sofronie."

"Will you buy my hair?" asked Della.

"I buy hair," said Madame. "Take yer hat off and let's have a sight at the looks of it."

Down rippled the brown cascade.

"Twenty dollars," said Madame, lifting the mass with a practised hand.

"Give it to me quick" said Della.

Oh, and the next two hours tripped by on rosy wings. Forget the hashed metaphor. She was ransacking the stores for Jim's present.

She found it at last. It surely had been made for Jim and no one else. There was no other like it in any of the stores, and she had turned all of them inside out. It was a platinum fob chain simple and chaste in design, properly proclaiming its value by substance alone and not by meretricious ornamentation--as all good things should do. It was even worthy of The Watch. As soon as she saw it she knew that it must be Jim's. It was like him. Quietness and value--the description applied to both. Twenty-one dollars they took from her for it, and she hurried home with the 78 cents. With that chain on his watch Jim might be properly anxious about the time in any company. Grand as the watch was, he sometimes looked at it on the sly on account of the old leather strap that he used in place of a chain.

When Della reached home her intoxication gave way a little to prudence and reason. She got out her curling irons and lighted the gas and went to work repairing the ravages made by generosity added to love. Which is always a tremendous task dear friends--a mammoth task.

Within forty minutes her head was covered with tiny, close-lying curls that made her look wonderfully like a truant schoolboy. She looked at her reflection in the mirror long, carefully, and critically.

"If Jim doesn't kill me," she said to herself, "before he takes a second look at me, he'll say I look like a Coney Island chorus girl. But what could I do--oh! what could I do with a dollar and eighty-seven cents?"

At 7 o'clock the coffee was made and the frying-pan was on the back of the stove hot and ready to cook the chops.

Jim was never late. Della doubled the fob chain in her hand and sat on the corner of the table near the door that he always entered. Then she heard his step on the stair away down on the first flight, and she turned white for just a moment. She had a habit of saying little silent prayers about the simplest everyday things, and now she whispered: "Please, God, make him think I am still pretty."

The door opened and Jim stepped in and closed it. He looked thin and very serious. Poor fellow, he was only twenty-two--and to be burdened with a family! He needed a new overcoat and he was with out gloves.

Jim stepped inside the door, as immovable as a setter at the scent of quail. His eyes were fixed upon Della, and there was an expression in them that she could not read, and it terrified her. It was not anger, nor surprise, nor disapproval, nor horror, nor any of the sentiments that she had been prepared for. He simply stared at her fixedly with that peculiar expression on his face.

Della wriggled off the table and went for him.

"Jim, darling," she cried, "don't look at me that way. I had my hair cut off and sold it because I couldn't have lived through Christmas without giving you a present. It'll grow out again--you won't mind, will you? I just had to do it. My hair grows awfully fast. Say 'Merry Christmas!' Jim, and let's be happy. You don't know what a nice-what a beautiful, nice gift I've got for you."

"You've cut off your hair?" asked Jim, laboriously, as if he had not arrived at that patent fact yet, even after the hardest mental labour.

"Cut it off and sold it," said Della. "Don't you like me just as well, anyhow? I'm me without my hair, ain't I?"

Jim looked about the room curiously.

"You say your hair is gone?" he said, with an air almost of idiocy.

"You needn't look for it," said Della. "It's sold, I tell you--sold and gone, too. It's Christmas Eve, boy. Be good to me, for it went for you. Maybe the hairs of my head were numbered," she went on with a sudden serious sweetness, "but nobody could ever count my love for you. Shall I put the chops on, Jim?"

Out of his trance Jim seemed quickly to wake. He enfolded his Della. For ten seconds let us regard with discreet scrutiny some inconsequential object in the other direction. Eight dollars a week or a million a year-- what is the difference? A mathematician or a wit would give you the wrong answer. The magi brought valuable gifts, but that was not among them. I his dark assertion will be illuminated later on.

Jim drew a package from his overcoat pocket and threw it upon the table.

"Don't make any mistake, Dell," he said, "about me. I don't think there's anything in the way of a haircut or a shave or a shampoo that could make me like my girl any less. But if you'll unwrap that package you may see why you had me going a while at first."

White fingers and nimble tore at the string and paper. And then an ecstatic scream of joy; and then, alas! a quick feminine change to hysterical tears and wails, necessitating the immediate employment of all the comforting powers of the lord of the flat.

For there lay The Combs--the set of combs, side and back, that Della had worshipped for long in a Broadway window. Beautiful combs, pure tortoise-shell, with jewelled rims--just the shade to wear in the beautiful vanished hair. They were expensive combs, she knew, and her heart had simply craved and yearned over them without the least hope of possession. And now, they were hers, but the tresses that should have adorned the coveted adornments were gone.

But she hugged them to her bosom, and at length she was able to look up with dim eyes and a smile and say: "My hair grows so fast, Jim!"

And then Della leaped up like a little singed cat and cried, "Oh, oh!"

Jim had not yet seen his beautiful present. She held it out to him eagerly upon her open palm. The dull precious metal seemed to flash with a reflection of her bright and ardent spirit.

"Isn't it a dandy, Jim? I hunted all over town to find it. You'll have to look at the time a hundred times a day now. Give me your watch. I want to see how it looks on it."

Instead of obeying, Jim tumbled down on the couch and put his hands under the back of his head and smiled.

"Dell," said he, "let's put our Christmas presents away and keep 'em a while. They're too nice to use just at present. I sold the watch to get the money to buy your combs. And now suppose you put the chops on."

The magi, as you know, were wise men--wonderfully wise men-who brought gifts to the Babe in the manger. They invented the art of giving Christmas presents. Being wise, their gifts were no doubt wise ones, possibly bearing the privilege of exchange in case of duplication. And here I have lamely related to you the uneventful chronicle of two foolish children in a flat who most unwisely sacrificed for each other the greatest treasures of their house. But in a last word to the wise of these days let it be said that of all who give gifts these two were the wisest. Of all who give and receive gifts, such as they are wisest. Everywhere they are wisest. They are the magi.

THE SKYLIGHT ROOM

First Mrs. Parker would show you the double parlours. You would not dare to interrupt her description of their advantages and of the merits of the gentleman who had occupied them for eight years. Then you would manage to stammer forth the confession that you were neither a doctor nor a dentist. Mrs. Parker's manner of receiving the admission was such that you could never afterward entertain the same feeling toward your parents, who had neglected to train you up in one of the professions that fitted Mrs. Parker's parlours.

Next you ascended one flight of stairs and looked at the second- floor-back at $8. Convinced by her second-floor manner that it was worth the $12 that Mr. Toosenberry always paid for it until he left to take charge of his brother's orange plantation in Florida near Palm Beach, where Mrs. McIntyre always spent the winters that had the double front room with private bath, you managed to babble that you wanted something still cheaper.

If you survived Mrs. Parker's scorn, you were taken to look at Mr.

Skidder's large hall room on the third floor. Mr. Skidder's room was not vacant. He wrote plays and smoked cigarettes in it all day long. But every room-hunter was made to visit his room to admire the lambrequins. After each visit, Mr. Skidder, from the fright caused by possible eviction, would pay something on his rent.

Then--oh, then--if you still stood on one foot, with your hot hand clutching the three moist dollars in your pocket, and hoarsely proclaimed your hideous and culpable poverty, nevermore would Mrs. Parker be cicerone of yours. She would honk loudly the word" Clara," she would show you her back, and march downstairs. Then Clara, the coloured maid, would escort you up the carpeted ladder that served for the fourth flight, and show you the Skylight Room. It occupied 7x8 feet of floor space at the middle of the hall. On each side of it was a dark lumber closet or storeroom.

In it was an iron cot, a washstand and a chair. A shelf was the dresser. Its four bare walls seemed to close in upon you like the sides of a coffin. Your hand crept to your throat, you gasped, you looked up as from a well--and breathed once more. Through the glass of the little skylight you saw a square of blue infinity.

"Two dollars, suh," Clara would say in her half-contemptuous, half-Tuskegeenial tones.

One day Miss Leeson came hunting for a room. She carried a typewriter made to be lugged around by a much larger lady. She was a very little girl, with eyes and hair that had kept on growing after she had stopped and that always looked as if they were saying: "Goodness me ! Why didn't you keep up with us?"

Mrs. Parker showed her the double parlours. "In this closet," she said, "one could keep a skeleton or anaesthetic or coal "

"But I am neither a doctor nor a dentist," said Miss Leeson, with a shiver.

Mrs. Parker gave her the incredulous, pitying, sneering, icy stare that she kept for those who failed to qualify as doctors or dentists, and led the way to the second floor back.

"Eight dollars?" said Miss Leeson. "Dear me! I'm not Hetty if I do look green. I'm just a poor little working girl. Show me something higher and lower."

Mr. Skidder jumped and strewed the floor with cigarette stubs at the rap on his door.

"Excuse me, Mr. Skidder," said Mrs. Parker, with her demon's smile at his pale looks. "I didn't know you were in. I asked the lady to have a look at your lambrequins."

"They're too lovely for anything," said Miss Leeson, smiling in exactly the way the angels do.

After they had gone Mr. Skidder got very busy erasing the tall, black-haired heroine from his latest (unproduced) play and inserting a small, roguish one with heavy, bright hair and vivacious features.

"Anna Held'll jump at it," said Mr. Skidder to himself, putting his feet up against the lambrequins and disappearing in a cloud of smoke like an aerial cuttlefish.

Presently the tocsin call of "Clara!" sounded to the world the state of Miss Leeson's purse. A dark goblin seized her, mounted a Stygian stairway, thrust her into a vault with a glimmer of light in its top and muttered the menacing and cabalistic words "Two dollars!"

"I'll take it!" sighed Miss Leeson, sinking down upon the squeaky iron bed.

Every day Miss Leeson went out to work. At night she brought home papers with handwriting on them and made copies with her typewriter. Sometimes she had no work at night, and then she would sit on the steps of the high stoop with the other roomers. Miss Leeson was not intended for a sky-light room when the plans were drawn for her creation. She was gay-hearted and full of tender, whimsical fancies. Once she let Mr. Skidder read to her three acts of his great (unpublished) comedy, "It's No Kid; or, The Heir of the Subway."

There was rejoicing among the gentlemen roomers whenever Miss Leeson had time to sit on the steps for an hour or two. But Miss Longnecker, the tall blonde who taught in a public school and said, "Well, really!" to everything you said, sat on the top step and sniffed. And Miss Dorn, who shot at the moving ducks at Coney every Sunday and worked in a department store, sat on the bottom step and sniffed. Miss Leeson sat on the middle step and the men would quickly group around her.

Especially Mr. Skidder, who had cast her in his mind for the star part in a private, romantic (unspoken) drama in real life. And especially Mr. Hoover, who was forty-five, fat, flush and foolish. And especially very young Mr. Evans, who set up a hollow cough to induce her to ask him to leave off cigarettes. The men voted her "the funniest and jolliest ever," but the sniffs on the top step and the lower step were implacable.

* * * * * *

I pray you let the drama halt while Chorus stalks to the footlights and drops an epicedian tear upon the fatness of Mr. Hoover. Tune the pipes to

11

the tragedy of tallow, the bane of bulk, the calamity of corpulence. Tried out, Falstaff might have rendered more romance to the ton than would have Romeo's rickety ribs to the ounce. A lover may sigh, but he must not puff. To the train of Momus are the fat men remanded. In vain beats the faithfullest heart above a 52-inch belt. Avaunt, Hoover! Hoover, forty-five, flush and foolish, might carry off Helen herself; Hoover, forty-five, flush, foolish and fat is meat for perdition. There was never a chance for you, Hoover.

As Mrs. Parker's roomers sat thus one summer's evening, Miss Leeson looked up into the firmament and cried with her little gay laugh:

"Why, there's Billy Jackson! I can see him from down here, too."

All looked up--some at the windows of skyscrapers, some casting about for an airship, Jackson-guided.

"It's that star," explained Miss Leeson, pointing with a tiny finger. "Not the big one that twinkles--the steady blue one near it. I can see it every night through my skylight. I named it Billy Jackson."

"Well, really!" said Miss Longnecker. "I didn't know you were an astronomer, Miss Leeson."

"Oh, yes," said the small star gazer, "I know as much as any of them about the style of sleeves they're going to wear next fall in Mars."

"Well, really!" said Miss Longnecker. "The star you refer to is Gamma, of the constellation Cassiopeia. It is nearly of the second magnitude, and its meridian passage is--"

"Oh," said the very young Mr. Evans, "I think Billy Jackson is a much better name for it."

"Same here," said Mr. Hoover, loudly breathing defiance to Miss Longnecker. "I think Miss Leeson has just as much right to name stars as any of those old astrologers had."

"Well, really!" said Miss Longnecker.

"I wonder whether it's a shooting star," remarked Miss Dorn. "I hit nine ducks and a rabbit out of ten in the gallery at Coney Sunday."

"He doesn't show up very well from down here," said Miss Leeson. "You ought to see him from my room. You know you can see stars even in the daytime from the bottom of a well. At night my room is like the shaft of a coal mine, and it makes Billy Jackson look like the big diamond pin that Night fastens her kimono with."

There came a time after that when Miss Leeson brought no formidable papers home to copy. And when she went out in the morning, instead of working, she went from office to office and let her heart melt away in the drip of cold refusals transmitted through insolent office boys. This went on.

There came an evening when she wearily climbed Mrs. Parker's stoop at the hour when she always returned from her dinner at the restaurant. But she had had no dinner.

As she stepped into the hall Mr. Hoover met her and seized his chance. He asked her to marry him, and his fatness hovered above her like an avalanche. She dodged, and caught the balustrade. He tried for her hand, and she raised it and smote him weakly in the face. Step by step she went up, dragging herself by the railing. She passed Mr. Skidder's door as he was red-inking a stage direction for Myrtle Delorme (Miss Leeson) in his (unaccepted) comedy, to "pirouette across stage from L to the side of the Count." Up the carpeted ladder she crawled at last and opened the door of the skylight room.

She was too weak to light the lamp or to undress. She fell upon the iron cot, her fragile body scarcely hollowing the worn springs. And in that Erebus of the skylight room, she slowly raised her heavy eyelids, and smiled.

For Billy Jackson was shining down on her, calm and bright and constant through the skylight. There was no world about her. She was sunk in a pit of blackness, with but that small square of pallid light framing the star that she had so whimsically and oh, so ineffectually named. Miss Longnecker must be right; it was Gamma, of the constellation Cassiopeia, and not Billy Jackson. And yet she could not let it be Gamma.

As she lay on her back she tried twice to raise her arm. The third time she got two thin fingers to her lips and blew a kiss out of the black pit to Billy Jackson. Her arm fell back limply.

"Good-bye, Billy," she murmured faintly. "You're millions of miles away and you won't even twinkle once. But you kept where I could see you most of the time up there when there wasn't anything else but darkness to look at, didn't you? . . . Millions of miles. . . . Good-bye, Billy Jackson."

Clara, the coloured maid, found the door locked at 10 the next day, and they forced it open. Vinegar, and the slapping of wrists and burnt feathers proving of no avail, some one ran to 'phone for an ambulance.

In due time it backed up to the door with much gong-clanging, and the capable young medico, in his white linen coat, ready, active, confident, with his smooth face half debonair, half grim, danced up the steps.

"Ambulance call to 49," he said briefly. "What's the trouble?"

"Oh, yes, doctor," sniffed Mrs. Parker, as though her trouble that there should be trouble in the house was the greater. "I can't think what can be the matter with her. Nothing we could do would bring her to. It's a young woman, a Miss Elsie--yes, a Miss Elsie Leeson. Never before in my house--"

"What room?" cried the doctor in a terrible voice, to which Mrs. Parker was a stranger.

"The skylight room. It--

Evidently the ambulance doctor was familiar with the location of skylight rooms. He was gone up the stairs, four at a time. Mrs. Parker followed slowly, as her dignity demanded.

On the first landing she met him coming back bearing the astronomer in his arms. He stopped and let loose the practised scalpel of his tongue, not loudly. Gradually Mrs. Parker crumpled as a stiff garment that slips down from a nail. Ever afterward there remained crumples in her mind and body. Sometimes her curious roomers would ask her what the doctor said to her.

"Let that be," she would answer. "If I can get forgiveness for having heard it I will be satisfied."

The ambulance physician strode with his burden through the pack of hounds that follow the curiosity chase, and even they fell back along the sidewalk abashed, for his face was that of one who bears his own dead.

They noticed that he did not lay down upon the bed prepared for it in the ambulance the form that he carried, and all that he said was: "Drive like h**l, Wilson," to the driver.

That is all. Is it a story? In the next morning's paper I saw a little news item, and the last sentence of it may help you (as it helped me) to weld the incidents together.

It recounted the reception into Bellevue Hospital of a young woman who had been removed from No. 49 East -- street, suffering from debility induced by starvation. It concluded with these words:

"Dr. William Jackson, the ambulance physician who attended the case, says the patient will recover."

THE CACTUS

The most notable thing about Time is that it is so purely relative. A large amount of reminiscence is, by common consent, conceded to the drowning man; and it is not past belief that one may review an entire courtship while removing one's gloves.

That is what Trysdale was doing, standing by a table in his bachelor apartments. On the table stood a singular-looking green plant in a red earthen jar. The plant was one of the species of cacti, and was provided with long, tentacular leaves that perpetually swayed with the slightest breeze with a peculiar beckoning motion.

Trysdale's friend, the brother of the bride, stood at a sideboard complaining at being allowed to drink alone. Both men were in evening dress. White favors like stars upon their coats shone through the gloom of the apartment.

As he slowly unbuttoned his gloves, there passed through Trysdale's mind a swift, scarifying retrospect of the last few hours. It seemed that in his nostrils was still the scent of the flowers that had been banked in odorous masses about the church, and in his ears the lowpitched hum of a thousand well-bred voices, the rustle of crisp garments, and, most insistently recurring, the drawling words of the minister irrevocably binding her to another.

From this last hopeless point of view he still strove, as if it had become a habit of his mind, to reach some conjecture as to why and how he had lost her. Shaken rudely by the uncompromising fact, he had suddenly found himself confronted by a thing he had never before faced --his own innermost, unmitigated, arid unbedecked self. He saw all the garbs of pretence and egoism that he had worn now turn to rags of folly. He shuddered at the thought that to others, before now, the garments of his soul must have appeared sorry and threadbare. Vanity and conceit? These were the joints in his armor. And how free from either she had always been--But why--

As she had slowly moved up the aisle toward the altar he had felt an unworthy, sullen exultation that had served to support him. He had told himself that her paleness was from thoughts of another than the man to whom she was about to give herself. But even that poor consolation had been wrenched from him. For, when he saw that swift, limpid, upward look that she gave the man when he took her hand, he knew himself to be forgotten. Once that same look had been raised to him, and he had gauged its meaning. Indeed, his conceit had crumbled; its last prop was gone. Why had it ended thus? There had been no quarrel between them, nothing--

For the thousandth time he remarshalled in his mind the events of those last few days before the tide had so suddenly turned.

She had always insisted upon placing him upon a pedestal, and he had accepted her homage with royal grandeur. It had been a very sweet incense that she had burned before him; so modest (he told himself); so childlike and worshipful, and (he would once have sworn) so sincere. She had invested him with an almost supernatural number of high attributes and excellencies and talents, and he had absorbed the oblation as a desert drinks the rain that can coax from it no promise of blossom or fruit.

As Trysdale grimly wrenched apart the seam of his last glove, the crowning instance of his fatuous and tardily mourned egoism came vividly back to him. The scene was the night when he had asked her to come up on his pedestal with him and share his greatness. He could not, now, for the pain of it, allow his mind to dwell upon the memory of her convincing beauty that night--the careless wave of her hair, the tenderness and virginal charm of her looks and words. But they had been enough, and they had brought him to speak. During their conversation she had said:

"And Captain Carruthers tells me that you speak the Spanish language like a native. Why have you hidden this accomplishment from me? Is there anything you do not know?"

Now, Carruthers was an idiot. No doubt he (Trysdale) had been guilty (he sometimes did such things) of airing at the club some old, canting Castilian proverb dug from the hotchpotch at the back of dictionaries. Carruthers, who was one of his incontinent admirers, was the very man to have magnified this exhibition of doubtful erudition.

But, alas! the incense of her admiration had been so sweet and flattering. He allowed the imputation to pass without denial. Without protest, he allowed her to twine about his brow this spurious bay of Spanish scholarship. He let it grace his conquering head, and, among its soft convolutions, he did not feel the prick of the thorn that was to pierce him later.

How glad, how shy, how tremulous she was! How she fluttered like a snared bird when he laid his mightiness at her feet! He could have sworn, and he could swear now, that unmistakable consent was in her eyes, but, coyly, she would give him no direct answer. "I will send you my answer to-morrow," she said; and he, the indulgent, confident victor, smilingly granted the delay. The next day he waited, impatient, in his rooms for the word. At noon her groom came to the door and left the strange cactus in the red earthen jar. There was no note, no message, merely a tag upon the plant bearing a barbarous foreign or botanical name. He waited until night, but her answer did not come. His large pride and hurt vanity kept him from seeking her. Two evenings later they met at a dinner. Their greetings were conventional, but she looked at him, breathless, wondering, eager. He was courteous, adamant, waiting her explanation. With womanly swiftness she took her cue from his manner, and turned to snow and ice. Thus, and wider from this on, they had drifted apart. Where was his fault? Who had been to blame? Humbled now, he sought the answer amid the ruins of his self-conceit. If--

The voice of the other man in the room, querulously intruding upon his thoughts, aroused him.

"I say, Trysdale, what the deuce is the matter with you? You look unhappy as if you yourself had been married instead of having acted merely as an accomplice. Look at me, another accessory, come two thousand miles on a garlicky, cockroachy banana steamer all the way from South America to connive at the sacrifice--please to observe how lightly my guilt rests upon my shoulders. Only little sister I had, too, and now she's gone. Come now! take something to ease your conscience."

"I don't drink just now, thanks," said Trysdale.

"Your brandy," resumed the other, coming over and joining him, "is abominable. Run down to see me some time at Punta Redonda, and try some of our stuff that old Garcia smuggles in. It's worth the, trip. Hallo! here's an old acquaintance. Wherever did you rake up this cactus, Trysdale?"

"A present," said Trysdale, "from a friend. Know the species?"

"Very well. It's a tropical concern. See hundreds of 'em around Punta every day. Here's the name on this tag tied to it. Know any Spanish, Trysdale?"

"No," said Trysdale, with the bitter wraith of a smile--"Is it Spanish?"

"Yes. The natives imagine the leaves are reaching out and beckoning to you. They call it by this name--Ventomarme. Name means in English, 'Come and take me.'"

Jack London

TO BUILD A FIRE

Day had broken cold and grey, exceedingly cold and grey, when the man turned aside from the main Yukon trail and climbed the high earth-bank, where a dim and little-travelled trail led eastward through the fat spruce timberland. It was a steep bank, and he paused for breath at the top, excusing the act to himself by looking at his watch. It was nine o'clock. There was no sun nor hint of sun, though there was not a cloud in the sky. It was a clear day, and yet there seemed an intangible pall over the face of things, a subtle gloom that made the day dark, and that was due to the absence of sun. This fact did not worry the man. He was used to the lack of sun. It had been days since he had seen the sun, and he knew that a few more days must pass before that cheerful orb, due south, would just peep above the sky- line and dip immediately from view.

The man flung a look back along the way he had come. The Yukon lay a mile wide and hidden under three feet of ice. On top of this ice were as many feet of snow. It was all pure white, rolling in gentle undulations where the ice-jams of the freeze-up had formed. North and south, as far as his eye could see, it was unbroken white, save for a dark hair-line that curved and twisted from around the spruce- covered island to the south, and that curved and twisted away into the north, where it disappeared behind another spruce-covered island. This dark hair-line was the trail-- the main trail--that led south five hundred miles to the Chilcoot Pass, Dyea, and salt water; and that led north seventy miles to Dawson, and still on to the north a thousand miles to Nulato, and finally to St. Michael on Bering Sea, a thousand miles and half a thousand more.

But all this--the mysterious, far-reaching hairline trail, the absence of sun from the sky, the tremendous cold, and the strangeness and weirdness of it all--made no impression on the man. It was not because he was long used to it. He was a new-comer in the land, a chechaquo, and this was his first winter. The trouble with him was that he was without imagination. He was quick and alert in the things of life, but only in the things, and not in the significances. Fifty degrees below zero meant eighty odd degrees of frost. Such fact impressed him as being cold and uncomfortable, and that was all. It did not lead him to meditate upon his frailty as a creature of temperature, and upon man's frailty in general, able only to live within certain narrow limits of heat and cold; and from there on it did not lead him to the conjectural field of immortality and man's place in the universe. Fifty degrees below zero stood for a bite of frost that hurt and that must be guarded against by the use of mittens, ear-flaps, warm moccasins, and thick socks. Fifty degrees below zero was to him just precisely fifty degrees below zero. That there should be anything more to it than that was a thought that never entered his head.

As he turned to go on, he spat speculatively. There was a sharp, explosive crackle that startled him. He spat again. And again, in the air, before it could fall to the snow, the spittle crackled. He knew that at fifty below spittle crackled on the snow, but this spittle had crackled in the air. Undoubtedly it was colder than fifty below--how much colder he did not know. But the temperature did not matter. He was bound for the old claim on the left fork of Henderson Creek, where the boys were already. They had come over across the divide from the Indian Creek country, while he had come the roundabout way to take a look at the possibilities of getting out logs in the spring from the islands in the Yukon. He would be in to camp by six o'clock; a bit after dark, it was true, but the boys would be there, a fire would be going, and a hot supper would be ready. As for lunch, he pressed his hand against the protruding bundle under his jacket. It was also under his shirt, wrapped up in a handkerchief and lying against the naked skin. It was the only way to keep the biscuits from freezing. He smiled agreeably to himself as he thought of those biscuits, each cut open and sopped in bacon grease, and each enclosing a generous slice of fried bacon.

He plunged in among the big spruce trees. The trail was faint. A foot of snow had fallen since the last sled had passed over, and he was glad he was without a sled, travelling light. In fact, he carried nothing but the lunch wrapped in the handkerchief. He was surprised, however, at the cold. It certainly was cold, he concluded, as he rubbed his numbed nose and cheek-bones with his mittened hand. He was a warm-whiskered man, but the hair on his face did not protect the high cheek-bones and the eager nose that thrust itself aggressively into the frosty air.

At the man's heels trotted a dog, a big native husky, the proper wolf-dog, grey-coated and without any visible or temperamental difference from its brother, the wild wolf. The animal was depressed by the tremendous cold. It knew that it was no time for travelling. Its instinct told it a truer tale than was told to the man by the man's judgment. In reality, it was not merely colder than fifty below zero; it was colder than sixty below, than seventy below. It was seventy-five below zero. Since the freezing-point is thirty-two above zero, it meant that one hundred and seven degrees of frost obtained. The dog did not know anything about thermometers. Possibly in its brain there was no sharp consciousness of a condition of very cold such as was in the man's brain. But the brute had its instinct. It experienced a vague but menacing apprehension that subdued it and made it slink along at the man's heels, and that made it question eagerly every unwonted movement of the man as if expecting him to go into camp or to seek shelter somewhere and build a fire. The dog had learned fire, and it wanted fire, or else to burrow under the snow and cuddle its warmth away from the air.

The frozen moisture of its breathing had settled on its fur in a fine powder of frost, and especially were its jowls, muzzle, and eyelashes whitened by its crystalled breath. The man's red beard and moustache were likewise frosted, but more solidly, the deposit taking the form of ice and increasing with every warm, moist breath he exhaled. Also, the man was chewing tobacco, and the muzzle of ice held his lips so rigidly that he was unable to clear his chin when he expelled the juice. The result was that a crystal beard of the colour and solidity of amber was increasing its length on his chin. If he fell down it would shatter itself, like glass, into brittle fragments. But he did not mind the appendage. It was the penalty all tobacco- chewers paid in that country, and he had been out before in two cold snaps. They had not been so cold as this, he knew, but by the spirit thermometer at Sixty Mile he knew they had been registered at fifty below and at fifty-five.

He held on through the level stretch of woods for several miles, crossed a wide flat of nigger-heads, and dropped down a bank to the frozen bed of a small stream. This was Henderson Creek, and he knew he was ten miles from the forks. He looked at his watch. It was ten o'clock. He was making four miles an hour, and he calculated that he would arrive at the forks at half-past twelve. He decided to celebrate that event by eating his lunch there.

The dog dropped in again at his heels, with a tail drooping discouragement, as the man swung along the creek-bed. The furrow of the old sled-trail was plainly visible, but a dozen inches of snow covered the marks of the last runners. In a month no man had come up or down that silent creek. The man held steadily on. He was not much given to thinking, and just then particularly he had nothing to think about save that he would eat lunch at the forks and that at six o'clock he would be in camp with the boys. There was nobody to talk to and, had there been, speech would have been impossible because of the ice-muzzle on his mouth. So he continued monotonously to chew tobacco and to increase the length of his amber beard.

Once in a while the thought reiterated itself that it was very cold and that he had never experienced such cold. As he walked along he rubbed his cheek-bones and nose with the back of his mittened hand. He did this automatically, now and again changing hands. But rub as he would, the instant he stopped his cheek-bones went numb, and the following instant the end of his nose went numb. He was sure to frost his cheeks; he knew that, and experienced a pang of regret that he had not devised a nose-strap of the sort Bud wore in cold snaps. Such a strap passed across the cheeks, as well, and saved them. But it didn't matter much, after all. What were frosted cheeks? A bit painful, that was all; they were never serious.

Empty as the man's mind was of thoughts, he was keenly observant, and he noticed the changes in the creek, the curves and bends and timber-jams, and always he sharply noted where he placed his feet. Once, coming around a bend, he shied abruptly, like a startled horse, curved away from the place where he had been walking, and retreated several paces back along the trail. The creek he knew was frozen clear to the bottom--no creek could contain water in that arctic winter--but he knew also that there were springs that bubbled out from the hillsides and ran along under the snow and on top the ice of the creek. He knew that the coldest snaps never froze these springs, and he knew likewise their danger. They were traps. They hid pools of water under the snow that might be three inches deep, or three feet. Sometimes a skin of ice half an inch thick covered them, and in turn was covered by the snow. Sometimes there were alternate layers of water and ice-skin, so that when one broke through he kept on breaking through for a while, sometimes wetting himself to the waist.

That was why he had shied in such panic. He had felt the give under his feet and heard the crackle of a snow-hidden ice-skin. And to get his feet wet in such a temperature meant trouble and danger. At the very least it meant delay, for he would be forced to stop and build a fire, and under its protection to bare his feet while he dried his socks and moccasins. He stood and studied the creek-bed and its banks, and decided that the flow of water came from the right. He reflected awhile, rubbing his nose and cheeks, then skirted to the left, stepping gingerly and testing the footing for each step. Once clear of the danger, he took a fresh chew of tobacco and swung along at his four-mile gait.

In the course of the next two hours he came upon several similar traps. Usually the snow above the hidden pools had a sunken, candied appearance that advertised the danger. Once again, however, he had a close call; and once, suspecting danger, he compelled the dog to go on in front. The dog did not want to go. It hung back until the man shoved it forward, and then it went quickly across the white, unbroken surface. Suddenly it broke through, floundered to one side, and got away to firmer footing. It had wet its forefeet and legs, and almost immediately the water that clung to it turned to ice. It made quick efforts to lick the ice off its legs, then dropped down in the snow and began to bite out the ice that had formed between the toes. This was a matter of instinct. To permit the ice to remain would mean sore feet. It did not know this. It merely obeyed the mysterious prompting that arose from the deep crypts of its being. But the man knew, having achieved a judgment on the subject, and he removed the mitten from his right hand and helped tear out the ice- particles. He did not expose his fingers more than a minute, and was astonished at the swift numbness that smote them. It certainly was cold. He pulled on the mitten hastily, and beat the hand savagely across his chest.

At twelve o'clock the day was at its brightest. Yet the sun was too far south on its winter journey to clear the horizon. The bulge of the earth intervened between it and Henderson Creek, where the man walked under a clear sky at noon and cast no shadow. At half-past twelve, to the minute, he arrived at the forks of the creek. He was pleased at the speed he had made. If he kept it up, he would certainly be with the boys by six. He unbuttoned his jacket and shirt and drew forth his lunch. The action consumed no more than a quarter of a minute, yet in that brief moment the numbness laid hold of the exposed fingers. He did not put the mitten on, but, instead, struck the fingers a dozen sharp smashes against his leg. Then he sat down on a snow-covered log to eat. The sting that followed upon the striking of his fingers against his leg ceased so quickly that he was startled, he had had no chance to take a bite of biscuit. He struck the fingers repeatedly and returned them to the mitten, baring the other hand for the purpose of eating. He tried to take a mouthful, but the ice-muzzle prevented. He had forgotten to build a fire and thaw out. He chuckled at his foolishness, and as he chuckled he noted the numbness creeping into the exposed fingers. Also, he noted that the stinging which had first come to his toes when he sat down was already passing away. He wondered whether the toes were warm or numbed. He moved them inside the moccasins and decided that they were numbed.

He pulled the mitten on hurriedly and stood up. He was a bit frightened. He stamped up and down until the stinging returned into the feet. It certainly was cold, was his thought. That man from Sulphur Creek had spoken the truth when telling how cold it sometimes got in the country. And he had laughed at him at the time! That showed one must not be too sure of things. There was no mistake about it, it was cold. He strode up and down, stamping his feet and threshing his arms, until reassured by the returning warmth. Then he got out matches and proceeded to make a fire. From the undergrowth, where high water of the previous spring had lodged a supply of seasoned twigs, he got his firewood. Working carefully from a small beginning, he soon had a roaring fire, over which he thawed the ice from his face and in the protection of which he ate his biscuits. For the moment the cold of space was outwitted. The dog took satisfaction in the fire, stretching out close enough for warmth and far enough away to escape being singed.

When the man had finished, he filled his pipe and took his comfortable time over a smoke. Then he pulled on his mittens, settled the ear-flaps of his cap firmly about his ears, and took the creek trail up the left fork. The dog was disappointed and yearned back toward the fire. This man did not know cold. Possibly all the generations of his ancestry had been ignorant of cold, of real cold, of cold one hundred and seven degrees below freezing-point. But the dog knew; all its ancestry knew, and it had inherited the knowledge. And it knew that it was not good to walk abroad in such fearful cold. It was the time to lie snug in a hole in the snow and wait for a curtain of cloud to be drawn across the face of outer space whence this cold came. On the other hand, there was keen intimacy between the dog and the man. The one was the toil-slave of the other, and the only caresses it had ever received were the caresses of the whip-lash and of harsh and menacing throat-sounds that threatened the whip-lash. So the dog made no effort to communicate its apprehension to the man. It was not concerned in the welfare of the man; it was for its own sake that it yearned back toward the fire. But the man whistled, and spoke to it with the sound of whip-lashes, and the dog swung in at the man's heels and followed after.

The man took a chew of tobacco and proceeded to start a new amber beard. Also, his moist breath quickly powdered with white his moustache, eyebrows, and lashes. There did not seem to be so many springs on the left fork of the Henderson, and for half an hour the man saw no signs of any. And then it happened. At a place where there were no signs, where the soft, unbroken snow seemed to advertise solidity beneath, the man broke through. It was not deep. He wetted himself half-way to the knees before he floundered out to the firm crust.

He was angry, and cursed his luck aloud. He had hoped to get into camp with the boys at six o'clock, and this would delay him an hour, for he would have to build a fire and dry out his foot-gear. This was imperative at that low temperature--he knew that much; and he turned aside to the bank, which he climbed. On top, tangled in the underbrush about the trunks of several small spruce trees, was a high-water deposit of dry firewood--sticks and twigs principally, but also larger portions of seasoned branches and fine, dry, last-year's grasses. He threw down several large pieces on top of the snow. This served for a foundation and prevented the young flame from drowning itself in the snow it otherwise would melt. The flame he got by touching a match to a small shred of birch-bark that he took from his pocket. This burned even more readily than paper. Placing it on the foundation, he fed the young flame with wisps of dry grass and with the tiniest dry twigs.

He worked slowly and carefully, keenly aware of his danger. Gradually, as the flame grew stronger, he increased the size of the twigs with which he fed it. He squatted in the snow, pulling the twigs out from their entanglement in the brush and feeding directly to the flame. He knew there must be no failure. When it is seventy-five below zero, a man must not fail in his first attempt to build a fire--that is, if his feet are wet. If his feet are dry, and he fails, he can run along the trail for half a mile and restore his circulation. But the circulation of wet and freezing feet cannot be restored by running when it is seventy-five below. No matter how fast he runs, the wet feet will freeze the harder.

All this the man knew. The old-timer on Sulphur Creek had told him about it the previous fall, and now he was appreciating the advice. Already all sensation had gone out of his feet. To build the fire he had been forced to remove his mittens, and the fingers had quickly gone numb. His pace of four miles an hour had kept his heart pumping blood to the surface of his body and to all the extremities. But the instant he stopped, the action of the pump eased down. The cold of space smote the unprotected tip of the planet, and he, being on that unprotected tip, received the full force of the blow. The blood of his body recoiled before it. The blood was alive, like the dog, and like the dog it wanted to hide away and cover itself up from the fearful cold. So long as he walked four miles an hour, he pumped that blood, willy-nilly, to the surface; but now it ebbed away and sank down into the recesses of his body. The extremities were the first to feel its absence. His wet feet froze the faster, and his exposed fingers numbed the faster, though they had not yet begun to freeze. Nose and cheeks were already freezing, while the skin of all his body chilled as it lost its blood.

But he was safe. Toes and nose and cheeks would be only touched by the frost, for the fire was beginning to burn with strength. He was feeding it with twigs the size of his finger. In another minute he would be able to feed it with branches the size of his wrist, and then he could remove his wet foot-gear, and, while it dried, he could keep his naked feet warm by the fire, rubbing them at first, of course, with snow. The fire was a success. He was safe. He remembered the advice of the old-timer on Sulphur Creek, and smiled. The old-timer had been very serious in laying down the law that no man must travel alone in the Klondike after fifty below. Well, here he was; he had had the accident; he was alone; and he had saved himself. Those old-timers were rather womanish, some of them, he thought. All a man had to do was to keep his head, and he was all right. Any man who was a man could travel alone. But it was surprising, the rapidity with which his cheeks and nose were freezing. And he had not thought his fingers could go lifeless in so short a time. Lifeless they were, for he could scarcely make them move together to grip a twig, and they seemed remote from his body and from him. When he touched a twig, he had to look and see whether or not he had hold of it. The wires were pretty well down between him and his finger-ends.

All of which counted for little. There was the fire, snapping and crackling and promising life with every dancing flame. He started to untie his moccasins. They were coated with ice; the thick German socks were like sheaths of iron half-way to the knees; and the mocassin strings were like rods of steel all twisted and knotted as by some conflagration. For a moment he tugged with his numbed fingers, then, realizing the folly of it, he drew his sheath-knife.

But before he could cut the strings, it happened. It was his own fault or, rather, his mistake. He should not have built the fire under the spruce tree. He should have built it in the open. But it had been easier to pull the twigs from the brush and drop them directly on the fire. Now the tree under which he had done this carried a weight of snow on its boughs. No wind had blown for weeks, and each bough was fully freighted. Each time he had pulled a twig he had communicated a slight agitation to the tree-- an imperceptible agitation, so far as he was concerned, but an agitation sufficient to bring about the disaster. High up in the tree one bough capsized its load of snow. This fell on the boughs beneath, capsizing them. This process continued, spreading out and involving the whole tree. It grew like an avalanche, and it descended without warning upon the man and the fire, and the fire was blotted out! Where it had burned was a mantle of fresh and disordered snow.

The man was shocked. It was as though he had just heard his own sentence of death. For a moment he sat and stared at the spot where the fire had been. Then he grew very calm. Perhaps the old-timer on Sulphur Creek was right. If he had only had a trail-mate he would have been in no danger now. The trail-mate could have built the fire. Well, it was up to him to build the fire over again, and this second time there must be no failure. Even if he succeeded, he would most likely lose some toes. His feet must be badly frozen by now, and there would be some time before the second fire was ready.

Such were his thoughts, but he did not sit and think them. He was busy all the time they were passing through his mind, he made a new foundation for a fire, this time in the open; where no treacherous tree could blot it out. Next, he gathered dry grasses and tiny twigs from the high-water flotsam. He could not bring his fingers together to pull them out, but he was able to gather them by the handful. In this way he got many rotten twigs and bits of green moss that were undesirable, but it was the best he could do. He worked methodically, even collecting an armful of the larger branches to be used later when the fire gathered strength. And all the while the dog sat and watched him, a certain yearning wistfulness in its eyes, for it looked upon him as the fire-provider, and the fire was slow in coming.

When all was ready, the man reached in his pocket for a second piece of birch-bark. He knew the bark was there, and, though he could not feel it with his fingers, he could hear its crisp rustling as he fumbled for it. Try as he would, he could not clutch hold of it. And all the time, in his consciousness, was the knowledge that each instant his feet were freezing. This thought tended to put him in a panic, but he fought against it and kept calm. He pulled on his mittens with his teeth, and threshed his arms back and forth, beating his hands with all his might against his sides. He did this sitting down, and he stood up to do it; and all the while the dog sat in the snow, its wolf-brush of a tail curled around warmly over its forefeet, its sharp wolf-ears pricked forward intently as it watched the man. And the man as he beat and threshed with his arms and hands, felt a great surge of envy as he regarded the creature that was warm and secure in its natural covering.

After a time he was aware of the first far-away signals of sensation in his beaten fingers. The faint tingling grew stronger till it evolved into a stinging ache that was excruciating, but which the man hailed with satisfaction. He stripped the mitten from his right hand and fetched forth the birch-bark. The exposed fingers were quickly going numb again. Next he brought out his bunch of sulphur matches. But the tremendous cold had already driven the life out of his fingers. In his effort to separate one match from the others, the whole bunch fell in the snow. He tried to pick it out of the snow, but failed. The dead fingers could neither touch nor clutch. He was very careful. He drove the thought of his freezing feet; and nose, and cheeks, out of his mind, devoting his whole soul to the matches. He watched, using the sense of vision in place of that of touch, and when he saw his fingers on each side the bunch, he closed them--that is, he willed to close them, for the wires were drawn, and the fingers did not obey. He pulled the mitten on the right hand, and beat it fiercely against his knee. Then, with both mittened hands, he scooped the bunch of matches, along with much snow, into his lap. Yet he was no better off. After some manipulation he managed to get the bunch between the heels of his mittened hands. In this fashion he carried it to his mouth. The ice crackled and snapped when by a violent effort he opened his mouth. He drew the lower jaw in, curled the upper lip out of the way, and scraped the bunch with his upper teeth in order to separate a match. He succeeded in getting one, which he dropped on his lap. He was no better off. He could not pick it up. Then he devised a way. He picked it up in his teeth and scratched it on his leg. Twenty times he scratched before he succeeded in lighting it. As it flamed he held it with his teeth to the birch-bark. But the burning brimstone went up his nostrils and into his lungs, causing him to cough spasmodically. The match fell into the snow and went out.

The old-timer on Sulphur Creek was right, he thought in the moment of controlled despair that ensued: after fifty below, a man should travel with a partner. He beat his hands, but failed in exciting any sensation. Suddenly he bared both hands, removing the mittens with his teeth. He caught the whole bunch between the heels of his hands. His arm-muscles not being frozen enabled him to press the hand-heels tightly against the matches. Then he scratched the bunch along his leg. It flared into flame, seventy sulphur matches at once! There was no wind to blow them out. He kept his head to one side to escape the strangling fumes, and held the blazing bunch to the birch-bark. As he so held it, he became aware of sensation in his hand. His flesh was burning. He could smell it. Deep down below the surface he could feel it. The sensation developed into pain that grew acute. And still he endured it, holding the flame of the matches clumsily to the bark that would not light readily because his own burning hands were in the way, absorbing most of the flame.

At last, when he could endure no more, he jerked his hands apart. The blazing matches fell sizzling into the snow, but the birch-bark was alight. He began laying dry grasses and the tiniest twigs on the flame. He could not pick and choose, for he had to lift the fuel between the heels of his hands. Small pieces of rotten wood and green moss clung to the twigs, and he bit them off as well as he could with his teeth. He cherished the flame carefully and awkwardly. It meant life, and it must not perish. The withdrawal of blood from the surface of his body now made him begin to shiver, and he grew more awkward. A large piece of green moss fell squarely on the little fire. He tried to poke it out with his fingers, but his shivering frame made him poke too far, and he disrupted the nucleus of the little fire, the burning grasses and tiny twigs separating and scattering. He tried to poke them together again, but in spite of the tenseness of the effort, his shivering got away with him, and the twigs were hopelessly scattered. Each twig gushed a puff of smoke and went out. The fire-provider had failed. As he looked apathetically about him, his eyes chanced on the dog, sitting across the ruins of the fire from him, in the snow, making restless, hunching movements, slightly lifting one forefoot and then the other, shifting its weight back and forth on them with wistful eagerness.

The sight of the dog put a wild idea into his head. He remembered the tale of the man, caught in a blizzard, who killed a steer and crawled inside the carcass, and so was saved. He would kill the dog and bury his hands in the warm body until the numbness went out of them. Then he could build another fire. He spoke to the dog, calling it to him; but in his voice was a strange note of fear that frightened the animal, who had never known the man to speak in such way before. Something was the matter, and its suspicious nature sensed danger,--it knew not what danger but somewhere, somehow, in its brain arose an apprehension of the man. It flattened its ears down at the sound of the man's voice, and its restless, hunching movements and the liftings and shiftings of its forefeet became more pronounced but it would not come to the man. He got on his hands and knees and crawled toward the dog. This unusual posture again excited suspicion, and the animal sidled mincingly away.

The man sat up in the snow for a moment and struggled for calmness. Then he pulled on his mittens, by means of his teeth, and got upon his feet. He glanced down at first in order to assure himself that he was really standing up, for the absence of sensation in his feet left him unrelated to the earth. His erect position in itself started to drive the webs of suspicion from the dog's mind; and when he spoke peremptorily, with the sound of whip-lashes in his voice, the dog rendered its customary allegiance and came to him. As it came within reaching distance, the man lost his control. His arms flashed out to the dog, and he experienced genuine surprise when he discovered that his hands could not clutch, that there was neither bend nor feeling in the lingers. He had forgotten for the moment that they were frozen and that they were freezing more and more. All this happened quickly, and before the animal could get away, he encircled its body with his arms. He sat down in the snow, and in this fashion held the dog, while it snarled and whined and struggled.

But it was all he could do, hold its body encircled in his arms and sit there. He realized that he could not kill the dog. There was no way to do it. With his helpless hands he could neither draw nor hold his sheath-knife nor throttle the animal. He released it, and it plunged wildly away, with tail between its legs, and still snarling. It halted forty feet away and surveyed him curiously, with ears sharply pricked forward. The man looked down at his hands in order to locate them, and found them hanging on the ends of his arms. It struck him as curious that one should have to use his eyes in order to find out where his hands were. He began threshing his arms back and forth, beating the mittened hands against his sides. He did this for five minutes, violently, and his heart pumped enough blood up to the surface to put a stop to his shivering. But no sensation was aroused in the hands. He had an impression that they hung like weights on the ends of his arms, but when he tried to run the impression down, he could not find it.

A certain fear of death, dull and oppressive, came to him. This fear quickly became poignant as he realized that it was no longer a mere matter of freezing his fingers and toes, or of losing his hands and feet, but that it was a matter of life and death with the chances against him. This threw him into a panic, and he turned and ran up the creek-bed along the old, dim trail. The dog joined in behind and kept up with him. He ran blindly, without intention, in fear such as he had never known in his life. Slowly, as he ploughed and floundered through the snow, he began to see things again--the banks of the creek, the old timber-jams, the leafless aspens, and the sky. The running made him feel better. He did not shiver. Maybe, if he ran on, his feet would thaw out; and, anyway, if he ran far enough, he would reach camp and the boys. Without doubt he would lose some fingers and toes and some of his face; but the boys would take care of him, and save the rest of him when he got there. And at the same time there was another thought in his mind that said he would never get to the camp and the boys; that it was too many miles away, that the freezing had too great a start on him, and that he would soon be stiff and dead. This thought he kept in the background and refused to consider. Sometimes it pushed itself forward and demanded to be heard, but he thrust it back and strove to think of other things.

It struck him as curious that he could run at all on feet so frozen that he could not feel them when they struck the earth and took the weight of his body. He seemed to himself to skim along above the surface and to have no connection with the earth. Somewhere he had once seen a winged Mercury, and he wondered if Mercury felt as he felt when skimming over the earth.

His theory of running until he reached camp and the boys had one flaw in it: he lacked the endurance. Several times he stumbled, and finally he tottered, crumpled up, and fell. When he tried to rise, he failed. He must sit and rest, he decided, and next time he would merely walk and keep on going. As he sat and regained his breath, he noted that he was feeling quite warm and comfortable. He was not shivering, and it even seemed that a warm glow had come to his chest and trunk. And yet, when he touched his nose or cheeks, there was no sensation. Running would not thaw them out. Nor would it thaw out his hands and feet. Then the thought came to him that the frozen portions of his body must be extending. He tried to keep this thought down, to forget it, to think of something else; he was aware of the panicky feeling that it caused, and he was afraid of the panic. But the thought asserted itself, and persisted, until it produced a vision of his body totally frozen. This was too much, and he made another wild run along the trail. Once he slowed down to a walk, but the thought of the freezing extending itself made him run again.

And all the time the dog ran with him, at his heels. When he fell down a second time, it curled its tail over its forefeet and sat in front of him facing him curiously eager and intent. The warmth and security of the animal angered him, and he cursed it till it flattened down its ears appeasingly. This time the shivering came more quickly upon the man. He was losing in his battle with the frost. It was creeping into his body from all sides. The thought of it drove him on, but he ran no more than a hundred feet, when he staggered and pitched headlong. It was his last panic. When he had recovered his breath and control, he sat up and entertained in his mind the conception of meeting death with dignity. However, the conception did not come to him in such terms. His idea of it was that he had been making a fool of himself, running around like a chicken with its head cut off--such was the simile that occurred to him. Well, he was bound to freeze anyway, and he might as well take it decently. With this new-found peace of mind came the first glimmerings of drowsiness. A good idea, he thought, to sleep off to death. It was like taking an anaesthetic. Freezing was not so bad as people thought. There were lots worse ways to die.

He pictured the boys finding his body next day. Suddenly he found himself with them, coming along the trail and looking for himself. And, still with them, he came around a turn in the trail and found himself lying in the snow. He did not belong with himself any more, for even then he was out of himself, standing with the boys and looking at himself in the snow. It certainly was cold, was his thought. When he got back to the States he could tell the folks what real cold was. He drifted on from this to a vision of the old-timer on Sulphur Creek. He could see him quite clearly, warm and comfortable, and smoking a pipe.

"You were right, old hoss; you were right," the man mumbled to the old-timer of Sulphur Creek.

Then the man drowsed off into what seemed to him the most comfortable and satisfying sleep he had ever known. The dog sat facing him and waiting. The brief day drew to a close in a long, slow twilight. There were no signs of a fire to be made, and, besides, never in the dog's experience had it known a man to sit like that in the snow and make no fire. As the twilight drew on, its eager yearning for the fire mastered it, and with a great lifting and shifting of forefeet, it whined softly, then flattened its ears down in anticipation of being chidden by the man. But the man remained silent. Later, the dog whined loudly. And still later it crept close to the man and caught the scent of death. This made the animal bristle and back away. A little longer it delayed, howling under the stars that leaped and danced and shone brightly in the cold sky. Then it turned and trotted up the trail in the direction of the camp it knew, where were the other food-providers and fire-providers.

Ambrose Bierce

AN OCCURRENCE AT OWL CREEK BRIDGE

I

A man stood upon a railroad bridge in northern Alabama, looking down into the swift water twenty feet below. The man's hands were behind his back, the wrists bound with a cord. A rope closely encircled his neck. It was attached to a stout cross-timber above his head and the slack fell to the level of his knees. Some loose boards laid upon the sleepers supporting the metals of the railway supplied a footing for him and his executioners--two private soldiers of the Federal army, directed by a sergeant who in civil life may have been a deputy sheriff. At a short remove upon the same temporary platform was an officer in the uniform of his rank, armed. He was a captain. A sentinel at each end of the bridge stood with his rifle in the position known as "support," that is to say, vertical in front of the left shoulder, the hammer resting on the forearm thrown straight across the chest--a formal and unnatural position, enforcing an erect carriage of the body. It did not appear to be the duty of these two men to know what was occurring at the center of the bridge; they merely blockaded the two ends of the foot planking that traversed it. Beyond one of the sentinels nobody was in sight; the railroad ran straight away into a forest for a hundred yards, then, curving, was lost to view.

Doubtless there was an outpost farther along. The other bank of the stream was open ground--a gentle acclivity topped with a stockade of vertical tree trunks, loopholed for rifles, with a single embrasure through which protruded the muzzle of a brass cannon commanding the bridge. Midway of the slope between the bridge and fort were the spectators--a single company of infantry in line, at "parade rest," the butts of the rifles on the ground, the barrels inclining slightly backward against the right shoulder, the hands crossed upon the stock. A lieutenant stood at the right of the line, the point of his sword upon the ground, his left hand resting upon his right. Excepting the group of four at the center of the bridge, not a man moved. The company faced the bridge, staring stonily, motionless. The sentinels, facing the banks of the stream, might have been statues to adorn the bridge. The captain stood with folded arms, silent, observing the work of his subordinates, but making no sign. Death is a dignitary who when he comes announced is to be received with formal manifestations of respect, even by those most familiar with him. In the code of military etiquette silence and fixity are forms of deference.

The man who was engaged in being hanged was apparently about thirty-five years of age. He was a civilian, if one might judge from his habit, which was that of a planter. His features were good--a straight nose, firm mouth, broad forehead, from which his long, dark hair was combed straight back, falling behind his ears to the collar of his well-fitting frock coat. He wore a mustache and pointed beard, but no whiskers; his eyes were large and dark gray, and had a kindly expression which one would hardly have expected in one whose neck was in the hemp. Evidently this was no vulgar assassin. The liberal military code makes provision for hanging many kinds of persons, and gentlemen are not excluded.

The preparations being complete, the two private soldiers stepped aside and each drew away the plank upon which he had been standing. The sergeant turned to the captain, saluted and placed himself immediately behind that officer, who in turn moved apart one pace. These movements left the condemned man and the sergeant standing on the two ends of the same plank, which spanned three of the cross-ties of the bridge. The end upon which the civilian stood almost, but not quite, reached a fourth. This plank had been held in place by the weight of the captain; it was now held by that of the sergeant. At a signal from the former the latter would step aside, the plank would tilt and the condemned man go down between two ties. The arrangement commended itself to his judgment as simple and effective. His face had not been covered nor his eyes bandaged. He looked a moment at his "unsteadfast footing," then let his gaze wander to the swirling water of the stream racing madly beneath his feet. A piece of dancing driftwood caught his attention and his eyes followed it down the current. How slowly it appeared to move, What a sluggish stream!

He closed his eyes in order to fix his last thoughts upon his wife and children. The water, touched to gold by the early sun, the brooding mists under the banks at some distance down the stream, the fort, the soldiers, the piece of drift--all had distracted him. And now he became conscious of a new disturbance. Striking through the thought of his dear ones was a sound which he could neither ignore nor understand, a sharp, distinct, metallic percussion like the stroke of a blacksmith's hammer upon the anvil; it had the same ringing quality. He wondered what it was, and whether immeasurably distant or near by--it seemed both. Its recurrence was regular, but as slow as the tolling of a death knell. He awaited each stroke with impatience and--he knew not why--apprehension. The intervals of silence grew progressively longer, the delays became maddening. With their greater infrequency the sounds increased in strength and sharpness. They hurt his ear like the thrust of a knife; he feared he would shriek. What he heard was the ticking of his watch.

He unclosed his eyes and saw again the water below him. "If I could free my hands," he thought, "I might throw off the noose and spring into the stream. By diving I could evade the bullets and, swimming vigorously, reach the bank, take to the woods and get away home. My home, thank God, is as yet outside their lines; my wife and little ones are still beyond the invader's farthest advance."

As these thoughts, which have here to be set down in words, were flashed into the doomed man's brain rather than evolved from it the captain nodded to the sergeant. The sergeant stepped aside.

II

Peyton Farquhar was a well-to-do planter, of an old and highly respected Alabama family. Being a slave owner and like other slave owners a politician he was naturally an original secessionist and ardently devoted to the Southern cause. Circumstances of an imperious nature, which it is unnecessary to relate here, had prevented him from taking service with the gallant army that had fought the disastrous campaigns ending with the fall of Corinth, and he chafed under the inglorious restraint, longing for the release of his energies, the larger life of the soldier, the opportunity for distinction. That opportunity, he felt, would come, as it comes to all in war time. Meanwhile he did what he could. No service was too humble for him to perform in aid of the South, no adventure too perilous for him to undertake if consistent with the character of a civilian who was at heart a soldier, and who in good faith and without too much qualification assented to at least a part of the frankly villainous dictum that all is fair in love and war.

One evening while Farquhar and his wife were sitting on a rustic bench near the entrance to his grounds, a gray-clad soldier rode up to the gate and asked for a drink of water. Mrs. Farquhar was only too happy to serve him with her own white hands. While she was fetching the water her husband approached the dusty horseman and inquired eagerly for news from the front.

"The Yanks are repairing the railroads," said the man, "and are getting ready for another advance. They have reached the Owl Creek bridge, put it in order and built a stockade on the north bank. The commandant has issued an order, which is posted everywhere, declaring that any civilian caught interfering with the railroad, its bridges, tunnels or trains will be summarily hanged. I saw the order."

"How far is it to the Owl Creek bridge?" Farquhar asked.

"About thirty miles."

"Is there no force on this side the creek?"

"Only a picket post half a mile out, on the railroad, and a single sentinel at this end of the bridge."

"Suppose a man--a civilian and student of hanging--should elude the picket post and perhaps get the better of the sentinel," said Farquhar, smiling, "what could he accomplish?"

The soldier reflected. "I was there a month ago," he replied. "I observed that the flood of last winter had lodged a great quantity of driftwood against the wooden pier at this end of the bridge. It is now dry and would burn like tow."

The lady had now brought the water, which the soldier drank. He thanked her ceremoniously, bowed to her husband and rode away. An hour later, after nightfall, he repassed the plantation, going northward in the direction from which he had come. He was a Federal scout.

III

As Peyton Farquhar fell straight downward through the bridge he lost consciousness and was as one already dead. From this state he was awakened--ages later, it seemed to him--by the pain of a sharp pressure upon his throat, followed by a sense of suffocation. Keen, poignant agonies seemed to shoot from his neck downward through every fiber of his body and limbs. These pains appeared to flash along well-defined lines of ramification and to beat with an inconceivably rapid periodicity. They seemed like streams of pulsating fire heating him to an intolerable temperature. As to his head, he was conscious of nothing but a feeling of fulness--of congestion. These sensations were unaccompanied by thought. The intellectual part of his nature was already effaced; he had power only to feel, and feeling was torment. He was conscious of motion. Encompassed in a luminous cloud, of which he was now merely the fiery heart, without material substance, he swung through unthinkable arcs of oscillation, like a vast pendulum. Then all at once, with terrible suddenness, the light about him shot upward with the noise of a loud splash; a frightful roaring was in his ears, and all was cold and dark. The power of thought was restored; he knew that the rope had broken and he had fallen into the stream. There was no additional strangulation; the noose about his neck was already suffocating him and kept the water from his lungs. To die of hanging at the bottom of a river!--the idea seemed to him ludicrous. He opened his eyes in the darkness and saw above him a gleam of light, but how distant, how inaccessible! He was still sinking, for the light became fainter and fainter until it was a mere glimmer. Then it began to grow and brighten, and he knew that he was rising toward the surface--knew it with reluctance, for he was now very comfortable. "To be hanged and drowned," he thought? "that is not so bad; but I do not wish to be shot. No; I will not be shot; that is not fair."

He was not conscious of an effort, but a sharp pain in his wrist apprised him that he was trying to free his hands. He gave the struggle his attention, as an idler might observe the feat of a juggler, without interest in the outcome. What splendid effort!--what magnificent, what superhuman strength! Ah, that was a fine endeavor! Bravo! The cord fell away; his arms parted and floated upward, the hands dimly seen on each side in the growing light. He watched them with a new interest as first one and then the other pounced upon the noose at his neck. They tore it away and thrust it fiercely aside, its undulations resembling those of a water snake. "Put it back, put it back!" He thought he shouted these words to his hands, for the undoing of the noose had been succeeded by the direst pang that he had yet experienced. His neck ached horribly; his brain was on fire; his heart, which had been fluttering faintly, gave a great leap, trying to force itself out at his mouth. His whole body was racked and wrenched with an insupportable anguish! But his disobedient hands gave no heed to the command. They beat the water vigorously with quick, downward strokes, forcing him to the surface. He felt his head emerge; his eyes were blinded by the sunlight; his chest expanded convulsively, and with a supreme and crowning agony his lungs engulfed a great draught of air, which instantly he expelled in a shriek!

He was now in full possession of his physical senses. They were, indeed, preternaturally keen and alert. Something in the awful disturbance of his organic system had so exalted and refined them that they made record of things never before perceived. He felt the ripples upon his face and heard their separate sounds as they struck. He looked at the forest on the bank of the stream, saw the individual trees, the leaves and the veining of each leaf--saw the very insects upon them: the locusts, the brilliant-bodied flies, the grey spiders stretching their webs from twig to twig. He noted the prismatic colors in all the dewdrops upon a million blades of grass. The humming of the gnats that danced above the eddies of the stream, the beating of the dragon flies' wings, the strokes of the water-spiders' legs, like oars which had lifted their boat--all these made audible music. A fish slid along beneath his eyes and he heard the rush of its body parting the water.

He had come to the surface facing down the stream; in a moment the visible world seemed to wheel slowly round, himself the pivotal point, and he saw the bridge, the fort, the soldiers upon the bridge, the captain, the sergeant, the two privates, his executioners. They were in silhouette against the blue sky. They shouted and gesticulated, pointing at him. The captain had drawn his pistol, but did not fire; the others were unarmed. Their movements were grotesque and horrible, their forms gigantic.

Suddenly he heard a sharp report and something struck the water smartly within a few inches of his head, spattering his face with spray. He heard a second report, and saw one of the sentinels with his rifle at his shoulder, a light cloud of blue smoke rising from the muzzle. The man in the water saw the eye of the man on the bridge gazing into his own through the sights of the rifle. He observed that it was a grey eye and remembered having read that grey eyes were keenest, and that all famous marksmen had them. Nevertheless, this one had missed.

A counter-swirl had caught Farquhar and turned him half round; he was again looking into the forest on the bank opposite the fort. The sound of a clear, high voice in a monotonous singsong now rang out behind him and came across the water with a distinctness that pierced and subdued all other sounds, even the beating of the ripples in his ears. Although no soldier, he had frequented camps enough to know the dread significance of that deliberate, drawling, aspirated chant; the lieutenant on shore was taking a part in the morning's work. How coldly and pitilessly--with what an even, calm intonation, presaging, and enforcing tranquillity in the men--with what accurately measured intervals fell those cruel words: "Attention, company! . . Shoulder arms! . . . Ready! . . . Aim! . . . Fire!" Farquhar dived--dived as deeply as he could. The water roared in his ears like the voice of Niagara, yet he heard the dulled thunder of the volley and, rising again toward the surface, met shining bits of metal, singularly flattened, oscillating slowly downward. Some of them touched him on the face and hands, then fell away, continuing their descent. One lodged between his collar and neck; it was uncomfortably warm and he snatched it out.

As he rose to the surface, gasping for breath, he saw that he had been a long time under water; he was perceptibly farther down stream nearer to safety. The soldiers had almost finished reloading; the metal ramrods flashed all at once in the sunshine as they were drawn from the barrels, turned in the air, and thrust into their sockets. The two sentinels fired again, independently and ineffectually.

The hunted man saw all this over his shoulder; he was now swimming vigorously with the current. His brain was as energetic as his arms and legs; he thought with the rapidity of lightning.

The officer," he reasoned, "will not make that martinet's error a second time. It is as easy to dodge a volley as a single shot. He has probably already given the command to fire at will. God help me, I cannot dodge them all!"

An appalling splash within two yards of him was followed by a loud, rushing sound, diminuendo, which seemed to travel back through the air to the fort and died in an explosion which stirred the very river to its deeps!

A rising sheet of water curved over him, fell down upon him, blinded him, strangled him! The cannon had taken a hand in the game. As he shook his head free from the commotion of the smitten water he heard the deflected shot humming through the air ahead, and in an instant it was cracking and smashing the branches in the forest beyond.

"They will not do that again," he thought; "the next time they will use a charge of grape. I must keep my eye upon the gun; the smoke will apprise me--the report arrives too late; it lags behind the missile. That is a good gun."

Suddenly he felt himself whirled round and round--spinning like a top. The water, the banks, the forests, the now distant bridge, fort and men-- all were commingled and blurred. Objects were represented by their colors only; circular horizontal streaks of color--that was all he saw. He

37

had been caught in a vortex and was being whirled on with a velocity of advance and gyration that made him giddy and sick. In a few moments he was flung upon the gravel at the foot of the left bank of the stream-- the southern bank--and behind a projecting point which concealed him from his enemies. The sudden arrest of his motion, the abrasion of one of his hands on the gravel, restored him, and he wept with delight. He dug his fingers into the sand, threw it over himself in handfuls and audibly blessed it. It looked like diamonds, rubies, emeralds; he could think of nothing beautiful which it did not resemble. The trees upon the bank were giant garden plants; he noted a definite order in their arrangement, inhaled the fragrance of their blooms. A strange, roseate light shone through the spaces among their trunks and the wind made in their branches the music of olian harps. He had no wish to perfect his escape-- was content to remain in that enchanting spot until retaken.

A whiz and rattle of grapeshot among the branches high above his head roused him from his dream. The baffled cannoneer had fired him a random farewell. He sprang to his feet, rushed up the sloping bank, and plunged into the forest.

All that day he traveled, laying his course by the rounding sun. The forest seemed interminable; nowhere did he discover a break in it, not even a woodman's road. He had not known that he lived in so wild a region. There was something uncanny in the revelation.

By nightfall he was fatigued, footsore, famishing. The thought of his wife and children urged him on. At last he found a road which led him in what he knew to be the right direction. It was as wide and straight as a city street, yet it seemed untraveled. No fields bordered it, no dwelling anywhere. Not so much as the barking of a dog suggested human habitation. The black bodies of the trees formed a straight wall on both sides, terminating on the horizon in a point, like a diagram in a lesson in perspective. Overhead, as he looked up through this rift in the wood, shone great garden stars looking unfamiliar and grouped in strange constellations. He was sure they were arranged in some order which had a secret and malign significance. The wood on either side was full of singular noises, among which--once, twice, and again--he distinctly heard whispers in an unknown tongue.

His neck was in pain and lifting his hand to it found it horribly swollen. He knew that it had a circle of black where the rope had bruised it. His eyes felt congested; he could no longer close them. His tongue was swollen with thirst; he relieved its fever by thrusting it forward from between his teeth into the cold air. How softly the turf had carpeted the untraveled avenue--he could no longer feel the roadway beneath his feet! Doubtless, despite his suffering, he had fallen asleep while walking, for now he sees another scene--perhaps he has merely recovered from a delirium. He stands at the gate of his own home. All is as he left it, and all bright and beautiful in the morning sunshine. He must have traveled the entire night. As he pushes open the gate and passes up the wide white walk, he sees a flutter of female garments; his wife, looking fresh and cool and sweet, steps down from the veranda to meet him. At the bottom of the steps she stands waiting, with a smile of ineffable joy, an attitude of matchless grace and dignity. Ah, how beautiful she is! He springs forward with extended arms. As he is about to clasp her he feels a stunning blow upon the back of the neck; a blinding white light blazes all about him with a sound like the shock of a cannon--then all is darkness and silence!

Peyton Farquhar was dead; his body, with a broken neck, swung gently from side to side beneath the timbers of the Owl Creek bridge.

A Horseman in the Sky

I

One sunny afternoon in the autumn of the year 1861 a soldier lay in a clump of laurel by the side of a road in western Virginia. He lay at full length upon his stomach, his feet resting upon the toes, his head upon the left forearm. His extended right hand loosely grasped his rifle. But for the somewhat methodical disposition of his limbs and a slight rhythmic movement of the cartridge-box at the back of his belt he might have been thought to be dead. He was asleep at his post of duty. But if detected he would be dead shortly afterward, death being the just and legal penalty of his crime.

The clump of laurel in which the criminal lay was in the angle of a road which after ascending southward a steep acclivity to that point turned sharply to the west, running along the summit for perhaps one hundred yards. There it turned southward again and went zigzagging downward through the forest. At the salient of that second angle was a large flat rock, jutting out northward, overlooking the deep valley from which the road ascended. The rock capped a high cliff; a stone dropped from its outer edge would have fallen sheer downward one thousand feet to the tops of the pines. The angle where the soldier lay was on another spur of the same cliff. Had he been awake he would have commanded a view, not only of the short arm of the road and the jutting rock, but of the entire profile of the cliff below it. It might well have made him giddy to look.

The country was wooded everywhere except at the bottom of the valley to the northward, where there was a small natural meadow, through which flowed a stream scarcely visible from the valley's rim. This open ground looked hardly larger than an ordinary door-yard, but was really several acres in extent. Its green was more vivid than that of the inclosing forest. Away beyond it rose a line of giant cliffs similar to those upon which we are supposed to stand in our survey of the savage scene, and through which the road had somehow made its climb to the summit. The configuration of the valley, indeed, was such that from this point of observation it seemed entirely shut in, and one could but have wondered how the road which found a way out of it had found a way into it, and whence came and whither went the waters of the stream that parted the meadow more than a thousand feet below.

No country is so wild and difficult but men will make it a theatre of war; concealed in the forest at the bottom of that military rat-trap, in which half a hundred men in possession of the exits might have starved an army to submission, lay five regiments of Federal infantry. They had marched all the previous day and night and were resting. At nightfall they would take to the road again, climb to the place where their unfaithful sentinel now slept, and descending the other slope of the ridge fall upon a camp of the enemy at about midnight. Their hope was to surprise it, for the road led to the rear of it. In case of failure, their position would be perilous in the extreme; and fail they surely would should accident or vigilance apprise the enemy of the movement.

II

The sleeping sentinel in the clump of laurel was a young Virginian named Carter Druse. He was the son of wealthy parents, an only child, and had known such ease and cultivation and high living as wealth and taste were able to command in the mountain country of western Virginia. His home was but a few miles from where he now lay. One morning he had risen from the breakfast-table and said, quietly but gravely: "Father, a Union regiment has arrived at Grafton. I am going to join it."

The father lifted his leonine head, looked at the son a moment in silence, and replied: "Well, go, sir, and whatever may occur do what you conceive to be your duty. Virginia, to which you are a traitor, must get on without you. Should we both live to the end of the war, we will speak further of the matter. Your mother, as the physician has informed you, is in a most critical condition; at the best she cannot be with us longer than a few weeks, but that time is precious. It would be better not to disturb her."

So Carter Druse, bowing reverently to his father, who returned the salute with a stately courtesy that masked a breaking heart, left the home of his childhood to go soldiering. By conscience and courage, by deeds of devotion and daring, he soon commended himself to his fellows and his officers; and it was to these qualities and to some knowledge of the country that he owed his selection for his present perilous duty at the extreme outpost. Nevertheless, fatigue had been stronger than resolution and he had fallen asleep. What good or bad angel came in a dream to rouse him from his state of crime, who shall say? Without a movement, without a sound, in the profound silence and the languor of the late afternoon, some invisible messenger of fate touched with unsealing finger the eyes of his consciousness--whispered into the ear of his spirit the mysterious awakening word which no human lips ever have spoken, no human memory ever has recalled. He quietly raised his forehead from his arm and looked between the masking stems of the laurels, instinctively closing his right hand about the stock of his rifle.

His first feeling was a keen artistic delight. On a colossal pedestal, the cliff,--motionless at the extreme edge of the capping rock and sharply outlined against the sky,--was an equestrian statue of impressive dignity. The figure of the man sat the figure of the horse, straight and soldierly, but with the repose of a Grecian god carved in the marble which limits the suggestion of activity. The gray costume harmonized with its arial background; the metal of accoutrement and caparison was softened and subdued by the shadow; the animal's skin had no points of high light. A carbine strikingly foreshortened lay across the pommel of the saddle, kept in place by the right hand grasping it at the "grip"; the left hand, holding the bridle rein, was invisible. In silhouette against the sky the profile of the horse was cut with the sharpness of a cameo; it looked across the heights of air to the confronting cliffs beyond. The face of the rider, turned slightly away, showed only an outline of temple and beard; he was looking downward to the bottom of the valley. Magnified by its lift against the sky and by the soldier's testifying sense of the formidableness of a near enemy the group appeared of heroic, almost colossal, size.

For an instant Druse had a strange, half-defined feeling that he had slept to the end of the war and was looking upon a noble work of art reared upon that eminence to commemorate the deeds of an heroic past of which he had been an inglorious part. The feeling was dispelled by a slight movement of the group: the horse, without moving its feet, had drawn its body slightly backward from the verge; the man remained immobile as before. Broad awake and keenly alive to the significance of the situation, Druse now brought the butt of his rifle against his cheek by cautiously pushing the barrel forward through the bushes, cocked the piece, and glancing through the sights covered a vital spot of the horseman's breast. A touch upon the trigger and all would have been well with Carter Druse. At that instant the horseman turned his head and looked in the direction of his concealed foeman--seemed to look into his very face, into his eyes, into his brave, compassionate heart.

Is it then so terrible to kill an enemy in war--an enemy who has surprised a secret vital to the safety of one's self and comrades--an enemy more formidable for his knowledge than all his army for its numbers? Carter Druse grew pale; he shook in every limb, turned faint, and saw the statuesque group before him as black figures, rising, falling, moving unsteadily in arcs of circles in a fiery sky. His hand fell away from his weapon, his head slowly dropped until his face rested on the leaves in which he lay. This courageous gentleman and hardy soldier was near swooning from intensity of emotion.

It was not for long; in another moment his face was raised from earth, his hands resumed their places on the rifle, his forefinger sought the trigger; mind, heart, and eyes were clear, conscience and reason sound. He could not hope to capture that enemy; to alarm him would but send him dashing to his camp with his fatal news. The duty of the soldier was plain: the man must be shot dead from ambush--without warning, without a moment's spiritual preparation, with never so much as an unspoken prayer, he must be sent to his account. But no--there is a hope; he may have discovered nothing--perhaps he is but admiring the sublimity of the landscape. If permitted, he may turn and ride carelessly away in the direction whence he came. Surely it will be possible to judge at the instant of his withdrawing whether he knows. It may well be that his fixity of attention--Druse turned his head and looked through the deeps of air downward, as from the surface to the bottom of a translucent sea. He saw creeping across the green meadow a sinuous line of figures of men and horses--some foolish commander was permitting the soldiers of his escort to water their beasts in the open, in plain view from a dozen summits!

Druse withdrew his eyes from the valley and fixed them again upon the group of man and horse in the sky, and again it was through the sights of his rifle. But this time his aim was at the horse. In his memory, as if they were a divine mandate, rang the words of his father at their parting: "Whatever may occur, do what you conceive to be your duty." He was calm now. His teeth were firmly but not rigidly closed; his nerves were as tranquil as a sleeping babe's--not a tremor affected any muscle of his body; his breathing, until suspended in the act of taking aim, was regular and slow. Duty had conquered; the spirit had said to the body: "Peace, be still." He fired.

III

An officer of the Federal force, who in a spirit of adventure or in quest of knowledge had left the hidden *bivouac* in the valley, and with aimless feet had made his way to the lower edge of a small open space near the foot of the cliff, was considering what he had to gain by pushing his exploration further. At a distance of a quarter-mile before him, but apparently at a stone's throw, rose from its fringe of pines the gigantic face of rock, towering to so great a height above him that it made him giddy to look up to where its edge cut a sharp, rugged line against the sky. It presented a clean, vertical profile against a background of blue sky to a point half the way down, and of distant hills, hardly less blue, thence to the tops of the trees at its base. Lifting his eyes to the dizzy altitude of its summit the officer saw an astonishing sight--a man on horseback riding down into the valley through the air!

Straight upright sat the rider, in military fashion, with a firm seat in the saddle, a strong clutch upon the rein to hold his charger from too impetuous a plunge. From his bare head his long hair streamed upward, waving like a plume. His hands were concealed in the cloud of the horse's lifted mane. The animal's body was as level as if every hoof-stroke encountered the resistant earth. Its motions were those of a wild gallop, but even as the officer looked they ceased, with all the legs thrown sharply forward as in the act of alighting from a leap. But this was a flight!

Filled with amazement and terror by this apparition of a horseman in the sky--half believing himself the chosen scribe of some new Apocalypse, the officer was overcome by the intensity of his emotions; his legs failed him and he fell. Almost at the same instant he heard a crashing sound in the trees--a sound that died without an echo--and all was still.

The officer rose to his feet, trembling. The familiar sensation of an abraded shin recalled his dazed faculties. Pulling himself together he ran rapidly obliquely away from the cliff to a point distant from its foot; thereabout he expected to find his man; and thereabout he naturally failed. In the fleeting instant of his vision his imagination had been so wrought upon by the apparent grace and ease and intention of the marvelous performance that it did not occur to him that the line of march of arial cavalry is directly downward, and that he could find the objects of his search at the very foot of the cliff. A half-hour later he returned to camp.

This officer was a wise man; he knew better than to tell an incredible truth. He said nothing of what he had seen. But when the commander asked him if in his scout he had learned anything of advantage to the expedition he answered:

"Yes, sir; there is no road leading down into this valley from the southward."

The commander, knowing better, smiled.

IV

After firing his shot, Private Carter Druse reloaded his rifle and resumed his watch. Ten minutes had hardly passed when a Federal sergeant crept cautiously to him on hands and knees. Druse neither turned his head nor looked at him, but lay without motion or sign of recognition.

"Did you fire?" the sergeant whispered.

"Yes."

"At what?"

"A horse. It was standing on yonder rock--pretty far out. You see it is no longer there. It went over the cliff."

The man's face was white, but he showed no other sign of emotion. Having answered, he turned away his eyes and said no more. The sergeant did not understand.

"See here, Druse," he said, after a moment's silence, "it's no use making a mystery. I order you to report. Was there anybody on the horse?"

"Yes."

"Well?"

"My father."

The sergeant rose to his feet and walked away. "Good God!" he said.

Stephen Crane

A DARK BROWN DOG

A Child was standing on a street-corner. He leaned with one shoulder against a high board-fence and swayed the other to and fro, the while kicking carelessly at the gravel.

Sunshine beat upon the cobbles, and a lazy summer wind raised yellow dust which trailed in clouds down the avenue. Clattering trucks moved with indistinctness through it. The child stood dreamily gazing.

After a time, a little dark-brown dog came trotting with an intent air down the sidewalk. A short rope was dragging from his neck. Occasionally he trod upon the end of it and stumbled.

He stopped opposite the child, and the two regarded each other. The dog hesitated for a moment, but presently he made some little advances with his tail. The child put out his hand and called him. In an apologetic manner the dog came close, and the two had an interchange of friendly pattings and waggles. The dog became more enthusiastic with each moment of the interview, until with his gleeful caperings he threatened to overturn the child. Whereupon the child lifted his hand and struck the dog a blow upon the head.

This thing seemed to overpower and astonish the little dark-brown dog, and wounded him to the heart. He sank down in despair at the child's feet. When the blow was repeated, together with an admonition in childish sentences, he turned over upon his back, and held his paws in a peculiar manner. At the same time with his ears and his eyes he offered a small prayer to the child.

He looked so comical on his back, and holding his paws peculiarly, that the child was greatly amused and gave him little taps repeatedly, to keep him so. But the little dark-brown dog took this chastisement in the most serious way, and no doubt considered that he had committed some grave crime, for he wriggled contritely and showed his repentance in every way that was in his power. He pleaded with the child and petitioned him, and offered more prayers.

At last the child grew weary of this amusement and turned toward home. The dog was praying at the time. He lay on his back and turned his eyes upon the retreating form.

Presently he struggled to his feet and started after the child. The latter wandered in a perfunctory way toward his home, stopping at times to investigate various matters. During one of these pauses he discovered the little dark-brown dog who was following him with the air of a footpad.

The child beat his pursuer with a small stick he had found. The dog lay down and prayed until the child had finished, and resumed his journey. Then he scrambled erect and took up the pursuit again.

On the way to his home the child turned many times and beat the dog, proclaiming with childish gestures that he held him in contempt as an unimportant dog, with no value save for a moment. For being this quality of animal the dog apologized and eloquently expressed regret, but he continued stealthily to follow the child. His manner grew so very guilty that he slunk like an assassin.

When the child reached his door-step, the dog was industriously ambling a few yards in the rear. He became so agitated with shame when he again confronted the child that he forgot the dragging rope. He tripped upon it and fell forward.

The child sat down on the step and the two had another interview. During it the dog greatly exerted himself to please the child. He performed a few gambols with such abandon that the child suddenly saw him to be a valuable thing. He made a swift, avaricious charge and seized the rope.

He dragged his captive into a hall and up many long stairways in a dark tenement. The dog made willing efforts, but he could not hobble very skillfully up the stairs because he was very small and soft, and at last the pace of the engrossed child grew so energetic that the dog became panic-stricken. In his mind he was being dragged toward a grim unknown. His eyes grew wild with the terror of it. He began to wiggle his head frantically and to brace his legs.

The child redoubled his exertions. They had a battle on the stairs. The child was victorious because he was completely absorbed in his purpose, and because the dog was very small. He dragged his acquirement to the door of his home, and finally with triumph across the threshold.

No one was in. The child sat down on the floor and made overtures to the dog. These the dog instantly accepted. He beamed with affection upon his new friend. In a short time they were firm and abiding comrades.

When the child's family appeared, they made a great row. The dog was examined and commented upon and called names. Scorn was leveled at him from all eyes, so that he became much embarrassed and drooped like a scorched plant. But the child went sturdily to the center of the floor, and, at the top of his voice, championed the dog. It happened that he was roaring protestations, with his arms clasped about the dog's neck, when the father of the family came in from work.

The parent demanded to know what the blazes they were making the kid howl for. It was explained in many words that the infernal kid wanted to introduce a disreputable dog into the family.

A family council was held. On this depended the dog's fate, but he in no way heeded, being busily engaged in chewing the end of the child's dress.

The affair was quickly ended. The father of the family, it appears, was in a particularly savage temper that evening, and when he perceived that it would amaze and anger everybody if such a dog were allowed to remain, he decided that it should be so. The child, crying softly, took his friend off to a retired part of the room to hobnob with him, while the father quelled a fierce rebellion of his wife. So it came to pass that the dog was a member of the household.

He and the child were associated together at all times save when the child slept. The child became a guardian and a friend. If the large folk kicked the dog and threw things at him, the child made loud and violent objections. Once when the child had run, protesting loudly, with tears raining down his face and his arms outstretched, to protect his friend, he had been struck in the head with a very large saucepan from the hand of his father, enraged at some seeming lack of courtesy in the dog. Ever after, the family were careful how they threw things at the dog. Moreover, the latter grew very skilful in avoiding missiles and feet. In a small room containing a stove, a table, a bureau and some chairs, he would display strategic ability of a high order, dodging, feinting and scuttling about among the furniture. He could force three or four people armed with brooms, sticks and handfuls of coal, to use all their ingenuity to get in a blow. And even when they did, it was seldom that they could do him a serious injury or leave any imprint.

But when the child was present, these scenes did not occur. It came to be recognized that if the dog was molested, the child would burst into sobs, and as the child, when started, was very riotous and practically unquenchable, the dog had therein a safeguard.

However, the child could not always be near. At night, when he was asleep, his dark-brown friend would raise from some black corner a wild, wailful cry, a song of infinite lowliness and despair, that would go shuddering and sobbing among the buildings of the block and cause people to swear. At these times the singer would often be chased all over the kitchen and hit with a great variety of articles.

Sometimes, too, the child himself used to beat the dog, although it is not known that he ever had what could be truly called a just cause. The dog always accepted these thrashings with an air of admitted guilt. He was too much of a dog to try to look to be a martyr or to plot revenge. He received the blows with deep humility, and furthermore he forgave his friend the moment the child had finished, and was ready to caress the child's hand with his little red tongue.

When misfortune came upon the child, and his troubles overwhelmed him, he would often crawl under the table and lay his small distressed head on the dog's back. The dog was ever sympathetic. It is not to be supposed that at such times he took occasion to refer to the unjust beatings his friend, when provoked, had administered to him.

He did not achieve any notable degree of intimacy with the other members of the family. He had no confidence in them, and the fear that he would express at their casual approach often exasperated them exceedingly. They used to gain a certain satisfaction in underfeeding him, but finally his friend the child grew to watch the matter with some care, and when he forgot it, the dog was often successful in secret for himself.

So the dog prospered. He developed a large bark, which came wondrously from such a small rug of a dog. He ceased to howl persistently at night. Sometimes, indeed, in his sleep, he would utter little yells, as from pain, but that occurred, no doubt, when in his dreams he encountered huge flaming dogs who threatened him direfully.

His devotion to the child grew until it was a sublime thing. He wagged at his approach; he sank down in despair at his departure. He could detect the sound of the child's step among all the noises of the neighborhood. It was like a calling voice to him.

The scene of their companionship was a kingdom governed by this terrible potentate, the child; but neither criticism nor rebellion ever lived for an instant in the heart of the one subject. Down in the mystic, hidden fields of his little dog-soul bloomed flowers of love and fidelity and perfect faith.

The child was in the habit of going on many expeditions to observe strange things in the vicinity. On these occasions his friend usually jogged aimfully along behind. Perhaps, though, he went ahead. This necessitated his turning around every quarter-minute to make sure the child was coming. He was filled with a large idea of the importance of these journeys. He would carry himself with such an air! He was proud to be the retainer of so great a monarch.

One day, however, the father of the family got quite exceptionally drunk. He came home and held carnival with the cooking utensils, the furniture and his wife. He was in the midst of this recreation when the child, followed by the dark-brown dog, entered the room. They were returning from their voyages.

The child's practised eye instantly noted his father's state. He dived under the table, where experience had taught him was a rather safe place. The dog, lacking skill in such matters, was, of course, unaware of the true condition of affairs. He looked with interested eyes at his friend's sudden dive. He interpreted it to mean: Joyous gambol. He started to patter across the floor to join him. He was the picture of a little dark-brown dog en route to a friend.

The head of the family saw him at this moment. He gave a huge howl of joy, and knocked the dog down with a heavy coffee-pot. The dog, yelling in supreme astonishment and fear, writhed to his feet and ran for cover. The man kicked out with a ponderous foot. It caused the dog to swerve as if caught in a tide. A second blow of the coffee-pot laid him upon the floor.

Here the child, uttering loud cries, came valiantly forth like a knight. The father of the family paid no attention to these calls of the child, but advanced with glee upon the dog. Upon being knocked down twice in swift succession, the latter apparently gave up all hope of escape. He rolled over on his back and held his paws in a peculiar manner. At the same time with his eyes and his ears he offered up a small prayer.

But the father was in a mood for having fun, and it occurred to him that it would be a fine thing to throw the dog out of the window. So he reached down and grabbing the animal by a leg, lifted him, squirming, up. He swung him two or three times hilariously about his head, and then flung him with great accuracy through the window.

The soaring dog created a surprise in the block. A woman watering plants in an opposite window gave an involuntary shout and dropped a flower-pot. A man in another window leaned perilously out to watch the flight of the dog. A woman, who had been hanging out clothes in a yard, began to caper wildly. Her mouth was filled with clothes-pins, but her arms gave vent to a sort of exclamation. In appearance she was like a gagged prisoner. Children ran whooping.

The dark-brown body crashed in a heap on the roof of a shed five stories below. From thence it rolled to the pavement of an alleyway.

The child in the room far above burst into a long, dirgelike cry, and toddled hastily out of the room. It took him a long time to reach the alley, because his size compelled him to go downstairs backward, one step at a time, and holding with both hands to the step above.

When they came for him later, they found him seated by the body of his dark-brown friend.

Edgar Allan Poe

THE CASK OF AMONTILLADO

The thousand injuries of Fortunato I had borne as I best could, but when he ventured upon insult I vowed revenge. You, who so well know the nature of my soul, will not suppose, however, that gave utterance to a threat. At length I would be avenged; this was a point definitely, settled

--but the very definitiveness with which it was resolved precluded the idea of risk. I must not only punish but punish with impunity. A wrong is unredressed when retribution overtakes its redresser. It is equally unredressed when the avenger fails to make himself felt as such to him who has done the wrong.

It must be understood that neither by word nor deed had I given Fortunato cause to doubt my good will. I continued, as was my in to smile in his face, and he did not perceive that my to smile now was at the thought of his immolation.

He had a weak point --this Fortunato --although in other regards he was a man to be respected and even feared. He prided himself on his connoisseurship in wine. Few Italians have the true virtuoso spirit. For the most part their enthusiasm is adopted to suit the time and opportunity, to practise imposture upon the British and Austrian millionaires. In painting and gemmary, Fortunato, like his countrymen, was a quack, but in the matter of old wines he was sincere. In this respect I did not differ from him materially; --I was skilful in the Italian vintages myself, and bought largely whenever I could.

It was about dusk, one evening during the supreme madness of the carnival season, that I encountered my friend. He accosted me with excessive warmth, for he had been drinking much. The man wore motley. He had on a tight-fitting parti-striped dress, and his head was surmounted by the conical cap and bells. I was so pleased to see him that I thought I should never have done wringing his hand.

I said to him --"My dear Fortunato, you are luckily met. How remarkably well you are looking to-day. But I have received a pipe of what passes for Amontillado, and I have my doubts."

"How?" said he. "Amontillado, A pipe? Impossible! And in the middle of the carnival!"

"I have my doubts," I replied; "and I was silly enough to pay the full Amontillado price without consulting you in the matter. You were not to be found, and I was fearful of losing a bargain."

"Amontillado!"

"I have my doubts."

"Amontillado!"

"And I must satisfy them."

"Amontillado!"

"As you are engaged, I am on my way to Luchresi. If any one has a critical turn it is he. He will tell me --"

"Luchresi cannot tell Amontillado from Sherry."

"And yet some fools will have it that his taste is a match for your own.

"Come, let us go."

"Whither?"

"To your vaults."

"My friend, no; I will not impose upon your good nature. I perceive you have an engagement. Luchresi--"

"I have no engagement; --come."

"My friend, no. It is not the engagement, but the severe cold with which I perceive you are afflicted. The vaults are insufferably damp. They are encrusted with nitre."

"Let us go, nevertheless. The cold is merely nothing. Amontillado! You have been imposed upon. And as for Luchresi, he cannot distinguish Sherry from Amontillado."

Thus speaking, Fortunato possessed himself of my arm; and putting on a mask of black silk and drawing a roquelaire closely about my person, I suffered him to hurry me to my palazzo.

There were no attendants at home; they had absconded to make merry in honour of the time. I had told them that I should not return until the morning, and had given them explicit orders not to stir from the house. These orders were sufficient, I well knew, to insure their immediate disappearance, one and all, as soon as my back was turned.

I took from their sconces two flambeaux, and giving one to Fortunato, bowed him through several suites of rooms to the archway that led into the vaults. I passed down a long and winding staircase, requesting him to be cautious as he followed. We came at length to the foot of the descent, and stood together upon the damp ground of the catacombs of the Montresors.

The gait of my friend was unsteady, and the bells upon his cap jingled as he strode.

"The pipe," he said.

"It is farther on," said I; "but observe the white web-work which gleams from these cavern walls."

He turned towards me, and looked into my eyes with two filmy orbs that distilled the rheum of intoxication.

"Nitre?" he asked, at length.

"Nitre," I replied. "How long have you had that cough?"

"Ugh! ugh! ugh! --ugh! ugh! ugh! --ugh! ugh! ugh! --ugh! ugh! ugh! --ugh! ugh! ugh!"

My poor friend found it impossible to reply for many minutes.

"It is nothing," he said, at last.

"Come," I said, with decision, "we will go back; your health is precious. You are rich, respected, admired, beloved; you are happy, as once I was. You are a man to be missed. For me it is no matter. We will go back; you will be ill, and I cannot be responsible. Besides, there is Luchresi --"

"Enough," he said; "the cough's a mere nothing; it will not kill me. I shall not die of a cough."

"True --true," I replied; "and, indeed, I had no intention of alarming you unnecessarily --but you should use all proper caution. A draught of this Medoc will defend us from the damps."

Here I knocked off the neck of a bottle which I drew from a long row of its fellows that lay upon the mould.

"Drink," I said, presenting him the wine. He raised it to his lips with a leer. He paused and nodded to me familiarly, while his bells jingled.

"I drink," he said, "to the buried that repose around us."

"And I to your long life."

He again took my arm, and we proceeded.

"These vaults," he said, "are extensive."

"The Montresors," I replied, "were a great and numerous family."

"I forget your arms."

"A huge human foot d'or, in a field azure; the foot crushes a serpent rampant whose fangs are imbedded in the heel."

"And the motto?"

"Nemo me impune lacessit."

"Good!" he said.

The wine sparkled in his eyes and the bells jingled. My own fancy grew warm with the Medoc. We had passed through long walls of piled skeletons, with casks and puncheons intermingling, into the inmost recesses of the catacombs. I paused again, and this time I made bold to seize Fortunato by an arm above the elbow.

"The nitre!" I said; "see, it increases. It hangs like moss upon the vaults. We are below the river's bed. The drops of moisture trickle among the bones. Come, we will go back ere it is too late. Your cough --"

"It is nothing," he said; "let us go on. But first, another draught of the Medoc."

I broke and reached him a flagon of De Grave. He emptied it at a breath. His eyes flashed with a fierce light. He laughed and threw the bottle upwards with a gesticulation I did not understand.

I looked at him in surprise. He repeated the movement --a grotesque one.

"You do not comprehend?" he said.

"Not I," I replied.

"Then you are not of the brotherhood."

"How?"

"You are not of the masons."

"Yes, yes," I said; "yes, yes."

"You? Impossible! A mason?"

"A mason," I replied.

"A sign," he said, "a sign."

"It is this," I answered, producing from beneath the folds of my roquelaire a trowel.

"You jest," he exclaimed, recoiling a few paces. "But let us proceed to the Amontillado."

"Be it so," I said, replacing the tool beneath the cloak and again offering him my arm. He leaned upon it heavily. We continued our route in search of the Amontillado. We passed through a range of low arches, descended, passed on, and descending again, arrived at a deep crypt, in which the foulness of the air caused our flambeaux rather to glow than flame.

At the most remote end of the crypt there appeared another less spacious. Its walls had been lined with human remains, piled to the vault overhead, in the fashion of the great catacombs of Paris. Three sides of this interior crypt were still ornamented in this manner. From the fourth side the bones had been thrown down, and lay promiscuously upon the earth, forming at one point a mound of some size. Within the wall thus exposed by the displacing of the bones, we perceived a still interior crypt or recess, in depth about four feet, in width three, in height six or seven. It seemed to have been constructed for no especial use within itself, but formed merely the interval between two of the colossal supports of the roof of the catacombs, and was backed by one of their circumscribing walls of solid granite.

It was in vain that Fortunato, uplifting his dull torch, endeavoured to pry into the depth of the recess. Its termination the feeble light did not enable us to see.

"Proceed," I said; "herein is the Amontillado. As for Luchresi --"

"He is an ignoramus," interrupted my friend, as he stepped unsteadily forward, while I followed immediately at his heels. In niche, and finding an instant he had reached the extremity of the niche, and finding his progress arrested by the rock, stood stupidly bewildered. A moment more and I had fettered him to the granite. In its surface were two iron staples, distant from each other about two feet, horizontally. From one of these depended a short chain, from the other a padlock. Throwing the links about his waist, it was but the work of a few seconds to secure it. He was too much astounded to resist. Withdrawing the key I stepped back from the recess.

"Pass your hand," I said, "over the wall; you cannot help feeling the nitre. Indeed, it is very damp. Once more let me implore you to return. No? Then I must positively leave you. But I must first render you all the little attentions in my power."

"The Amontillado!" ejaculated my friend, not yet recovered from his astonishment.

"True," I replied; "the Amontillado."

As I said these words I busied myself among the pile of bones of which I have before spoken. Throwing them aside, I soon uncovered a quantity of building stone and mortar. With these materials and with the aid of my trowel, I began vigorously to wall up the entrance of the niche.

I had scarcely laid the first tier of the masonry when I discovered that the intoxication of Fortunato had in a great measure worn off. The earliest indication I had of this was a low moaning cry from the depth of the recess. It was not the cry of a drunken man. There was then a long and obstinate silence. I laid the second tier, and the third, and the fourth; and then I heard the furious vibrations of the chain. The noise lasted for several minutes, during which, that I might hearken to it with the more satisfaction, I ceased my labours and sat down upon the bones. When at last the clanking subsided, I resumed the trowel, and finished without interruption the fifth, the sixth, and the seventh tier. The wall was now nearly upon a level with my breast. I again paused, and holding the flambeaux over the mason-work, threw a few feeble rays upon the figure within.

A succession of loud and shrill screams, bursting suddenly from the throat of the chained form, seemed to thrust me violently back. For a brief moment I hesitated, I trembled. Unsheathing my rapier, I began to grope with it about the recess; but the thought of an instant reassured me. I placed my hand upon the solid fabric of the catacombs, and felt satisfied. I reapproached the wall; I replied to the yells of him who clamoured. I re-echoed, I aided, I surpassed them in volume and in strength. I did this, and the clamourer grew still.

It was now midnight, and my task was drawing to a close. I had completed the eighth, the ninth and the tenth tier. I had finished a portion of the last and the eleventh; there remained but a single stone to be fitted and plastered in. I struggled with its weight; I placed it partially

54

in its destined position. But now there came from out the niche a low laugh that erected the hairs upon my head. It was succeeded by a sad voice, which I had difficulty in recognizing as that of the noble Fortunato. The voice said--

"Ha! ha! ha! --he! he! he! --a very good joke, indeed --an excellent jest. We will have many a rich laugh about it at the palazzo --he! he! he! --over our wine --he! he! he!"

"The Amontillado!" I said.

"He! he! he! --he! he! he! --yes, the Amontillado. But is it not getting late? Will not they be awaiting us at the palazzo, the Lady Fortunato and the rest? Let us be gone."

"Yes," I said, "let us be gone."

"For the love of God, Montresor!"

"Yes," I said, "for the love of God!"

But to these words I hearkened in vain for a reply. I grew impatient. I called aloud --

"Fortunato!"

No answer. I called again --

"Fortunato!"

No answer still. I thrust a torch through the remaining aperture and let it fall within. There came forth in return only a jingling of the bells. My heart grew sick; it was the dampness of the catacombs that made it so. I hastened to make an end of my labour. I forced the last stone into its position; I plastered it up. Against the new masonry I re-erected the old rampart of bones. For the half of a century no mortal has disturbed them. In pace requiescat!

THE TELL-TALE HEART

True!-nervous--very, very dreadfully nervous i had been and am! but why will you say that I am mad? The disease had sharpened my senses--not destroyed--not dulled them. Above all was the sense of hearing acute. I heard all things in the heaven and in the earth. I heard many things in hell. How, then, am I mad? Hearken! and observe how healthily--how calmly I can tell you the whole story.

It is impossible to tell how first the idea entered my brain; but once conceived, it haunted me day and night. Object there was none. Passion there was none. I loved the old man. He had never wronged me. He had never given me insult. For his gold I had no desire. I think it was his eye! Yes, it was this! One of his eyes resembled that of a vulture--a pale blue eye, with a film over it. Whenever it fell upon me, my blood ran cold; and so by degrees--very gradually--I made up my mind to take the life of the old man, and thus rid myself of the eye forever.

Now this is the point. You fancy me mad. Madmen know nothing. But you should have seen me. You should have seen how wisely I proceeded--with what caution--with what foresight--with what dissimulation I went to work!

I was never kinder to the old man than during the whole week before I killed him. And every night, about midnight, I turned the latch of his door and opened it--oh, so gently! And then, when I had made an opening sufficient for my head, I put in a dark lantern, all closed, closed, so that no light shone out, and then I thrust in my head. Oh, you would have laughed to see how cunningly I thrust it in! I moved it slowly--very, very slowly, so that I might not disturb the old man's sleep. It took me an hour to place my whole head within the opening so far that I could see him as he lay upon his bed. Ha!--would a madman have been so wise as this? And then, when my head was well in the room, I undid the lantern cautiously--oh, so cautiously--cautiously (for the hinges creaked)--I undid it just so much that a single thin ray fell upon the vulture eye. And this I did for seven long nights--every night just at midnight--but I found the eye always closed; and so it was impossible to do the work; for it was not the old man who vexed me, but his Evil Eye. And every morning, when the day broke, I went boldly into the chamber, and spoke courageously to him, calling him by name in a hearty tone, and inquiring how he had passed the night. So you see he would have been a very profound old man, indeed, to suspect that every night, just at twelve, I looked in upon him while he slept.

Upon the eighth night I was more than usually cautious in opening the door. A watch's minute hand moves more quickly than did mine. Never before that night had I felt the extent of my own powers--of my sagacity. I could scarcely contain my feelings of triumph. To think that there I was, opening the door, little by little, and he not even to dream of my secret deeds or thoughts. I fairly chuckled at the idea; and perhaps he heard me; for he moved on the bed suddenly, as if startled. Now you may think that I drew back--but no. His room was as black as pitch with the thick darkness (for the shutters were close fastened, through fear of robbers), and so I knew that he could not see the opening of the door, and I kept pushing it on steadily, steadily.

I had my head in, and was about to open the lantern, when my thumb slipped upon the tin fastening, and the old man sprang up in bed, crying out: "Who's there?"

I kept quite still and said nothing. For a whole hour I did not move a muscle, and in the meantime I did not hear him lie down. He was still sitting up in the bed listening;--just as I have done, night after night, hearkening to the death watches in the wall.

Presently I heard a slight groan, and I knew it was the groan of mortal terror. It was not a groan of pain or grief--oh no!--it was the low stifled sound that arises from the bottom of the soul when overcharged with awe. I knew the sound well. Many a night, just at midnight, when all the world slept, it has welled up from my own bosom, deepening, with its dreadful echo, the terrors that distracted me. I say I knew it well. I knew what the old man felt, and pitied him, although I chuckled at heart. I knew that he had been lying awake ever since the first slight noise, when he had turned in the bed. His fears had been ever since growing upon him. He had been trying to fancy them causeless, but could not. He had been saying to himself: "It is nothing but the wind in the chimney--it is only a mouse crossing the floor," or "it is merely a cricket which has made a single chirp." Yes, he had been trying to comfort himself with these suppositions; but he had found all in vain. All in vain; because Death, in approaching him. had stalked with his black shadow before him, and enveloped the victim. And it was the mournful influence of the unperceived shadow that caused him to feel--although he neither saw nor heard--to feel the presence of my head within the room.

When I had waited a long time, very patiently, without hearing him lie down, I resolved to open a little--a very, very little crevice in the lantern. So I opened it--you cannot imagine how stealthily, stealthily--until, at length, a single dim ray, like the thread of the spider, shot from out the crevice and full upon the vulture eye.

It was open--wide, wide open--and I grew furious as I gazed upon it. I saw it with perfect distinctness--all a dull blue, with a hideous veil over it that chilled the very marrow in my bones; but I could see nothing else of the old man's face or person: for I had directed the ray, as if by instinct, precisely upon the damned spot.

And now--have I not told you that what you mistake for madness is but over-acuteness of the senses?--now, I say, there came to my ears a low, dull, quick sound, such as a watch makes when enveloped in cotton. I knew that sound well too. It was the beating of the old man's heart. It increased my fury, as the beating of a drum stimulates the soldier into courage.

But even yet I refrained and kept still. I scarcely breathed. I held the lantern motionless. I tried how steadily I could maintain the ray upon the eye. Meantime the hellish tattoo of the heart increased. It grew quicker and quicker' and louder and louder every instant. The old man's terror must have been extreme! It grew louder, I say, louder every moment!--do you mark me well? I have told you that I am nervous: so I am. And now at the dead hour of night, amid the dreadful silence of that old house, so strange a noise as this excited me to uncontrollable terror. Yet, for some minutes longer I refrained and stood still. But the beating grew louder, louder! I thought the heart must burst. And now a new anxiety seized me--the sound would be heard by a neighbor! The old man's hour had come! With a loud yell, I threw open the lantern and leaped into the room. He shrieked once--once only. In an instant I dragged him to the floor, and pulled the heavy bed over him. I then smiled gaily, to find the deed so far done. But, for many minutes, the heart beat on with a muffled sound. This, however, did not vex me; it would not be heard through the wall. At length it ceased. The old man was dead. I removed the bed and examined the corpse. Yes, he was stone, stone dead. I placed my hand upon the heart and held it there many minutes. There was no pulsation. He was stone dead. His eye would trouble me no more.

If still you think me mad, you will think so no longer when I describe the wise precautions I took for the concealment of the body. The night waned, and I worked hastily, but in silence. First of all I dismembered the corpse. I cut off the head and the arms and the legs.

I then took up three planks from the flooring of the chamber, and deposited all between the scantlings. I then replaced the boards so cleverly, so cunningly, that no human eye--not even his--could have detected anything wrong. There was nothing to wash out--no stain of any kind--no blood-spot whatever. I had been too wary for that. A tub had caught all--ha! ha!

When I had made an end of these labors, it was four o'clock--still dark as midnight. As the bell sounded the hour, there came a knocking at the street door. I went down to open it with a light heart--for what had I now to fear? There entered three men, who introduced themselves, with perfect suavity, as officers of the police. A shriek had been heard by a neighbor during the night: suspicion of foul play had been aroused; information had been lodged at the police office, and they (the officers) had been deputed to search the premises.

I smiled--for what had I to fear? I bade the gentlemen welcome. The shriek, I said, was my own in a dream. The old man, I mentioned, was absent in the country. I took my visitors all over the house. I bade them search--search well. I led them, at length, to his chamber. I showed them his treasures, secure, undisturbed. In the enthusiasm of my confidence, I brought chairs into the room, and desired them here to rest from their fatigues, while I myself, in the wild audacity of my perfect triumph, placed my own seat upon the very spot beneath which reposed the corpse of the victim.

The officers were satisfied. My manner had convinced them. I was singularly at ease. They sat, and while I answered cheerily, they chatted familiar things. But, ere long, I felt myself getting pale and wished them gone. My head ached, and I fancied a ringing in my ears: but still they sat and still chatted. The ringing became more distinct:--it continued and became more distinct: I talked more freely to get rid of the feeling: but it continued and gained definiteness--until, at length, I found that the noise was not within my ears.

No doubt I now grew very pale,--but I talked more fluently, and with a heightened voice. Yet the sound increased--and what could I do? It was a low, dull, quick sound--much such a sound as a watch makes when enveloped in cotton. I gasped for breath--and yet the officers heard it not. I talked more quickly--more vehemently; but the noise steadily increased. Why would they not be gone? I paced the floor to and fro with heavy strides, as if excited to fury by the observation of the men--but the noise steadily increased. Oh, God; what could I do? I foamed--I raved--I swore! I swung the chair upon which I had been sitting, and grated it upon the boards, but the noise arose over all and continually increased. It grew louder--louder --louder! And still the men chatted pleasantly, and smiled. Was it possible they heard not? Almighty God!--no, no! They heard!--they suspected--they knew!--they were making a mockery of my horror!--this I thought, and this I think. But anything was better than this agony! Anything was more tolerable than this derision! I could bear those hypocritical smiles no longer! I felt that I must scream or die!--and now-- again!--hark! louder! louder! louder!

"Villains!" I shrieked, "dissemble no more! I admit the deed!--tear up the planks!--here, here!--it is the beating of his hideous heart!"

THE PURLOINED LETTER

At Paris, just after dark one gusty evening in the autumn of 18 -- , I was enjoying the twofold luxury of meditation and a meerschaum, in company with my friend, C. Auguste Dupin, in his little back library, or book-closet, au troisime, No. 33 Rue Dunt, Faubourg St. Germain. For one hour at least we had maintained a profound silence; while each, to any casual observer, might have seemed intently and exclusively occupied with the curling eddies of smoke that oppressed the atmosphere of the chamber. For myself, however, I was mentally discussing certain topics which had formed matter for conversation between us at an earlier period of the evening; I mean the affair of the Rue Morgue, and the mystery attending the murder of Marie Rogt. I looked upon it, therefore, as something of a coincidence, when the door of our apartment was thrown open and admitted our old acquaintance, Monsieur G -- -- , the Prefect of the Parisian police.

We gave him a hearty welcome; for there was nearly half as much of the entertaining as of the contemptible about the man, and we had not seen him for several years. We had been sitting in the dark, and Dupin now arose for the purpose of lighting a lamp, but sat down again, without doing so, upon G.'s saying that he had called to consult us, or rather to ask the opinion of my friend, about some official business which had occasioned a great deal of trouble.

"If it is any point requiring reflection," observed Dupin, as he forbore to enkindle the wick, "we shall examine it to better purpose in the dark."

"That is another one of your odd notions," said the Prefect, who had the fashion of calling everything "odd" that was beyond his comprehension, and thus lived amid an absolute legion of "oddities."

"Very true," said Dupin, as he supplied his visitor with a pipe, and rolled toward him a comfortable chair.

"And what is the difficulty now?" I asked. "Nothing more in the assassination way I hope?"

"Oh, no; nothing of that nature. The fact is, the business is very simple indeed, and I make no doubt that we can manage it sufficiently well ourselves; but then I thought Dupin would like to hear the details of it because it is so excessively odd."

"Simple and odd," said Dupin.

"Why, yes; and not exactly that either. The fact is, we have all been a good deal puzzled because the affair is so simple, and yet baffles us altogether."

"Perhaps it is the very simplicity of the thing which puts you at fault," said my friend.

"What nonsense you do talk!" replied the Prefect, laughing heartily.

"Perhaps the mystery is a little too plain," said Dupin.

"Oh, good heavens! who ever heard of such an idea?"

"A little too self-evident."

"Ha! ha! ha! -- ha! ha! ha! -- ho! ho! ho!" roared our visitor, profoundly amused, "oh, Dupin, you will be the death of me yet!"

"And what, after all, is the matter on hand?" I asked.

"Why, I will tell you," replied the Prefect, as he gave a long, steady, and contemplative puff, and settled himself in his chair. "I will tell you in a few words; but, before I begin, let me caution you that this is an affair demanding the greatest secrecy, and that I should most probably lose the position I now hold, were it known that I confided it to any one."

"Proceed," said I.

"Or not," said Dupin.

"Well, then; I have received personal information, from a very high quarter, that a certain document of the last importance has been purloined from the royal apartments. The individual who purloined it is known; that beyond a doubt; he was seen to take it. It is known, also, that it still remains in his possession."

"How is this known?" asked Dupin.

"It is clearly inferred," replied the Prefect, "from the nature of the document, and from the non-appearance of certain results which would at once arise from its passing out of the robber's possession -- that is to say, from his employing it as he must design in the end to employ it."

"Be a little more explicit," I said.

"Well, I may venture so far as to say that the paper gives its holder a certain power in a certain quarter where such power is immensely valuable." The Prefect was fond of the cant of diplomacy.

"Still I do not quite understand," said Dupin.

"No? Well; the disclosure of the document to a third person, who shall be nameless, would bring in question the honor of a personage of most exalted station; and this fact gives the holder of the document an ascendancy over the illustrious personage whose honor and peace are so jeopardized."

"But this ascendancy," I interposed, "would depend upon the robber's knowledge of the loser's knowledge of the robber. Who would dare -- "

"The thief," said G., "is the Minister D -- -- , who dares all things, those unbecoming as well as those becoming a man. The method of the theft was not less ingenious than bold. The document in question -- a letter, to be frank -- had been received by the personage robbed while alone in the royal boudoir. During its perusal she was suddenly interrupted by the entrance of the other exalted personage from whom especially it was her wish to conceal it. After a hurried and vain endeavor to thrust it in a drawer, she was forced to place it, open it was, upon a table. The address, however, was uppermost, and, the contents thus unexposed, the letter escaped notice. At this juncture enters the Minister D -- -- . His lynx eye immediately perceives the paper, recognizes the handwriting of the address, observes the confusion of the personage addressed, and fathoms her secret. After some business transactions, hurried through in his ordinary manner, he produces a letter somewhat similar to the one in question, opens it, pretends to read it, and then places it in close juxtaposition to the other. Again he converses, for some fifteen minutes, upon the public affairs. At length, in taking leave, he takes also from the table the letter to which he has no claim. Its rightful owner saw, but, of course, dared not call attention to the act, in the presence of the third person who stood at her elbow. The minister decamped; leaving his own letter -- of no importance -- upon the table."

"Here, then," said Dupin to me, "you have precisely what you demand to make the ascendancy complete -- the robber's knowledge of the loser's knowledge of the robber."

"Yes," replied the Prefect; "and the power thus attained has, for some months past, been wielded, for political purposes, to a very dangerous extent. The personage robbed is more thoroughly convinced, every day, of the necessity of reclaiming her letter. But this, of course, cannot be done openly. In fine, driven to despair, she has committed the matter to me."

"Than whom," said Dupin, amid a perfect whirlwind of smoke, "no more sagacious agent could, I suppose, be desired, or even imagined."

"You flatter me," replied the Prefect; "but it is possible that some such opinion may have been entertained."

"It is clear," said I, "as you observe, that the letter is still in the possession of the minister; since it is this possession, and not any employment of the letter, which bestows the power. With the employment the power departs."

"True," said G.; "and upon this conviction I proceeded. My first care was to make a thorough search of the minister's hotel; and here my chief embarrassment lay in the necessity of searching without his knowledge. Beyond all things, I have been warned of the danger which would result from giving him reason to suspect our design."

"But," said I, "you are quite au fait in these investigations. The parisian police have done this thing often before."

"Oh, yes; and for this reason I did not despair. The habits of the minister gave me, too, a great advantage. He is frequently absent from home all night. His servants are no means numerous. They sleep at a distance from their master's apartment, and, being chiefly Neapolitans, are readily made drunk. I have keys, as you know, with which I can open any chamber or cabinet in Paris. For three months a night has not passed, during the greater part of which I have not been engaged, personally, in ransacking the D -- -- Hotel. My honor is interested, and, to mention a great secret, the reward is enormous. So I did not abandon the search until I had become fully satisfied that the thief is a more astute man than myself. I fancy that I have investigated every nook and corner of the premises in which it is possible that the paper can be concealed."

"But is it not possible," I suggested, "that although the letter may be in possession of the minister, as it unquestionably is, he may have concealed it elsewhere than upon his own premises?"

"This is barely possible," said Dupin. "The present peculiar condition of affairs at court, and especially of those intrigues in which D -- -- is known to be involved, would render the instant availability of the document -- its susceptibility of being produced at a moments notice -- a point of nearly equal importance with its possession."

"Its susceptibility of being produced?" said I.

"That is to say, of being destroyed," said Dupin.

"True," I observed; "the paper is clearly then upon the premises. As for its being upon the person of the minister, we may consider that as out of the question."

"Entirely," said the Prefect. "He has been twice waylaid, as if by footpads, and his person rigidly searched for my own inspection."

"You might have spared yourself this trouble," said Dupin. "D -- -- , I presume, is not altogether a fool, and, if not, must have anticipated these waylayings, as a matter of course."

"Not altogether a fool," said G., "but then he is a poet, which I take to be only one removed from a fool."

"True," said Dupin, after a long and thoughtful whiff from his meerschaum, "although I have been guilty of certain doggerel myself."

"Suppose you detail," said I, "the particulars of your search."

"Why, the fact is, we took our time, and we searched everywhere. I have had long experience in these affairs. I took the entire building, room by room; devoting the nights of a whole week to each. We examined, first the furniture of each apartment. We opened every possible drawer; and I presume you know that, to a properly trained police-agent, such a thing as a 'secret' drawer is impossible. Any man is a dolt who permits a 'secret' drawer to escape him in a search of this kind. The thing is so plain. There is a certain amount of bulk -- of space -- to be accounted for in every cabinet. Then we have accurate rules. The fiftieth part of a line could not escape us. After the cabinets we took the chairs. The cushions we probed with the fine ling needles you have seen me employ. From the tables we removed the tops."

"Why so?"

"Sometimes the top of a table, or other similarly arranged piece of furniture, is removed by the person wishing to conceal an article; then the leg is excavated, the article deposited within the cavity, and the top replaced. The bottoms and tops of bedposts are employed in the same way."

"But could not the cavity be detected by sounding?" I asked.

"By no means, if, when the article is deposited, a sufficient wadding of cotton be placed around it. Besides, in our case, we were obliged to proceed without noise."

"But you could not have removed -- you could not have taken to pieces all articles of furniture in which it would have been possible to make a deposit in the manner you mention. A letter may be compressed into a thin spiral roll, not differing much in shape or bulk from a large knitting-needle, and in this form it might be inserted into the rung of a chair, for example. You did not take to pieces all the chairs?"

"Certainly not; but we did better -- we examined the rungs of every chair in the hotel, and, indeed, the jointings of every description of furniture, by the aid of a most powerful microscope. Had there been any traces of recent disturbance we should not have failed to detect it instantly. A single grain of gimlet-dust, for example, would have been as obvious as an apple. Any disorder in the gluing -- any unusual gap in the joints -- would have sufficed to insure detection."

"I presume you looked to the mirrors, between the boards and the plates, and you probed the beds and the bedclothes, as well as the curtains and carpets."

"That of course; and when we had absolutely completed every particle of the furniture in this way, then we examined the house itself. We divided its entire surface into compartments, which we numbered, so that none might be missed; then we scrutinized each individual square inch throughout the premises, including the two houses immediately adjoining, with the microscope, as before."

"The two houses adjoining!" I exclaimed; "you must have had a great deal of trouble."

"We had; but the reward offered is prodigious."

"You included the grounds about the houses?"

"All the grounds are paved with brick. They give us comparatively little trouble. We examined the moss between the bricks, and found it undisturbed."

"You looked among D -- -- 's papers, of course, and into the books of the library?"

"Certainly; we opened every package and parcel; we not only opened every book, but we turned over every leaf in each volume, not contenting ourselves with a mere shake, according to the fashion of some of our police officers. We also measured the thickness of every book-cover, with the most accurate admeasurement, and applied to each the most jealous scrutiny of the microscope. Had any of the bindings been recently meddled with, it would have been utterly impossible that the fact should have escaped observation. Some five or six volumes, just from the hands of the binder, we carefully probed, longitudinally, with the needles."

"You explored the floors beneath the carpets?"

"Beyond doubt. We removed every carpet, and examined the boards with the microscope."

"And the paper on the walls?"

"Yes."

"You looked into the cellars?"

"We did."

"Then," I said, "you have been making a miscalculation, and the letter is not upon the premises, as you suppose."

"I fear you are right there," said the Prefect. "And now, Dupin, what would you advise me to do?"

"To make a thorough research of the premises."

"That is absolutely needless," replied G -- -- . "I am not more sure that I breathe than I am that the letter is not at the hotel."

"I have no better advice to give you," said Dupin. "You have, of course, an accurate description of the letter?"

"Oh, yes!" -- And here the Prefect, producing a memorandum-book, proceeded to read aloud a minute account of the internal, and especially of the external, appearance of the missing document. Soon after finishing the perusal of this description, he took his departure, more entirely depressed in spirits than I have ever known the good gentleman before.

In about a month afterward he paid another visit, and found us occupied very nearly as before. He took a pipe and a chair and entered into some ordinary conversation. At length I said:

"Well, but G., what of the purloined letter? I presume you have at last made up your mind that there is no such thing as overreaching the Minister?"

"Confound him, say I -- yes; I made the re-examination, however, as Dupin suggested -- but it was all labor lost, as I knew it would be."

"How much was the reward offered, did you say?" asked Dupin.

"Why, a very great deal -- a very liberal reward -- I don't like to say how much precisely; but one thing I will say, that I wouldn't mind giving my individual check for fifty thousand francs to any one who could obtain me that letter. The fact is, it is becoming of more and more importance every day; and the reward has been lately doubled. If it were trebled, however, I could do no more than I have done."

"Why, yes," said Dupin, drawlingly, between the whiffs of his meerschaum, "I really -- think, G., you have not exerted yourself -- to the utmost in the matter. You might -- do a little more, I think, eh?"

"How? -- in what way?"

"Why -- puff, puff -- you might -- puff, puff -- employ counsel in the matter, eh? -- puff, puff, puff. Do you remember the story they tell of Abernethy?"

"No; hang Abernethy!"

"To be sure! hang him and welcome. But, once upon a time, a certain rich miser conceived the design of spunging upon this Abernethy for a medical opinion. Getting up, for this purpose, an ordinary conversation in a private company, he insinuated his case to the physician, as that of an imaginary individual.

"'We will suppose,' said the miser, 'that his symptoms are such and such; now, doctor, what would you have directed him to take?'

"'Take!' said Abernethy, 'why, take advice, to be sure.'"

"But," said the Prefect, a little discomposed, "I am perfectly willing to take advice, and to pay for it. I would really give fifty thousand francs to any one who would aid me in the matter."

"In that case," replied Dupin, opening a drawer, and producing a check-book, "you may as well fill me up a check for the amount mentioned. When you have signed it, I will hand you the letter."

I was astonished. The Prefect appeared absolutely thunder-stricken. For some minutes he remained speechless and motionless, looking incredulously at my friend with open mouth, and eyes that seemed startling from their sockets; then apparently recovering himself in some measure, he seized a pen, and after several pauses and vacant stares, finally filled up and signed a check for fifty thousand francs, and handed it across the table to Dupin. The latter examined it carefully and deposited it in his pocket-book; then, unlocking an escritoire, took thence a letter and gave it to the Prefect. This functionary grasped it in a perfect agony of joy, opened it with a trembling hand, cast a rapid glance at its contents, and then, scrambling and struggling to the door, rushed at length unceremoniously from the room and from the house, without having uttered a syllable since Dupin had requested him to fill up the check.

When he had gone, my friend entered into some explanations.

"The Parisian police," he said, "are exceedingly able in their way. They are persevering, ingenious, cunning, and thoroughly versed in the knowledge which their duties seem chiefly to demand. Thus, when G -- -- detailed to us his mode of searching the premises at the Hotel D -- -- , I felt entire confidence in his having made a satisfactory investigation -- so far as his labors extended."

"So far as his labors extended?" said I.

"Yes," said Dupin. "The measures adopted were not only the best of their kind, but carried out to absolute perfection. Had the letter been deposited within the range of their search, these fellows would, beyond a question, have found it."

I merely laughed -- but he seemed quite serious in all that he said.

"The measures, then," he continued, "were good in their kind, and well executed; their defect lay in their being inapplicable to the case and to the man. A certain set of highly ingenious resources are, with the Prefect, a sort of Procrustean bed, to which he forcibly adapts his designs. But he perpetually errs by being too deep or too shallow for the matter in hand; and many a school-boy is a better reasoner than he. I knew one about eight years of age, whose success at guessing in the game of 'even and odd' attracted universal admiration. This game is simple, and is played with marbles. One player holds in his hand a number of these toys, and demands of another whether that number is even or odd. If the guess is right, the guesser wins one; if wrong, he loses one. The boy to whom I allude won all the marbles of the school. Of course he had some principle of guessing; and this lay in mere observation and admeasurement of the astuteness of his opponents. For example, an arrant simpleton is his opponent, and, holding up his closed hand, asks, 'Are they even or odd?' Our school-boy replies, 'Odd,' and loses; but upon the second trial he wins, for he then says to himself: 'The simpleton had them even upon the first trial, and his amount of cunning is just sufficient to make him have them odd upon the second; I will therefore guess odd'; -- he guesses odd and wins. Now, with a simpleton a degree above the first, he would have reasoned thus: 'This fellow finds that in the first instance I guessed odd, and, in the second, he will propose to himself, upon the first impulse, a simple variation from even to odd, as did the first simpleton; but then a second thought will suggest that this is too simple a variation, and finally he will decide upon putting it even as before. I will therefore guess even'; -- he guesses even, and wins. Now this mode of reasoning in the school-boy, whom his fellows termed 'lucky,' -- what, in its last analysis, is it?"

"It is merely," I said, "an identification of the reasoner's intellect with that of his opponent."

"It is," said Dupin; "and, upon inquiring of the boy by what means he effected the thorough identification in which his success consisted, I received answer as follows: 'When I wish to find out how wise, or how stupid, or how good, or how wicked is any one, or what are his thoughts at the moment, I fashion the expression of my face, as accurately as possible, in accordance with the expression of his, and then wait to see what thoughts or sentiments arise in my mind or heart, as if to match or correspond with the expression.' This response of the school-boy lies at the bottom of all the spurious profundity which has been attributed to Rochefoucault, to La Bougive, to Machiavelli, and to Campanella."

"And the identification," I said, "of the reasoner's intellect with that of his opponent, depends, if I understand you aright, upon the accuracy with which the opponent's intellect is admeasured."

"For its practical value it depends upon this," replied Dupin; "and the Prefect and his cohort fail so frequently, first, by default of this identification, and, secondly, by ill-admeasurement, or rather through non-admeasurement, of the intellect with which they are engaged. They consider only their own ideas of ingenuity; and, in searching for any thing hidden, advert only to the modes in which they would have hidden it. They are right in this much -- that their own ingenuity is a faithful representative of that of the mass; but when the cunning of the individual felon is diverse in character from their own, the felon foils them, of course. This always happens when it is above their own, and very usually when it is below. They have no variation of principle in their investigations; at best, when urged by some unusual emergency -- by some extraordinary reward -- they extend or exaggerate their old modes of practice, without touching their principles. What, for example, in this case of D -- -- , has been done to vary the principle of action? What is all this boring, and probing, and sounding, and scrutinizing with the microscope, and dividing the surface of the building into registered square inches -- what is it all but an exaggeration of the application of the one principle or set of principles of search, which are based upon the one set of notions regarding human ingenuity, to which the Prefect, in the long routine of his duty, has been accustomed? Do you not see he has taken it for granted that all men proceed to conceal a letter, not exactly in a gimlet-hole bored in a chair-leg, but, at least, in some out-of-the-way hole or corner suggested by the same tenor of thought which would urge a man to secrete a letter in a gimlet-hole bored in a chair-leg? And do you not see also, that such recherchs nooks for concealment ar adapted only for ordinary occasions, and would be adopted by ordinary intellects; for, in all cases of concealment, a disposal of the article concealed -- a disposal in this recherch manner, -- is, in the very first instance, presumable and presumed; and thus its discovery depends, not at all upon the acumen, but altogether upon the mere care, patience, and determination of the seekers; and where the case is of importance -- or, what amounts to the same thing in the political eyes, when the reward is of magnitude, -- the qualities in question have never been known to fail. You will now understand what I mean in suggesting that, had the purloined letter been hidden anywhere within the limits of the Prefect's examination -- in other words, had the principle of its concealment been comprehended within the principles of the Prefect -- its discovery would have been a matter altogether beyond question. This functionary, however, has been thoroughly mystified; and the remote source of his defeat lies in the supposition that the Minister is a fool, because he has acquired renown as a poet. All fools are poets; this the Prefect feels; and he is merely guilty of a non distributio medii in thence inferring that all poets are fools."

"But is this really the poet?" I asked. "There are two brothers, I know; and both have attained reputation in letters. The minister I believe has written learnedly on the Differential Calculus. He is a mathematician, and no poet."

"You are mistaken; I know him well; he is both. As a poet and as a mathematician, he would reason well; as a mere mathematician, he could not have reasoned at all, and thus would have been at the mercy of the Prefect."

"You surprise me," I said, "by these opinions, which have been contradicted by the voice of the world. You do not mean to set at naught the well-digested ideas of centuries. The mathematical reason has long been regarded as the reason par excellence."

"'Il y a parier,'" replied Dupin, quoting from Chamfort, "'que toute ide publique, toute convention reue, est une sottise, cor elle a convenue au plus grand nombre.' The mathematicians, I grant you, have done their best to promulgate the popular error to which you allude, and which is none the less an error for its promulgation as truth. With an art worthy a better cause, for example, they have insinuated the term 'analysis' into application to algebra. The French are the originators of this particular deception; but if a term is of any importance -- if words derive any value from applicability -- then 'analysis' conveys 'algebra' about as much as, in Latin, 'ambitus' implies 'ambition,' 'religio' 'religion,' or 'homines honesti' a set of honorable men."

"You have a quarrel on hand, I see," said I, "with some of the algebraists of Paris; but proceed."

"I dispute the availability, and thus the value, of that reason which is cultivated in any especial form other than the abstractly logical. I dispute, in particular, the reason educed by mathematical study. The mathematics are the science of form and quantity; mathematical reasoning is merely logic applied to observation upon form and quantity. The great error lies in supposing that even the truths of what is called pure algebra are abstract or general truths. And this error is so egregious that I am confounded at the universality with which it has been received. Mathematical axioms are not axioms of general truth. What is true of relation -- of form and quantity -- is often grossly false in regard to morals, for example. In this latter science it is very usually untrue that the aggregated parts are equal to the whole. In chemistry also the axiom fails. In the consideration of motive it fails; for two motives, each of a given value, have not, necessarily, a value when united, equal to the sum of their values apart. There are numerous other mathematical truths which are only truths within the limits of relation. But the mathematician argues from his finite truths, through habit, as if they were of an absolutely general applicability -- as the world indeed imagines them to be. Bryant, in his very learned 'Mythology,' mentions an analogous source of error, when he says that 'although the pagan fables are not believed, yet we forget ourselves continually, and make inferences from them as existing realities.' With the algebraists, however, who are pagans themselves, the 'pagan fables' are believed, and the inferences are made, not so much through lapse of memory as through an unaccountable addling of the brains. In short, I never yet encountered the mere mathematician who would be trusted out of equal roots, or one who did not clandestinely hold it as a point of his faith that $x2 + px$ was absolutely and unconditionally equal to q. Say to one of these gentlemen, by way of experiment, if you please, that you believe occasions may occur when $x2 + px$ is not altogether equal to q, and, having made him understand what you mean, get out of his reach as speedily as convenient, for beyond doubt, he will endeavor to knock you down.

"I mean to say," continued Dupin, while I merely laughed at his last observations, "that if the Minister had been no more than a mathematician, the Prefect would have been under no necessity of giving me this check. I knew him, however, as both mathematician and poet, and my measures were adapted to his capacity, with reference to the circumstances by which he was surrounded. I knew him as a courtier, too, and as a bold intriguant. Such a man, I considered, could not fail to be aware of the ordinary political modes of action. He could not fail to be anticipate -- and events have proved he did not fail to anticipate -- the waylayings to which he was subjected. He must have foreseen, I reflected, the secret investigations of his premises. His frequent absences from home at night, which were hailed by the Prefect as certain aids to his success, I regarded only as ruses, to afford opportunity for thorough search to the police, and thus sooner to impress them with the conviction to which G -- -- , in fact, did finally arrive -- the conviction that the letter was not upon the premises. I felt, also, that the whole train of thought, which I was at some pains in detailing to you just now, concerning the invariable principle of political action in searches for articles concealed -- I felt that this whole train of thought would necessarily pass through the mind of the minister. It would imperatively lead him to despise all the ordinary nooks of concealment. He could not, I reflected, be so weak as not to see that the most intricate and remote recess of his hotel would be as open as his commonest closets to the eyes, to the probes, to the gimlets, and to the microscopes of the Prefect. I saw, in fine, that he would be driven, as a matter of course, to simplicity, if not deliberately induced to it as a matter of choice. You will remember, perhaps, how desperately the Prefect laughed when I suggested, upon our first interview, that it was just possible this mystery troubled him so much on account of its being so very self-evident."

"Yes," said I, "I remember his merriment well. I really thought he would have fallen into convulsions."

"The material world," continued Dupin, "abounds with very strict analogies to the immaterial; and thus some color of truth has been given to the rhetorical dogma, that metaphor, or simile, may be made to strengthen an argument as well as to embellish a description. The principle of the vis inertiae, for example, seems to be identical in physics and metaphysics. It is not more true in the former, than a large body is with more difficulty set in motion than a smaller one, and that its subsequent momentum is commensurate with this difficulty, than it is, in the latter, that intellects of the vaster capacity, while more forcible, more constant, and more eventful in their movements than those of inferior grade, are yet the less readily moved, and more embarrassed, and full of hesitation in the first few steps of their progress. Again: have you ever noticed which of the street signs, over the shop doors, are the most attractive of attention?"

"I have never given the matter a thought," I said.

"There is a game of puzzles," he resumed, "which is played upon a map. One party playing requires another to find a given word -- the name of town, river, state, or empire -- any word, in short, upon the motley and perplexed surface of the chart. A novice in the game generally seeks to embarrass his opponents by giving them the most minutely lettered names; but the adept selects such words as stretch, in large characters, from one end of the chart to the other. These, like the over-largely lettered signs and placards of the street, escape observation by dint of being excessively obvious; and here the physical oversight is precisely analogous with the moral inapprehension by which the intellect suffers to pass unnoticed those considerations which are too obtrusively and too palpably self-evident. But this is a point, it appears, somewhat above or beneath the understanding of the Prefect. He never once thought it probable, or possible, that the minister had deposited the letter immediately beneath the nose of the whole world, by way of best preventing any portion of that world from perceiving it.

"But the more I reflected upon the daring, dashing, and discriminating ingenuity of D -- -- ; upon the fact that the document must always have been at hand, if he intended to use it to good purpose; and upon the decisive evidence, obtained by the Prefect, that it was not hidden within the limits of that dignitary's ordinary search -- the more satisfied I became that, to conceal this letter, the minister had resorted to the comprehensive and sagacious expedient of not attempting to conceal it at all.

"Full of these ideas, I prepared myself with a pair of green spectacles, and called one fine morning, quite by accident, at the Ministerial hotel. I found D -- -- at home, yawning, lounging, and dawdling, as usual, and pretending to be in the last extremity of ennui. He is, perhaps, the most really energetic human being now alive -- but that is only when nobody sees him.

"To be even with him, I complained of my weak eyes, and lamented the necessity of the spectacles, under cover of which I cautiously and thoroughly surveyed the whole apartment, while seemingly intent only upon the conversation of my host.

"I paid especial attention to a large writing-table near where he sat, and upon which lay confusedly, some miscellaneous letters and other papers, with one or two musical instruments and a few books. Here, however, after a long and very deliberate scrutiny, I saw nothing to excite particular suspicion.

"At length my eyes, in going the circuit of the room, fell upon a trumpery filigree card-rack of pasteboard, that hung dangling by a dirty blue ribbon, from a little brass knob just beneath the middle of the mantelpiece. In this rack, which had three or four compartments, were five or six visiting cards and a solitary letter. The last was much soiled and crumpled. It was torn nearly in two, across the middle -- as if a design, in the first instance, to tear it entirely up as worthless, had been altered, or stayed, in the second. It had a large black seal, bearing the D -- -- cipher very conspicuously, and was addressed, in a diminutive female hand, to D -- -- , the minister, himself. It was thrust carelessly, and even, as it seemed, contemptuously, into one of the uppermost divisions of the rack.

"No sooner had I glanced at this letter than I concluded it to be that of which I was in search. To be sure, it was, to all appearance, radically different from the one of which the Prefect had read to us so minute a description. Here the seal was large and black, with the D -- -- cipher; there it was small and read, with the ducal arms of the S -- -- family. Here, the address, to the minister, was diminutive and feminine; there the superscription, to a certain royal personage, was markedly bold and decided; the size alone formed a point of correspondence. But, then, the radicalness of these differences, which was excessive; the dirt; the soiled and torn condition of the paper, so inconsistent with the true methodical habits of D -- -- , and so suggestive of a design to delude the beholder into an idea of the worthlessness of the document; -- these things, together with the hyperobtrusive situation of this document, full in the view of every visitor, and thus exactly in accordance with the conclusions to which I had previously arrived; these things, I say, were strongly corroborative of suspicion, in one who came with the intention to suspect.

"I protracted my visit as long as possible, and, while I maintained a most animated discussion with the minister, upon a topic which I knew well had never failed to interest and excite him, I kept my attention really riveted upon the letter. In examination, I committed to memory its external appearance and arrangement in the rack; and also fell, at length, upon a discovery which set at rest whatever trivial doubt I might have entertained. In scrutinizing the edges of the paper, I observed them to be more chafed than seemed necessary. They presented the broken appearance which is manifested when a stiff paper, having been once folded and pressed with a folder, is refolded in a reversed direction, in the same creases or edges which had formed the original fold. This discovery was sufficient. It was clear to me that the letter had been turned, as a glove, inside out, re-directed and re-sealed. I bade the minister good-morning, and took my departure at once, leaving a gold snuff-box upon the table.

"The next morning I called for the snuff-box, when we resumed, quite eagerly, the conversation of the preceding day. While thus engaged, however, a large report, as if of a pistol, was heard immediately beneath the windows of the hotel, and was succeeded by a series of fearful screams, and the shoutings of a terrified mod. D -- -- rushed to a casement, threw it open, and looked out. In the meantime I stepped to the card-rack, took the letter, put it in my pocket, and replaced it by a fac-simile, (so far as regards externals) which I had carefully prepared at my lodgings -- imitating the D -- -- cipher, very readily, by means of a seal formed of bread.

"The disturbance in the street had been occasioned by the frantic behavior of a man with a musket. He had fired it among a crowd of women and children. It proved, however, to have been without ball, and the fellow was suffered to go his way as a lunatic or a drunkard. When he had gone, D -- -- came from the window, whither I had followed him immediately upon securing the object in view. Soon afterward I bade him farewell. The pretended lunatic was a man in my own pay."

"But what purpose had you," I asked, "in replacing the letter by a fac-simile? Would it not have been better, at the first visit, to have seized it openly, and departed?"

"D -- -- ," replied Dupin, "is a desperate man, and a man of nerve. His hotel, too, is not without attendants devoted to his interests. Had I made the wild attempt you suggest, I might never have left the Ministerial presence alive. The good people of Paris might have heard of me no more. But I had an object apart from these considerations. You know my political prepossessions. In this matter, I act as a partisan of the lady concerned. For eighteen months the Minister has had her in his power. She has now him in hers -- since, being unaware that the letter is not in his possession, he will proceed with his exactions as if it was. Thus will he inevitably commit himself, at once, to his political destruction. His downfall, too, will not be more precipitate than awkward. It is all very well to talk about the facilis descensus Averni; but in all kinds of climbing, as Catalani said of singing, it is far more easy to get up than to come down. In the present instance I have no sympathy -- at least no pity -- for him who descends. He is that monstrum horrendum, an unprincipled man of genius. I confess, however, that I should like very well to know the precise character of his thoughts, when, being defied by her whom the Prefect terms 'a certain personage,' he is reduced to opening the letter which I left for him in the card-rack."

"How? did you put any thing particular in it?"

"Why -- it did not seem altogether right to leave the interior blank -- that would have been insulting. D -- -- , at Vienna once, did me an evil turn, which I told him, quite good-humoredly, that I should remember. So, as I knew he would feel some curiosity in regard to the identity of the person who had outwitted him, I thought it a pity not to give him a clew. He is well acquainted with my MS., and I just copied into the middle of the blank sheet the words --

"' -- -- -- -- Un dessein si funeste, S'il n'est digne d'Atre, est digne de Thyeste.'

They are to be found in Crbillon's 'Atre.'"

Mark Twain

EVE'S DIARY (Translated from the original)

SATURDAY.--I am almost a whole day old, now. I arrived yesterday. That is as it seems to me. And it must be so, for if there was a day-before-yesterday I was not there when it happened, or I should remember it. It could be, of course, that it did happen, and that I was not noticing. Very well; I will be very watchful now, and if any day-before-yesterdays happen I will make a note of it. It will be best to start right and not let the record get confused, for some instinct tells me that these details are going to be important to the historian some day. For I feel like an experiment, I feel exactly like an experiment; it would be impossible for a person to feel more like an experiment than I do, and so I am coming to feel convinced that that is what I AM--an experiment; just an experiment, and nothing more.

Then if I am an experiment, am I the whole of it? No, I think not; I think the rest of it is part of it. I am the main part of it, but I think the rest of it has its share in the matter. Is my position assured, or do I have to watch it and take care of it? The latter, perhaps. Some instinct tells me that eternal vigilance is the price of supremacy. [That is a good phrase, I think, for one so young.]

Everything looks better today than it did yesterday. In the rush of finishing up yesterday, the mountains were left in a ragged condition, and some of the plains were so cluttered with rubbish and remnants that the aspects were quite distressing. Noble and beautiful works of art should not be subjected to haste; and this majestic new world is indeed a most noble and beautiful work. And certainly marvelously near to being perfect, notwithstanding the shortness of the time. There are too many stars in some places and not enough in others, but that can be remedied presently, no doubt. The moon got loose last night, and slid down and fell out of the scheme --a very great loss; it breaks my heart to think of it. There isn't another thing among the ornaments and decorations that is comparable to it for beauty and finish. It should have been fastened better. If we can only get it back again-- But of course there is no telling where it went to. And besides, whoever gets it will hide it; I know it because I would do it myself. I believe I can be honest in all other matters, but I already begin to realize that the core and center of my nature is love of the beautiful, a passion for the beautiful, and that it would not be safe to trust me with a moon that belonged to another person and that person didn't know I had it. I could give up a moon that I found in the daytime, because I should be afraid some one was looking; but if I found it in the dark, I am sure I should find some kind of an excuse for not saying anything about it. For I do love moons, they are so pretty and so romantic. I wish we had five or six; I would never go to bed; I should never get tired lying on the moss-bank and looking up at them.

Stars are good, too. I wish I could get some to put in my hair. But I suppose I never can. You would be surprised to find how far off they are, for they do not look it. When they first showed, last night, I tried to knock some down with a pole, but it didn't reach, which astonished me; then I tried clouds till I was all tired out, but I never got one. It was because I am left-handed and cannot throw good. Even when I aimed at the one I wasn't after I couldn't hit the other one, though I did make some close shots, for I saw the black blot of the cloud sail right into the midst of the golden clusters forty or fifty times, just barely missing them, and if I could have held out a little longer maybe I could have got one.

So I cried a little, which was natural, I suppose, for one of my age, and after I was rested I got a basket and started for a place on the extreme rim of the circle, where the stars were close to the ground and I could get them with my hands, which would be better, anyway, because I could gather them tenderly then, and not break them. But it was farther than I thought, and at last I had go give it up; I was so tired I couldn't drag my feet another step; and besides, they were sore and hurt me very much.

I couldn't get back home; it was too far and turning cold; but I found some tigers and nestled in among them and was most adorably comfortable, and their breath was sweet and pleasant, because they live on strawberries. I had never seen a tiger before, but I knew them in a minute by the stripes. If I could have one of those skins, it would make a lovely gown.

Today I am getting better ideas about distances. I was so eager to get hold of every pretty thing that I giddily grabbed for it, sometimes when it was too far off, and sometimes when it was but six inches away but seemed a foot--alas, with thorns between! I learned a lesson; also I made an axiom, all out of my own head --my very first one; *THE SCRATCHED EXPERIMENT SHUNS THE THORN*. I think it is a very good one for one so young.

I followed the other Experiment around, yesterday afternoon, at a distance, to see what it might be for, if I could. But I was not able to make out. I think it is a man. I had never seen a man, but it looked like one, and I feel sure that that is what it is. I realize that I feel more curiosity about it than about any of the other reptiles. If it is a reptile, and I suppose it is; for it has frowzy hair and blue eyes, and looks like a reptile. It has no hips; it tapers like a carrot; when it stands, it spreads itself apart like a derrick; so I think it is a reptile, though it may be architecture.

I was afraid of it at first, and started to run every time it turned around, for I thought it was going to chase me; but by and by I found it was only trying to get away, so after that I was not timid any more, but tracked it along, several hours, about twenty yards behind, which made it nervous and unhappy. At last it was a good deal worried, and climbed a tree. I waited a good while, then gave it up and went home.

Today the same thing over. I've got it up the tree again.

SUNDAY.--It is up there yet. Resting, apparently. But that is a subterfuge: Sunday isn't the day of rest; Saturday is appointed for that. It looks to me like a creature that is more interested in resting than it anything else. It would tire me to rest so much. It tires me just to sit around and watch the tree. I do wonder what it is for; I never see it do anything.

They returned the moon last night, and I was SO happy! I think it is very honest of them. It slid down and fell off again, but I was not distressed; there is no need to worry when one has that kind of neighbors; they will fetch it back. I wish I could do something to show my appreciation. I would like to send them some stars, for we have more than we can use. I mean I, not we, for I can see that the reptile cares nothing for such things.

It has low tastes, and is not kind. When I went there yesterday evening in the gloaming it had crept down and was trying to catch the little speckled fishes that play in the pool, and I had to clod it to make it go up the tree again and let them alone. I wonder if THAT is what it is for? Hasn't it any heart? Hasn't it any compassion for those little creature? Can it be that it was designed and manufactured for such ungentle work? It has the look of it. One of the clods took it back of the ear, and it used language. It gave me a thrill, for it was the first time I had ever heard speech, except my own. I did not understand the words, but they seemed expressive.

When I found it could talk I felt a new interest in it, for I love to talk; I talk, all day, and in my sleep, too, and I am very interesting, but if I had another to talk to I could be twice as interesting, and would never stop, if desired.

If this reptile is a man, it isn't an IT, is it? That wouldn't be grammatical, would it? I think it would be HE. I think so. In that case one would parse it thus: nominative, HE; dative, HIM; possessive, HIS'N. Well, I will consider it a man and call it he until it turns out to be something else. This will be handier than having so many uncertainties.

NEXT WEEK SUNDAY.--All the week I tagged around after him and tried to get acquainted. I had to do the talking, because he was shy, but I didn't mind it. He seemed pleased to have me around, and I used the sociable "we" a good deal, because it seemed to flatter him to be included.

WEDNESDAY.--We are getting along very well indeed, now, and getting better and better acquainted. He does not try to avoid me any more, which is a good sign, and shows that he likes to have me with him. That pleases me, and I study to be useful to him in every way I can, so as to increase his regard. During the last day or two I have taken all the work of naming things off his hands, and this has been a great relief to him, for he has no gift in that line, and is evidently very grateful. He can't think of a rational name to save him, but I do not let him see that I am aware of his defect. Whenever a new creature comes along I name it before he has time to expose himself by an awkward silence. In this way I have saved him many embarrassments. I have no defect like this. The minute I set eyes on an animal I know what it is. I don't have to reflect a moment; the right name comes out instantly, just as if it were an inspiration, as no doubt it is, for I am sure it wasn't in me half a minute before. I seem to know just by the shape of the creature and the way it acts what animal it is.

When the dodo came along he thought it was a wildcat--I saw it in his eye. But I saved him. And I was careful not to do it in a way that could hurt his pride. I just spoke up in a quite natural way of pleasing surprise, and not as if I was dreaming of conveying information, and said, "Well, I do declare, if there isn't the dodo!" I explained--without seeming to be explaining --how I know it for a dodo, and although I thought maybe he was a little piqued that I knew the creature when he didn't, it was quite evident that he admired me. That was very agreeable, and I thought of it more than once with gratification before I slept. How little a thing can make us happy when we feel that we have earned it!

THURSDAY.--my first sorrow. Yesterday he avoided me and seemed to wish I would not talk to him. I could not believe it, and thought there was some mistake, for I loved to be with him, and loved to hear him talk, and so how could it be that he could feel unkind toward me when I had not done anything? But at last it seemed true, so I went away and sat lonely in the place where I first saw him the morning that we were made and I did not know what he was and was indifferent about him; but now it was a mournful place, and every little thing spoke of him, and my heart was very sore. I did not know why very clearly, for it was a new feeling; I had not experienced it before, and it was all a mystery, and I could not make it out.

But when night came I could not bear the lonesomeness, and went to the new shelter which he has built, to ask him what I had done that was wrong and how I could mend it and get back his kindness again; but he put me out in the rain, and it was my first sorrow.

SUNDAY.--It is pleasant again, now, and I am happy; but those were heavy days; I do not think of them when I can help it.

I tried to get him some of those apples, but I cannot learn to throw straight. I failed, but I think the good intention pleased him. They are forbidden, and he says I shall come to harm; but so I come to harm through pleasing him, why shall I care for that harm?

MONDAY.--This morning I told him my name, hoping it would interest him. But he did not care for it. It is strange. If he should tell me his name, I would care. I think it would be pleasanter in my ears than any other sound.

He talks very little. Perhaps it is because he is not bright, and is sensitive about it and wishes to conceal it. It is such a pity that he should feel so, for brightness is nothing; it is in the heart that the values lie. I wish I could make him understand that a loving good heart is riches, and riches enough, and that without it intellect is poverty.

Although he talks so little, he has quite a considerable vocabulary. This morning he used a surprisingly good word. He evidently recognized, himself, that it was a good one, for he worked in in twice afterward, casually. It was good casual art, still it showed that he possesses a certain quality of perception. Without a doubt that seed can be made to grow, if cultivated.

Where did he get that word? I do not think I have ever used it.

No, he took no interest in my name. I tried to hide my disappointment, but I suppose I did not succeed. I went away and sat on the moss-bank with my feet in the water. It is where I go when I hunger for companionship, some one to look at, some one to talk to. It is not enough--that lovely white body painted there in the pool --but it is something, and something is better than utter loneliness. It talks when I talk; it is sad when I am sad; it comforts me with its sympathy; it says, "Do not be downhearted, you poor friendless girl; I will be your friend." It IS a good friend to me, and my only one; it is my sister.

That first time that she forsook me! ah, I shall never forget that --never, never. My heart was lead in my body! I said, "She was all I had, and now she is gone!" In my despair I said, "Break, my heart; I cannot bear my life any more!" and hid my face in my hands, and there was no solace for me. And when I took them away, after a little, there she was again, white and shining and beautiful, and I sprang into her arms!

That was perfect happiness; I had known happiness before, but it was not like this, which was ecstasy. I never doubted her afterward. Sometimes she stayed away--maybe an hour, maybe almost the whole day, but I waited and did not doubt; I said, "She is busy, or she is gone on a journey, but she will come." And it was so: she always did. At night she would not come if it was dark, for she was a timid little thing; but if there was a moon she would come. I am not afraid of the dark, but she is younger than I am; she was born after I was. Many and many are the visits I have paid her; she is my comfort and my refuge when my life is hard--and it is mainly that.

TUESDAY.--All the morning I was at work improving the estate; and I purposely kept away from him in the hope that he would get lonely and come. But he did not.

At noon I stopped for the day and took my recreation by flitting all about with the bees and the butterflies and reveling in the flowers, those beautiful creatures that catch the smile of God out of the sky and preserve it! I gathered them, and made them into wreaths and garlands and clothed myself in them while I ate my luncheon --apples, of course; then I sat in the shade and wished and waited. But he did not come.

But no matter. Nothing would have come of it, for he does not care for flowers. He called them rubbish, and cannot tell one from another, and thinks it is superior to feel like that. He does not care for me, he does not care for flowers, he does not care for the painted sky at eventide--is there anything he does care for, except building shacks to coop himself up in from the good clean rain, and thumping the melons, and sampling the grapes, and fingering the fruit on the trees, to see how those properties are coming along?

I laid a dry stick on the ground and tried to bore a hole in it with another one, in order to carry out a scheme that I had, and soon I got an awful fright. A thin, transparent bluish film rose out of the hole, and I dropped everything and ran! I thought it was a spirit, and I WAS so frightened! But I looked back, and it was not coming; so I leaned against a rock and rested and panted, and let my limps go on trembling until they got steady again; then I crept warily back, alert, watching, and ready to fly if there was occasion; and when I was come near, I parted the branches of a rose-bush and peeped through--wishing the man was about, I was looking so cunning and pretty--but the sprite was gone. I went there, and there was a pinch of delicate pink dust in the hole. I put my finger in, to feel it, and said OUCH! and took it out again. It was a cruel pain. I put my finger in my mouth; and by standing first on one foot and then the other, and grunting, I presently eased my misery; then I was full of interest, and began to examine.

I was curious to know what the pink dust was. Suddenly the name of it occurred to me, though I had never heard of it before. It was FIRE! I was as certain of it as a person could be of anything in the world. So without hesitation I named it that--fire.

I had created something that didn't exist before; I had added a new thing to the world's uncountable properties; I realized this, and was proud of my achievement, and was going to run and find him and tell him about it, thinking to raise myself in his esteem --but I reflected, and did not do it. No--he would not care for it. He would ask what it was good for, and what could I answer? for if it was not GOOD for something, but only beautiful, merely beautiful-- So I sighed, and did not go. For it wasn't good for anything; it could not build a shack, it could not improve melons, it could not hurry a fruit crop; it was useless, it was a foolishness and a vanity; he would despise it and say cutting words. But to me it was not despicable; I said, "Oh, you fire, I love you, you dainty pink creature, for you are BEAUTIFUL--and that is enough!" and was going to gather it to my breast. But refrained. Then I made another maxim out of my head, though it was so nearly like the first one that I was afraid it was only a plagiarism: *"THE BURNT EXPERIMENT SHUNS THE FIRE."*

I wrought again; and when I had made a good deal of fire-dust I emptied it into a handful of dry brown grass, intending to carry it home and keep it always and play with it; but the wind struck it and it sprayed up and spat out at me fiercely, and I dropped it and ran. When I looked back the blue spirit was towering up and stretching and rolling away like a cloud, and instantly I thought of the name of it--SMOKE!--though, upon my word, I had never heard of smoke before.

Soon brilliant yellow and red flares shot up through the smoke, and I named them in an instant--FLAMES--and I was right, too, though these were the very first flames that had ever been in the world. They climbed the trees, then flashed splendidly in and out of the vast and increasing volume of tumbling smoke, and I had to clap my hands and laugh and dance in my rapture, it was so new and strange and so wonderful and so beautiful!

He came running, and stopped and gazed, and said not a word for many minutes. Then he asked what it was. Ah, it was too bad that he should ask such a direct question. I had to answer it, of course, and I did. I said it was fire. If it annoyed him that I should know and he must ask; that was not my fault; I had no desire to annoy him. After a pause he asked:

"How did it come?"

Another direct question, and it also had to have a direct answer.

"I made it."

The fire was traveling farther and farther off. He went to the edge of the burned place and stood looking down, and said:

"What are these?"

"Fire-coals."

He picked up one to examine it, but changed his mind and put it down again. Then he went away. NOTHING interests him.

But I was interested. There were ashes, gray and soft and delicate and pretty--I knew what they were at once. And the embers; I knew the embers, too. I found my apples, and raked them out, and was glad; for I am very young and my appetite is active. But I was disappointed; they were all burst open and spoiled. Spoiled apparently; but it was not so; they were better than raw ones. Fire is beautiful; some day it will be useful, I think.

FRIDAY.--I saw him again, for a moment, last Monday at nightfall, but only for a moment. I was hoping he would praise me for trying to improve the estate, for I had meant well and had worked hard. But he was not pleased, and turned away and left me. He was also displeased on another account: I tried once more to persuade him to stop going over the Falls. That was because the fire had revealed to me a new passion-- quite new, and distinctly different from love, grief, and those others which I had already discovered--FEAR. And it is horrible!--I wish I had never discovered it; it gives me dark moments, it spoils my happiness, it makes me shiver and tremble and shudder. But I could not persuade him, for he has not discovered fear yet, and so he could not understand me.

Extract from Adam's Diary

Perhaps I ought to remember that she is very young, a mere girl and make allowances. She is all interest, eagerness, vivacity, the world is to her a charm, a wonder, a mystery, a joy; she can't speak for delight when she finds a new flower, she must pet it and caress it and smell it and talk to it, and pour out endearing names upon it. And she is color-mad: brown rocks, yellow sand, gray moss, green foliage, blue sky; the pearl of the dawn, the purple shadows on the mountains, the golden islands floating in crimson seas at sunset, the pallid moon sailing through the shredded cloud-rack, the star-jewels glittering in the wastes of space--none of them is of any practical value, so far as I can see, but because they have color and majesty, that is enough for her, and she loses her mind over them. If she could quiet down and keep still a couple minutes at a time, it would be a reposeful spectacle. In that case I think I could enjoy looking at her; indeed I am sure I could, for I am coming to realize that she is a quite remarkably comely creature --lithe, slender, trim, rounded, shapely, nimble, graceful; and once when she was standing marble-white and sun- drenched on a boulder, with her young head tilted back and her hand shading her eyes, watching the flight of a bird in the sky, I recognized that she was beautiful.

MONDAY NOON.--If there is anything on the planet that she is not interested in it is not in my list. There are animals that I am indifferent to, but it is not so with her. She has no discrimination, she takes to all of them, she thinks they are all treasures, every new one is welcome.

When the mighty brontosaurus came striding into camp, she regarded it as an acquisition, I considered it a calamity; that is a good sample of the lack of harmony that prevails in our views of things. She wanted to domesticate it, I wanted to make it a present of the homestead and move out. She believed it could be tamed by kind treatment and would be a good pet; I said a pet twenty-one feet high and eighty-four feet long would be no proper thing to have about the place, because, even with the best intentions and without meaning any harm, it could sit down on the house and mash it, for any one could see by the look of its eye that it was absent-minded.

Still, her heart was set upon having that monster, and she couldn't give it up. She thought we could start a dairy with it, and wanted me to help milk it; but I wouldn't; it was too risky. The sex wasn't right, and we hadn't any ladder anyway. Then she wanted to ride it, and look at the scenery. Thirty or forty feet of its tail was lying on the ground, like a fallen tree, and she thought she could climb it, but she was mistaken; when she got to the steep place it was too slick and down she came, and would have hurt herself but for me.

Was she satisfied now? No. Nothing ever satisfies her but demonstration; untested theories are not in her line, and she won't have them. It is the right spirit, I concede it; it attracts me; I feel the influence of it; if I were with her more I think I should take it up myself. Well, she had one theory remaining about this colossus: she thought that if we could tame it and make him friendly we could stand in the river and use him for a bridge. It turned out that he was already plenty tame enough--at least as far as she was concerned --so she tried her theory, but it failed: every time she got him properly placed in the river and went ashore to cross over him, he came out and followed her around like a pet mountain. Like the other animals. They all do that.

FRIDAY.--Tuesday--Wednesday--Thursday--and today: all without seeing him. It is a long time to be alone; still, it is better to be alone than unwelcome.

I HAD to have company--I was made for it, I think--so I made friends with the animals. They are just charming, and they have the kindest disposition and the politest ways; they never look sour, they never let you feel that you are intruding, they smile at you and wag their tail, if they've got one, and they are always ready for a romp or an excursion or anything you want to propose. I think they are perfect gentlemen. All these days we have had such good times, and it hasn't been lonesome for me, ever. Lonesome! No, I should say not. Why, there's always a swarm of them around --sometimes as much as four or five acres--you can't count them; and when you stand on a rock in the midst and look out over the furry expanse it is so mottled and splashed and gay with color and frisking sheen and sun-flash, and so rippled with stripes, that you might think it was a lake, only you know it isn't; and there's storms of sociable birds, and hurricanes of whirring wings; and when the sun strikes all that feathery commotion, you have a blazing up of all the colors you can think of, enough to put your eyes out.

We have made long excursions, and I have seen a great deal of the world; almost all of it, I think; and so I am the first traveler, and the only one. When we are on the march, it is an imposing sight --there's nothing like it anywhere. For comfort I ride a tiger or a leopard, because it is soft and has a round back that fits me, and because they are such pretty animals; but for long distance or for scenery I ride the elephant. He hoists me up with his trunk, but I can get off myself; when we are ready to camp, he sits and I slide down the back way.

The birds and animals are all friendly to each other, and there are no disputes about anything. They all talk, and they all talk to me, but it must be a foreign language, for I cannot make out a word they say; yet they often understand me when I talk back, particularly the dog and the elephant. It makes me ashamed. It shows that they are brighter than I am, for I want to be the principal Experiment myself--and I intend to be, too.

I have learned a number of things, and am educated, now, but I wasn't at first. I was ignorant at first. At first it used to vex me because, with all my watching, I was never smart enough to be around when the water was running uphill; but now I do not mind it. I have experimented and experimented until now I know it never does run uphill, except in the dark. I know it does in the dark, because the pool never goes dry, which it would, of course, if the water didn't come back in the night. It is best to prove things by actual experiment; then you KNOW; whereas if you depend on guessing and supposing and conjecturing, you never get educated.

Some things you CAN'T find out; but you will never know you can't by guessing and supposing: no, you have to be patient and go on experimenting until you find out that you can't find out. And it is delightful to have it that way, it makes the world so interesting. If there wasn't anything to find out, it would be dull. Even trying to find out and not finding out is just as interesting as trying to find out and finding out, and I don't know but more so. The secret of the water was a treasure until I GOT it; then the excitement all went away, and I recognized a sense of loss.

By experiment I know that wood swims, and dry leaves, and feathers, and plenty of other things; therefore by all that cumulative evidence you know that a rock will swim; but you have to put up with simply knowing it, for there isn't any way to prove it--up to now. But I shall find a way-- then THAT excitement will go. Such things make me sad; because by and by when I have found out everything there won't be any more excitements, and I do love excitements so! The other night I couldn't sleep for thinking about it.

At first I couldn't make out what I was made for, but now I think it was to search out the secrets of this wonderful world and be happy and thank the Giver of it all for devising it. I think there are many things to learn yet--I hope so; and by economizing and not hurrying too fast I think they will last weeks and weeks. I hope so. When you cast up a feather it sails away on the air and goes out of sight; then you throw up a clod and it doesn't. It comes down, every time. I have tried it and tried it, and it is always so. I wonder why it is? Of course it DOESN'T come down, but why should it SEEM to? I suppose it is an optical illusion. I mean, one of them is. I don't know which one. It may be the feather, it may be the clod; I can't prove which it is, I can only demonstrate that one or the other is a fake, and let a person take his choice.

By watching, I know that the stars are not going to last. I have seen some of the best ones melt and run down the sky. Since one can melt, they can all melt; since they can all melt, they can all melt the same night. That sorrow will come--I know it. I mean to sit up every night and look at them as long as I can keep awake; and I will impress those sparkling fields on my memory, so that by and by when they are taken away I can by my fancy restore those lovely myriads to the black sky and make them sparkle again, and double them by the blur of my tears.

After the Fall

When I look back, the Garden is a dream to me. It was beautiful, surpassingly beautiful, enchantingly beautiful; and now it is lost, and I shall not see it any more.

The Garden is lost, but I have found HIM, and am content. He loves me as well as he can; I love him with all the strength of my passionate nature, and this, I think, is proper to my youth and sex. If I ask myself why I love him, I find I do not know, and do not really much care to know; so I suppose that this kind of love is not a product of reasoning and statistics, like one's love for other reptiles and animals. I think that this must be so. I love certain birds because of their song; but I do not love Adam on account of his singing--no, it is not that; the more he sings the more I do not get reconciled to it. Yet I ask him to sing, because I wish to learn to like everything he is interested in. I am sure I can learn, because at first I could not stand it, but now I can. It sours the milk, but it doesn't matter; I can get used to that kind of milk.

It is not on account of his brightness that I love him--no, it is not that. He is not to blame for his brightness, such as it is, for he did not make it himself; he is as God make him, and that is sufficient. There was a wise purpose in it, THAT I know. In time it will develop, though I think it will not be sudden; and besides, there is no hurry; he is well enough just as he is.

It is not on account of his gracious and considerate ways and his delicacy that I love him. No, he has lacks in this regard, but he is well enough just so, and is improving.

It is not on account of his industry that I love him--no, it is not that. I think he has it in him, and I do not know why he conceals it from me. It is my only pain. Otherwise he is frank and open with me, now. I am sure he keeps nothing from me but this. It grieves me that he should have a secret from me, and sometimes it spoils my sleep, thinking of it, but I will put it out of my mind; it shall not trouble my happiness, which is otherwise full to overflowing.

It is not on account of his education that I love him--no, it is not that. He is self-educated, and does really know a multitude of things, but they are not so.

It is not on account of his chivalry that I love him--no, it is not that. He told on me, but I do not blame him; it is a peculiarity of sex, I think, and he did not make his sex. Of course I would not have told on him, I would have perished first; but that is a peculiarity of sex, too, and I do not take credit for it, for I did not make my sex.

Then why is it that I love him? MERELY BECAUSE HE IS MASCULINE, I think.

At bottom he is good, and I love him for that, but I could love him without it. If he should beat me and abuse me, I should go on loving him. I know it. It is a matter of sex, I think.

He is strong and handsome, and I love him for that, and I admire him and am proud of him, but I could love him without those qualities. He he were plain, I should love him; if he were a wreck, I should love him; and I would work for him, and slave over him, and pray for him, and watch by his bedside until I died.

Yes, I think I love him merely because he is MINE and is MASCULINE. There is no other reason, I suppose. And so I think it is as I first said: that this kind of love is not a product of reasonings and statistics. It just COMES--none knows whence--and cannot explain itself. And doesn't need to.

It is what I think. But I am only a girl, the first that has examined this

matter, and it may turn out that in my ignorance and inexperience I have
not got it right.

Forty Years Later

It is my prayer, it is my longing, that we may pass from this life
together--a longing which shall never perish from the earth, but shall
have place in the heart of every wife that loves, until the end of time; and
it shall be called by my name.

But if one of us must go first, it is my prayer that it shall be I; for he is
strong, I am weak, I am not so necessary to him as he is to me--life
without him would not be life; now could I endure it? This prayer is also
immortal, and will not cease from being offered up while my race
continues. I am the first wife; and in the last wife I shall be repeated.

At Eve's Grave

ADAM: Wheresoever she was, THERE was Eden.

THE CELEBRATED JUMPING FROG OF CALAVERAS COUNTY

In compliance with the request of a friend of mine, who wrote me from
the East, I called on good-natured, garrulous old Simon Wheeler, and
inquired after my friend's friend, Leonidas W. Smiley, as requested to do,
and I hereunto append the result. I have a lurking suspicion
that *Leonidas W.* Smiley is a myth; and that my friend never knew such a
personage; and that he only conjectured that if I asked old Wheeler about
him, it would remind him of his infamous *Jim Smiley*, and he would go
to work and bore me to death with some exasperating reminiscence of
him as long and as tedious as it should be useless to me. If that was the
design, it succeeded.

I found Simon Wheeler dozing comfortably by the barroom stove of the
dilapidated tavern in the decayed mining camp of Angel's, and I noticed
that he was fat and bald-headed, and had an expression of winning
gentleness and simplicity upon his tranquil countenance. He roused up,
and gave me good-day. I told him a friend had commissioned me to make
some inquiries about a cherished companion of his boyhood
named *Leonidas W.* Smiley--*Rev. Leonidas W.* Smiley, a young minister
of the Gospel, who he had heard was at one time a resident of Angel's
Camp. I added that if Mr. Wheeler could tell me anything about this Rev.
Leonidas W. Smiley, I would feel under many obligations to him.

Simon Wheeler backed me into a corner and blockaded me there with his chair, and then sat down and reeled off the monotonous narrative which follows this paragraph. He never smiled, he never frowned, he never changed his voice from the gentle-flowing key to which he tuned his initial sentence, he never betrayed the slightest suspicion of enthusiasm; but all through the interminable narrative there ran a vein of impressive earnestness and sincerity, which showed me plainly that, so far from his imagining that there was anything ridiculous or funny about his story, he regarded it as a really important matter, and admired its two heroes as men of transcendent genius in *finesse*. I let him go on in his own way, and never interrupted him once.

"Rev. Leonidas W. H'm, Reverend Le--well, there was a feller here once by the name of *Jim* Smiley, in the winter of '49--or may be it was the spring of '50--I don't recollect exactly, somehow, though what makes me think it was one or the other is because I remember the big flume warn't finished when he first came to the camp; but any way, he was the curiousest man about always betting on anything that turned up you ever see, if he could get anybody to bet on the other side; and if he couldn't he'd change sides. Any way that suited the other man would suit *him*-- any way just so's he got a bet, *he* was satisfied. But still he was lucky, uncommon lucky; he most always come out winner. He was always ready and laying for a chance; there couldn't be no solit'ry thing mentioned but that feller'd offer to bet on it, and take any side you please, as I was just telling you. If there was a horse-race, you'd find him flush or you'd find him busted at the end of it; if there was a dog-fight, he'd bet on it; if there was a cat-fight, he'd bet on it; if there was a chicken-fight, he'd bet on it; why, if there was two birds setting on a fence, he would bet you which one would fly first; or if there was a camp-meeting, he would be there reg'lar to bet on Parson Walker, which he judged to be the best exhorter about here, and he was, too, and a good man. If he even see a straddle-bug start to go anywheres, he would bet you how long it would take him to get to--to wherever he *was* going to, and if you took him up, he would foller that straddle-bug to Mexico but what he would find out where he was bound for and how long he was on the road.Lots of the boys here has seen that Smiley and can tell you about him. Why, it never made no difference to *him*--he'd bet on *any* thing--the dangest feller. Parson Walker's wife laid very sick once, for a good while, and it seemed as if they warn't going to save her; but one morning he come in, and Smiley up and asked him how she was, and he said she was considerable better--thank the Lord for his inf'nit' mercy--and coming on so smart that with the blessing of Prov'dence she'd get well yet; and Smiley, before he thought, says, Well, I'll risk two-and-a-half she don't anyway.'"

Thish-yer Smiley had a mare--the boys called her the fifteen-minute nag, but that was only in fun, you know, because, of course, she was faster than that--and he used to win money on that horse, for all she was so slow and always had the asthma, or the distemper, or the consumption, or something of that kind. They used to give her two or three hundred yards start, and then pass her under way; but always at the fag-end of the race she'd get excited and desperate-like, and come cavorting and straddling up, and scattering her legs around limber, sometimes in the air, and sometimes out to one side amongst the fences, and kicking up m-o-r-e dust and raising m-o-r-e racket with her coughing and sneezing and blowing her nose--and always fetch up at the stand just about a neck ahead, as near as you could cipher it down.

And he had a little small bull-pup, that to look at him you'd think he warn't worth a cent but to set around and look ornery and lay for a chance to steal something. But as soon as money was up on him he was a different dog; his under-jaw'd begin to stick out like the fo'-castle of a steamboat, and his teeth would uncover and shine like the furnaces. And a dog might tackle him and bully-rag him, and bite him, and throw him over his shoulder two or three times, and Andrew Jackson--which was the name of the pup--Andrew Jackson would never let on but what *he* was satisfied, and hadn't expected nothing else--and the bets being doubled and doubled on the other side all the time, till the money was all up; and then all of a sudden he would grab that other dog jest by the j'int of his hind leg and freeze to it--not chaw, you understand, but only just grip and hang on till they throwed up the sponge, if it was a year. Smiley always come out winner on that pup, till he harnessed a dog once that didn't have no hind legs, because they'd been sawed off in a circular saw, and when the thing had gone along far enough, and the money was all up, and he come to make a snatch for his pet holt, he see in a minute how he'd been imposed on, and how the other dog had him in the door, so to speak, and he 'peared surprised, and then he looked sorter discouraged-like, and didn't try no more to win the fight, and so he got shucked out bad. He gave Smiley a look, as much as to say his heart was broke, and it was *his* fault, for putting up a dog that hadn't no hind legs for him to take holt of, which was his main dependence in a fight, and then he limped off a piece and laid down and died. It was a good pup, was that Andrew Jackson, and would have made a name for hisself if he'd lived, for the stuff was in him and he had genius--I know it, because he hadn't no opportunities to speak of, and it don't stand to reason that a dog could make such a fight as he could under them circumstances if he hadn't no talent. It always makes me feel sorry when I think of that last fight of his'n, and the way it turned out.

Well, thish-yer Smiley had rat-tarriers, and chicken cocks, and tom-cats and all of them kind of things, till you couldn't rest, and you couldn't fetch nothing for him to bet on but he'd match you. He ketched a frog one day, and took him home, and said he cal'lated to educate him; and so he never done nothing for three months but set in his back yard and learn that frog to jump. And you bet you he *did* learn him, too. He'd give him a little punch behind, and the next minute you'd see that frog whirling in the air like a doughnut--see him turn one summerset, or may be a couple, if he got a good start, and come down flat-footed and all right, like a cat.

He got him up so in the matter of ketching flies, and kep' him in practice so constant, that he'd nail a fly every time as fur as he could see him. Smiley said all a frog wanted was education, and he could do 'most anything--and I believe him. Why, I've seen him set Dan'l Webster down here on this floor--Dan'l Webster was the name of the frog--and sing out, "Flies, Dan'l, flies!" and quicker'n you could wink he'd spring straight up and snake a fly off'n the counter there, and flop down on the floor ag'in as solid as a gob of mud, and fall to scratching the side of his head with his hind foot as indifferent as if he hadn't no idea he'd been doin' any more'n any frog might do. You never see a frog so modest and straightfor'ard as he was, for all he was so gifted. And when it come to fair and square jumping on a dead level, he could get over more ground at one straddle than any animal of his breed you ever see. Jumping on a dead level was his strong suit, you understand; and when it come to that, Smiley would ante up money on him as long as he had a red. Smiley was monstrous proud of his frog, and well he might be, for fellers that had traveled and been everywheres, all said he laid over any frog that ever *they* see.

Well, Smiley kep' the beast in a little lattice box, and he used to fetch him downtown sometimes and lay for a bet. One day a feller--a stranger in the camp, he was--come acrost him with his box, and says:

"What might be that you've got in the box?"

And Smiley says, sorter indifferent-like, "It might be a parrot, or it might be a canary, maybe, but it ain't--it's only just a frog."

And the feller took it, and looked at it careful, and turned it round this way and that, and says, "H'm--so 'tis. Well, what's *he* good for?"

"Well," Smiley says, easy and careless, "he's good enough for *one* thing, I should judge--he can outjump any frog in Calaveras county."

The feller took the box again, and took another long, particular look, and give it back to Smiley, and says, very deliberate, "Well," he says, "I don't see no p'ints about that frog that's any better'n any other frog."

"Maybe you don't," Smiley says. "Maybe you understand frogs and maybe you don't understand 'em; maybe you've had experience, and maybe you ain't only a amature, as it were. Anyways, I've got *my* opinion and I'll risk forty dollars that he can outjump any frog in Calaveras County."

And the feller studied a minute, and then says, kinder sad like, "Well, I'm only a stranger here, and I ain't got no frog; but if I had a frog, I'd bet you."

And then Smiley says, "That's all right--that's all right--if you'll hold my box a minute, I'll go and get you a frog." And so the feller took the box, and put up his forty dollars along with Smiley's, and set down to wait.

So he set there a good while thinking and thinking to his-self, and then he got the frog out and prized his mouth open and took a teaspoon and filled him full of quail shot--filled! him pretty near up to his chin--and set him on the floor. Smiley he went to the swamp and slopped around in the mud for a long time, and finally he ketched a frog, and fetched him in, and give him to this feller, and says:

"Now, if you're ready, set him alongside of Dan'l, with his forepaws just even with Dan'l's, and I'll give the word." Then he says, "One--two--three--*git!*" and him and the feller touched up the frogs from behind, and the new frog hopped off lively, but Dan'l give a heave, and hysted up his shoulders--so--like a Frenchman, but it warn't no use--he couldn't budge; he was planted as solid as a church, and he couldn't no more stir than if he was anchored out. Smiley was a good deal surprised, and he was disgusted too, but he didn't have no idea what the matter was, of course.

The feller took the money and started away; and when he was going out at the door, he sorter jerked his thumb over his shoulder--so--at Dan'l, and says again, very deliberate, "Well," he says, "*I* don't see no p'ints about that frog that's any better'n any other frog."

Smiley he stood scratching his head and looking down at Dan'l a long time, and at last says, "I do wonder what in the nation that frog throwed off for--I wonder if there ain't something the matter with him--he 'pears to look mighty baggy, somehow." And he ketched Dan'l up by the nap of the neck, and hefted him, and says, "Why blame my cats if he don't weigh five pounds!" and turned him upside down and he belched out a double handful of shot. And then he see how it was, and he was the maddest man--he set the frog down and took out after that feller, but he never ketched him. And----

(Here Simon Wheeler heard his name called from the front yard, and got up to see what was wanted.) And turning to me as he moved away, he said: "Just set where you are, stranger, and rest easy--I ain't going to be gone a second."

But, by your leave, I did not think that a continuation of the history of the enterprising vagabond *Jim* Smiley would be likely to afford me much information concerning the Rev. *Leonidas W.* Smiley, and so I started away.

At the door I met the sociable Wheeler returning, and he buttonholed me and recommenced:

"Well, thish-yer Smiley had a yaller, one-eyed cow that didn't have no tail, only jest a short stump like a bannanner, and----"

However, lacking both time and inclination, I did not wait to hear about the afflicted cow, but took my leave.

Kate Chopin

THE STORY OF AN HOUR

Knowing that Mrs. Mallard was afflicted with a heart trouble, great care was taken to break to her as gently as possible the news of her husband's death.

It was her sister Josephine who told her, in broken sentences; veiled hints that revealed in half concealing. Her husband's friend Richards was there, too, near her. It was he who had been in the newspaper office when intelligence of the railroad disaster was received, with Brently Mallard's name leading the list of "killed." He had only taken the time to assure himself of its truth by a second telegram, and had hastened to forestall any less careful, less tender friend in bearing the sad message.

She did not hear the story as many women have heard the same, with a paralyzed inability to accept its significance. She wept at once, with sudden, wild abandonment, in her sister's arms. When the storm of grief had spent itself she went away to her room alone. She would have no one follow her.

There stood, facing the open window, a comfortable, roomy armchair. Into this she sank, pressed down by a physical exhaustion that haunted her body and seemed to reach into her soul.

She could see in the open square before her house the tops of trees that were all aquiver with the new spring life. The delicious breath of rain was in the air. In the street below a peddler was crying his wares. The notes of a distant song which someone was singing reached her faintly, and countless sparrows were twittering in the eaves.

There were patches of blue sky showing here and there through the clouds that had met and piled one above the other in the west facing her window.

She sat with her head thrown back upon the cushion of the chair, quite motionless, except when a sob came up into her throat and shook her, as a child who has cried itself to sleep continues to sob in its dreams.

She was young, with a fair, calm face, whose lines bespoke repression and even a certain strength. But now there was a dull stare in her eyes, whose gaze was fixed away off yonder on one of those patches of blue sky. It was not a glance of reflection, but rather indicated a suspension of intelligent thought.

There was something coming to her and she was waiting for it, fearfully. What was it? She did not know; it was too subtle and elusive to name. But she felt it, creeping out of the sky, reaching toward her through the sounds, the scents, the color that filled the air.

Now her bosom rose and fell tumultuously. She was beginning to recognize this thing that was approaching to possess her, and she was striving to beat it back with her will--as powerless as her two white slender hands would have been. When she abandoned herself a little whispered word escaped her slightly parted lips. She said it over and over under the breath: "free, free, free!" The vacant stare and the look of terror that had followed it went from her eyes. They stayed keen and bright. Her pulses beat fast, and the coursing blood warmed and relaxed every inch of her body.

She did not stop to ask if it were or were not a monstrous joy that held her. A clear and exalted perception enabled her to dismiss the suggestion as trivial. She knew that she would weep again when she saw the kind, tender hands folded in death; the face that had never looked save with love upon her, fixed and gray and dead. But she saw beyond that bitter moment a long procession of years to come that would belong to her absolutely. And she opened and spread her arms out to them in welcome.

There would be no one to live for during those coming years; she would live for herself. There would be no powerful will bending hers in that blind persistence with which men and women believe they have a right to impose a private will upon a fellow-creature. A kind intention or a cruel intention made the act seem no less a crime as she looked upon it in that brief moment of illumination.

And yet she had loved him--sometimes. Often she had not. What did it matter! What could love, the unsolved mystery, count for in the face of this possession of self-assertion which she suddenly recognized as the strongest impulse of her being!

"Free! Body and soul free!" she kept whispering.

Josephine was kneeling before the closed door with her lips to the keyhole, imploring for admission. "Louise, open the door! I beg; open the door--you will make yourself ill. What are you doing, Louise? For heaven's sake open the door."

"Go away. I am not making myself ill." No; she was drinking in a very elixir of life through that open window.

Her fancy was running riot along those days ahead of her. Spring days, and summer days, and all sorts of days that would be her own. She breathed a quick prayer that life might be long. It was only yesterday she had thought with a shudder that life might be long.

She arose at length and opened the door to her sister's importunities. There was a feverish triumph in her eyes, and she carried herself unwittingly like a goddess of Victory. She clasped her sister's waist, and together they descended the stairs. Richards stood waiting for them at the bottom.

Someone was opening the front door with a latchkey. It was Brently Mallard who entered, a little travel-stained, composedly carrying his grip-sack and umbrella. He had been far from the scene of the accident, and did not even know there had been one. He stood amazed at Josephine's piercing cry; at Richards' quick motion to screen him from the view of his wife.

When the doctors came they said she had died of heart disease--of the joy that kills.

REGRET

MAMZELLE AURLIE possessed a good strong figure, ruddy cheeks, hair that was changing from brown to gray, and a determined eye. She wore a man's hat about the farm, and an old blue army overcoat when it was cold, and sometimes top-boots.

Mamzelle Aurlie had never thought of marrying. She had never been in love. At the age of twenty she had received a proposal, which she had promptly declined, and at the age of fifty she had not yet lived to regret it.

So she was quite alone in the world, except for her dog Ponto, and the negroes who lived in her cabins and worked her crops, and the fowls, a few cows, a couple of mules, her gun (with which she shot chicken-hawks), and her religion.

One morning Mamzelle Aurlie stood upon her gallery, contemplating, with arms akimbo, a small band of very small children who, to all intents and purposes, might have fallen from the clouds, so unexpected and bewildering was their coming, and so unwelcome. They were the children of her nearest neighbor, Odile, who was not such a near neighbor, after all.

The young woman had appeared but five minutes before, accompanied by these four children. In her arms she carried little Lodie; she dragged Ti Nomme by an unwilling hand; while Marcline and Marclette followed with irresolute steps.

Her face was red and disfigured from tears and excitement. She had been summoned to a neighboring parish by the dangerous illness of her mother; her husband was away in Texas -- it seemed to her a million miles away; and Valsin was waiting with the mule-cart to drive her to the station.

"It's no question, Mamzelle Aurlie; you jus' got to keep those youngsters fo' me tell I come back. Dieu sait, I wouldn' botha you with 'em if it was any otha way to do! Make 'em mine you, Mamzelle Aurlie; don' spare 'em. Me, there, I'm half crazy between the chil'ren, an' Lon not home, an' maybe not even to fine po' maman alive encore!" -- a harrowing possibility which drove Odile to take a final hasty and convulsive leave of her disconsolate family.

She left them crowded into the narrow strip of shade on the porch of the long, low house; the white sunlight was beating in on the white old boards; some chickens were scratching in the grass at the foot of the steps, and one had boldly mounted, and was stepping heavily, solemnly, and aimlessly across the gallery. There was a pleasant odor of pinks in the air, and the sound of negroes' laughter was coming across the flowering cotton-field.

Mamzelle Aurlie stood contemplating the children. She looked with a critical eye upon Marcline, who had been left staggering beneath the weight of the chubby Lodie. She surveyed with the same calculating air Marclette mingling her silent tears with the audible grief and rebellion of Ti Nomme. During those few contemplative moments she was collecting herself, determining upon a line of action which should be identical with a line of duty. She began by feeding them.

If Mamzelle Aurlie's responsibilities might have begun and ended there, they could easily have been dismissed; for her larder was amply provided against an emergency of this nature. But little children are not little pigs: they require and demand attentions which were wholly unexpected by Mamzelle Aurlie, and which she was ill prepared to give.

She was, indeed, very inapt in her management of Odile's children during the first few days. How could she know that Marclette always wept when spoken to in a loud and commanding tone of voice? It was a peculiarity of Marclette's. She became acquainted with Ti Nomme's passion for flowers only when he had plucked all the choicest gardenias and pinks for the apparent purpose of critically studying their botanical construction.

"'T ain't enough to tell 'im, Mamzelle Aurlie," Marcline instructed her; "you got to tie 'im in a chair. It's w'at maman all time do w'en he's bad: she tie 'im in a chair." The chair in which Mamzelle Aurlie tied Ti Nomme was roomy and comfortable, and he seized the opportunity to take a nap in it, the afternoon being warm.

At night, when she ordered them one and all to bed as she would have shooed the chickens into the hen-house, they stayed uncomprehending before her. What about the little white nightgowns that had to be taken from the pillow-slip in which they were brought over, and shaken by some strong hand till they snapped like ox-whips? What about the tub of water which had to be brought and set in the middle of the floor, in which the little tired, dusty, sun-browned feet had every one to be washed sweet and clean? And it made Marcline and Marclette laugh merrily -- the idea that Mamzelle Aurlie should for a moment have believed that Ti Nomme could fall asleep without being told the story of Croque-mitaine or Loup-garou, or both; or that Iodie could fall asleep at all without being rocked and sung to.

"I tell you, Aunt Ruby," Mamzelle Aurlie informed her cook in confidence; "me, I'd rather manage a dozen plantation' than fo' chil'ren. It's terrassent! Bont! don't talk to me about chil'ren!"

"T ain' ispected sich as you would know airy thing 'bout 'em, Mamzelle Aurlie. I see dat plainly yistiddy w'en I spy dat li'le chile playin' wid yo' baskit o' keys. You don' know dat makes chillun grow up hard-headed, to play wid keys? Des like it make 'em teeth hard to look in a lookin'-glass. Them's the things you got to know in the raisin' an' manigement o' chillun."

Mamzelle Aurlie certainly did not pretend or aspire to such subtle and far-reaching knowledge on the subject as Aunt Ruby possessed, who had "raised five an' buried six" in her day. She was glad enough to learn a few little mother-tricks to serve the moment's need.

Ti Nomme's sticky fingers compelled her to unearth white aprons that she had not worn for years, and she had to accustom herself to his moist kisses -- the expressions of an affectionate and exuberant nature. She got down her sewing-basket, which she seldom used, from the top shelf of the armoire, and placed it within the ready and easy reach which torn slips and buttonless waists demanded. It took her some days to become accustomed to the laughing, the crying, the chattering that echoed through the house and around it all day long. And it was not the first or the second night that she could sleep comfortably with little Lodie's hot, plump body pressed close against her, and the little one's warm breath beating her cheek like the fanning of a bird's wing.

But at the end of two weeks Mamzelle Aurlie had grown quite used to these things, and she no longer complained.

It was also at the end of two weeks that Mamzelle Aurlie, one evening, looking away toward the crib where the cattle were being fed, saw Valsin's blue cart turning the bend of the road. Odile sat beside the mulatto, upright and alert. As they drew near, the young woman's beaming face indicated that her home-coming was a happy one.

But this coming, unannounced and unexpected, threw Mamzelle Aurlie into a flutter that was almost agitation. The children had to be gathered. Where was Ti Nomme? Yonder in the shed, putting an edge on his knife at the grindstone. And Marcline and Marclette? Cutting and fashioning doll-rags in the corner of the gallery. As for Lodie, she was safe enough in Mamzelle Aurlie's arms; and she had screamed with delight at sight of the familiar blue cart which was bringing her mother back to her.

THE excitement was all over, and they were gone. How still it was when they were gone! Mamzelle Aurlie stood upon the gallery, looking and listening. She could no longer see the cart; the red sunset and the blue-gray twilight had together flung a purple mist across the fields and road that hid it from her view. She could no longer hear the wheezing and creaking of its wheels. But she could still faintly hear the shrill, glad voices of the children.

She turned into the house. There was much work awaiting her, for the children had left a sad disorder behind them; but she did not at once set about the task of righting it. Mamzelle Aurlie seated herself beside the table. She gave one slow glance through the room, into which the evening shadows were creeping and deepening around her solitary figure. She let her head fall down upon her bended arm, and began to cry. Oh, but she cried! Not softly, as women often do. She cried like a man, with sobs that seemed to tear her very soul. She did not notice Ponto licking her hand.

Bert Harte

THE LUCK OF THE ROARING CAMP

There was commotion in Roaring Camp. It could not have been a fight, for in 1850 that was not novel enough to have called together the entire settlement. The ditches and claims were not only deserted, but "Tuttle's grocery" had contributed its gamblers, who, it will be remembered, calmly continued their game the day that French Pete and Kanaka Joe shot each other to death over the bar in the front room. The whole camp was collected before a rude cabin on the outer edge of the clearing. Conversation was carried on in a low tone, but the name of a woman was frequently repeated. It was a name familiar enough in the camp,--"Cherokee Sal."

Perhaps the less said of her the better. She was a coarse and, it is to be feared, a very sinful woman. But at that time she was the only woman in Roaring Camp, and was just then lying in sore extremity, when she most needed the ministration of her own sex. Dissolute, abandoned, and irreclaimable, she was yet suffering a martyrdom hard enough to bear even when veiled by sympathizing womanhood, but now terrible in her loneliness. The primal curse had come to her in that original isolation which must have made the punishment of the first transgression so dreadful. It was, perhaps, part of the expiation of her sin that, at a moment when she most lacked her sex's intuitive tenderness and care, she met only the half-contemptuous faces of her masculine associates. Yet a few of the spectators were, I think, touched by her sufferings. Sandy Tipton thought it was "rough on Sal," and, in the contemplation of her condition, for a moment rose superior to the fact that he had an ace and two bowers in his sleeve.

It will be seen also that the situation was novel. Deaths were by no means uncommon in Roaring Camp, but a birth was a new thing. People had been dismissed the camp effectively, finally, and with no possibility of return; but this was the first time that anybody had been introduced AB INITIO. Hence the excitement.

"You go in there, Stumpy," said a prominent citizen known as "Kentuck," addressing one of the loungers. "Go in there, and see what you kin do. You've had experience in them things."

Perhaps there was a fitness in the selection. Stumpy, in other climes, had been the putative head of two families; in fact, it was owing to some legal informality in these proceedings that Roaring Camp--a city of refuge--was indebted to his company. The crowd approved the choice, and Stumpy was wise enough to bow to the majority. The door closed on the extempore surgeon and midwife, and Roaring Camp sat down outside, smoked its pipe, and awaited the issue.

The assemblage numbered about a hundred men. One or two of these were actual fugitives from justice, some were criminal, and all were reckless. Physically they exhibited no indication of their past lives and character. The greatest scamp had a Raphael face, with a profusion of blonde hair; Oakhurst, a gambler, had the melancholy air and intellectual abstraction of a Hamlet; the coolest and most courageous man was scarcely over five feet in height, with a soft voice and an embarrassed, timid manner. The term "roughs" applied to them was a distinction rather than a definition. Perhaps in the minor details of fingers, toes, ears, etc., the camp may have been deficient, but these slight omissions did not detract from their aggregate force. The strongest man had but three fingers on his right hand; the best shot had but one eye.

Such was the physical aspect of the men that were dispersed around the cabin. The camp lay in a triangular valley between two hills and a river. The only outlet was a steep trail over the summit of a hill that faced the cabin, now illuminated by the rising moon. The suffering woman might have seen it from the rude bunk whereon she lay,--seen it winding like a silver thread until it was lost in the stars above.

A fire of withered pine boughs added sociability to the gathering. By degrees the natural levity of Roaring Camp returned. Bets were freely offered and taken regarding the result. Three to five that "Sal would get through with it;" even that the child would survive; side bets as to the sex and complexion of the coming stranger. In the midst of an excited discussion an exclamation came from those nearest the door, and the camp stopped to listen. Above the swaying and moaning of the pines, the swift rush of the river, and the crackling of the fire rose a sharp, querulous cry,--a cry unlike anything heard before in the camp. The pines stopped moaning, the river ceased to rush, and the fire to crackle. It seemed as if Nature had stopped to listen too.

The camp rose to its feet as one man! It was proposed to explode a barrel of gunpowder; but in consideration of the situation of the mother, better counsels prevailed, and only a few revolvers were discharged; for whether owing to the rude surgery of the camp, or some other reason, Cherokee

Sal was sinking fast. Within an hour she had climbed, as it were, that rugged road that led to the stars, and so passed out of Roaring Camp, its sin and shame, forever. I do not think that the announcement disturbed them much, except in speculation as to the fate of the child. "Can he live now?" was asked of Stumpy. The answer was doubtful. The only other being of Cherokee Sal's sex and maternal condition in the settlement was an ass. There was some conjecture as to fitness, but the experiment was tried. It was less problematical than the ancient treatment of Romulus and Remus, and apparently as successful.

When these details were completed, which exhausted another hour, the door was opened, and the anxious crowd of men, who had already formed themselves into a queue, entered in single file. Beside the low bunk or shelf, on which the figure of the mother was starkly outlined below the blankets, stood a pine table. On this a candle- box was placed, and within it, swathed in staring red flannel, lay the last arrival at Roaring Camp. Beside the candle-box was placed a hat. Its use was soon indicated. "Gentlemen," said Stumpy, with a singular mixture of authority and EX OFFICIO complacency,-- "gentlemen will please pass in at the front door, round the table, and out at the back door. Them as wishes to contribute anything toward the orphan will find a hat handy." The first man entered with his hat on; he uncovered, however, as he looked about him, and so unconsciously set an example to the next. In such communities good and bad actions are catching. As the procession filed in comments were audible,--criticisms addressed perhaps rather to Stumpy in the character of showman; "Is that him?" "Mighty small specimen;" "Has n't more 'n got the color;" "Ain't bigger nor a derringer." The contributions were as characteristic: A silver tobacco box; a doubloon; a navy revolver, silver mounted; a gold specimen; a very beautifully embroidered lady's handkerchief (from Oakhurst the gambler); a diamond breastpin; a diamond ring (suggested by the pin, with the remark from the giver that he "saw that pin and went two diamonds better"); a slung-shot; a Bible (contributor not detected); a golden spur; a silver teaspoon (the initials, I regret to say, were not the giver's); a pair of surgeon's shears; a lancet; a Bank of England note for 5 pounds; and about $200 in loose gold and silver coin. During these proceedings Stumpy maintained a silence as impassive as the dead on his left, a gravity as inscrutable as that of the newly born on his right. Only one incident occurred to break the monotony of the curious procession. As Kentuck bent over the candle-box half curiously, the child turned, and, in a spasm of pain, caught at his groping finger, and held it fast for a moment. Kentuck looked foolish and embarrassed. Something like a blush tried to assert itself in his weather-beaten cheek. "The damned little cuss!" he said, as he extricated his finger, with perhaps more tenderness and care than he might have been deemed capable of showing. He held that finger a little apart from its fellows as he went out, and examined it curiously. The examination provoked the same original remark in regard to the child. In fact, he seemed to enjoy repeating it. "He rastled with my finger," he remarked to Tipton, holding up the member, "the damned little cuss!"

It was four o'clock before the camp sought repose. A light burnt in the cabin where the watchers sat, for Stumpy did not go to bed that night. Nor did Kentuck. He drank quite freely, and related with great gusto his experience, invariably ending with his characteristic condemnation of the newcomer. It seemed to relieve him of any unjust implication of sentiment, and Kentuck had the weaknesses of the nobler sex. When everybody else had gone to bed, he walked down to the river and whistled reflectingly. Then he walked up the gulch past the cabin, still whistling with demonstrative unconcern. At a large redwood-tree he paused and retraced his steps, and again passed the cabin. Halfway down to the river's bank he again paused, and then returned and knocked at the door. It was opened by Stumpy. "How goes it?" said Kentuck, looking past Stumpy toward the candle-box. "All serene!" replied Stumpy. "Anything up?" "Nothing." There was a pause--an embarrassing one--Stumpy still holding the door. Then Kentuck had recourse to his finger, which he held up to Stumpy. "Rastled with it,--the damned little cuss," he said, and retired.

The next day Cherokee Sal had such rude sepulture as Roaring Camp afforded. After her body had been committed to the hillside, there was a formal meeting of the camp to discuss what should be done with her infant. A resolution to adopt it was unanimous and enthusiastic. But an animated discussion in regard to the manner and feasibility of providing for its wants at once sprang up. It was remarkable that the argument partook of none of those fierce personalities with which discussions were usually conducted at Roaring Camp. Tipton proposed that they should send the child to Red Dog,--a distance of forty miles,--where female attention could be procured. But the unlucky suggestion met with fierce and unanimous opposition. It was evident that no plan which entailed parting from their new acquisition would for a moment be entertained. "Besides," said Tom Ryder, "them fellows at Red Dog would swap it, and ring in somebody else on us." A disbelief in the honesty of other camps prevailed at Roaring Camp, as in other places.

The introduction of a female nurse in the camp also met with objection. It was argued that no decent woman could be prevailed to accept Roaring Camp as her home, and the speaker urged that "they didn't want any more of the other kind." This unkind allusion to the defunct mother, harsh as it may seem, was the first spasm of propriety,--the first symptom of the camp's regeneration. Stumpy advanced nothing. Perhaps he felt a certain delicacy in interfering with the selection of a possible successor in office. But when questioned, he averred stoutly that he and "Jinny"--the mammal before alluded to--could manage to rear the child. There was something original, independent, and heroic about the plan that pleased the camp. Stumpy was retained. Certain articles were sent for to Sacramento. "Mind," said the treasurer, as he pressed a bag of gold-dust into the expressman's hand, "the best that can be got,--lace, you know, and filigree-work and frills,--damn the cost!"

Strange to say, the child thrived. Perhaps the invigorating climate of the mountain camp was compensation for material deficiencies. Nature took the foundling to her broader breast. In that rare atmosphere of the Sierra foothills,--that air pungent with balsamic odor, that ethereal cordial at once bracing and exhilarating,--he may have found food and nourishment, or a subtle chemistry that transmuted ass's milk to lime and phosphorus. Stumpy inclined to the belief that it was the latter and good nursing. "Me and that ass," he would say, "has been father and mother to him! Don't you," he would add, apostrophizing the helpless bundle before him, "never go back on us."

By the time he was a month old the necessity of giving him a name became apparent. He had generally been known as "The Kid," "Stumpy's Boy," "The Coyote" (an allusion to his vocal powers), and even by Kentuck's endearing diminutive of "The damned little cuss." But these were felt to be vague and unsatisfactory, and were at last dismissed under another influence. Gamblers and adventurers are generally superstitious, and Oakhurst one day declared that the baby had brought "the luck" to Roaring Camp. It was certain that of late they had been successful. "Luck" was the name agreed upon, with the prefix of Tommy for greater convenience. No allusion was made to the mother, and the father was unknown. "It's better," said the philosophical Oakhurst, "to take a fresh deal all round. Call him Luck, and start him fair." A day was accordingly set apart for the christening. What was meant by this ceremony the reader may imagine who has already gathered some idea of the reckless irreverence of Roaring Camp. The master of ceremonies was one

"Boston," a noted wag, and the occasion seemed to promise the greatest facetiousness. This ingenious satirist had spent two days in preparing a burlesque of the Church service, with pointed local allusions. The choir was properly trained, and Sandy Tipton was to stand godfather. But after the procession had marched to the grove with music and banners, and the child had been deposited before a mock altar, Stumpy stepped before the expectant crowd. "It ain't my style to spoil fun, boys," said the little man, stoutly eyeing the faces around him," but it strikes me that this thing ain't exactly on the squar. It's playing it pretty low down on this yer baby to ring in fun on him that he ain't goin' to understand. And ef there's goin' to be any godfathers round, I'd like to see who's got any better rights than me." A silence followed Stumpy's speech. To the credit of all humorists be it said that the first man to acknowledge its justice was the satirist thus stopped of his fun. "But," said Stumpy, quickly following up his advantage, "we're here for a christening, and we'll have it. I proclaim you Thomas Luck, according to the laws of the United States and the State of California, so help me God." It was the first time that the name of the Deity had been otherwise uttered than profanely in the camp. The form of christening was perhaps even more ludicrous than the satirist had conceived; but strangely enough, nobody saw it and nobody laughed. "Tommy" was christened as seriously as he would have been under a Christian roof and cried and was comforted in as orthodox fashion.

And so the work of regeneration began in Roaring Camp. Almost imperceptibly a change came over the settlement. The cabin assigned to "Tommy Luck"--or "The Luck," as he was more frequently called--first showed signs of improvement. It was kept scrupulously clean and whitewashed. Then it was boarded, clothed, and papered. The rose wood cradle, packed eighty miles by mule, had, in Stumpy's way of putting it, "sorter killed the rest of the furniture." So the rehabilitation of the cabin became a necessity. The men who were in the habit of lounging in at Stumpy's to see "how 'The Luck' got on" seemed to appreciate the change, and in self-defense the rival establishment of "Tuttle's grocery" bestirred itself and imported a carpet and mirrors. The reflections of the latter on the appearance of Roaring Camp tended to produce stricter habits of personal cleanliness. Again Stumpy imposed a kind of quarantine upon those who aspired to the honor and privilege of holding The Luck. It was a cruel mortification to Kentuck--who, in the carelessness of a large nature and the habits of frontier life, had begun to regard all garments as a second cuticle, which, like a snake's, only sloughed off through decay--to be debarred this privilege from certain prudential reasons. Yet such was the subtle influence of innovation that he thereafter appeared regularly every afternoon in a clean shirt and face still shining from his ablutions. Nor were moral and social sanitary laws neglected. "Tommy," who was supposed to spend his whole existence in a persistent attempt to repose, must not be disturbed by noise. The shouting and yelling, which had gained the camp its infelicitous title, were not permitted within hearing distance of Stumpy's. The men conversed in whispers or smoked with Indian gravity. Profanity was tacitly given up in these sacred precincts, and throughout the camp a popular form of expletive, known as "D--n the luck!" and "Curse the luck!" was abandoned, as having a new personal bearing. Vocal music was not interdicted, being supposed to have a soothing, tranquilizing quality; and one song, sung by "Man-o'-War Jack," an English sailor from her Majesty's Australian colonies, was quite popular as a lullaby. It was a lugubrious recital of the exploits of "the Arethusa, Seventy-four," in a muffled minor, ending with a prolonged dying fall at the burden of each verse, "On b-oo-o-ard of the Arethusa." It was a fine sight to see Jack holding The Luck, rocking from side to side as if with the motion of a ship, and crooning forth this naval ditty. Either through the peculiar rocking of Jack or the length of his song,--it contained ninety stanzas, and was continued with conscientious deliberation to the bitter end,--the lullaby generally had the desired effect. At such times the men would lie at full length under the trees in the soft summer twilight, smoking their pipes and drinking in the melodious utterances. An indistinct idea that this was pastoral happiness pervaded the camp. "This 'ere kind o' think," said the Cockney Simmons, meditatively reclining on his elbow, "is 'evingly." It reminded him of Greenwich.

On the long summer days The Luck was usually carried to the gulch from whence the golden store of Roaring Camp was taken. There, on a blanket spread over pine boughs, he would lie while the men were working in the ditches below. Latterly there was a rude attempt to decorate this bower with flowers and sweet-smelling shrubs, and generally some one would bring him a cluster of wild honeysuckles, azaleas, or the painted blossoms of Las Mariposas. The men had suddenly awakened to the fact that there were beauty and significance in these trifles, which they had so long trodden carelessly beneath their feet. A flake of glittering mica, a fragment of variegated quartz, a bright pebble from the bed of the creek, became beautiful to eyes thus cleared and strengthened, and were invariably pat aside for The Luck. It was wonderful how many treasures the woods and hillsides yielded that "would do for Tommy." Surrounded by playthings such as never child out of fairyland had before, it is to he hoped that Tommy was content. He appeared to be serenely happy, albeit there was an infantine gravity about him, a contemplative light in his round gray eyes, that sometimes worried Stumpy. He was always tractable and quiet, and it is recorded that once, having crept beyond his "corral,"--a hedge of tessellated pine boughs, which surrounded his bed,-- he dropped over the bank on his head in the soft earth, and remained with his mottled legs in the air in that position for at least five minutes with unflinching gravity. He was extricated without a murmur. I hesitate to record the many other instances of his sagacity, which rest, unfortunately, upon the statements of prejudiced friends. Some of them were not without a tinge of superstition. "I crep' up the bank just now," said Kentuck one day, in a breathless state of excitement "and dern my skin if he was a-talking to a jay bird as was a-sittin' on his lap. There they was, just as free and sociable as anything you please, a- jawin' at each other just like two cherrybums." Howbeit, whether creeping over the pine boughs or lying lazily on his back blinking at the leaves above him, to him the birds sang, the squirrels chattered, and the flowers bloomed. Nature was his nurse and playfellow. For him she would let slip between the leaves golden shafts of sunlight that fell just within his grasp; she would send wandering breezes to visit him with the balm of bay and resinous gum; to him the tall redwoods nodded familiarly and sleepily, the bumblebees buzzed, and the rooks cawed a slumbrous accompaniment.

Such was the golden summer of Roaring Camp. They were "flush times," and the luck was with them. The claims had yielded enormously. The camp was jealous of its privileges and looked suspiciously on strangers. No encouragement was given to immigration, and, to make their seclusion more perfect, the land on either side of the mountain wall that surrounded the camp they duly preempted. This, and a reputation for singular proficiency with the revolver, kept the reserve of Roaring Camp inviolate. The expressman--their only connecting link with the surrounding world-- sometimes told wonderful stories of the camp. He would say, "They've a street up there in 'Roaring' that would lay over any street in Red Dog. They've got vines and flowers round their houses, and they wash themselves twice a day. But they're mighty rough on strangers, and they worship an Ingin baby."

With the prosperity of the camp came a desire for further improvement. It was proposed to build a hotel in the following spring, and to invite one or two decent families to reside there for the sake of The Luck, who might perhaps profit by female companionship. The sacrifice that this concession to the sex cost these men, who were fiercely skeptical in regard to its general virtue and usefulness, can only be accounted for by their affection for Tommy. A few still held out. But the resolve could not be carried into effect for three months, and the minority meekly yielded in the hope that something might turn up to prevent it. And it did.

The winter of 1851 will long be remembered in the foothills. The snow lay deep on the Sierras, and every mountain creek became a river, and every river a lake. Each gorge and gulch was transformed into a tumultuous watercourse that descended the hillsides, tearing down giant trees and scattering its drift and debris along the plain. Red Dog had been twice under water, and Roaring Camp had been forewarned. "Water put the gold into them gulches," said Stumpy. "It been here once and will be here again!" And that night the North Fork suddenly leaped over its banks and swept up the triangular valley of Roaring Camp.

In the confusion of rushing water, crashing trees, and crackling timber, and the darkness which seemed to flow with the water and blot out the fair valley, but little could be done to collect the scattered camp. When the morning broke, the cabin of Stumpy, nearest the river-bank, was gone. Higher up the gulch they found the body of its unlucky owner; but the pride, the hope, the joy, The Luck, of Roaring Camp had disappeared. They were returning with sad hearts when a shout from the bank recalled them.

It was a relief-boat from down the river. They had picked up, they said, a man and an infant, nearly exhausted, about two miles below. Did anybody know them, and did they belong here?

It needed but a glance to show them Kentuck lying there, cruelly crushed and bruised, but still holding The Luck of Roaring Camp in his arms. As they bent over the strangely assorted pair, they saw that the child was cold and pulseless. "He is dead," said one. Kentuck opened his eyes. "Dead?" he repeated feebly. "Yes, my man, and you are dying too." A smile lit the eyes of the expiring Kentuck. "Dying!" he repeated; "he's a-taking me with him. Tell the boys I've got The Luck with me now;" and the strong man, clinging to the frail babe as a drowning man is said to cling to a straw, drifted away into the shadowy river that flows forever to the unknown sea.

Washington Irving

THE LEGEND OF THE SLEEPY HOLLOW

Found among the papers of the late Diedrech Knickerbocker.
A pleasing land of drowsy head it was,
Of dreams that wave before the half-shut eye;
And of gay castles in the clouds that pass,
Forever flushing round a summer sky.
- ***Castle of Indolence.***
In the bosom of one of those spacious coves which indent the eastern
shore of the Hudson, at that broad expansion of the river denominated by
the ancient Dutch navigators the Tappan Zee, and where they always
prudently shortened sail and implored the protection of St. Nicholas
when they crossed, there lies a small market town or rural port, which by
some is called Greensburgh, but which is more generally and properly
known by the name of Tarry Town. This name was given, we are told, in
former days, by the good housewives of the adjacent country, from the
inveterate propensity of their husbands to linger about the village tavern
on market days. Be that as it may, I do not vouch for the fact, but merely
advert to it, for the sake of being precise and authentic. Not far from this
village, perhaps about two miles, there is a little valley or rather lap of
land among high hills, which is one of the quietest places in the whole
world. A small brook glides through it, with just murmur enough to lull
one to repose; and the occasional whistle of a quail or tapping of a
woodpecker is almost the only sound that ever breaks in upon the
uniform tranquillity.
 I recollect that, when a stripling, my first exploit in squirrel-shooting was
in a grove of tall walnut-trees that shades one side of the valley. I had
wandered into it at noontime, when all nature is peculiarly quiet, and was
startled by the roar of my own gun, as it broke the Sabbath stillness
around and was prolonged and reverberated by the angry echoes. If ever I
should wish for a retreat whither I might steal from the world and its
distractions, and dream quietly away the remnant of a troubled life, I
know of none more promising than this little valley.
 From the listless repose of the place, and the peculiar character of its
inhabitants, who are descendants from the original Dutch settlers, this
sequestered glen has long been known by the name of SLEEPY
HOLLOW, and its rustic lads are called the Sleepy Hollow Boys
throughout all the neighboring country. A drowsy, dreamy influence

seems to hang over the land, and to pervade the very atmosphere. Some say that the place was bewitched by a High German doctor, during the early days of the settlement; others, that an old Indian chief, the prophet or wizard of his tribe, held his powwows there before the country was discovered by Master Hendrick Hudson. Certain it is, the place still continues under the sway of some witching power, that holds a spell over the minds of the good people, causing them to walk in a continual reverie. They are given to all kinds of marvelous beliefs; are subject to trances and visions, and frequently see strange sights, and hear music and voices in the air. The whole neighborhood abounds with local tales, haunted spots, and twilight superstitions; stars shoot and meteors glare oftener across the valley than in any other part of the country, and the nightmare, with her whole ninefold, seems to make it the favorite scene of her gambols.

The dominant spirit, however, that haunts this enchanted region, and seems to be commander-in-chief of all the powers of the air, is the apparition of a figure on horseback, without a head. It is said by some to be the ghost of a Hessian trooper, whose head had been carried away by a cannon-ball, in some nameless battle during the Revolutionary War, and who is ever and anon seen by the country folk hurrying along in the gloom of night, as if on the wings of the wind. His haunts are not confined to the valley, but extend at times to the adjacent roads, and especially to the vicinity of a church at no great distance. Indeed, certain of the most authentic historians of those parts, who have been careful in collecting and collating the floating facts concerning this spectre, allege that the body of the trooper having been buried in the churchyard, the ghost rides forth to the scene of battle in nightly quest of his head, and that the rushing speed with which he sometimes passes along the Hollow, like a midnight blast, is owing to his being belated, and in a hurry to get back to the churchyard before daybreak.

Such is the general purport of this legendary superstition, which has furnished materials for many a wild story in that region of shadows; and the spectre is known at all the country firesides, by the name of the Headless Horseman of Sleepy Hollow.

It is remarkable that the visionary propensity I have mentioned is not confined to the native inhabitants of the valley, but is unconsciously imbibed by every one who resides there for a time. However wide awake they may have been before they entered that sleepy region, they are sure, in a little time, to inhale the witching influence of the air, and begin to grow imaginative, to dream dreams, and see apparitions.

I mention this peaceful spot with all possible laud for it is in such little retired Dutch valleys, found here and there embosomed in the great State of New York, that population, manners, and customs remain fixed, while the great torrent of migration and improvement, which is making such incessant changes in other parts of this restless country, sweeps by them unobserved. They are like those little nooks of still water, which border a rapid stream, where we may see the straw and

bubble riding quietly at anchor, or slowly revolving in their mimic harbor, undisturbed by the rush of the passing current. Though many years have elapsed since I trod the drowsy shades of Sleepy Hollow, yet I question whether I should not still find the same trees and the same families vegetating in its sheltered bosom.

In this by-place of nature there abode, in a remote period of American history, that is to say, some thirty years since, a worthy wight of the name of Ichabod Crane, who sojourned, or, as he expressed it, "tarried," in Sleepy Hollow, for the purpose of instructing the children of the vicinity. He was a native of Connecticut, a State which supplies the Union with pioneers for the mind as well as for the forest, and sends forth yearly its legions of frontier woodmen and country schoolmasters. The cognomen of Crane was not inapplicable to his person. He was tall, but exceedingly lank, with narrow shoulders, long arms and legs, hands that dangled a mile out of his sleeves, feet that might have served for shovels, and his whole frame most loosely hung together. His head was small, and flat at top, with huge ears, large green glassy eyes, and a long snipe nose, so that it looked like a weather-cock perched upon his spindle neck to tell which way the wind blew. To see him striding along the profile of a hill on a windy day, with his clothes bagging and fluttering about him, one might have mistaken him for the genius of famine descending upon the earth, or some scarecrow eloped from a cornfield.

His schoolhouse was a low building of one large room, rudely constructed of logs; the windows partly glazed, and partly patched with leaves of old copybooks. It was most ingeniously secured at vacant hours, by a *withe twisted in the handle of the door, and stakes set against the window shutters; so that though a thief might get in with perfect ease, he would find some embarrassment in getting out, --an idea most probably borrowed by the architect, Yost Van Houten, from the mystery of an eelpot. The schoolhouse stood in a rather lonely but pleasant situation, just at the foot of a woody hill, with a brook running close by, and a formidable birch-tree growing at one end of it. From hence the low murmur of his pupils' voices, conning over their lessons, might be heard in a drowsy summer's day, like the hum of a beehive; interrupted now and then by the authoritative voice of the master, in the tone of menace or command, or, peradventure, by the appalling sound of the birch, as he urged some tardy loiterer along the flowery path of knowledge. Truth to say, he was a conscientious man, and ever bore in mind the golden maxim, "Spare the rod and spoil the child." Ichabod Crane's scholars certainly were not spoiled.

I would not have it imagined, however, that he was one of those cruel potentates of the school who joy in the smart of their subjects; on the contrary, he administered justice with discrimination rather than severity; taking the burden off the backs of the weak, and laying it on those of the strong. Your mere puny stripling, that winced at the least flourish of the rod, was passed by with indulgence; but the claims of justice were satisfied by inflicting a double portion on some little tough wrong headed, broad-skirted Dutch urchin, who sulked and swelled and grew dogged and sullen beneath the birch. All this he called "doing his duty by their parents;" and he never inflicted a chastisement without following it by the assurance, so consolatory to the smarting urchin, that "he would remember it and thank him for it the longest day he had to live."

When school hours were over, he was even the companion and playmate of the larger boys; and on holiday afternoons would convoy some of the smaller ones home, who happened to have pretty sisters, or good housewives for mothers, noted for the comforts of the cupboard. Indeed, it behooved him to keep on good terms with his pupils. The revenue arising from his school was small, and would have been scarcely sufficient to furnish him with daily bread, for he was a huge feeder, and, though lank, had the dilating powers of an anaconda; but to help out his maintenance, he was, according to country custom in those parts, boarded and lodged at the houses of the farmers whose children he instructed. With these he lived successively a week at a time, thus going the rounds of the neighborhood, with all his worldly effects tied up in a cotton handkerchief.

That all this might not be too onerous on the purses of his rustic patrons, who are apt to considered the costs of schooling a grievous burden, and schoolmasters as mere drones he had various ways of rendering himself both useful and agreeable. He assisted the farmers occasionally in the lighter labors of their farms, helped to make hay, mended the fences, took the horses to water, drove the cows from pasture, and cut wood for the winter fire. He laid aside, too, all the dominant dignity and absolute sway with which he lorded it in his little empire, the school, and became wonderfully gentle and ingratiating. He found favor in the eyes of the mothers by petting the children, particularly the youngest; and like the lion bold, which whilom so magnanimously the lamb did hold, he would sit with a child on one knee, and rock a cradle with his foot for whole hours together.

In addition to his other vocations, he was the singing- master of the neighborhood, and picked up many bright shillings by instructing the young folks in psalmody. It was a matter of no little vanity to him on Sundays, to take his station in front of the church gallery, with a band of chosen singers; where, in his own mind, he completely carried away the palm from the parson. Certain it is, his voice resounded far above all the rest of the congregation; and there are peculiar quavers still to be heard in that church, and which may even be heard half a mile off, quite to the opposite side of the mill-pond, on a still Sunday morning, which are said to be legitimately descended from the nose of Ichabod Crane. Thus, by divers little makeshifts, in that ingenious way which is commonly denominated "by hook and by crook," the worthy pedagogue got on tolerably enough, and was thought, by all who understood nothing of the labor of headwork, to have a wonderfully easy life of it.

The schoolmaster is generally a man of some importance in the female circle of a rural neighborhood; being considered a kind of idle, gentlemanlike personage, of vastly superior taste and accomplishments to the rough country swains, and, indeed, inferior in learning only to the parson. His appearance, therefore, is apt to occasion some little stir at the tea-table of a farmhouse, and the addition of a supernumerary dish of cakes or sweetmeats, or, peradventure, the parade of a silver teapot. Our man of letters, therefore, was peculiarly happy in the smiles of all the country damsels. How he would figure among them in the churchyard, between services on Sundays; gathering grapes for them from the wild vines that overran the surrounding trees; reciting for their amusement all the epitaphs on the tombstones; or sauntering, with a whole bevy of them, along the banks of the adjacent mill-pond; while the more bashful country bumpkins hung sheepishly back, envying his superior elegance and address.

From his half-itinerant life, also, he was a kind of traveling gazette, carrying the whole budget of local gossip from house to house, so that his appearance was always greeted with satisfaction. He was, moreover, esteemed by the women as a man of great erudition, for he had read several books quite through, and was a perfect master of Cotton Mather's "History of New England Witchcraft," in which, by the way, he most firmly and potently believed.

He was, in fact, an odd mixture of small shrewdness and simple credulity. His appetite for the marvelous, and his powers of digesting it, were equally extraordinary; and both had been increased by his residence in this spell-bound region. No tale was too gross or monstrous for his capacious swallow. It was often his delight, after his school was dismissed in the afternoon, to stretch himself on the rich bed of clover bordering the little brook that whimpered by his school-house, and there con over old Mather's direful tales, until the gathering dusk of evening made the printed page a mere mist before his eyes. Then, as he wended his way by swamp and stream and awful woodland, to the farmhouse where he happened to be quartered, every sound of nature, at that witching hour, fluttered his excited imagination, --the moan of the whip-poor-will from the hillside, the boding cry of the tree toad, that harbinger of storm, the dreary hooting of the screech owl, to the sudden rustling in the thicket of birds frightened from their roost. The fireflies, too, which sparkled most vividly in the darkest places, now and then startled him, as one of uncommon brightness would stream across his path; and if, by chance, a huge blockhead of a beetle came winging his blundering flight against him, the poor varlet was ready to give up the ghost, with the idea that he was struck with a witch's token. His only resource on such occasions, either to drown thought or drive away evil spirits, was to sing psalm tunes and the good people of Sleepy Hollow, as they sat by their doors of an evening, were often filled with awe at hearing his nasal melody, "in linked sweetness long drawn out," floating from the distant hill, or along the dusky road.

Another of his sources of fearful pleasure was to pass long winter evenings with the old Dutch wives, as they sat spinning by the fire, with a row of apples roasting and spluttering along the hearth, and listen to their marvellous tales of ghosts and goblins, and haunted fields, and haunted brooks, and haunted bridges, and haunted houses, and particularly of the headless horseman, or Galloping Hessian of the Hollow, as they sometimes called him. He would delight them equally by his anecdotes of witchcraft, and of the direful omens and portentous sights and sounds in the air, which prevailed in the earlier times of Connecticut; and would frighten them woefully with speculations upon comets and shooting stars; and with the alarming fact that the world did absolutely turn round, and that they were half the time topsy-turvy!

But if there was a pleasure in all this, while snugly cuddling in the chimney corner of a chamber that was all of a ruddy glow from the crackling wood fire, and where, of course, no spectre dared to show its face, it was dearly purchased by the terrors of his subsequent walk homewards. What fearful shapes and shadows beset his path, amidst the dim and ghastly glare of a snowy night! With what wistful look did he eye every trembling ray of light streaming across the waste fields from some distant window! How often was he appalled by some shrub covered with snow, which, like a sheeted spectre, beset his very path! How often did he shrink with curdling awe at the sound of his own steps on the frosty crust beneath his feet; and dread to look over his shoulder, lest he should behold some uncouth being tramping close behind him! and how often was he thrown into complete dismay by some rushing blast, howling among the trees, in the idea that it was the Galloping Hessian on one of his nightly scourings!

All these, however, were mere terrors of the night, phantoms of the mind that walk in darkness; and though he had seen many spectres in his time, and been more than once beset by Satan in divers shapes, in his lonely perambulations, yet daylight put an end to all these evils; and he would have passed a pleasant life of it, in despite of the Devil and all his works, if his path had not been crossed by a being that causes more perplexity to mortal man than ghosts, goblins, and the whole race of witches put together, and that was--a woman.

Among the musical disciples who assembled, one evening in each week, to receive his instructions in psalmody, was Katrina Van Tassel, the daughter and only child of a substantial Dutch farmer. She was a booming lass of fresh eighteen; plump as a partridge; ripe and melting and rosy-cheeked as one of her father's peaches, and universally famed, not merely for her beauty, but her vast expectations. She was withal a little of a coquette, as might be perceived even in her dress, which was a mixture of ancient and modern fashions, as most suited to set of her charms. She wore the ornaments of pure yellow gold, which her great-great-grandmother had brought over from Saar dam; the tempting stomacher of the olden time, and withal a provokingly short petticoat, to display the prettiest foot and ankle in the country round.

Ichabod Crane had a soft and foolish heart towards the sex; and it is not to be wondered at, that so tempting a morsel soon found favor in his eyes, more especially after he had visited her in her paternal mansion. Old Baltus Van Tassel was a perfect picture of a thriving, contented, liberal-hearted farmer. He seldom, it is true, sent either his eyes or his thoughts beyond the boundaries of his own farm; but within those everything was snug, happy and well-conditioned. He was satisfied with his wealth, but not proud of it; and piqued himself upon the hearty abundance, rather than the style in which he lived. His stronghold was situated on the banks of the Hudson, in one of those green, sheltered, fertile nooks in which the Dutch farmers are so fond of nestling. A great elm tree spread its broad branches over it, at the foot of which bubbled up a spring of the softest and sweetest water, in a little well formed of a barrel; and then stole sparkling away through the grass, to a neighboring brook, that babbled along among alders and dwarf willows. Hard by the farmhouse was a vast barn, that might have served for a church; every window and crevice of which seemed bursting forth with the treasures of the farm; the flail was busily resounding within it from morning to night; swallows and martins skimmed twittering about the eaves; an rows of pigeons, some with one eye turned up, as if watching the weather, some with their heads under their wings or buried in their bosoms, and others swelling, and cooing, and bowing about their dames, were enjoying the sunshine on the roof. Sleek unwieldy porkers were grunting in the repose and abundance of their pens, from whence sallied forth, now and then, troops of sucking pigs, as if to snuff the air. A stately squadron of snowy geese were riding in an adjoining pond, convoying whole fleets of ducks; regiments of turkeys were gobbling through the farmyard, and Guinea fowls fretting about it, like ill-tempered housewives, with their peevish, discontented cry. Before the barn door strutted the gallant cock, that pattern of a husband, a warrior and a fine gentleman, clapping his burnished wings and crowing in the pride and gladness of his heart, --sometimes tearing up the earth with his feet, and then generously calling his ever-hungry family of wives and children to enjoy the rich morsel which he had discovered.

The pedagogue's mouth watered as he looked upon this sumptuous promise of luxurious winter fare. In his devouring mind's eye, he pictured to himself every roasting-pig running about with a pudding in his belly, and an apple in his mouth; the pigeons were snugly put to bed in a comfortable pie, and tucked in with a coverlet of crust; the geese were swimming in their own gravy; and the ducks pairing cosily in dishes, like snug married couples, with a decent competency of onion sauce. In the porkers he saw carved out the future sleek side of bacon, and juicy relishing ham; not a turkey but he beheld daintily trussed up, with its gizzard under its wing, and, peradventure, a necklace of savory sausages; and even bright chanticleer himself lay sprawling on his back, in a side dish, with uplifted claws, as if craving that quarter which his chivalrous spirit disdained to ask while living.

As the enraptured Ichabod fancied all this, and as he rolled his great green eyes over the fat meadow lands, the rich fields of wheat, of rye, of buckwheat, and Indian corn, and the orchards burdened with ruddy fruit, which surrounded the warm tenement of Van Tassel, his heart yearned after the damsel who was to inherit these domains, and his imagination expanded with the idea, how they might be readily turned into cash, and the money invested in immense tracts of wild land, and shingle palaces in the wilderness. Nay, his busy fancy already realized his hopes, and presented to him the blooming Katrina, with a whole family of children, mounted on the top of a wagon loaded with household trumpery, with pots and kettles dangling beneath; and he beheld himself bestriding a pacing mare, with a colt at her heels, setting out for Kentucky, Tennessee, --or the Lord knows where!

When he entered the house, the conquest of his heart was complete. It was one of those spacious farmhouses, with high- ridged but lowly sloping roofs, built in the style handed down from the first Dutch settlers; the low projecting eaves forming a piazza along the front, capable of being closed up in bad weather. Under this were hung flails, harness, various utensils of husbandry, and nets for fishing in the neighboring river. Benches were built along the sides for summer use; and a great spinning-wheel at one end, and a churn at the other, showed the various uses to which this important porch might be devoted. From this piazza the wondering Ichabod entered the hall, which formed the centre of the mansion, and the place of usual residence. Here rows of resplendent pewter, ranged on a long dresser, dazzled his eyes. In one corner stood a huge bag of wool, ready to be spun; in another, a quantity of linsey-woolsey just from the loom; ears of Indian corn, and strings of dried apples and peaches, hung in gay festoons along the walls, mingled with the gaud of red peppers; and a door left ajar gave him a peep into the best parlor, where the claw-footed chairs and dark mahogany tables shone like mirrors; andirons, with their accompanying shovel and tongs, glistened from their covert of asparagus tops; mock- oranges and conch - shells decorated the mantelpiece; strings of various-colored birds eggs were suspended above it; a great ostrich egg was hung from the centre of the room, and a corner cupboard, knowingly left open, displayed immense treasures of old silver and well-mended china.

From the moment Ichabod laid his eyes upon these regions of delight, the peace of his mind was at an end, and his only study was how to gain the affections of the peerless daughter of Van Tassel. In this enterprise, however, he had more real difficulties than generally fell to the lot of a knight-errant of yore, who seldom had anything but giants, enchanters, fiery dragons, and such like easily conquered adversaries, to contend with and had to make his way merely through gates of iron and brass, and walls of adamant to the castle keep, where the lady of his heart was confined; all which he achieved as easily as a man would carve his way to the centre of a Christmas pie; and then the lady gave him her hand as a matter of course. Ichabod, on the contrary, had to win his way to the heart of a country coquette, beset with a labyrinth of whims and caprices, which were forever presenting new difficulties and impediments; and he had to encounter a host of fearful adversaries of real flesh and blood, the numerous rustic admirers, who beset every portal to her heart, keeping a watchful and angry eye upon each other, but ready to fly out in the common cause against any new competitor.

Among these, the most formidable was a burly, roaring, roystering blade, of the name of Abraham, or, according to the Dutch abbreviation, Brom Van Brunt, the hero of the country round which rang with his feats of strength and hardihood. He was broad-shouldered and double-jointed, with short curly black hair, and a bluff but not unpleasant countenance, having a mingled air of fun and arrogance From his Herculean frame and great powers of limb he had received the nickname of BROM BONES, by which he was universally known. He was famed for great knowledge and skill in horsemanship, being as dexterous on horseback as a Tartar. He was foremost at all races and cock fights; and, with the ascendancy which bodily strength always acquires in rustic life, was the umpire in all disputes, setting his hat on one side, and giving his decisions with an air and tone that admitted of no gainsay or appeal. He was always ready for either a fight or a frolic; but had more mischief than ill-will in his composition; and with all his overbearing roughness, there was a strong dash of waggish good humor at bottom. He had three or four boon companions, who regarded him as their model, and at the head of whom he scoured the country, attending every scene of feud or merriment for miles round. In cold weather he was distinguished by a fur cap, surmounted with a flaunting fox's tail; and when the folks at a country gathering descried this well-known crest at a distance, whisking about among a squad of hard riders, they always stood by for a squall. Sometimes his crew would be heard dashing along past the farmhouses at midnight, with whoop and halloo, like a troop of Don Cossacks; and the old dames, startled out of their sleep, would listen for a moment till the hurry-scurry had clattered by, and then exclaim, "Ay, there goes Brom Bones and his gang!" The neighbors looked upon him with a mixture of awe, admiration, and good-will; and, when any madcap prank or rustic brawl occurred in the vicinity, always shook their heads, and warranted Brom Bones was at the bottom of it.

This rantipole hero had for some time singled out the blooming Katrina for the object of his uncouth gallantries, and though his amorous toyings were something like the gentle caresses and endearments of a bear, yet it was whispered that she did not altogether discourage his hopes. Certain it is, his advances were signals for rival candidates to retire, who felt no inclination to cross a lion in his amours; insomuch, that when his horse was seen tied to Van Tassel's paling, on a Sunday night, a sure sign that his master was courting, or, as it is termed, " sparking," within, all other suitors passed by in despair, and carried the war into other quarters.

Such was the formidable rival with whom Ichabod Crane had to contend, and, considering, all things, a stouter man than he would have shrunk from the competition, and a wiser man would have despaired. He had, however, a happy mixture of pliability and perseverance in his nature; he was in form and spirit like a supple-jackyielding, but tough; though he bent, he never broke; and though he bowed beneath the slightest pressure, yet, the moment it was away--jerk!--he was as erect, and carried his head as high as ever.

To have taken the field openly against his rival would have been madness; for he was not a man to be thwarted in his amours, any more than that stormy lover, Achilles. Ichabod, therefore, made his advances in a quiet and gently insinuating manner. Under cover of his character of singing-master, he made frequent visits at the farmhouse; not that he had anything to apprehend from the meddlesome interference of parents, which is so often a stumbling-block in the path of lovers. Balt Van Tassel was an easy indulgent soul; he loved his daughter better even than his pipe, and, like a reasonable man and an excellent father, let her have her way in everything. His notable little wife, too, had enough to do to attend to her housekeeping and manage her poultry; for, as she sagely observed, ducks and geese are foolish things, and must be looked after, but girls can take care of themselves. Thus, while the busy dame bustled about the house, or plied her spinning-wheel at one end of the piazza, honest Balt would sit smoking his evening pipe at the other, watching the achievements of a little wooden warrior, who, armed with a sword in each hand, was most valiantly fighting the wind on the pinnacle of the barn. In the mean time, Ichabod would carry on his suit with the daughter by the side of the spring under the great elm, or sauntering along in the twilight, that hour so favorable to the lover's eloquence.

I profess not to know how women's hearts are wooed and won. To me they have always been matters of riddle and admiration. Some seem to have but one vulnerable point, or door of access; while others have a thousand avenues, and may be captured in a thousand different ways. It is a great triumph of skill to gain the former, but a still greater proof of generalship to maintain possession of the latter, for man must battle for his fortress at every door and window. He who wins a thousand common hearts is therefore entitled to some renown; but he who keeps undisputed sway over the heart of a coquette is indeed a hero. Certain it is, this was not the case with the redoubtable Brom Bones; and from the moment Ichabod Crane made his advances, the interests of the former evidently declined: his horse was no longer seen tied to the palings on Sunday nights, and a deadly feud gradually arose between him and the preceptor of Sleepy Hollow.

Brom, who had a degree of rough chivalry in his nature, would fain have carried matters to open warfare and have settled their pretensions to the lady, according to the mode of those most concise and simple reasoners, the knights-errant of yore, -- by single combat; but Ichabod was too conscious of the superior might of his adversary to enter the lists against him; he had overheard a boast of Bones, that he would "double the schoolmaster up, and lay him on a shelf of his own schoolhouse;" and he was too wary to give him an opportunity. There was something extremely provoking, in this obstinately pacific system; it left Brom no alternative but to draw upon the funds of rustic waggery in his disposition, and to play off boorish practical jokes upon his rival. Ichabod became the object of whimsical persecution to Bones and his gang of rough riders. They harried his hitherto peaceful domains, smoked out his singing- school by stopping up the chimney, broke into the schoolhouse at night, in spite of its formidable fastenings of withe and window stakes, and turned everything topsy-turvy, so that the poor schoolmaster began to think all the witches in the country held their meetings there. But what was still more annoying, Brom took all Opportunities of turning him into ridicule in presence of his mistress, and had a scoundrel dog whom he taught to whine in the most ludicrous manner, and introduced as a rival of Ichabod's, to instruct her in psalmody.

In this way matters went on for some time, without producing any material effect on the relative situations of the contending powers. On a fine autumnal afternoon, Ichabod, in pensive mood, sat enthroned on the lofty stool from whence he usually watched all the concerns of his little literary realm. In his hand he swayed a ferule, that sceptre of despotic power; the birch of justice reposed on three nails behind the throne, a constant terror to evil doers, while on the desk before him might be seen sundry contraband articles and prohibited weapons, detected upon the persons of idle urchins, such as half-munched apples, popguns, whirligigs, fly-cages, and whole legions of rampant little paper game-cocks. Apparently there had been some appalling act of justice recently inflicted, for his scholars were all busily intent upon their books, or slyly whispering behind them with one eye kept upon the master; and a kind of buzzing stillness reigned throughout the schoolroom. It was suddenly interrupted by the appearance of a negro in tow-cloth jacket and trowsers. a round-crowned fragment of a hat, like the cap of Mercury, and mounted on the back of a ragged, wild, half-broken colt, which he managed with a rope by way of halter. He came clattering up to the school-door with an invitation to Ichabod to attend a merry - making or "quilting-frolic," to be held that evening at Mynheer Van Tassel's; and having, delivered his message with that air of importance and effort at fine language which a negro is apt to display on petty embassies of the kind, he dashed over the brook, and was seen scampering, away up the Hollow, full of the importance and hurry of his mission.

All was now bustle and hubbub in the late quiet schoolroom. The scholars were hurried through their lessons without stopping at trifles; those who were nimble skipped over half with impunity, and those who were tardy had a smart application now and then in the rear, to quicken their speed or help them over a tall word. Books were flung aside without being put away on the shelves, inkstands were overturned, benches thrown down, and the whole school was turned loose an hour before the usual time, bursting forth like a legion of young imps, yelping and racketing about the green in joy at their early emancipation.

The gallant Ichabod now spent at least an extra half hour at his toilet, brushing and furbishing up his best, and indeed only suit of rusty black, and arranging his locks by a bit of broken looking-glass that hung up in the schoolhouse. That he might make his appearance before his mistress in the true style of a cavalier, he borrowed a horse from the farmer with whom he was domiciliated, a choleric old Dutchman of the name of Hans Van Ripper, and, thus gallantly mounted, issued forth like a knight-errant in quest of adventures. But it is meet I should, in the true spirit of romantic story, give some account of the looks and equipments of my hero and his steed. The animal he bestrode was a broken-down plow-horse, that had outlived almost everything but its viciousness. He was gaunt and shagged, with a ewe neck, and a head like a hammer; his rusty mane and tail were tangled and knotted with burs; one eye had lost its pupil, and was glaring and spectral, but the other had the gleam of a genuine devil in it. Still he must have had fire and mettle in his day, if we may judge from the name he bore of Gunpowder. He had, in fact, been a favorite steed of his master's, the choleric Van Ripper, who was a furious rider, and had infused, very probably, some of his own spirit into the animal; for, old and broken-down as he looked, there was more of the lurking devil in him than in any young filly in the country.

Ichabod was a suitable figure for such a steed . He rode with short stirrups, which brought his knees nearly up to the pommel of the saddle; his sharp elbows stuck out like grasshoppers'; he carried his whip perpendicularly in his hand, like a sceptre, and as his horse jogged on, the motion of his arms was not unlike the flapping of a pair of wings. A small wool hat rested on the top of his nose, for so his scanty strip of forehead might be called, and the skirts of his black coat fluttered out almost to the horses tail. Such was the appearance of Ichabod and his steed as they shambled out of the gate of Hans Van Ripper, and it was altogether such an apparition as is seldom to be met with in broad daylight.

It was, as I have said, a fine autumnal day; the sky was clear and serene, and nature wore that rich and golden livery which we always associate with the idea of abundance. The forests had put on their sober brown and yellow, while some trees of the tenderer kind had been nipped by the frosts into brilliant dyes of orange, purple, and scarlet. Streaming files of wild ducks began to make their appearance high in the air; the bark of the squirrel might be heard from the groves of beech and hickory- nuts, and the pensive whistle of the quail at intervals from the neighboring stubble field.

The small birds were taking their farewell banquets. In the fullness of their revelry, they fluttered, chirping and frolicking from bush to bush, and tree to tree, capricious from the very profusion and variety around them. There was the honest cockrobin, the favorite game of stripling sportsmen, with its loud querulous note; and the twittering blackbirds flying in sable clouds, and the golden- winged woodpecker with his crimson crest, his broad black gorget, and splendid plumage; and the cedar-bird, with its red tipt wings and yellow-tipt tail and its little monteiro cap of feathers; and the blue jay, that noisy coxcomb, in his gay light blue coat and white underclothes, screaming and chattering, nodding and bobbing and bowing, and pretending to be on good terms with every songster of the grove.

As Ichabod jogged slowly on his way, his eye, ever open to every symptom of culinary abundance, ranged with delight over the treasures of jolly autumn. On all sides he beheld vast store of apples: some hanging in oppressive opulence on the trees; some gathered into baskets and barrels for the market; others heaped up in rich piles for the cider-press. Farther on he beheld great fields of Indian corn, with its golden ears peeping from their leafy coverts, and holding out the promise of cakes and hasty-pudding; and the yellow pumpkins lying beneath them, turning up their fair round bellies to the sun, and giving ample prospects of the most luxurious of pies; and anon he passed the fragrant buckwheat fields breathing the odor of the beehive, and as he beheld them, soft anticipations stole over his mind of dainty slap-jacks, well buttered, and garnished with honey or treacle, by the delicate little dimpled hand of Katrina Van Tassel.

Thus feeding his mind with many sweet thoughts and "sugared suppositions," he journeyed along the sides of a range of hills which look out upon some of the goodliest scenes of the mighty Hudson. The sun gradually wheeled his broad disk down in the west. The wide bosom of the Tappan Zee lay motionless and glassy, excepting that here and there a gentle undulation waved and prolonged the blue shallow of the distant mountain. A few amber clouds floated in the sky, without a breath of air to move them. The horizon was of a fine golden tint, changing gradually into a pure apple green, and from that into the deep blue of the mid-heaven. A slanting ray lingered on the woody crests of the precipices that overhung some parts of the river, giving greater depth to the dark gray and purple of their rocky sides. A sloop was loitering in the distance, dropping slowly down with the tide, her sail hanging uselessly against the mast; and as the reflection of the sky gleamed along the still water, it seemed as if the vessel was suspended in the air.

It was toward evening that Ichabod arrived at the castle of the Heer Van Tassel, which he found thronged with the pride and flower of the adjacent country Old farmers, a spare leathern- faced race, in homespun coats and breeches, blue stockings, huge shoes, and magnificent pewter buckles. Their brisk, withered little dames, in close crimped caps, long waisted short-gowns, homespun petticoats, with scissors and pin-cushions, and gay calico pockets hanging on the outside. Buxom lasses, almost as antiquated as their mothers, excepting where a straw hat, a fine ribbon, or perhaps a white frock, gave symptoms of city innovation. The sons, in short square-skirted coats, with rows of stupendous brass buttons, and their hair generally queued in the fashion of the times, especially if they could procure an eelskin for the purpose, it being esteemed throughout the country as a potent nourisher and strengthener of the hair.

Brom Bones, however, was the hero of the scene, having come to the gathering on his favorite steed Daredevil, a creature, like himself, full of mettle and mischief, and which no one but himself could manage. He was, in fact, noted for preferring vicious animals, given to all kinds of tricks which kept the rider in constant risk of his neck, for he held a tractable, wellbroken horse as unworthy of a lad of spirit.

Fain would I pause to dwell upon the world of charms that burst upon the enraptured gaze of my hero, as he entered the state parlor of Van Tassel's mansion. Not those of the bevy of buxom lasses, with their luxurious display of red and white; but the ample charms of a genuine Dutch country tea-table, in the sumptuous time of autumn. Such heaped up platters of cakes of various and almost indescribable kinds, known only to experienced Dutch housewives! There was the doughty doughnut, the tender olykoek, and the crisp and crumbling cruller; sweet cakes and short cakes, ginger cakes and honey cakes, and the whole family of cakes. And then there were apple pies, and peach pies, and pumpkin pies; besides slices of ham and smoked beef; and moreover delectable dishes of preserved plums, and peaches, and pears, and quinces; not to mention broiled shad and roasted chickens; together with bowls of milk and cream, all mingled higgledy- pigglely, pretty much as I have enumerated them, with the motherly teapot sending up its clouds of vapor from the midst-- Heaven bless the mark! I want breath and time to discuss this banquet as it deserves, and am too eager to get on with my story. Happily, Ichabod Crane was not in so great a hurry as his historian, but did ample justice to every dainty.

He was a kind and thankful creature, whose heart dilated in proportion as his skin was filled with good cheer, and whose spirits rose with eating, as some men's do with drink. He could not help, too, rolling his large eyes round him as he ate, and chuckling with the possibility that he might one day be lord of all this scene of almost unimaginable luxury and splendor. Then, he thought, how soon he'd turn his back upon the old schoolhouse; snap his fingers in the face of Hans Van Ripper, and every other niggardly patron, and kick any itinerant pedagogue out of doors that should dare to call him comrade!

Old Baltus Van Tassel moved about among his guests with a face dilated with content and goodhumor, round and jolly as the harvest moon. His hospitable attentions were brief, but expressive, being confined to a shake of the hand, a slap on the shoulder, a loud laugh, and a pressing invitation to "fall to, and help themselves."

And now the sound of the music from the common room, or hall, summoned to the dance. The musician was an old gray-headed negro, who had been the itinerant orchestra of the neighborhood for more than half a century. His instrument was as old and battered as himself. The greater part of the time he scraped on two or three strings, accompanying every movement of the bow with a motion of the head; bowing almost to the ground, and stamping with his foot whenever a fresh couple were to start.

Ichabod prided himself upon his dancing as much as upon his vocal powers. Not a limb, not a fibre about him was idle; and to have seen his loosely hung frame in full motion, and clattering about the room, you would have thought St. Vitus himself, that blessed patron of the dance, was figuring before you in person. He was the admiration of all the negroes; who, having gathered, of all ages and sizes, from the farm and the neighborhood, stood forming a pyramid of shining black faces at every door and window; gazing with delight at the scene; rolling their white eye-balls, and showing grinning rows of ivory from ear to ear. How could the flogger of urchins be otherwise than animated and joyous? the lady of his heart was his partner in the dance, and smiling graciously in reply to all his amorous oglings; while Brom Bones, sorely smitten with love and jealousy, sat brooding by himself in one corner.

When the dance was at an end, Ichabod was attracted to a knot of the sager folks, who, with Old Van Tassel, sat smoking at one end of the piazza, gossiping over former times, and drawing out long stories about the war. This neighborhood, at the time of which I am speaking, was one of those highly favored places which abound with chronicle and great men. The British and American line had run near it during the war; it had, therefore], been the scene of marauding and infested with refugees, cow-boys, and all kinds of border chivalry. Just sufficient time had elapsed to enable each story-teller to dress up his tale with a little becoming fiction, and, in the indistinctness of his recollection, to make himself the hero of every exploit.

There was the story of Doffue Martling, a large blue-bearded Dutchman, who had nearly taken a British frigate with an old iron nine-pounder from a mud breastwork, only that his gun burst at the sixth discharge. And there was an old gentleman who shall be nameless, being too rich a mynheer to be lightly mentioned, who, in the battle of White Plains, being an excellent master of defence, parried a musket-ball with a small-sword, insomuch that he absolutely felt it whiz round the blade, and glance off at the hilt; in proof of which he was ready at any time to show the sword, with the hilt a little bent. There were several more that had been equally great in the field, not one of whom but was persuaded that he had a considerable hand in bringing the war to a happy termination. But all these were nothing to the tales of ghosts and apparitions that succeeded. The neighborhood is rich in legendary treasures of the kind. Local tales and superstitions thrive best in these sheltered, long settled retreats; but are trampled under foot by the shifting throng that forms the population of most of our country places. Besides, there is no encouragement for ghosts in most of our villages, for they have scarcely had time to finish their first nap and turn themselves in their graves, before their surviving friends have travelled away from the neighborhood; so that when they turn out at night to walk their rounds, they have no acquaintance left to call upon. This is perhaps the reason why we so seldom hear of ghosts except in our long-established Dutch communities.

The immediate cause, however, of the prevalence of supernatural stories in these parts, was doubtless owing to the vicinity of Sleepy Hollow. There was a contagion in the very air that blew from that haunted region; it breathed forth an atmosphere of dreams and fancies infecting all the land. Several of the Sleepy Hollow people were present at Van Tassel's, and, as usual, were doling out their wild and wonderful legends. Many dismal tales were told about funeral trains, and mourning cries and wailings heard and seen about the great tree where the unfortunate Major Andre was taken, and which stood in the neighborhood. Some mention was made also of the woman in white, that haunted the dark glen at Raven Rock, and was often heard to shriek on winter nights before a storm, having perished there in the snow. The chief part of the stories, however, turned upon the favorite spectre of Sleepy Hollow, the Headless Horseman, who had been heard several times of late, patrolling the country; and, it was said, tethered his horse nightly among the graves in the churchyard.

The sequestered situation of this church seems always to have made it a favorite haunt of troubled spirits. It stands on a knoll, surrounded by locust, trees and lofty elms, from among which its decent, whitewashed walls shine modestly forth, like Christian purity beaming through the shades of retirement. A gentle slope descends from it to a silver sheet of water, bordered by high trees, between which, peeps may be caught at the blue hills of the Hudson. To look upon its grass-grown yard, where the sunbeams seem to sleep so quietly, one would think that there at least the dead might rest in peace. On one side of the church extends a wide woody dell, along which raves a large brook among broken rocks and trunks of fallen trees. Over a deep black part of the stream, not far from the church, was formerly thrown a wooden bridge; the road that led to it, and the bridge itself, were thickly shaded by overhanging trees, which cast a gloom about it, even in the daytime; but occasioned a fearful darkness at night. Such was one of the favorite haunts of the Headless Horseman, and the place where he was most frequently encountered. The tale was told of old Brouwer, a most heretical disbeliever in ghosts, how he met the Horseman returning from his foray into Sleepy Hollow, and was obliged to get up behind him; how they galloped over bush and brake, over hill and swamp, until they reached the bridge; when the Horseman suddenly turned into a skeleton, threw old Brouwer into the brook, and sprang away over the tree-tops with a clap of thunder.

This story was immediately matched by a thrice marvellous adventure of Brom Bones, who made light of the Galloping Hessian as an arrant jockey. He affirmed that on returning one night from the neighboring village of Sing Sing, he had been overtaken by this midnight trooper; that he had offered to race with him for a bowl of punch, and should have won it too, for Daredevil beat the goblin horse all hollow, but just as they came to the church bridge, the Hessian bolted, and vanished in a flash of fire.

All these tales, told in that drowsy undertone with which men talk in the dark, the countenances of the listeners only now and then receiving a casual gleam from the glare of a pipe, sank deep in the mind of Ichabod. He repaid them in kind with large extracts from his invaluable author, Cotton Mather, and added many marvellous events that had taken place in his native State of Connecticut, and fearful sights which he had seen in his nightly walks about Sleepy Hollow.

The revel now gradually broke up. The old farmers gathered together their families in their wagons, and were heard for some time rattling along the hollow roads, and over the distant hills. Some of the damsels mounted on pillions behind their favorite swains, and their light-hearted laughter, mingling with the clatter of hoofs, echoed along the silent woodlands, sounding fainter and fainter, until they gradually died away, --and the late scene of noise and frolic was all silent and deserted. Ichabod only lingered behind, according to the custom of country lovers, to have a tete-a-tete with the heiress; fully convinced that he was now on the high road to success. What passed at this interview I will not pretend to say, for in fact I do not know. Something, however, I fear me, must have gone wrong, for he certainly sallied forth, after no very great interval, with an air quite desolate and chapfallen. Oh, these women! these women! Could that girl have been playing off any of her coquettish tricks? Was her encouragement of the poor pedagogue all a mere sham to secure her conquest of his rival? Heaven only knows, not I! Let it suffice to say, Ichabod stole forth with the air of one who had been sacking a henroost, rather than a fair lady's heart. Without looking to the right or left to notice the scene of rural wealth, on which he had so often gloated, he went straight to the stable, and with several hearty cuffs and kicks roused his steed most uncourteously from the comfortable quarters in which he was soundly sleeping, dreaming of mountains of corn and oats, and whole valleys of timothy and clover.

It was the very witching time of night that Ichabod, heavy hearted and crest-fallen, pursued his travels homewards, along the sides of the lofty hills which rise above Tarry Town, and which he had traversed so cheerily in the afternoon. The hour was as dismal as himself. Far below him the Tappan Zee spread its dusky and indistinct waste of waters, with here and there the tall mast of a sloop, riding quietly at anchor under the land. In the dead hush of midnight, he could even hear the barking of the watchdog from the opposite shore of the Hudson; but it was so vague and faint as only to give an idea of his distance from this faithful companion of man. Now and then, too, the long-drawn crowing of a cock, accidentally awakened, would sound far, far off, from some farmhouse away among the hills--but it was like a dreaming sound in his ear. No signs of life occurred near him, but occasionally the melancholy chirp of a cricket, or perhaps the guttural twang of a bull-frog from a neighboring marsh, as if sleeping uncomfortably and turning suddenly in his bed.

All the stories of ghosts and goblins that he had heard in the afternoon now came crowding upon his recollection. The night grew darker and darker; the stars seemed to sink deeper in the sky, and driving clouds occasionally hid them from his sight. He had never felt so lonely and dismal. He was, moreover, approaching the very place where many of the scenes of the ghost stories had been laid. In the centre of the road stood an enormous tulip-tree, which towered like a giant above all the other trees of the neighborhood, and formed a kind of landmark. Its limbs were gnarled and fantastic, large enough to form trunks for ordinary trees, twisting down almost to the earth, and rising again into the air. It was connected with the tragical story of the unfortunate Andre, who had been taken prisoner hard by; and was universally known by the name of Major Andre's tree. The common people regarded it with a mixture of respect and superstition, partly out of sympathy for the fate of its ill- starred namesake, and partly from the tales of strange sights, and doleful lamentations, told concerning it.

As Ichabod approached this fearful tree, he began to whistle; he thought his whistle was answered; it was but a blast sweeping sharply through the dry branches. As he approached a little nearer, he thought he saw something white, hanging in the midst of the tree: he paused, and ceased whistling but, on looking more narrowly, perceived that it was a place where the tree had been scathed by lightning, and the white wood laid bare. Suddenly he heard a groan--his teeth chattered, and his knees smote against the saddle: it was but the rubbing of one huge bough upon another, as they were swayed about by the breeze. He passed the tree in safety, but new perils lay before him.

About two hundred yards from the tree, a small brook crossed the road, and ran into a marshy and thickly-wooded glen, known by the name of Wiley's Swamp. A few rough logs, laid side by side, served for a bridge over this stream. On that side of the road where the brook entered the wood, a group of oaks and chestnuts, matted thick with wild grape-vines, threw a cavernous gloom over it. To pass this bridge was the severest trial. It was at this identical spot that the unfortunate Andre was captured, and under the covert of those chestnuts and vines were the sturdy yeomen concealed who surprised him. This has ever since been considered a haunted stream, and fearful are the feelings of the school-boy who has to pass it alone after dark.

As he approached the stream, his heart began to thump he summoned up, however, all his resolution, gave his horse half a score of kicks in the ribs, and attempted to dash briskly across the bridge; but instead of starting forward, the perverse old animal made a lateral movement, and ran broadside against the fence. Ichabod, whose fears increased with the delay, jerked the reins on the other side, and kicked lustily with the contrary foot: it was all in vain; his steed started, it is true, but it was only to plunge to the opposite side of the road into a thicket of brambles and alder-bushes. The schoolmaster now bestowed both whip and heel upon the starveling ribs of old Gunpowder, who dashed forward, snuffling and snorting, but came to a stand just by the bridge, with a suddenness that had nearly sent his rider sprawling over his head. Just at this moment a plashy tramp by the side of the bridge caught the sensitive ear of Ichabod. In the dark shadow of the grove, on the margin of the brook, he beheld something huge, misshapen and towering. It stirred not, but seemed gathered up in the gloom, like some gigantic monster ready to spring upon the traveller.

The hair of the affrighted pedagogue rose upon his head with terror. What was to be done? To turn and fly was now too late; and besides, what chance was there of escaping ghost or goblin, if such it was, which could ride upon the wings of the wind? Summoning up, therefore, a show of courage, he demanded in stammering accents, " Who are you?" He received no reply. He repeated his demand in a still more agitated voice. Still there was no answer. Once more he cudgelled the sides of the inflexible Gunpowder, and, shutting his eyes, broke forth with involuntary fervor into a psalm tune. Just then the shadowy object of alarm put itself in motion, and with a scramble and a bound stood at once in the middle of the road. Though the night was dark and dismal, yet the form of the unknown might now in some degree be ascertained. He appeared to be a horseman of large dimensions, and mounted on a black horse of powerful frame. He made no offer of molestation or sociability, but kept aloof on one side of the road, jogging along on the blind side of old Gunpowder, who had now got over his fright and waywardness.

Ichabod, who had no relish for this strange midnight companion, and bethought himself of the adventure of Brom Bones with the Galloping Hessian, now quickened his steed in hopes of leaving him behind. The stranger, however, quickened his horse to an equal pace. Ichabod pulled up, and fell into a walk, thinking to lag behind, the other did the same. His heart began to sink within him; he endeavored to resume his psalm tune, but his parched tongue clove to the roof of his mouth, and he could not utter a stave. There was something in the moody and dogged silence of this pertinacious companion that was mysterious and appalling. It was soon fearfully accounted for. On mounting a rising ground, which brought the figure of his fellow-traveller in relief against the sky, gigantic in height, and muffled in a cloak, Ichabod was horror-struck on perceiving that he was headless! but his horror was still more increased on observing that the head, which should have rested on his shoulders, was carried before him on the pommel of his saddle! His terror rose to desperation; he rained a shower of kicks and blows upon Gunpowder, hoping by a sudden movement to give his companion the slip; but the spectre started full jump with him. Away, then, they dashed through thick and thin; stones flying and sparks flashing at every bound. Ichabod's flimsy garments fluttered in the air, as he stretched his long lank body away over his horse's head, in the eagerness of his flight.

They had now reached the road which turns off to Sleepy Hollow; but Gunpowder, who seemed possessed with a demon, instead of keeping up it, made an opposite turn, and plunged headlong down hill to the left. This road leads through a sandy hollow shaded by trees for about a quarter of a mile, where it crosses the bridge famous in goblin story; and just beyond swells the green knoll on which stands the whitewashed church.

As yet the panic of the steed had given his unskilful rider an apparent advantage in the chase, but just as he had got half way through the hollow, the girths of the saddle gave way, and he felt it slipping from under him. He seized it by the pommel, and endeavored to hold it firm, but in vain; and had just time to save himself by clasping old Gunpowder round the neck, when the saddle fell to the earth, and he heard it trampled under foot by his pursuer. For a moment the terror of Hans Van Ripper's wrath passed across his mind, --for it was his Sunday saddle; but this was no time for petty fears; the goblin was hard on his haunches; and (unskilful rider that he was!) he had much ado to maintain his seat; sometimes slipping on one side, sometimes on another, and sometimes jolted on the high ridge of his horse's backbone, with a violence that he verily feared would cleave him asunder.

An opening, in the trees now cheered him with the hopes that the church bridge was at hand. The wavering reflection of a silver star in the bosom of the brook told him that he was not mistaken. He saw the walls of the church dimly glaring under the trees beyond. He recollected the place where Brom Bones' ghostly competitor had disappeard. "If I can but reach that bridge," thought Ichabod, " I am safe." Just then he heard the black steed panting and blowing close behind him; he even fancied that he felt his hot breath. Another convulsive kick in the ribs, and old Gunpowder sprang upon the bridge; he thundered over the resounding planks; he gained the opposite side; and now Ichabod cast a look behind to see if his pursuer should vanish, according to rule, in a flash of fire and brimstone. Just then he saw the goblin rising in his stirrups, and in the very act of hurling his head at him. Ichabod endeavored to dodge the horrible missile, but too late. It encountered his cranium with a tremendous crash, --he was tumbled headlong into the dust, and Gunpowder, the black steed, and the goblin rider, passed by like a whirlwind.

The next morning the old horse was found without his saddle, and with the bridle under his feet, soberly cropping the grass at his master's gate. Ichabod did not make his appearance at breakfast; dinner-hour came, but no Ichabod. The boys assembled at the schoolhouse, and strolled idly about the banks of the brook; but no schoolmaster. Hans Van Ripper now began to feel some uneasiness about the fate of poor Ichabod, and his saddle. An inquiry was set on foot, and after diligent investigation they came upon his traces. In one part of the road leading to the church was found the saddle trampled in the dirt; the tracks of horses' hoofs deeply dented in the road, and evidently at furious speed, were traced to the bridge, beyond which, on the bank of a broad part of the brook, where the water ran deep and black, was found the head of the unfortunate Ichabod, and close beside it a shattered pumpkin.

The brook was searched, but the body of the schoolmaster was not to be discovered. Hans Van Ripper as executor of his estate, examined the bundle which contained all his worldly effects. They consisted of two shirts and a half; two stocks for the neck; a pair or two of worsted stockings; an old pair of corduroy small- clothes; a rusty razor; a book of psalm tunes full of dog's-ears; and a broken pitch-pipe. As to the books and furniture of the schoolhouse, they belonged to the community, excepting Cotton Mather's History of Witchcraft, a New England Almanac, and book of dreams and fortune-telling; in which last was a sheet of foolscap much scribbled and blotted in several fruitless attempts to make a copy of verses in honor of the heiress of Van Tassel. These magic books and the poetic scrawl were forthwith consigned to the flames by Hans Van Ripper; who, from that time forward, determined to send his children no more to school; observing that he never knew any good come of this same reading and writing. Whatever money the schoolmaster possessed, and he had received his quarter's pay but a day or two before, he must have had about his person at the time of his disappearance.

The mysterious event caused much speculation at the church on the following Sunday. Knots of gazers and gossips were collected in the churchyard, at the bridge, and at the spot where the hat and pumpkin had been found. The stories of Brouwer, of Bones, and a whole budget of others were called to mind; and when they had diligently considered them all, and compared them with the symptoms of the present case, they shook their heads, and came to the conclusion chat Ichabod had been carried off by the Galloping Hessian. As he was a bachelor, and in nobody's debt, nobody troubled his head any more about him; the school was removed to a different quarter of the Hollow, and another pedagogue reigned in his stead.

It is true, an old farmer, who had been down to New York on a visit several years after, and from whom this account of the ghostly adventure was received, brought home the intelligence that Ichabod Crane was still alive; that he had left the neighborhood partly through fear of the goblin and Hans Van Ripper, and partly in mortification at having been suddenly dismissed by the heiress; that he had changed his quarters to a distant part of the country; had kept school and studied law at the same time; had been admitted to the bar; turned politician; electioneered; written for the newspapers; and finally had been made a justice of the ten pound court. Brom Bones, too, who, shortly after his rival's disappearance conducted the blooming Katrina in triumph to the altar, was observed to look exceedingly knowing whenever the story of Ichabod was related, and always burst into a hearty laugh at the mention of the pumpkin; which led some to suspect that he knew more about the matter than he chose to tell.

The old country wives, however, who are the best judges of these matters, maintain to this day that Ichabod was spirited away by supernatural means; and it is a favorite story often told about the neighborhood round the winter evening fire. The bridge became more than ever an object of superstitious awe; and that may be the reason why the road has been altered of late years, so as to approach the church by the border of the mill-pond. The schoolhouse being deserted soon fell to decay, and was reported to be haunted by the ghost of the unfortunate pedagogue and the plough-boy, loitering homeward of a still summer evening, has often fancied his voice at a distance, chanting a melancholy psalm tune among the tranquil solitudes of Sleepy Hollow.

Nathaniel Hawthorne

MY KINSMAN, MAJOR MOLINEUX

AFTER the kings of Great Britain had assumed the right of appointing the colonial governors, the measures of the latter seldom met with the ready and generous approbation which had been paid to those of their predecessors, under the original charters. The people looked with most jealous scrutiny to the exercise of power which did not emanate from themselves, and they usually rewarded their rulers with slender gratitude for the compliances by which, in softening their instructions from beyond the sea, they had incurred the reprehension of those who gave them. The annals of Massachusetts Bay will inform us, that of six governors in the space of about forty years from the surrender of the old charter, under James II., two were imprisoned by a popular insurrection; a third, as Hutchinson inclines to believe, was driven from the province by the whizzing of a musket-ball; a fourth, in the opinion of the same historian, was hastened to his grave by continual bickerings with the House of Representatives; and the remaining two, as well as their successors, till the Revolution, were favored with few and brief intervals of peaceful sway. The inferior members of the court party, in times of high political excitement, led scarcely a more desirable life. These remarks may serve as a preface to the following adventures, which chanced upon a summer night, not far from a hundred years ago. The reader, in order to avoid a long and dry detail of colonial affairs, is requested to dispense with an account of the train of circumstances that had caused much temporary inflammation of the popular mind.

It was near nine o'clock of a moonlight evening, when a boat crossed the ferry with a single passenger, who had obtained his conveyance at that unusual hour by the promise of an extra fare. While he stood on the landing-place, searching in either pocket for the means of fulfilling his agreement, the ferryman lifted a lantern, by the aid of which, and the newly risen moon, he took a very accurate survey of the stranger's figure. He was a youth of barely eighteen years, evidently country-bred, and now, as it should seem, upon his first visit to town. He was clad in a coarse gray coat, well worn, but in excellent repair; his under garments were durably constructed of leather, and fitted tight to a pair of serviceable and well-shaped limbs; his stockings of blue yarn were the incontrovertible work of a mother or a sister; and on his head was a three-cornered hat, which in its better days had perhaps sheltered the graver brow of the lad's father. Under his left arm was a heavy cudgel formed of an oak sapling, and retaining a part of the hardened root; and his equipment was completed by a wallet, not so abundantly stocked as to incommode the vigorous shoulders on which it hung. Brown, curly hair, well-shaped features, and bright, cheerful eyes were nature's gifts, and worth all that art could have done for his adornment.

The youth, one of whose names was Robin, finally drew from his pocket the half of a little province bill of five shillings, which, in the depreciation in that sort of currency, did but satisfy the ferryman's demand, with the surplus of a sexangular piece of parchment, valued at three pence. He then walked forward into the town, with as light a step as if his day's journey had not already exceeded thirty miles, and with as eager an eye as if he were entering London city, instead of the little metropolis of a New England colony. Before Robin had proceeded far, however, it occurred to him that he knew not whither to direct his steps; so he paused, and looked up and down the narrow street, scrutinizing the small and mean wooden buildings that were scattered on either side.

"This low hovel cannot be my kinsman's dwelling," thought he, "nor yonder old house, where the moonlight enters at the broken casement; and truly I see none hereabouts that might be worthy of him. It would have been wise to inquire my way of the ferryman, and doubtless he would have gone with me, and earned a shilling from the Major for his pains. But the next man I meet will do as well."

He resumed his walk, and was glad to perceive that the street now became wider, and the houses more respectable in their appearance. He soon discerned a figure moving on moderately in advance, and hastened his steps to overtake it. As Robin drew nigh, he saw that the passenger was a man in years, with a full periwig of gray hair, a wide-skirted coat of dark cloth, and silk stockings rolled above his knees. He carried a long and polished cane, which he struck down perpendicularly before him at every step; and at regular intervals he uttered two successive hems, of a peculiarly solemn and sepulchral intonation. Having made these observations, Robin laid hold of the skirt of the old man's coat just when the light from the open door and windows of a barber's shop fell upon both their figures.

"Good evening to you, honored sir," said he, making a low bow, and still retaining his hold of the skirt. "I pray you tell me whereabouts is the dwelling of my kinsman, Major Molineux."

The youth's question was uttered very loudly; and one of the barbers, whose razor was descending on a well-soaped chin, and another who was dressing a Ramillies wig, left their occupations, and came to the door. The citizen, in the mean time, turned a long-favored countenance upon Robin, and answered him in a tone of excessive anger and annoyance. His two sepulchral hems, however, broke into the very centre of his rebuke, with most singular effect, like a thought of the cold grave obtruding among wrathful passions.

"Let go my garment, fellow! I tell you, I know not the man you speak of. What! I have authority, I have -- hem, hem -- authority; and if this be the respect you show for your betters, your feet shall be brought acquainted with the stocks by daylight, tomorrow morning!"

Robin released the old man's skirt, and hastened away, pursued by an ill-mannered roar of laughter from the barber's shop. He was at first considerably surprised by the result of his question, but, being a shrewd youth, soon thought himself able to account for the mystery.

"This is some country representative," was his conclusion, "who has never seen the inside of my kinsman's door, and lacks the breeding to answer a stranger civilly. The man is old, or verily -- I might be tempted to turn back and smite him on the nose. Ah, Robin, Robin! even the barber's boys laugh at you for choosing such a guide! You will be wiser in time, friend Robin."

He now became entangled in a succession of crooked and narrow streets, which crossed each other, and meandered at no great distance from the water-side. The smell of tar was obvious to his nostrils, the masts of vessels pierced the moonlight above the tops of the buildings, and the numerous signs, which Robin paused to read, informed him that he was near the centre of business. But the streets were empty, the shops were closed, and lights were visible only in the second stories of a few dwelling-houses. At length, on the corner of a narrow lane, through which he was passing, he beheld the broad countenance of a British hero swinging before the door of an inn, whence proceeded the voices of many guests. The casement of one of the lower windows was thrown back, and a very thin curtain permitted Robin to distinguish a party at supper, round a well-furnished table. The fragrance of the good cheer steamed forth into the outer air, and the youth could not fail to recollect that the last remnant of his travelling stock of provision had yielded to his morning appetite, and that noon had found and left him dinnerless.

"Oh, that a parchment three-penny might give me a right to sit down at yonder table!'" said Robin, with a sigh. "But the Major will make me welcome to the best of his victuals; so I will even step boldly in, and inquire my way to his dwelling.'"

He entered the tavern, and was guided by the murmur of voices and the fumes of tobacco to the public-room. It was a long and low apartment, with oaken walls, grown dark in the continual smoke, and a floor which was thickly sanded, but of no immaculate purity. A number of persons -- the larger part of whom appeared to be mariners, or in some way connected with the sea -- occupied the wooden benches, or leather-bottomed chairs, conversing on various matters, and occasionally lending their attention to some topic of general interest. Three or four little groups were draining as many bowls of punch, which the West India trade had long since made a familiar drink in the colony. Others, who had the appearance of men who lived by regular and laborious handicraft, preferred the insulated bliss of an unshared potation, and became more taciturn under its influence. Nearly all, in short, evinced a predilection for the Good Creature in some of its various shapes, for this is a vice to which, as Fast Day sermons of a hundred years ago will testify, we have a long hereditary claim. The only guests to whom Robin's sympathies inclined him were two or three sheepish countrymen, who were using the inn somewhat after the fashion of a Turkish caravansary; they had gotten themselves into the darkest corner of the room, and heedless of the Nicotian atmosphere, were supping on the bread of their own ovens, and the bacon cured in their own chimney-smoke. But though Robin felt a sort of brotherhood with these strangers, his eyes were attracted from them to a person who stood near the door, holding whispered conversation with a group of ill-dressed associates. His features were separately striking almost to grotesqueness, and the whole face left a deep impression on the memory. The forehead bulged out into a double prominence, with a vale between; the nose came boldly forth in an irregular curve, and its bridge was of more than a finger's breadth; the eyebrows were deep and shaggy, and the eyes glowed beneath them like fire in a cave.

While Robin deliberated of whom to inquire respecting his kinsman's dwelling, he was accosted by the innkeeper, a little man in a stained white apron, who had come to pay his professional welcome to the stranger. Being in the second generation from a French Protestant, he seemed to have inherited the courtesy of his parent nation; but no variety of circumstances was ever known to change his voice from the one shrill note in which he now addressed Robin.

"From the country, I presume, sir?" said he, with a profound bow. "Beg leave to congratulate you on your arrival, and trust you intend a long stay with us. Fine town here, sir, beautiful buildings, and much that may interest a stranger. May I hope for the honor of your commands in respect to supper?"

"The man sees a family likeness! the rogue has guessed that I am related to the Major!" thought Robin, who had hitherto experienced little superfluous civility.

All eyes were now turned on the country lad, standing at the door, in his worn three-cornered hat, gray coat, leather breeches, and blue yarn stockings, leaning on an oaken cudgel, and bearing a wallet on his back.

Robin replied to the courteous innkeeper, with such an assumption of confidence as befitted the Major's relative. "My honest friend," he said, "I shall make it a point to patronize your house on some occasion, when" -- here he could not help lowering his voice -- "when I may have more than a parchment three-pence in my pocket. My present business," continued he, speaking with lofty confidence, "is merely to inquire my way to the dwelling of my kinsman, Major Molineux."

There was a sudden and general movement in the room, which Robin interpreted as expressing the eagerness of each individual to become his guide. But the innkeeper turned his eyes to a written paper on the wall, which he read, or seemed to read, with occasional recurrences to the young man's figure.

"What have we here?" said he, breaking his speech into little dry fragments. "Left the house of the subscriber, bounden servant, Hezekiah Mudge, -- had on, when he went away, gray coat, leather breeches, master's third-best hat. One pound currency reward to whosoever shall lodge him in any jail of the providence.' Better trudge, boy; better trudge!"

Robin had begun to draw his hand towards the lighter end of the oak cudgel, but a strange hostility in every countenance induced him to relinquish his purpose of breaking the courteous innkeeper's head. As he turned to leave the room, he encountered a sneering glance from the bold-featured personage whom he had before noticed; and no sooner was he beyond the door, than he heard a general laugh, in which the innkeeper's voice might be distinguished, like the dropping of small stones into a kettle.

"Now, is it not strange," thought Robin, with his usual shrewdness, -- "is it not strange that the confession of an empty pocket should outweigh the name of my kinsman, Major Molineux? Oh, if I had one of those grinning rascals in the woods, where I and my oak sapling grew up together, I would teach him that my arm is heavy though my purse be light!"

On turning the corner of the narrow lane, Robin found himself in a spacious street, with an unbroken line of lofty houses on each side, and a steepled building at the upper end, whence the ringing of a bell announced the hour of nine. The light of the moon, and the lamps from the numerous shop-windows, discovered people promenading on the pavement, and amongst them Robin had hoped to recognize his hitherto inscrutable relative. The result of his former inquiries made him unwilling to hazard another, in a scene of such publicity, and he determined to walk slowly and silently up the street, thrusting his face close to that of every elderly gentleman, in search of the Major's lineaments. In his progress, Robin encountered many gay and gallant figures. Embroidered garments of showy colors, enormous periwigs, gold-laced hats, and silver-hilted swords glided past him and dazzled his optics. Travelled youths, imitators of the European fine gentlemen of the period, trod jauntily along, half dancing to the fashionable tunes which they hummed, and making poor Robin ashamed of his quiet and natural gait.

At length, after many pauses to examine the gorgeous display of goods in the shop-windows, and after suffering some rebukes for the impertinence of his scrutiny into people's faces, the Major's kinsman found himself near the steepled building, still unsuccessful in his search. As yet, however, he had seen only one side of the thronged street; so Robin crossed, and continued the same sort of inquisition down the opposite pavement, with stronger hopes than the philosopher seeking an honest man, but with no better fortune. He had arrived about midway towards the lower end, from which his course began, when he overheard the approach of some one who struck down a cane on the flag-stones at every step, uttering at regular intervals, two sepulchral hems.

"Mercy on us!" quoth Robin, recognizing the sound.

Turning a corner, which chanced to be close at his right hand, he hastened to pursue his researches in some other part of the town. His patience now was wearing low, and he seemed to feel more fatigue from his rambles since he crossed the ferry, than from his journey of several days on the other side. Hunger also pleaded loudly within him, and Robin began to balance the propriety of demanding, violently, and with lifted cudgel, the necessary guidance from the first solitary passenger whom he should meet. While a resolution to this effect was gaining strength, he entered a street of mean appearance, on either side of which a row of ill-built houses was straggling towards the harbor. The moonlight fell upon no passenger along the whole extent, but in the third domicile which Robin passed there was a half-opened door, and his keen glance detected a woman's garment within.

"My luck may be better here," said he to himself.

Accordingly, he approached the doors and beheld it shut closer as he did so; yet an open space remained, sufficing for the fair occupant to observe the stranger, without a corresponding display on her part. All that Robin could discern was a strip of scarlet petticoat, and the occasional sparkle of an eye, as if the moonbeams were trembling on some bright thing.

"Pretty mistress," for I may call her so with a good conscience thought the shrewd youth, since I know nothing to the contrary, -- "my sweet pretty mistress, will you be kind enough to tell me whereabouts I must seek the dwelling of my kinsman, Major Molineux?"

Robin's voice was plaintive and winning, and the female, seeing nothing to be shunned in the handsome country youth, thrust open the door, and came forth into the moonlight. She was a dainty little figure with a white neck, round arms, and a slender waist, at the extremity of which her scarlet petticoat jutted out over a hoop, as if she were standing in a balloon. Moreover, her face was oval and pretty, her hair dark beneath the little cap, and her bright eyes possessed a sly freedom, which triumphed over those of Robin.

"Major Molineux dwells here," said this fair woman.

Now, her voice was the sweetest Robin had heard that night, yet he could not help doubting whether that sweet voice spoke Gospel truth. He looked up and down the mean street, and then surveyed the house before which they stood. It was a small, dark edifice of two stories, the second of which projected over the lower floor, and the front apartment had the aspect of a shop for petty commodities.

"Now, truly, I am in luck," replied Robin, cunningly, "and so indeed is my kinsman, the Major, in having so pretty a housekeeper. But I prithee trouble him to step to the door; I will deliver him a message from his friends in the country, and then go back to my lodgings at the inn."

"Nay, the Major has been abed this hour or more," said the lady of the scarlet petticoat; "and it would be to little purpose to disturb him to-night, seeing his evening draught was of the strongest. But he is a kind-hearted man, and it would be as much as my life's worth to let a kinsman of his turn away from the door. You are the good old gentleman's very picture, and I could swear that was his rainy-weather hat. Also he has garments very much resembling those leather small-clothes. But come in, I pray, for I bid you hearty welcome in his name."

So saying, the fair and hospitable dame took our hero by the hand; and the touch was light, and the force was gentleness, and though Robin read in her eyes what he did not hear in her words, yet the slender-waisted woman in the scarlet petticoat proved stronger than the athletic country youth. She had drawn his half-willing footsteps nearly to the threshold, when the opening of a door in the neighborhood startled the Major's housekeeper, and, leaving the Major's kinsman, she vanished speedily into her own domicile. A heavy yawn preceded the appearance of a man, who, like the Moonshine of Pyramus and Thisbe, carried a lantern, needlessly aiding his sister luminary in the heavens. As he walked sleepily up the street, he turned his broad, dull face on Robin, and displayed a long staff, spiked at the end.

"Home, vagabond, home!" said the watchman, in accents that seemed to fall asleep as soon as they were uttered. "Home, or we'll set you in the stocks by peep of day!"

"This is the second hint of the kind," thought Robin. "I wish they would end my difficulties, by setting me there to-night."

Nevertheless, the youth felt an instinctive antipathy towards the guardian of midnight order, which at first prevented him from asking his usual question. But just when the man was about to vanish behind the corner, Robin resolved not to lose the opportunity, and shouted lustily after him, --

"I say, friend! will you guide me to the house of my kinsman, Major Molineux?"

The watchman made no reply, but turned the corner and was gone; yet Robin seemed to hear the sound of drowsy laughter stealing along the solitary street. At that moment, also, a pleasant titter saluted him from the open window above his head; he looked up, and caught the sparkle of a saucy eye; a round arm beckoned to him, and next he heard light footsteps descending the staircase within. But Robin, being of the household of a New England clergyman, was a good youth, as well as a shrewd one; so he resisted temptation, and fled away.

He now roamed desperately, and at random, through the town, almost ready to believe that a spell was on him, like that by which a wizard of his country had once kept three pursuers wandering, a whole winter night, within twenty paces of the cottage which they sought. The streets lay before him, strange and desolate, and the lights were extinguished in almost every house. Twice, however, little parties of men, among whom Robin distinguished individuals in outlandish attire, came hurrying along; but, though on both occasions, they paused to address him such intercourse did not at all enlighten his perplexity. They did but utter a few words in some language of which Robin knew nothing, and perceiving his inability to answer, bestowed a curse upon him in plain English and hastened away. Finally, the lad determined to knock at the door of every mansion that might appear worthy to be occupied by his kinsman, trusting that perseverance would overcome the fatality that had hitherto thwarted him. Firm in this resolve, he was passing beneath the walls of a church, which formed the corner of two streets, when, as he turned into the shade of its steeple, he encountered a bulky stranger muffled in a cloak. The man was proceeding with the speed of earnest business, but Robin planted himself full before him, holding the oak cudgel with both hands across his body as a bar to further passage

"Halt, honest man, and answer me a question," said he, very resolutely, "Tell me, this instant, whereabouts is the dwelling of my kinsman, Major Molineux!"

"Keep your tongue between your teeth, fool, and let me pass!" said a deep, gruff voice, which Robin partly remembered. "Let me pass, or I'll strike you to the earth!"

"No, no, neighbor!" cried Robin, flourishing his cudgel, and then thrusting its larger end close to the man's muffled face. "No, no, I'm not the fool you take me for, nor do you pass till I have an answer to my question. Whereabouts is the dwelling of my kinsman, Major Molineux?" The stranger, instead of attempting to force his passage, stepped back into the moonlight, unmuffled his face, and stared full into that of Robin.

"Watch here an hour, and Major Molineux will pass by," said he.

Robin gazed with dismay and astonishment on the unprecedented physiognomy of the speaker. The forehead with its double prominence the broad hooked nose, the shaggy eyebrows, and fiery eyes were those which he had noticed at the inn, but the man's complexion had undergone a singular, or, more properly, a twofold change. One side of the face blazed an intense red, while the other was black as midnight, the division line being in the broad bridge of the nose; and a mouth which seemed to extend from ear to ear was black or red, in contrast to the color of the cheek. The effect was as if two individual devils, a fiend of fire and a fiend of darkness, had united themselves to form this infernal visage. The stranger grinned in Robin's face, muffled his party-colored features, and was out of sight in a moment.

"Strange things we travellers see!" ejaculated Robin.

He seated himself, however, upon the steps of the church-door, resolving to wait the appointed time for his kinsman. A few moments were consumed in philosophical speculations upon the species of man who had just left him; but having settled this point shrewdly, rationally, and satisfactorily, he was compelled to look elsewhere for his amusement. And first he threw his eyes along the street. It was of more respectable appearance than most of those into which he had wandered, and the moon, creating, like the imaginative power, a beautiful strangeness in familiar objects, gave something of romance to a scene that might not have possessed it in the light of day. The irregular and often quaint architecture of the houses, some of whose roofs were broken into numerous little peaks, while others ascended, steep and narrow, into a single point, and others again were square; the pure snow-white of some of their complexions, the aged darkness of others, and the thousand sparklings, reflected from bright substances in the walls of many; these matters engaged Robin's attention for a while, and then began to grow wearisome. Next he endeavored to define the forms of distant objects, starting away, with almost ghostly indistinctness, just as his eye appeared to grasp them, and finally he took a minute survey of an edifice which stood on the opposite side of the street, directly in front of the church-door, where he was stationed. It was a large, square mansion, distinguished from its neighbors by a balcony, which rested on tall pillars, and by an elaborate Gothic window, communicating therewith.

"Perhaps this is the very house I have been seeking," thought Robin.

Then he strove to speed away the time, by listening to a murmur which swept continually along the street, yet was scarcely audible, except to an unaccustomed ear like his; it was a low, dull, dreamy sound, compounded of many noises, each of which was at too great a distance to be separately heard. Robin marvelled at this snore of a sleeping town, and marvelled more whenever its continuity was broken by now and then a distant shout, apparently loud where it originated. But altogether it was a sleep-inspiring sound, and, to shake off its drowsy influence, Robin arose, and climbed a window-frame, that he might view the interior of the church. There the moonbeams came trembling in, and fell down upon the deserted pews, and extended along the quiet aisles. A fainter yet more awful radiance was hovering around the pulpit, and one solitary ray had dared to rest upon the open page of the great Bible. Had nature, in that deep hour, become a worshipper in the house which man had builded? Or was that heavenly light the visible sanctity of the place, -- visible because no earthly and impure feet were within the walls? The scene made Robin's heart shiver with a sensation of loneliness stronger than he had ever felt in the remotest depths of his native woods; so he turned away and sat down again before the door. There were graves around the church, and now an uneasy thought obtruded into Robin's breast. What if the object of his search, which had been so often and so strangely thwarted, were all the time mouldering in his shroud? What if his kinsman should glide through yonder gate, and nod and smile to him in dimly passing by?

"Oh that any breathing thing were here with me!" said Robin.

Recalling his thoughts from this uncomfortable track, he sent them over forest, hill, and stream, and attempted to imagine how that evening of ambiguity and weariness had been spent by his father's household. He pictured them assembled at the door, beneath the tree, the great old tree, which had been spared for its huge twisted trunk and venerable shade, when a thousand leafy brethren fell. There, at the going down of the summer sun, it was his father's custom to perform domestic worship that the neighbors might come and join with him like brothers of the family, and that the wayfaring man might pause to drink at that fountain, and keep his heart pure by freshening the memory of home. Robin distinguished the seat of every individual of the little audience; he saw the good man in the midst, holding the Scriptures in the golden light that fell from the western clouds; he beheld him close the book and all rise up to pray. He heard the old thanksgivings for daily mercies, the old supplications for their continuance to which he had so often listened in weariness, but which were now among his dear remembrances. He perceived the slight inequality of his father's voice when he came to speak of the absent one; he noted how his mother turned her face to the broad and knotted trunk; how his elder brother scorned, because the beard was rough upon his upper lip; to permit his features to be moved; how the younger sister drew down a low hanging branch before her eyes; and how the little one of all, whose sports had hitherto broken the decorum of the scene, understood the prayer for her playmate, and burst into clamorous grief. Then he saw them go in at the door; and when Robin would have entered also, the latch tinkled into its place, and he was excluded from his home.

"Am I here, or there?" cried Robin, starting; for all at once, when his thoughts had become visible and audible in a dream, the long, wide, solitary street shone out before him.

He aroused himself, and endeavored to fix his attention steadily upon the large edifice which he had surveyed before. But still his mind kept vibrating between fancy and reality; by turns, the pillars of the balcony lengthened into the tall, bare stems of pines, dwindled down to human figures, settled again into their true shape and size, and then commenced a new succession of changes. For a single moment, when he deemed himself awake, he could have sworn that a visage -- one which he seemed to remember, yet could not absolutely name as his kinsman's -- was looking towards him from the Gothic window. A deeper sleep wrestled with and nearly overcame him, but fled at the sound of footsteps along the opposite pavement. Robin rubbed his eyes, discerned a man passing at the foot of the balcony, and addressed him in a loud, peevish, and lamentable cry.

"Hallo, friend! must I wait here all night for my kinsman, Major Molineux?"

The sleeping echoes awoke, and answered the voice; and the passenger, barely able to discern a figure sitting in the oblique shade of the steeple, traversed the street to obtain a nearer view. He was himself a gentleman in his prime, of open, intelligent, cheerful, and altogether pre-possessing countenance. Perceiving a country youth, apparently homeless and without friends, he accosted him in a tone of real kindness, which had become strange to Robin's ears.

"Well, my good lad, why are you sitting here?" inquired he. "Can I be of service to you in any way?"

"I am afraid not, sir," replied Robin, despondingly; "yet I shall take it kindly, if you'll answer me a single question. I've been searching, half the night, for one Major Molineux, now, sir, is there really such a person in these parts, or am I dreaming?"

"Major Molineux! The name is not altogether strange to me," said the gentleman, smiling. "Have you any objection to telling me the nature of your business with him?"

Then Robin briefly related that his father was a clergyman, settled on a small salary, at a long distance back in the country, and that he and Major Molineux were brothers' children. The Major, having inherited riches, and acquired civil and military rank, had visited his cousin, in great pomp, a year or two before; had manifested much interest in Robin and an elder brother, and, being childless himself, had thrown out hints respecting the future establishment of one of them in life. The elder brother was destined to succeed to the farm which his father cultivated in the interval of sacred duties; it was therefore determined that Robin should profit by his kinsman's generous intentions, especially as he seemed to be rather the favorite, and was thought to possess other necessary endowments.

"For I have the name of being a shrewd youth," observed Robin, in this part of his story.

"I doubt not you deserve it," replied his new friend, good-naturedly; "but pray proceed."

"Well, sir, being nearly eighteen years old, and well grown, as you see," continued Robin, drawing himself up to his full height, "I thought it high time to begin in the world. So my mother and sister put me in handsome trim, and my father gave me half the remnant of his last year's salary, and five days ago I started for this place, to pay the Major a visit. But, would you believe it, sir! I crossed the ferry a little after dark, and have yet found nobody that would show me the way to his dwelling; only, an hour or two since, I was told to wait here, and Major Molineux would pass by."

"Can you describe the man who told you this?" inquired the gentleman.

"Oh, he was a very ill-favored fellow, sir," replied Robin, "with two great bumps on his forehead, a hook nose, fiery eyes; and, what struck me as the strangest, his face was of two different colors. Do you happen to know such a man, sir?"

"Not intimately," answered the stranger, "but I chanced to meet him a little time previous to your stopping me. I believe you may trust his word, and that the Major will very shortly pass through this street. In the mean time, as I have a singular curiosity to witness your meeting, I will sit down here upon the steps and bear you company."

He seated himself accordingly, and soon engaged his companion in animated discourse. It was but of brief continuance, however, for a noise of shouting, which had long been remotely audible, drew so much nearer that Robin inquired its cause.

"What may be the meaning of this uproar?" asked he. "Truly, if your town be always as noisy, I shall find little sleep while I am an inhabitant."

"Why, indeed, friend Robin, there do appear to be three or four riotous fellows abroad to-night," replied the gentleman. "You must not expect all the stillness of your native woods here in our streets. But the watch will shortly be at the heels of these lads and" --

"Ay, and set them in the stocks by peep of day," interrupted Robin recollecting his own encounter with the drowsy lantern-bearer. "But, dear sir, if I may trust my ears, an army of watchmen would never make head against such a multitude of rioters. There were at least a thousand voices went up to make that one shout."

"May not a man have several voices, Robin, as well as two complexions? said his friend.

"Perhaps a man may; but Heaven forbid that a woman should!" responded the shrewd youth, thinking of the seductive tones of the Major's housekeeper.

The sounds of a trumpet in some neighboring street now became so evident and continual, that Robin's curiosity was strongly excited. In addition to the shouts, he heard frequent bursts from many instruments of discord, and a wild and confused laughter filled up the intervals. Robin rose from the steps, and looked wistfully towards a point whither people seemed to be hastening

"Surely some prodigious merry-making is going on," exclaimed he "I have laughed very little since I left home, sir, and should be sorry to lose an opportunity. Shall we step round the corner by that darkish house and take our share of the fun?"

"Sit down again, sit down, good Robin," replied the gentleman, laying his hand on the skirt of the gray coat. "You forget that we must wait here for your kinsman; and there is reason to believe that he will pass by, in the course of a very few moments."

The near approach of the uproar had now disturbed the neighborhood; windows flew open on all sides; and many heads, in the attire of the pillow, and confused by sleep suddenly broken, were protruded to the gaze of whoever had leisure to observe them. Eager voices hailed each other from house to house, all demanding the explanation, which not a soul could give. Half-dressed men hurried towards the unknown commotion stumbling as they went over the stone steps that thrust themselves into the narrow foot-walk. The shouts, the laughter, and the tuneless bray the antipodes of music, came onwards with increasing din, till scattered individuals, and then denser bodies, began to appear round a corner at the distance of a hundred yards

"Will you recognize your kinsman, if he passes in this crowd?" inquired the gentleman

"Indeed, I can't warrant it, sir; but I'll take my stand here, and keep a bright lookout," answered Robin, descending to the outer edge.

A mighty stream of people now emptied into the street, and came rollmg slowly towards the church. A single horseman wheeled the corner in the midst of them, and close behind him came a band of fearful wind-instruments, sending forth a fresher discord now that no intervening buildings kept it from the ear. Then a redder light disturbed the moonbeams, and a dense multitude of torches shone along the street, concealing, by their glare, whatever object they illuminated. The single horseman, clad in a military dress, and bearing a drawn sword, rode onward as the leader, and, by his fierce and variegated countenance, appeared like war personified; the red of one cheek was an emblem of fire and sword; the blackness of the other betokened the mourning that attends them. In his train were wild figures in the Indian dress, and many fantastic shapes without a model, giving the whole march a visionary air, as if a dream had broken forth from some feverish brain, and were sweeping visibly through the midnight streets. A mass of people, inactive, except as applauding spectators, hemmed the procession in; and several women ran along the sidewalk, piercing the confusion of heavier sounds with their shrill voices of mirth or terror.

"The double-faced fellow has his eye upon me," muttered Robin, with an indefinite but an uncomfortable idea that he was himself to bear a part in the pageantry.

The leader turned himself in the saddle, and fixed his glance full upon the country youth, as the steed went slowly by. When Robin had freed his eyes from those fiery ones, the musicians were passing before him, and the torches were close at hand; but the unsteady brightness of the latter formed a veil which he could not penetrate. The rattling of wheels over the stones sometimes found its way to his ear, and confused traces of a human form appeared at intervals, and then melted into the vivid light. A moment more, and the leader thundered a command to halt: the trumpets vomited a horrid breath, and then held their peace; the shouts and laughter of the people died away, and there remained only a universal hum, allied to silence. Right before Robin's eyes was an uncovered cart. There the torches blazed the brightest, there the moon shone out like day, and there, in tar-and-feathery dignity, sat his kinsman, Major Molineux!

He was an elderly man, of large and majestic person, and strong, square features, betokening a steady soul; but steady as it was, his enemies had found means to shake it. His face was pale as death, and far more ghastly; the broad forehead was contracted in his agony, so that his eyebrows formed one grizzled line; his eyes were red and wild, and the foam hung white upon his quivering lip. His whole frame was agitated by a quick and continual tremor, which his pride strove to quell, even in those circumstances of overwhelming humiliation. But perhaps the bitterest pang of all was when his eyes met those of Robin; for he evidently knew him on the instant, as the youth stood witnessing the foul disgrace of a head grown gray in honor. They stared at each other in silence, and Robin's knees shook, and his hair bristled, with a mixture of pity and terror. Soon, however, a bewildering excitement began to seize upon his mind; the preceding adventures of the night, the unexpected appearance of the crowd, the torches, the confused din and the hush that followed, the spectre of his kinsman reviled by that great multitude, -- all this, and, more than all, a perception of tremendous ridicule in the whole scene, affected him with a sort of mental inebriety. At that moment a voice of sluggish merriment saluted Robin's ears; he turned instinctively, and just behind the corner of the church stood the lantern-bearer, rubbing his eyes, and drowsily enjoying the lad's amazement. Then he heard a peal of laughter like the ringing of silvery bells; a woman twitched his arm, a saucy eye met his, and he saw the lady of the scarlet petticoat. A sharp, dry cachinnation appealed to his memory, and, standing on tiptoe in the crowd, with his white apron over his head, he beheld the courteous little innkeeper. And lastly, there sailed over the heads of the multitude a great, broad laugh, broken in the midst by two sepulchral hems; thus, "Haw, haw, haw, -- hem, hem, -- haw, haw, haw, haw!"

The sound proceeded from the balcony of the opposite edifice, and thither Robin turned his eyes. In front of the Gothic window stood the old citizen, wrapped in a wide gown, his gray periwig exchanged for a nightcap, which was thrust back from his forehead, and his silk stockings hanging about his legs. He supported himself on his polished cane in a fit of convulsive merriment, which manifested itself on his solemn old features like a funny inscription on a tombstone. Then Robin seemed to hear the voices of the barbers, of the guests of the inn, and of all who had made sport of him that night. The contagion was spreading among the multitude, when all at once, it seized upon Robin, and he sent forth a shout of laughter that echoed through the street, -- every man shook his sides, every man emptied his lungs, but Robin's shout was the loudest there. The cloud-spirits peeped from their silvery islands, as the congregated mirth went roaring up the sky! The Man in the Moon heard the far bellow. "Oho," quoth he, "the old earth is frolicsome to-night!"

When there was a momentary calm in that tempestuous sea of sound, the leader gave the sign, the procession resumed its march. On they went, like fiends that throng in mockery around some dead potentate, mighty no more, but majestic still in his agony. On they went, in counterfeited pomp, in senseless uproar, in frenzied merriment, trampling all on an old man's heart. On swept the tumult, and left a silent street behind.

. . . .

"Well, Robin, are you dreaming?" inquired the gentleman, laying his hand on the youth's shoulder.

Robin started, and withdrew his arm from the stone post to which he had instinctively clung, as the living stream rolled by him. His cheek was somewhat pale, and his eye not quite as lively as in the earlier part of the evening.

"Will you be kind enough to show me the way to the ferry?" said he, after a moment's pause.

"You have, then, adopted a new subject of inquiry?" observed his companion, with a smile.

"Why, yes, sir," replied Robin, rather dryly. "Thanks to you, and to my other friends, I have at last met my kinsman, and he will scarce desire to see my face again. I begin to grow weary of a town life, sir. Will you show me the way to the ferry?"

"No, my good friend Robin, -- not to-night, at least," said the gentleman. "Some few days hence, if you wish it, I will speed you on your journey. Or, if you prefer to remain with us, perhaps, as you are a shrewd youth, you may rise in the world without the help of your kinsman, Major Molineux."

YOUNG GOODMAN BROWN

Young Goodman Brown came forth at sunset into the street at Salem village; but put his head back, after crossing the threshold, to exchange a parting kiss with his young wife. And Faith, as the wife was aptly named, thrust her own pretty head into the street, letting the wind play with the pink ribbons of her cap while she called to Goodman Brown.

"Dearest heart," whispered she, softly and rather sadly, when her lips were close to his ear, "prithee put off your journey until sunrise and sleep in your own bed to-night. A lone woman is troubled with such dreams and such thoughts that she's afeard of herself sometimes. Pray tarry with me this night, dear husband, of all nights in the year."

"My love and my Faith," replied young Goodman Brown, "of all nights in the year, this one night must I tarry away from thee. My journey, as thou callest it, forth and back again, must needs be done 'twixt now and sunrise. What, my sweet, pretty wife, dost thou doubt me already, and we but three months married?"

"Then God bless you!" said Faith, with the pink ribbons; "and may you find all well when you come back."

"Amen!" cried Goodman Brown. "Say thy prayers, dear Faith, and go to bed at dusk, and no harm will come to thee."

So they parted; and the young man pursued his way until, being about to turn the corner by the meeting-house, he looked back and saw the head of Faith still peeping after him with a melancholy air, in spite of her pink ribbons.

"Poor little Faith!" thought he, for his heart smote him. "What a wretch am I to leave her on such an errand! She talks of dreams, too. Methought as she spoke there was trouble in her face, as if a dream had warned her what work is to be done tonight. But no, no; 't would kill her to think it. Well, she's a blessed angel on earth; and after this one night I'll cling to her skirts and follow her to heaven."

With this excellent resolve for the future, Goodman Brown felt himself justified in making more haste on his present evil purpose. He had taken a dreary road, darkened by all the gloomiest trees of the forest, which barely stood aside to let the narrow path creep through, and closed immediately behind. It was all as lonely as could be; and there is this peculiarity in such a solitude, that the traveller knows not who may be concealed by the innumerable trunks and the thick boughs overhead; so that with lonely footsteps he may yet be passing through an unseen multitude.

"There may be a devilish Indian behind every tree," said Goodman Brown to himself; and he glanced fearfully behind him as he added, "What if the devil himself should be at my very elbow!"

His head being turned back, he passed a crook of the road, and, looking forward again, beheld the figure of a man, in grave and decent attire, seated at the foot of an old tree. He arose at Goodman Brown's approach and walked onward side by side with him.

"You are late, Goodman Brown," said he. "The clock of the Old South was striking as I came through Boston, and that is full fifteen minutes agone."

"Faith kept me back a while," replied the young man, with a tremor in his voice, caused by the sudden appearance of his companion, though not wholly unexpected.

It was now deep dusk in the forest, and deepest in that part of it where these two were journeying. As nearly as could be discerned, the second traveller was about fifty years old, apparently in the same rank of life as Goodman Brown, and bearing a considerable resemblance to him, though perhaps more in expression than features. Still they might have been taken for father and son. And yet, though the elder person was as simply clad as the younger, and as simple in manner too, he had an indescribable air of one who knew the world, and who would not have felt abashed at the governor's dinner table or in King William's court, were it possible that his affairs should call him thither. But the only thing about him that could be fixed upon as remarkable was his staff, which bore the likeness of a great black snake, so curiously wrought that it might almost be seen to twist and wriggle itself like a living serpent. This, of course, must have been an ocular deception, assisted by the uncertain light.

"Come, Goodman Brown," cried his fellow-traveller, "this is a dull pace for the beginning of a journey. Take my staff, if you are so soon weary."

"Friend," said the other, exchanging his slow pace for a full stop, "having kept covenant by meeting thee here, it is my purpose now to return whence I came. I have scruples touching the matter thou wot'st of."

"Sayest thou so?" replied he of the serpent, smiling apart. "Let us walk on, nevertheless, reasoning as we go; and if I convince thee not thou shalt turn back. We are but a little way in the forest yet."

"Too far! too far!" exclaimed the goodman, unconsciously resuming his walk. "My father never went into the woods on such an errand, nor his father before him. We have been a race of honest men and good Christians since the days of the martyrs; and shall I be the first of the name of Brown that ever took this path and kept"

"Such company, thou wouldst say," observed the elder person, interpreting his pause. "Well said, Goodman Brown! I have been as well acquainted with your family as with ever a one among the Puritans; and that's no trifle to say. I helped your grandfather, the constable, when he lashed the Quaker woman so smartly through the streets of Salem; and it was I that brought your father a pitch-pine knot, kindled at my own hearth, to set fire to an Indian village, in King Philip's war. They were my good friends, both; and many a pleasant walk have we had along this path, and returned merrily after midnight. I would fain be friends with you for their sake."

"If it be as thou sayest," replied Goodman Brown, "I marvel they never spoke of these matters; or, verily, I marvel not, seeing that the least rumor of the sort would have driven them from New England. We are a people of prayer, and good works to boot, and abide no such wickedness."

"Wickedness or not," said the traveller with the twisted staff, "I have a very general acquaintance here in New England. The deacons of many a church have drunk the communion wine with me; the selectmen of divers towns make me their chairman; and a majority of the Great and General Court are firm supporters of my interest. The governor and I, too—But these are state secrets."

"Can this be so?" cried Goodman Brown, with a stare of amazement at his undisturbed companion. "Howbeit, I have nothing to do with the governor and council; they have their own ways, and are no rule for a simple husbandman like me. But, were I to go on with thee, how should I meet the eye of that good old man, our minister, at Salem village? Oh, his voice would make me tremble both Sabbath day and lecture day."

Thus far the elder traveller had listened with due gravity; but now burst into a fit of irrepressible mirth, shaking himself so violently that his snake-like staff actually seemed to wriggle in sympathy.

"Ha! ha! ha!" shouted he again and again; then composing himself, "Well, go on, Goodman Brown, go on; but, prithee, don't kill me with laughing."

"Well, then, to end the matter at once," said Goodman Brown, considerably nettled, "there is my wife, Faith. It would break her dear little heart; and I'd rather break my own."

"Nay, if that be the case," answered the other, "e'en go thy ways, Goodman Brown. I would not for twenty old women like the one hobbling before us that Faith should come to any harm."

As he spoke he pointed his staff at a female figure on the path, in whom Goodman Brown recognized a very pious and exemplary dame, who had taught him his catechism in youth, and was still his moral and spiritual adviser, jointly with the minister and Deacon Gookin.

"A marvel, truly, that Goody Cloyse should be so far in the wilderness at nightfall," said he. "But with your leave, friend, I shall take a cut through the woods until we have left this Christian woman behind. Being a stranger to you, she might ask whom I was consorting with and whither I was going."

"Be it so," said his fellow-traveller. "Betake you to the woods, and let me keep the path."

Accordingly the young man turned aside, but took care to watch his companion, who advanced softly along the road until he had come within a staff's length of the old dame. She, meanwhile, was making the best of her way, with singular speed for so aged a woman, and mumbling some indistinct words—a prayer, doubtless—as she went. The traveller put forth his staff and touched her withered neck with what seemed the serpent's tail.

"The devil!" screamed the pious old lady.

"Then Goody Cloyse knows her old friend?" observed the traveller, confronting her and leaning on his writhing stick.

"Ah, forsooth, and is it your worship indeed?" cried the good dame. "Yea, truly is it, and in the very image of my old gossip, Goodman Brown, the grandfather of the silly fellow that now is. But—would your worship believe it?—my broomstick hath strangely disappeared, stolen, as I suspect, by that unhanged witch, Goody Cory, and that, too, when I was all anointed with the juice of smallage, and cinquefoil, and wolf's bane"

"Mingled with fine wheat and the fat of a new-born babe," said the shape of old Goodman Brown.

"Ah, your worship knows the recipe," cried the old lady, cackling aloud. "So, as I was saying, being all ready for the meeting, and no horse to ride on, I made up my mind to foot it; for they tell me there is a nice young man to be taken into communion to-night. But now your good worship will lend me your arm, and we shall be there in a twinkling."

"That can hardly be," answered her friend. "I may not spare you my arm, Goody Cloyse; but here is my staff, if you will."

So saying, he threw it down at her feet, where, perhaps, it assumed life, being one of the rods which its owner had formerly lent to the Egyptian magi. Of this fact, however, Goodman Brown could not take cognizance. He had cast up his eyes in astonishment, and, looking down again, beheld neither Goody Cloyse nor the serpentine staff, but his fellow-traveller alone, who waited for him as calmly as if nothing had happened.

"That old woman taught me my catechism," said the young man; and there was a world of meaning in this simple comment.

They continued to walk onward, while the elder traveller exhorted his companion to make good speed and persevere in the path, discoursing so aptly that his arguments seemed rather to spring up in the bosom of his auditor than to be suggested by himself. As they went, he plucked a branch of maple to serve for a walking stick, and began to strip it of the twigs and little boughs, which were wet with evening dew. The moment his fingers touched them they became strangely withered and dried up as with a week's sunshine. Thus the pair proceeded, at a good free pace, until suddenly, in a gloomy hollow of the road, Goodman Brown sat himself down on the stump of a tree and refused to go any farther.

"Friend," said he, stubbornly, "my mind is made up. Not another step will I budge on this errand. What if a wretched old woman do choose to go to the devil when I thought she was going to heaven: is that any reason why I should quit my dear Faith and go after her?"

"You will think better of this by and by," said his acquaintance, composedly. "Sit here and rest yourself a while; and when you feel like moving again, there is my staff to help you along."

Without more words, he threw his companion the maple stick, and was as speedily out of sight as if he had vanished into the deepening gloom. The young man sat a few moments by the roadside, applauding himself greatly, and thinking with how clear a conscience he should meet the minister in his morning walk, nor shrink from the eye of good old Deacon Gookin. And what calm sleep would be his that very night, which was to have been spent so wickedly, but so purely and sweetly now, in the arms of Faith! Amidst these pleasant and praiseworthy meditations, Goodman Brown heard the tramp of horses along the road, and deemed it advisable to conceal himself within the verge of the forest, conscious of the guilty purpose that had brought him thither, though now so happily turned from it.

On came the hoof tramps and the voices of the riders, two grave old voices, conversing soberly as they drew near. These mingled sounds appeared to pass along the road, within a few yards of the young man's hiding-place; but, owing doubtless to the depth of the gloom at that particular spot, neither the travellers nor their steeds were visible. Though their figures brushed the small boughs by the wayside, it could not be seen that they intercepted, even for a moment, the faint gleam from the strip of bright sky athwart which they must have passed. Goodman Brown alternately crouched and stood on tiptoe, pulling aside the branches and thrusting forth his head as far as he durst without discerning so much as a shadow. It vexed him the more, because he could have sworn, were such a thing possible, that he recognized the voices of the minister and Deacon Gookin, jogging along quietly, as they were wont to do, when bound to some ordination or ecclesiastical council. While yet within hearing, one of the riders stopped to pluck a switch.

"Of the two, reverend sir," said the voice like the deacon's, "I had rather miss an ordination dinner than to-night's meeting. They tell me that some of our community are to be here from Falmouth and beyond, and others from Connecticut and Rhode Island, besides several of the Indian powwows, who, after their fashion, know almost as much deviltry as the best of us. Moreover, there is a goodly young woman to be taken into communion."

"Mighty well, Deacon Gookin!" replied the solemn old tones of the minister. "Spur up, or we shall be late. Nothing can be done, you know, until I get on the ground."

The hoofs clattered again; and the voices, talking so strangely in the empty air, passed on through the forest, where no church had ever been gathered or solitary Christian prayed. Whither, then, could these holy men be journeying so deep into the heathen wilderness? Young Goodman Brown caught hold of a tree for support, being ready to sink down on the ground, faint and overburdened with the heavy sickness of his heart. He looked up to the sky, doubting whether there really was a heaven above him. Yet there was the blue arch, and the stars brightening in it.

"With heaven above and Faith below, I will yet stand firm against the devil!" cried Goodman Brown.

While he still gazed upward into the deep arch of the firmament and had lifted his hands to pray, a cloud, though no wind was stirring, hurried across the zenith and hid the brightening stars. The blue sky was still visible, except directly overhead, where this black mass of cloud was sweeping swiftly northward. Aloft in the air, as if from the depths of the cloud, came a confused and doubtful sound of voices. Once the listener fancied that he could distinguish the accents of towns-people of his own, men and women, both pious and ungodly, many of whom he had met at the communion table, and had seen others rioting at the tavern. The next moment, so indistinct were the sounds, he doubted whether he had heard aught but the murmur of the old forest, whispering without a wind. Then came a stronger swell of those familiar tones, heard daily in the sunshine at Salem village, but never until now from a cloud of night There was one voice of a young woman, uttering lamentations, yet with an uncertain sorrow, and entreating for some favor, which, perhaps, it

154

would grieve her to obtain; and all the unseen multitude, both saints and sinners, seemed to encourage her onward.

"Faith!" shouted Goodman Brown, in a voice of agony and desperation; and the echoes of the forest mocked him, crying, "Faith! Faith!" as if bewildered wretches were seeking her all through the wilderness.

The cry of grief, rage, and terror was yet piercing the night, when the unhappy husband held his breath for a response. There was a scream, drowned immediately in a louder murmur of voices, fading into far-off laughter, as the dark cloud swept away, leaving the clear and silent sky above Goodman Brown. But something fluttered lightly down through the air and caught on the branch of a tree. The young man seized it, and beheld a pink ribbon.

"My Faith is gone!" cried he, after one stupefied moment. "There is no good on earth; and sin is but a name. Come, devil; for to thee is this world given."

And, maddened with despair, so that he laughed loud and long, did Goodman Brown grasp his staff and set forth again, at such a rate that he seemed to fly along the forest path rather than to walk or run. The road grew wilder and drearier and more faintly traced, and vanished at length, leaving him in the heart of the dark wilderness, still rushing onward with the instinct that guides mortal man to evil. The whole forest was peopled with frightful sounds the creaking of the trees, the howling of wild beasts, and the yell of Indians; while sometimes the wind tolled like a distant church bell, and sometimes gave a broad roar around the traveller, as if all Nature were laughing him to scorn. But he was himself the chief horror of the scene, and shrank not from its other horrors.

"Ha! ha! ha!" roared Goodman Brown when the wind laughed at him. "Let us hear which will laugh loudest. Think not to frighten me with your deviltry. Come witch, come wizard, come Indian powwow, come devil himself, and here comes Goodman Brown. You may as well fear him as he fear you."

In truth, all through the haunted forest there could be nothing more frightful than the figure of Goodman Brown. On he flew among the black pines, brandishing his staff with frenzied gestures, now giving vent to an inspiration of horrid blasphemy, and now shouting forth such laughter as set all the echoes of the forest laughing like demons around him. The fiend in his own shape is less hideous than when he rages in the breast of man. Thus sped the demoniac on his course, until, quivering among the trees, he saw a red light before him, as when the felled trunks and branches of a clearing have been set on fire, and throw up their lurid blaze against the sky, at the hour of midnight. He paused, in a lull of the tempest that had driven him onward, and heard the swell of what seemed a hymn, rolling solemnly from a distance with the weight of many voices. He knew the tune; it was a familiar one in the choir of the village meeting-house. The verse died heavily away, and was lengthened by a chorus, not of human voices, but of all the sounds of the benighted wilderness pealing in awful harmony together. Goodman Brown cried out, and his cry was lost to his own ear by its unison with the cry of the desert.

In the interval of silence he stole forward until the light glared full upon his eyes. At one extremity of an open space, hemmed in by the dark wall of the forest, arose a rock, bearing some rude, natural resemblance either to an alter or a pulpit, and surrounded by four blazing pines, their tops aflame, their stems untouched, like candles at an evening meeting. The mass of foliage that had overgrown the summit of the rock was all on fire, blazing high into the night and fitfully illuminating the whole field. Each pendent twig and leafy festoon was in a blaze. As the red light arose and fell, a numerous congregation alternately shone forth, then disappeared in shadow, and again grew, as it were, out of the darkness, peopling the heart of the solitary woods at once.

"A grave and dark-clad company," quoth Goodman Brown.

In truth they were such. Among them, quivering to and fro between gloom and splendor, appeared faces that would be seen next day at the council board of the province, and others which, Sabbath after Sabbath, looked devoutly heavenward, and benignantly over the crowded pews, from the holiest pulpits in the land. Some affirm that the lady of the governor was there. At least there were high dames well known to her, and wives of honored husbands, and widows, a great multitude, and ancient maidens, all of excellent repute, and fair young girls, who trembled lest their mothers should espy them. Either the sudden gleams of light flashing over the obscure field bedazzled Goodman Brown, or he recognized a score of the church members of Salem village famous for their especial sanctity. Good old Deacon Gookin had arrived, and waited at the skirts of that venerable saint, his revered pastor. But, irreverently consorting with these grave, reputable, and pious people, these elders of the church, these chaste dames and dewy virgins, there were men of dissolute lives and women of spotted fame, wretches given over to all mean and filthy vice, and suspected even of horrid crimes. It was strange to see that the good shrank not from the wicked, nor were the sinners abashed by the saints. Scattered also among their pale-faced enemies were the Indian priests, or powwows, who had often scared their native forest with more hideous incantations than any known to English witchcraft.

"But where is Faith?" thought Goodman Brown; and, as hope came into his heart, he trembled.

Another verse of the hymn arose, a slow and mournful strain, such as the pious love, but joined to words which expressed all that our nature can conceive of sin, and darkly hinted at far more. Unfathomable to mere mortals is the lore of fiends. Verse after verse was sung; and still the chorus of the desert swelled between like the deepest tone of a mighty organ; and with the final peal of that dreadful anthem there came a sound, as if the roaring wind, the rushing streams, the howling beasts, and every other voice of the unconcerted wilderness were mingling and according with the voice of guilty man in homage to the prince of all. The four blazing pines threw up a loftier flame, and obscurely discovered shapes and visages of horror on the smoke wreaths above the impious assembly. At the same moment the fire on the rock shot redly forth and formed a glowing arch above its base, where now appeared a figure. With reverence be it spoken, the figure bore no slight similitude, both in garb and manner, to some grave divine of the New England churches.

"Bring forth the converts!" cried a voice that echoed through the field and rolled into the forest.

At the word, Goodman Brown stepped forth from the shadow of the trees and approached the congregation, with whom he felt a loathful brotherhood by the sympathy of all that was wicked in his heart. He could have well-nigh sworn that the shape of his own dead father beckoned him to advance, looking downward from a smoke wreath, while a woman, with dim features of despair, threw out her hand to warn him back. Was it his mother? But he had no power to retreat one step, nor to resist, even in thought, when the minister and good old Deacon Gookin seized his arms and led him to the blazing rock. Thither came also the slender form of a veiled female, led between Goody Cloyse, that pious teacher of the catechism, and Martha Carrier, who had received the devil's promise to be queen of hell. A rampant hag was she. And there stood the proselytes beneath the canopy of fire.

"Welcome, my children," said the dark figure, "to the communion of your race. Ye have found thus young your nature and your destiny. My children, look behind you!"

They turned; and flashing forth, as it were, in a sheet of flame, the fiend worshippers were seen; the smile of welcome gleamed darkly on every visage.

"There," resumed the sable form, "are all whom ye have reverenced from youth. Ye deemed them holier than yourselves, and shrank from your own sin, contrasting it with their lives of righteousness and prayerful aspirations heavenward. Yet here are they all in my worshipping assembly. This night it shall be granted you to know their secret deeds: how hoary-bearded elders of the church have whispered wanton words to the young maids of their households; how many a woman, eager for widows' weeds, has given her husband a drink at bedtime and let him sleep his last sleep in her bosom; how beardless youths have made haste to inherit their fathers' wealth; and how fair damsels—blush not, sweet ones—have dug little graves in the garden, and bidden me, the sole guest to an infant's funeral. By the sympathy of your human hearts for sin ye shall scent out all the places—whether in church, bedchamber, street, field, or forest— where crime has been committed, and shall exult to behold the whole earth one stain of guilt, one mighty blood spot. Far more than this. It shall be yours to penetrate, in every bosom, the deep mystery of sin, the fountain of all wicked arts, and which inexhaustibly supplies more evil impulses than human power—than my power at its utmost can make manifest in deeds. And now, my children, look upon each other."

They did so; and, by the blaze of the hell-kindled torches, the wretched man beheld his Faith, and the wife her husband, trembling before that unhallowed altar.

"Lo, there ye stand, my children," said the figure, in a deep and solemn tone, almost sad with its despairing awfulness, as if his once angelic nature could yet mourn for our miserable race. "Depending upon one another's hearts, ye had still hoped that virtue were not all a dream. Now are ye undeceived. Evil is the nature of mankind. Evil must be your only happiness. Welcome again, my children, to the communion of your race."

"Welcome," repeated the fiend worshippers, in one cry of despair and triumph.

And there they stood, the only pair, as it seemed, who were yet hesitating on the verge of wickedness in this dark world. A basin was hollowed, naturally, in the rock. Did it contain water, reddened by the lurid light? or was it blood? or, perchance, a liquid flame? Herein did the shape of evil dip his hand and prepare to lay the mark of baptism upon their foreheads, that they might be partakers of the mystery of sin, more conscious of the secret guilt of others, both in deed and thought, than they could now be of their own. The husband cast one look at his pale wife, and Faith at him. What polluted wretches would the next glance show them to each other, shuddering alike at what they disclosed and what they saw!

"Faith! Faith!" cried the husband, "look up to heaven, and resist the wicked one."

Whether Faith obeyed he knew not. Hardly had he spoken when he found himself amid calm night and solitude, listening to a roar of the wind which died heavily away through the forest. He staggered against the rock, and felt it chill and damp; while a hanging twig, that had been all on fire, besprinkled his cheek with the coldest dew.

The next morning young Goodman Brown came slowly into the street of Salem village, staring around him like a bewildered man. The good old minister was taking a walk along the graveyard to get an appetite for breakfast and meditate his sermon, and bestowed a blessing, as he passed, on Goodman Brown. He shrank from the venerable saint as if to avoid an anathema. Old Deacon Gookin was at domestic worship, and the holy words of his prayer were heard through the open window. "What God doth the wizard pray to?" quoth Goodman Brown. Goody Cloyse, that excellent old Christian, stood in the early sunshine at her own lattice, catechizing a little girl who had brought her a pint of morning's milk. Goodman Brown snatched away the child as from the grasp of the fiend himself. Turning the corner by the meeting-house, he spied the head of Faith, with the pink ribbons, gazing anxiously forth, and bursting into such joy at sight of him that she skipped along the street and almost kissed her husband before the whole village. But Goodman Brown looked sternly and sadly into her face, and passed on without a greeting.

Had Goodman Brown fallen asleep in the forest and only dreamed a wild dream of a witch-meeting?

Be it so if you will; but, alas! it was a dream of evil omen for young Goodman Brown. A stern, a sad, a darkly meditative, a distrustful, if not a desperate man did he become from the night of that fearful dream. On the Sabbath day, when the congregation were singing a holy psalm, he could not listen because an anthem of sin rushed loudly upon his ear and drowned all the blessed strain. When the minister spoke from the pulpit with power and fervid eloquence, and, with his hand on the open Bible, of the sacred truths of our religion, and of saint-like lives and triumphant deaths, and of future bliss or misery unutterable, then did Goodman Brown turn pale, dreading lest the roof should thunder down upon the gray blasphemer and his hearers. Often, waking suddenly at midnight, he shrank from the bosom of Faith; and at morning or eventide, when the family knelt down at prayer, he scowled and muttered to himself, and gazed sternly at his wife, and turned away. And when he had lived long, and was borne to his grave a hoary corpse, followed by Faith, an aged woman, and children and grandchildren, a goodly procession, besides neighbors not a few, they carved no hopeful verse upon his tombstone, for his dying hour was gloom.

Louisa May Alcott

SCARLET STOCKINGS

Chapter 1
I. HOW THEY WALKED INTO LENNOX'S LIFE.

"COME out for a drive, Harry?"

"Too cold."

"Have a game of billiards?"

"Too tired."

"Go and call on the Fairchilds?"

"Having an unfortunate prejudice against country girls, I respectfully decline."

"What will you do then?"

"Nothing, thank you."

And settling himself more luxuriously upon the couch, Lennox closed his eyes, and appeared to slumber tranquilly. Kate shook her head, and stood regarding her brother, despondently, till a sudden idea made her turn toward the window, exclaiming abruptly,

"Scarlet stockings, Harry!"

"Where?" and, as if the words were a spell to break the deepest day-dream, Lennox hurried to the window, with an unusual expression of interest in his listless face.

"I thought that would succeed! She isn't there, but I've got you up, and you are not to go down again," laughed Kate, taking possession of the sofa.

"Not a bad manoeuvre. I don't mind; it's about time for the one interesting event of the day to occur, so I'll watch for myself, thank you," and Lennox took the easy chair by the window with a shrug and a yawn.

"I'm glad any thing does interest you," said Kate, petulantly, "though I don't think it amounts to much, for, though you perch yourself at the window every day to see that girl pass, you don't care enough about it to ask her name."

"I've been waiting to be told."

"It's Belle Morgan, the Doctor's daughter, and my dearest friend."

"Then, of course, she is a blue-belle?"

"Don't try to be witty or sarcastic with her, for she will beat you at that."

"Not a dumb-belle then?"

"Quite the reverse; she talks a good deal, and very well too, when she likes."

"She is very pretty; has anybody the right to call her 'Ma belle'?"

"Many would be glad to do so, but she won't have any thing to say to them."

"A Canterbury belle in every sense of the word then?"

"She might be, for all Canterbury loves her, but she isn't fashionable, and has more friends among the poor than among the rich."

"Ah, I see, a diving-bell, who knows how to go down into a sea of troubles, and bring up the pearls worth having."

"I'll tell her that, it will please her. You are really waking up, Harry," and Kate smiled approvingly upon him.

"This page of 'Belle's Life' is rather amusing, so read away," said Lennox, glancing up the street, as if he awaited the appearance of the next edition with pleasure.

"There isn't much to tell; she is a nice, bright, energetic, warm-hearted dear; the pride of the Doctor's heart, and a favorite with every one, though she is odd.

"How odd?"

"Does and says what she likes, is very blunt and honest, has ideas and principles of her own, goes to parties in high dresses, won't dance round dances, and wears red stockings, though Mrs. Plantagenet says it's fast."

"Rather a jolly little person, I fancy. Why haven't we met her at some of the tea-fights and muffin-worries we've been to lately?"

"It may make you angry, but it will do you good, so I'll tell. She didn't care enough about seeing the distinguished stranger to come; that's the truth."

"Sensible girl, to spare herself hours of mortal dulness, gossip, and dyspepsia," was the placid reply.

"She has seen you, though, at church and dawdling about town, and she called you 'Sir Charles Coldstream' on the spot. How does that suit?" asked Kate, maliciously.

"Not bad, I rather like that. Wish she'd call some day, and stir us up."

"She won't; I asked her, but she said she was very busy, and told Jessy Tudor, she wasn't fond of peacocks."

"I don't exactly see the connection."

"Stupid boy! she meant you, of course."

"Oh, I'm peacocks, am I?"

"I don't wish to be rude, but I really do think you are vain of your good looks, elegant accomplishments, and the impression you make wherever you go. When it's worth while you exert yourself, and are altogether fascinating, but the 'I come -- see -- and -- conquer' air you put on, spoils it all for sensible people."

"It strikes me that Miss Morgan has slightly infected you with her oddity as far as bluntness goes. Fire away, it's rather amusing to be abused when one is dying of ennui."

"That's grateful and complimentary to me, when I have devoted myself to you ever since you came. But every thing bores you, and the only sign of interest you've shown is in those absurd red hose. I should like to know what the charm is," said Kate, sharply.

"Impossible to say; accept the fact calmly as I do, and be grateful that there is one glimpse of color, life, and spirit in this aristocratic tomb of a town."

"You are not obliged to stay in it!" fiercely.

"Begging your pardon, my dove, but I am. I promised to give you my enlivening society for a month, and a Lennox keeps his word, even at the cost of his life."

"I'm sorry I asked such a sacrifice; but I innocently thought that after being away for five long years, you might care to see your orphan sister," and the dove produced her handkerchief with a plaintive sniff.

"Now, my dear creature, don't be melodramatic, I beg of you," cried her brother, imploringly. "I wished to come, I pined to embrace you, and I give you my word, I don't blame you for the stupidity of this confounded place."

"It never was so gay as since you came, for every one has tried to make it pleasant for you," cried Kate, ruffled at his indifference to the hospitable efforts of herself and friends. "But you don't care for any of our simple amusements, because you are spoilt by the flattery, gayety, and nonsense of foreign society. If I didn't know it was half affectation, I should be in despair, you are so blase and absurd. It's always the way with men, if one happens to be handsome, accomplished, and talented, he puts on as many airs, and is as vain as any silly girl."

"Don't you think if you took breath, you'd get on faster, my dear?" asked the imperturbable gentleman, as Kate paused with a gasp.

"I know it's useless for me to talk, as you don't care a straw what I say, but it's true, and some day you'll wish you had done something worth doing all these years. I was so proud of you, so fond of you, that I can't help being disappointed, to find you with no more ambition than to kill time comfortably, no interest in any thing but your own pleasures, and only energy enough to amuse yourself with a pair of scarlet stockings."

Pathetic as poor Kate's face and voice were, it was impossible to help laughing at the comical conclusion of her lament. Lennox tried to hide the smile on his lips by affecting to curl his moustache with care, and to gaze pensively out as if touched by her appeal. But he wasn't, oh, bless you, no! she was only his sister, and, though she might have talked with the wisdom of Solomon, and the eloquence of Demosthenes, it wouldn't have done a particle of good. Sisters do very well to work for one, to pet one, and play confidante when one's love affairs need feminine wit to conduct them, but when they begin to reprove, or criticise or moralize, it won't do, and can't be allowed, of course. Lennox never snubbed anybody, but blandly extinguished them by a polite acquiescence in all their affirmations, for the time being, and then went on in his own way as if nothing had been said.

"I dare say you are right; I'll go and think over your very sensible advice," and, as if roused to unwonted exertion by the stings of an accusing conscience, he left the room abruptly.

"I do believe I've made an impression at last! He's actually gone out to think over what I've said. Dear Harry, I was sure he had a heart, if one only knew how to get at it!" and with a sigh of satisfaction Kate went to the window to behold the "dear Harry" going briskly down the street after a pair of scarlet stockings. A spark of anger kindled in her eyes as she watched him, and when he vanished, she still stood knitting her brows in deep thought, for a grand idea was dawning upon her.

It was a dull town; no one could deny that, for everybody was so intensely proper and well-born, that nobody dared to be jolly. All the houses were square, aristocratic mansions with Revolutionary elms in front and spacious coach-houses behind. The knockers had a supercilious perk to their bronze or brass noses, the dandelions on the lawns had a highly connected air, and the very pigs were evidently descended from "our first families." Stately dinner-parties, decorous dances, moral picnics, and much tea-pot gossiping were the social resources of the place. Of course, the young people flirted, for that diversion is apparently irradicable even in the "best society," but it was done with a propriety which was edifying to behold.

One can easily imagine that such a starched state of things would not be particularly attractive to a travelled young gentleman like Lennox, who, as

Kate very truly said, had been spoilt by the flattery, luxury, and gayety of foreign society. He did his best, but by the end of the first week ennui claimed him for its own, and passive endurance was all that was left him. From perfect despair he was rescued by the scarlet stockings, which went tripping by one day as he stood at the window, planning some means of escape.

A brisk, blithe-faced girl passed in a grey walking suit with a distracting pair of high-heeled boots and glimpses of scarlet at the ankle. Modest, perfectly so, I assure you, were the glimpses, but the feet were so decidedly pretty that one forgot to look at the face appertaining thereunto. It wasn't a remarkably lovely face, but it was a happy, wholesome one, with all sorts of good little dimples in cheek and chin, sunshiny twinkles in the black eyes, and a decided, yet lovable look about the mouth that was quite satisfactory. A busy, bustling little body she seemed to be, for sack-pockets and muff were full of bundles, and the trim boots tripped briskly over the ground, as if the girl's heart were as light as her heels. Somehow this active, pleasant figure seemed to wake up the whole street, and leave a streak of sunshine behind it, for every one nodded as it passed, and the primmest faces relaxed into smiles, which lingered when the girl had gone.

"Uncommonly pretty feet -- she walks well, which American girls seldom do -- all waddle or prance -- nice face, but the boots are French, and it does my heart good to see 'em."

Lennox made these observations to himself as the young lady approached, nodded to Kate at another window, gave a quick but comprehensive glance at himself and trotted round the corner, leaving the impression on his mind that a whiff of fresh spring air had blown through the street in spite of the December snow. He didn't trouble himself to ask who it was, but fell into the way of lounging in the bay-window at about three P. M., and watching the grey and scarlet figure pass with its blooming cheeks, bright eyes, and elastic step. Having nothing else to do, he took to petting this new whim, and quite depended on the daily stirring-up which the sight of the energetic damsel gave him. Kate saw it all, but took no notice till the day of the little tiff above recorded; after that she was as soft as a summer sea, and by some clever stroke had Belle Morgan to tea that very week.

Lennox was one of the best tempered fellows in the world, but the "peacocks" did rather nettle him because there was some truth in the insinuation; so he took care to put on no airs or try to be fascinating in the presence of Miss Belle. In truth he soon forgot himself entirely, and enjoyed her oddities with a relish, after the prim proprieties of the other young ladies who had simpered and sighed before him. For the first time in his life, the "Crusher," as his male friends called him, got crushed; for Belle, with the subtle skill of a quick-witted, keen-sighted girl, soon saw and condemned the elegant affectations which others called foreign polish. A look, a word, a gesture from a pretty woman is often more eloquent and impressive than moral essays or semi-occasional twinges of conscience, and in the presence of one satirical little person, Sir Charles Coldstream soon ceased to deserve the name.

Belle seemed to get over her hurry and to find time for occasional relaxation, but one never knew in what mood he might find her, for the weathercock was not more changeable than she. Lennox liked that, and found the muffin-worries quite endurable with this sauce piquante to relieve their insipidity. Presently he discovered that he was suffering for exercise, and formed the wholesome habit of promenading the town about three P. M.; Kate said, to follow the scarlet stockings.

Chapter 2
II. WHERE THEY LED HIM.

"WHITHER away, Miss Morgan?" asked Lennox, as he overtook her one bitter cold day.

"I'm taking my constitutional."

"So am I."

"With a difference," and Belle glanced at the blue-nosed, muffled-up gentleman strolling along beside her with an occasional shiver and shrug.

"After a winter in the south of France one don't find arctic weather like this easy to bear," he said, with a disgusted air.

"I like it, and do my five or six miles a day, which keeps me in what fine ladies call 'rude health,' answered Belle, walking him on at a pace which soon made his furs a burden.

She was a famous pedestrian, and a little proud of her powers, but she outdid all former feats that day, and got over the ground in gallant style. Something in her manner put her escort on his mettle, and his usual lounge was turned into a brisk march which set his blood dancing, face glowing, and spirits effervescing as they had not done for many a day.

"There! you look more like your real self now," said Belle, with the first sign of approval she had ever vouchsafed him, as he rejoined her after a race to recover her veil, which the wind whisked away over hedge and ditch.

"Are you sure you know what my real self is?" he asked, with a touch of the "conquering hero" air.

"Not a doubt of it. I always know a soldier when I see one," returned Belle, decidedly.

"A soldier! that's the last thing I should expect to be accused of," and Lennox looked both surprised and gratified.

"There's a flash in your eye and a ring to your voice, occasionally, which made me suspect that you had fire and energy enough if you only chose to show it, and the spirit with which you have just executed the 'Morgan Quick step' proves that I was right," returned Belle, laughing.

"Then I am not altogether a 'peacock?'" said Lennox, significantly, for during the chat, which had been as brisk as the walk, Belle had given his besetting sins several sly hits, and he couldn't resist one return shot, much as her unexpected compliment pleased him.

Poor Belle blushed up to her forehead, tried to look as if she did not understand, and gladly hid her confusion behind the recovered veil without a word.

There was a decided display both of the "flash" and the "ring," as Lennox looked at the suddenly subdued young lady, and, quite satisfied with his retaliation, gave the order -- "Forward, march!" which brought them to the garden-gate breathless, but better friends than before.

The next time the young people met, Belle was in such a hurry that she went round the corner with an abstracted expression which was quite a triumph of art. Just then, off tumbled the lid of the basket she carried, and Lennox, rescuing it from a puddle, obligingly helped readjust it over a funny collection of bottles, dishes, and tidy little rolls of all sorts.

"It's very heavy, mayn't I carry it for you?" he asked, in an insinuating manner.

"No, thank you," was on Belle's lips, but observing that he was got up with unusual elegance to pay calls, she couldn't resist the temptation of making a beast of burden of him, and took him at his word.

"You may, if you like. I've got more bundles to take from the store, and another pair of hands won't come amiss."

Lennox lifted his eyebrows, also the basket, and they went on again, Belle very much absorbed in her business, and her escort wondering where the dickens she was going with all that rubbish. Filling his unoccupied hand with sundry brown paper parcels, much to the detriment of the light kid that covered it, Belle paraded him down the main street before the windows of the most aristocratic mansions, and then dived into a dirty back-lane, where the want and misery of the town was decorously kept out of sight.

"You don't mind scarlet fever, I suppose?" observed Belle, as they approached the unsavory residence of Biddy O'Brien.

"Well, I'm not exactly partial to it," said Lennox, rather taken aback.

"You needn't go in if you are afraid, or speak to me afterwards, so no harm will be done -- except to your gloves."

"Why do you come here, if I may ask? It isn't the sort of amusement I should recommend," he began, evidently disapproving of the step.

"Oh, I'm used to it, and like to play nurse where father plays doctor. I'm fond of children, and Mrs. O'Brien's are little dears," returned Belle, briskly, threading her way between ash-heaps and mud-puddles as if bound to a festive scene.

"Judging from the row in there, I should infer that Mrs. O'Brien had quite a herd of little dears."

"Only nine."

"And all sick?"

"More or less."

"By Jove! it's perfectly heroic in you to visit this hole in spite of dirt, noise, fragrance, and infection," cried Lennox, who devoutly wished that the sense of smell if not of hearing were temporarily denied him.

"Bless you, it's the sort of thing I enjoy, for there's no nonsense here; the work you do is pleasant if you do it heartily, and the thanks you get are worth having, I assure you."

She put out her hand to relieve him of the basket, but he gave it an approving little shake, and said briefly --

"Not yet, I'm coming in."

It's all very well to rhapsodize about the exquisite pleasure of doing good, to give carelessly of one's abundance, and enjoy the delusion of having remembered the poor. But it is a cheap charity, and never brings the genuine satisfaction which those know who give their mite with heart as well as hand, and truly love their neighbor as themselves. Lennox had seen much fashionable benevolence, and laughed at it even while he imitated it, giving generously when it wasn't inconvenient. But this was a new sort of thing entirely, and in spite of the dirt, the noise, and the smells, he forgot the fever, and was glad he came when poor Mrs. O'Brien turned from her sick babies, exclaiming, with Irish fervor at sight of Belle,

"The Lord love ye, darlin, for remimberin us when ivery one, barrin' the doctor, and the praste, turns the cowld shouldther in our throuble!"

"Now if you really want to help, just keep this child quiet while I see to the sickest ones," said Belle, dumping a stout infant on to his knee, thrusting an orange into his hand, and leaving him aghast, while she unpacked her little messes, and comforted the maternal bird.

With the calmness of desperation, her aid-de-camp put down his best beaver on the rich soil which covered the floor, pocketed his Paris kids, and making a bib of his cambric handkerchief, gagged young Pat deliciously with bits of orange whenever he opened his mouth to roar. At her first leisure moment, Belle glanced at him to see how he was getting on, and found him so solemnly absorbed in his task that she went off into a burst of such infectious merriment that the O'Briens, sick and well, joined in it to a man.

"Good fun, isn't it?" she asked, turning down her cuffs when the last spoonful of gruel was administered.

"I've no doubt of it, when one is used to the thing. It comes a little hard at first, you know," returned Lennox, wiping his forehead, with a long breath, and seizing his hat as if quite ready to tear himself away.

"You've done very well for a beginner; so kiss the baby and come home," said Belle approvingly.

"No, thank you," muttered Lennox, trying to detach the bedaubed innocent. But little Pat had a grateful heart, and falling upon his new nurse's neck with a rapturous crow clung there like a burr.

"Take him off! Let me out of this! He's one too many for me!" cried the wretched young man in comic despair.

Being freed with much laughter, he turned and fled, followed by a shower of blessings, from Mrs. O'Brien.

As they came up again into the pleasant highways, Lennox said, awkwardly for him,

"The thanks of the poor are excellent things to have, but I think I'd rather receive them by proxy. Will you kindly spend this for me in making that poor soul comfortable?"

But Belle wouldn't take what he offered her, she put it back, saying earnestly,

"Give it yourself; one can't buy blessings, they must be earned or they are not worth having. Try it, please, and if you find it a failure, then I'll gladly be your almoner."

There was a significance in her words which he could not fail to understand. He neither shrugged, drawled, nor sauntered now, but gave her a look in which respect and self-reproach were mingled, and left her, simply saying, "I'll try it, Miss Morgan."

"Now isn't she odd?" whispered Kate to her brother, as Belle appeared at a little dance at Mrs. Plantagenet's in a high-necked dress, knitting away on an army-sock, as she greeted the friends who crowded round her.

"Charmingly so. Why don't you do that sort of thing when you can?" answered her brother, glancing at her thin, bare shoulders and hands, rendered nearly useless by the tightness of the gloves.

"Gracious, no! It's natural to her to do so, and she carries it off well; I couldn't, therefore I don't try, though I admire it in her. Go and ask her to dance, before she is engaged."

"She doesn't dance round dances you know."

"She is dreadfully prim about some things and so free and easy about others, I can't understand it, do you?"

"Well, yes, I think I do. Here's Forbes coming for you, I'll go and entertain Belle by a quarrel."

He found her in a recess out of the way of the rushing and romping, busy with her work, yet evidently glad to be amused.

"I admire your adherence to principles, Miss Belle, but don't you find it a little hard to sit still while your friends are enjoying themselves?" he asked, sinking luxuriously into the lounging chair beside her.

"Yes, very," answered Belle with characteristic candor. "But father don't approve of that sort of exercise, so I console myself with something useful till my chance comes."

"Your work can't exactly be called ornamental," said Lennox, looking at the big sock.

"Don't laugh at it, sir, it is for the foot of the brave fellow who is going to fight for me and his country."

"Happy fellow! May I ask who he is?" and Lennox sat up with an air of interest.

"My substitute; I don't know his name, for father has not got him yet, but I'm making socks, and towels, and a comfort-bag for him, so that when found he may be off at once."

"You really mean it?" cried Lennox.

"O course I do; I can't go myself, but I can buy a pair of strong arms to fight for me, and I intend to do it. I only hope he'll have the right sort of courage and be a credit to me."

"What do you call the right sort of courage?" asked Lennox, soberly.

"That which makes a man ready and glad to live or die for a principle. There's a chance for heroes now, if there ever was. When do you join your regiment?" she added abruptly.

"Haven't the least idea," and Lennox subsided again.

"But you intend to do so, of course?"

"Why should I?"

Belle dropped her work. "Why should you? What a question! Because you have health, and strength, and courage, and money to help on the good cause, and every man should give his best, and not dare to stay at home when he is needed."

"You forget that I am an Englishman, and we rather prefer to be strictly neutral just now."

"You are only half English, and for your mother's sake you should be proud and glad to fight for the North," cried Belle warmly.

"I don't remember my mother -- "

"That's evident!"

"But I was about to add, I've no objection to lend a hand if it isn't too much trouble to get off," said Lennox indifferently, for he liked to see Belle's color rise, and her eyes kindle while he provoked her.

"Do you expect to go South in a bandbox? You'd better join one of the kid-glove regiments, they say the dandies fight well when the time comes."

"I've been away so long, the patriotic fever hasn't seized me yet, and as the quarrel is none of mine, I think, perhaps I'd better take care of Kate, and let you fight it out among yourselves. Here's the Lancers, may I have the honor?"

But Belle, being very angry at this lukewarmness, answered in her bluntest manner.

"Having reminded me that you are a 'strictly neutral' Englishman, you must excuse me if I decline; I dance only with loyal Americans," and rolling up her work with a defiant flourish, she walked away, leaving him to lament his loss and wonder how he could retrieve it. She did not speak to him again till he stood in the hall waiting for Kate, then Belle came down in the charming little red hood, and going straight up to him with her hand out, a repentant look, and a friendly smile, said frankly --

"I was very rude; I want to beg pardon of the English, and shake hands with the American half."

So peace was declared, and lasted unbroken for the remaining week of his stay, when he proposed to take Kate to the city for a little gayety. Miss Morgan openly approved the plan, but secretly felt as if the town was about to be depopulated, and tried to hide her melancholy in her substitute's socks. They were not large enough, however, to absorb it all, and when Lennox went to make his adieu, it was perfectly evident that the Doctor's Belle was out of tune. The young gentleman basely exulted over this, till she gave him something else to think about by saying gravely,

"Before you go, I feel as if I ought to tell you something, since Kate won't. If you are offended about it please don't blame her; she meant it kindly and so did I." Belle paused as if it was not an easy thing to tell, and then went on quickly, with her eyes upon her work.

"Three weeks ago Kate asked me to help her in a little plot, and I consented, for the fun of the thing. She wanted something to amuse and stir you up, and finding that my queer ways diverted you, she begged me to be neighborly and let you do what you liked. I didn't care particularly about amusing you, but I did think you needed rousing, so for her sake I tried to do it, and you very good-naturedly bore my lecturing. I don't like deceit of any kind, so I confess, but I can't say I'm sorry, for I really think you are none the worse for the teasing and teaching you've had."

Belle didn't see him flush and frown as she made her confession, and when she looked up he only said, half gratefully, half reproachfully,

"I'm a good deal the better for it, I dare say, and ought to be very thankful for your friendly exertions. But two against one was hardly fair, now was it?"

"No, it was sly and sinful in the highest degree, but we did it for your good, so I know you'll forgive us, and as a proof of it sing one or two of my favorites for the last time."

"You don't deserve any favor, but I'll do it to show you how much more magnanimous men are than women."

Not at all loth to improve his advantages, Lennox warbled his most melting lays con amore, watching, as he sung, for any sign of sentiment in the girlish face opposite. But Belle wouldn't be sentimental; and sat rattling her knitting-needles industriously, though "The Harbor Bar was Moaning," dolefully, though "Douglas" was touchingly "tender and true," and the "Wind of the Summer Night" sighed romantically through the sitting-room.

"Much obliged. Must you go?" she said, without a sign of soft confusion as he rose.

"I must, but I shall come again before I leave the country. May I?" he asked, holding her hand.

"If you come in a uniform."

"Good night, Belle," tenderly. "Good-bye, Sir Charles," with a wicked twinkle of the eye, which lasted till he closed the hall-door, growling irefully,

"I thought I'd had some experience, but one never can understand these women."

Canterbury did become a desert to Belle after her dear friend had gone;

(of course the dear friend's brother had nothing to do with the desolation), and as the weeks dragged slowly, Belle took to reading poetry, practicing plaintive ballads, and dawdling over her work at a certain window which commanded a view of the railway station and hotel.

"You're dull, my dear, run up to town with me to-morrow, and see your young man off," said the Doctor, one evening as Belle sat musing with a half-mended red stocking in her hand.

"My young man?" she ejaculated, turning with a start and a blush.

"Your substitute, child. Stephens attended to the business for me, and he's off to-morrow. I began to tell you about the fellow last week, but you were wool-gathering, so I stopped."

"Yes, I remember, it was all very nice. Goes to-morrow, does he? I'd like to see him, but do you think we can both leave home at once? Some one might come you know, and I fancy it's going to snow," said Belle, putting her face behind the curtain to inspect the weather.

"You'd better go, the trip will do you good, you can take your things to Tom Jones, and see Kate on the way; she's got back from Philadelphia."

"Has she! I'll go, then; it will please her, and I do need change. You are an old dear, to think of it;" and giving her father a hasty glimpse of a suddenly excited countenance, Belle slipped out of the room to prepare her best array with a most reckless disregard of the impending storm.

It didn't snow on the morrow, and up they went to see the -- th regiment off. Belle did not see "her young man," however, for while her father went to carry him her comforts and a patriotic nosegay of red and white flowers, tied up with a smart blue ribbon, she called on Kate. But Miss Lennox was engaged, and sent an urgent request that her friend would call in the afternoon. Much disappointed and a little hurt, Belle then devoted herself to the departing regiment, wishing she was going with it, for she felt in a war-like mood. It was past noon when a burst of martial music, the measured tramp of many feet, and enthusiastic cheers announced that "the boys" were coming. From the balcony where she stood with her father, Belle looked down upon the living stream that flowed by like a broad river with a steely glitter above the blue. All her petty troubles vanished at the sight, her heart beat high, her face glowed, her eyes filled, and she waved her hat as zealously as if she had a dozen friends and lovers in the ranks below.

"Here comes your man; I told him to stick the posy where it would catch my eye, so I could point him out to you. Look, it's the tall fellow at the end of the front line," said the Doctor in an excited tone, as he pointed and beckoned.

172

Belle looked and gave a little cry, for there, in a private's uniform, with her nosegay at his buttonhole, and on his face a smile she never forgot, was Lennox! For an instant she stood staring at him as pale and startled as if he were a ghost, then the color rushed into her face, she kissed both hands to him, and cried bravely, "Good-bye, good-bye, God bless you, Harry!" and immediately laid her head on her father's shoulder, sobbing as if her heart was broken.

When she looked up, her substitute was lost in the undulating mass below, and for her the spectacle was over.

"Was it really he? Why wasn't I told? What does it all mean?" she demanded, looking bewildered, grieved, and ashamed.

"He's really gone, my dear. It's a surprise of his, and I was bound over to silence. Here, this will explain the joke, I suppose," and the Doctor handed her a cocked-hat note, done up like a military order.

"A Roland for your Oliver, Mademoiselle! I came home for the express purpose of enlisting, and only delayed a month on Kate's account. If I ever return, I will receive my bounty at your hands. Till then please comfort Kate, think as kindly as you can of 'Sir Charles,' and sometimes pray a little prayer for

"Your unworthy

"Substitute."

Belle looked very pale and meek when she put her note in her pocket, but she only said, "I must go and comfort Kate," and the Doctor gladly obeyed, feeling that the joke was more serious than he had imagined.

The moment her friend appeared, Miss Lennox turned on her tears, and "played away" pouring forth lamentations, reproaches, and regrets in a steady stream.

"I hope you are satisfied now, you cruel girl!" she began, refusing to be kissed. "You've sent him off with a broken heart to rush into danger and be shot, or get his arms and legs spoilt. You know he loved you and wanted to tell you so, but you wouldn't let him, and now you've driven him away, and he's gone as an insignificant private with his head shaved, and a heavy knapsack breaking his back, and a horrid gun that will be sure to explode, and he would wear those immense blue socks you sent, for he adores you, and you only teased and laughed at him, my poor deluded, deserted brother!" And quite overwhelmed by the afflicting picture, Kate lifted up her voice and wept again.

"I am satisfied; for he's done what I hoped he would, and he's none the less a gentleman because he's a private and wears my socks. I pray they will keep him safe and bring him home to us when he has done his duty like a man, as I know he will. I'm proud of my brave substitute, and I'll try to be worthy of him," cried Belle, kindling beautifully as she looked out into the wintry sunshine with a new softness in the eyes that still seemed watching that blue-coated figure marching away to danger, perhaps death.

"It's ill playing with edged tools; we meant to amuse him and we may have sent him to destruction. I'll never forgive you for your part, never!" said Kate, with the charming inconsistency of her sex.

But Belle turned away her wrath by a soft answer, as she whispered, with a tender choke in her voice,

"We both loved him, dear; let's comfort one another."

Chapter 3
III. WHAT BECAME OF THEM.

PRIVATE Lennox certainly had chosen pretty hard work, for the -- th was not a "kid-glove" regiment by any means; fighting in mid-winter was not exactly festive, and camps do not abound in beds of roses even at the best of times. But Belle was right in saying she knew a soldier when she saw him, for now that he was thoroughly waked up, he proved that there was plenty of courage, energy, and endurance in him.

It's my private opinion that he might now and then have slightly regretted the step he had taken, had it not been for certain recollections of a sarcastic tongue and a pair of keen eyes, not to mention the influence of one of the most potent rulers of the human heart, namely, the desire to prove himself worthy of the respect, if nothing more, of somebody at home. Belle's socks did seem to keep him safe, and lead him straight in the narrow path of duty. Belle's comfort-bag was such in very truth, for not one of the stout needles on the tricolored cushion but what seemed to wink its eye approvingly at him; not one of the tidy balls of thread that did not remind him of the little hand he coveted, and the impracticable scissors, were cherished as a good omen, though he felt that the sharpest steel that ever came from Sheffield couldn't cut his love in twain. And Belle's lessons, short as they had been, were not forgotten, but seemed to have been taken up by a sterner mistress, whose rewards were greater if not so sweet as those the girl could give. There was plenty of exercise now-a-days of hard work that left many a tired head asleep forever under the snow. There were many opportunities for diving "into the depths and bringing up pearls worth having" by acts of kindness among the weak, the wicked, and the suffering all about him. He learned now how to earn, not buy, the thanks of the poor, and unconsciously proved in the truest way that a private could be a gentleman. But best of all was the steadfast purpose "to live and die for a principle," which grew and strengthened with each month of bitter hardship, bloody strife, and dearly-bought success. Life grew earnest to him, time seemed precious, self was forgotten, and all that was best and bravest rallied round the flag on which his heart inscribed the motto, "Love and Liberty."

Praise and honor he could not fail to win, and had he never gone back to claim his bounty he would have earned the great "Well done," for he kept his oath loyally, did his duty manfully, and loved his lady faithfully, like a knight of the chivalrous times. He knew nothing of her secret, but wore her blue ribbon like an order, never went into battle without first, like many another poor fellow, kissing something which he carried next his heart, and with each day of absence felt himself a better man, and braver soldier, for the fondly foolish romance he had woven about the scarlet stockings.

Belle and Kate did comfort one another, not only with tears and kisses, but with womanly work which kept hearts happy and hands busy. How Belle bribed her to silence will always remain the ninth wonder of the world, but though reams of paper passed between brother and sister during those twelve months not a hint was dropped on one side in reply to artful inquiries from the other. Belle never told her love in words, but she stowed away an unlimited quantity of the article in the big boxes that went to gladden the eyes and -- alas for romance! -- the stomach of Private Lennox. If pickles could typify passion, cigars prove constancy, and gingerbread reveal the longings of the soul, then would the above-mentioned gentleman have been the happiest of lovers. But camp-life had doubtless dulled his finer intuitions, for he failed to understand the new language of love, and gave away these tender tokens with lavish prodigality. Concealment preyed a trifle on Belle's damask cheek it must be confessed, and the keen eyes grew softer with the secret tears that sometimes dimmed them; the sharp tongue seldom did mischief now, but uttered kindly words to every one as if doing penance for the past, and a sweet seriousness toned down the lively spirit which was learning many things in the sleepless nights that followed when the "little prayer" for the beloved substitute was done.

"I'll wait and see if he is all I hope he will be, before I let him know. I shall read the truth the instant I see him, and if he has stood the test I'll run into his arms and tell him everything," she said to herself with delicious thrills at the idea; but you may be sure she did nothing of the sort when the time came.

A rumor flew through the town one day that Lennox had arrived; upon receipt of which joyful tidings Belle had a panic and hid herself in the garret. But when she had quaked, and cried, and peeped, and listened for an hour or two, finding that no one came to hunt her up, she composed her nerves and descended to pass the afternoon in the parlor and a high state of dignity. All sorts of reports reached her -- he was mortally wounded, he had been made a major or a colonel, or a general, no one knew exactly which; he was dead, was going to be married, and hadn't come at all. Belle fully expiated all her small sins by the agonies of suspense she suffered that day, and when at last a note came from Kate begging her "to drop over to see Harry," she put her pride in her pocket and went at once.

The drawing-room was empty and in confusion, there was a murmur of voices up-stairs, a smell of camphor in the air, and an empty wine-glass on the table where a military cap was lying. Belle's heart sunk, and she covertly kissed the faded blue coat as she stood waiting breathlessly, wondering if Harry had any arms for her to run into. She heard the chuckling Biddy lumber up and announce her, then a laugh and a half fond, half exulting -- "Ah, ha, I thought she'd come!"

That spoilt it all; Belle took out her pride instanter, set her teeth, rubbed a quick color into her white cheeks, and snatching up a newspaper, sat herself down with as expressionless a face as it was possible for an excited young woman to possess. Lennox came running down -- "Thank heaven, his legs are safe!" sighed Belle, with her eyes glued to the price of beef. He entered with both hands extended, which relieved her mind upon another point, and he beamed upon her, looking so vigorous, manly, and martial that she cried within herself, "My beautiful brown soldier!" even while she greeted him with an unnecessarily brief "How do you do, Mr. Lennox?"

The sudden eclipse which passed over his joyful countenance would have been ludicrous if it hadn't been pathetic; but he was used to hard knocks now, and bore this, his hardest, like a man. He shook hands heartily, and as Belle sat down again (not to betray that she was trembling a good deal), he stood at ease before her, talking in a way which soon satisfied her that he had borne the test, and that bliss was waiting for her round the corner. But she had made it such a very sharp corner she couldn't turn it gracefully, and while she pondered how to do so he helped her with a cough. She looked up quickly, discovering all at once that he was very thin, rather pale in spite of the nice tan, and breathed hurriedly as he stood with one hand in his breast.

"Are you ill, wounded, in pain?" she asked, forgetting herself entirely.

"Yes, all three," he answered, after a curious look at her changing color and anxious eyes.

"Sit down -- tell me about it -- can I do any thing?" and Belle began to plump up the pillows on the couch with nervous eagerness.

"Thank you, I'm past help," was the mournful reply, accompanied by a hollow cough which made her shiver.

"Oh, don't say so! Let me bring father; he is very skilful. Shall I call Kate?"

"He can do nothing; Kate doesn't know this, and I beg you won't tell her. I got a shot in the breast and made light of it, but it will finish me sooner or later. I don't mind telling you, for you are one of the strong, cool sort, you know, and are not affected by such things. But Kate is so fond of me, I don't want to shock and trouble her yet awhile. Let her enjoy my little visit, and after I'm gone you can tell her the truth."

Belle had sat like a statue while he spoke with frequent pauses and an involuntary clutch or two at the suffering breast. As he stopped and passed his hand over his eyes, she said slowly, as if her white lips were stiff,

"Gone! where?"

"Back to my place. I'd rather die fighting than fussed and wailed over by a parcel of women. I expected to stay a week or so, but a battle is coming off sooner than we imagined, so I'm away again to-morrow. As I'm not likely ever to come back, I just wanted to ask you to stand by poor Kate when I'm finished, and to say good-bye to you, Belle, before I go." He put out his hand, but holding it fast in both her own, she laid her tearful face down on it, whispering imploringly,

"Oh, Harry, stay!"

Never mind what happened for the next ten minutes; suffice it to say that the enemy having surrendered, the victor took possession with great jubilation and showed no quarter.

"Bang the field piece, toot the fife, and beat the rolling drum, for ruse number three has succeeded! Come down, Kate, and give us your blessing," called Lennox, taking pity on his sister, who was anxiously awaiting the denouement on the stairs.

In she rushed, and the young ladies laughed and cried, kissed and talked tumultuously, while their idol benignantly looked on, vainly endeavoring to repress all vestiges of unmanly emotion.

"And you are not dying, really, truly?" cried Belle, when fair weather set in after the flurry.

"Bless your dear heart, no! I'm as sound as a nut, and haven't a wound to boast of, except this ugly slash on the head."

"It's a splendid wound, and I'm proud of it," and Belle set a rosy little seal on the scar which quite reconciled her lover to the disfigurement of his handsome forehead. "You've learned to fib in the army, and I'm disappointed in you," she added, trying to look reproachful and failing entirely.

"No, only the art of strategy. You quenched me by your frosty reception, and I thought it was all up till you put the idea of playing invalid into my head. It succeeded so well that I piled on the agony, resolving to fight it out on that line, and if I failed again to make a masterly retreat. You gave me a lesson in deceit once, so don't complain if I turned the tables and made your heart ache for a minute, as you've made mine for a year."

Belle's spirit was rapidly coming back, so she gave him a capital imitation of his French shrug, and drawled out in his old way --

"I have my doubts about that, mon ami."

"What do you say to this -- and this -- and this?" he retorted, pulling out and laying before her with a triumphant flourish, a faded blue ribbon, a fat pincushion with a hole through it, and a dainty-painted little picture of a pretty girl in scarlet stockings.

"There, I've carried those treasures in my breast-pocket for a year, and I'm firmly convinced that they have all done their part toward keeping me safe. The blue ribbon bound me fast to you, Belle; the funny cushion caught the bullet that otherwise might have finished me, and the blessed little picture was my comfort during those dreadful marches, my companion on picket-duty with treachery and danger all about me, and my inspiration when the word 'Charge!' went down the line, for in the thickest of the fight I always saw the little grey figure beckoning me on to my duty."

"Oh, Harry, you won't go back to all those horrors, will you? I'm sure you've done enough, and may rest now and enjoy your reward," said Kate, trying not to feel that "two is company and three is none."

"I've enlisted for the war, and shall not rest till either it or I come to an end. As for my reward, I had it when Belle kissed me."

"You are right, I'll wait for you, and love you all the better for the sacrifice," whispered Belle. "I only wish I could share your hardships, dear, for while you fight and suffer I can only love and pray."

"Waiting is harder than working to such as you, so be contented with your share, for the thought of you will glorify the world generally for me. I'll tell you what you can do while I'm away; it's both useful and amusing, so it will occupy and cheer you capitally. Just knit lots of red hose, because I don't intend you to wear any others hereafter, Mrs. Lennox."

"Mine are not worn out yet," laughed Belle, getting merry at the thought.

"No matter for that, those are sacred articles, and henceforth must be treasured as memorials of our love. Frame and hang 'em up; or, if the prejudices of society forbid that flight of romance, lay them carefully away where moths can't devour nor thieves steal 'em, so that years hence, when my descendants praise me for any virtues I may possess, any good I may have done, or any honor I may have earned, I can point to those precious relics and say proudly,

"My children, for all that I am, or hope to be, you must thank your honored mother's scarlet stockings."

T.S. Arthur

AN ANGEL IN DISGUISE

Idleness, vice, and intemperance had done their miserable work, and the dead mother lay cold and still amid her wretched children. She had fallen upon the threshold of her own door in a drunken fit, and died in the presence of her frightened little ones.

Death touches the spring of our common humanity. This woman had been despised, scoffed at, and angrily denounced by nearly every man, woman, and child in the village; but now, as the fact of her death was passed from lip to lip, in subdued tones, pity took the place of anger, and sorrow of denunciation. Neighbors went hastily to the old tumble-down hut, in which she had secured little more than a place of shelter from summer heats and winter cold: some with grave-clothes for a decent interment of the body; and some with food for the half-starving children, three in number. Of these, John, the oldest, a boy of twelve, was a stout lad, able to earn his living with any farmer. Kate, between ten and eleven, was bright, active girl, out of whom something clever might be made, if in good hands; but poor little Maggie, the youngest, was hopelessly diseased. Two years before a fall from a window had injured her spine, and she had not been able to leave her bed since, except when lifted in the arms of her mother.

"What is to be done with the children?" That was the chief question now. The dead mother would go underground, and be forever beyond all care or concern of the villagers. But the children must not be left to starve. After considering the matter, and talking it over with his wife, farmer Jones said that he would take John, and do well by him, now that his mother was out of the way; and Mrs. Ellis, who had been looking out for a bound girl, concluded that it would be charitable in her to make choice of Katy, even though she was too young to be of much use for several years.

"I could do much better, I know," said Mrs. Ellis; "but as no one seems inclined to take her, I must act from a sense of duty expect to have trouble with the child; for she's an undisciplined thing--used to having her own way."

But no one said "I'll take Maggie." Pitying glances were cast on her wan and wasted form and thoughts were troubled on her account. Mothers brought cast-off garments and, removing her soiled and ragged clothes, dressed her in clean attire. The sad eyes and patient face of the little one touched many hearts, and even knocked at them for entrance. But none opened to take her in. Who wanted a bed-ridden child?

"Take her to the poorhouse," said a rough man, of whom the question "What's to be done with Maggie?" was asked. "Nobody's going to be bothered with her."

"The poorhouse is a sad place for a sick and helpless child," answered one.

"For your child or mine," said the other, lightly speaking; "but for tis brat it will prove a blessed change, she will be kept clean, have healthy food, and be doctored, which is more than can be said of her past condition."

There was reason in that, but still it didn't satisfy. The day following the day of death was made the day of burial. A few neighbors were at the miserable hovel, but none followed dead cart as it bore the unhonored remains to its pauper grave. Farmer Jones, after the coffin was taken out, placed John in his wagon and drove away, satisfied that he had done his part. Mrs. Ellis spoke to Kate with a hurried air, "Bid your sister good by," and drew the tearful children apart ere scarcely their lips had touched in a sobbing farewell. Hastily others went out, some glancing at Maggie, and some resolutely refraining from a look, until all had gone. She was alone! Just beyond the threshold Joe Thompson, the wheelwright, paused, and said to the blacksmith's wife, who was hastening off with the rest,--

"It's a cruel thing to leave her so."

"Then take her to the poorhouse: she'll have to go there," answered the blacksmith's wife, springing away, and leaving Joe behind.

For a little while the man stood with a puzzled air; then he turned back, and went into the hovel again. Maggie with painful effort, had raised herself to an upright position and was sitting on the bed, straining her eyes upon the door out of which all had just departed, A vague terror had come into her thin white face.

"O, Mr. Thompson!" she cried out, catching her suspended breath, "don't leave me here all alone!"

Though rough in exterior, Joe Thompson, the wheelwright, had a heart, and it was very tender in some places. He liked children, and was pleased to have them come to his shop, where sleds and wagons were made or mended for the village lads without a draft on their hoarded sixpences.

"No, dear," he answered, in a kind voice, going to the bed, and stooping down over the child, "You sha'n't be left here alone." Then he wrapped her with the gentleness almost of a woman, in the clean bedclothes which some neighbor had brought; and, lifting her in his strong arms, bore her out into the air and across the field that lay between the hovel and his home.

Now, Joe Thompson's wife, who happened to be childless, was not a woman of saintly temper, nor much given to self-denial for others' good, and Joe had well-grounded doubts touching the manner of greeting he should receive on his arrival. Mrs. Thompson saw him approaching from the window, and with ruffling feathers met him a few paces from the door, as he opened the garden gate, and came in. He bore a precious burden, and he felt it to be so. As his arms held the sick child to his breast, a sphere of tenderness went out from her, and penetrated his feelings. A bond had already corded itself around them both, and love was springing into life.

"What have you there?" sharply questioned Mrs. Thompson.

Joe, felt the child start and shrink against him. He did not reply, except by a look that was pleading and cautionary, that said, "Wait a moment for explanations, and be gentle;" and, passing in, carried Maggie to the small chamber on the first floor, and laid her on a bed. Then, stepping back, he shut the door, and stood face to face with his vinegar-tempered wife in the passage-way outside.

"You haven't brought home that sick brat!" Anger and astonishment were in the tones of Mrs. Joe Thompson; her face was in a flame.

"I think women's hearts are sometimes very hard," said Joe. Usually Joe Thompson got out of his wife's way, or kept rigidly silent and non-combative when she fired up on any subject; it was with some surprise, therefore, that she now encountered a firmly-set countenance and a resolute pair of eyes.

"Women's hearts are not half so hard as men's!"

Joe saw, by a quick intuition, that his resolute bearing had impressed his wife and he answered quickly, and with real indignation, "Be that as it may, every woman at the funeral turned her eyes steadily from the sick child's face, and when the cart went off with her dead mother, hurried away, and left her alone in that old hut, with the sun not an hour in the sky."

"Where were John and Kate?" asked Mrs. Thompson.

"Farmer Jones tossed John into his wagon, and drove off. Katie went home with Mrs. Ellis; but nobody wanted the poor sick one. 'Send her to the poorhouse,' was the cry."

"Why didn't you let her go, then. What did you bring her here for?"

"She can't walk to the poorhouse," said Joe; "somebody's arms must carry her, and mine are strong enough for that task."

"Then why didn't you keep on? Why did you stop here?" demanded the wife.

"Because I'm not apt to go on fools' errands. The Guardians must first be seen, and a permit obtained."

There was no gainsaying this.

"When will you see the Guardians?" was asked, with irrepressible impatience.

"To-morrow."

"Why put it off till to-morrow? Go at once for the permit, and get the whole thing off of your hands to-night."

"Jane," said the wheelwright, with an impressiveness of tone that greatly subdued his wife, "I read in the Bible sometimes, and find much said about little children. How the Savior rebuked the disciples who would not receive them; how he took them up in his arms, and blessed them; and how he said that 'whosoever gave them even a cup of cold water should not go unrewarded.' Now, it is a small thing for us to keep this poor motherless little one for a single night; to be kind to her for a single night; to make her life comfortable for a single night."

The voice of the strong, rough man shook, and he turned his head away, so that the moisture in his eyes might not be seen. Mrs. Thompson did not answer, but a soft feeling crept into her heart.

"Look at her kindly, Jane; speak to her kindly," said Joe. "Think of her dead mother, and the loneliness, the pain, the sorrow that must be on all her coming life." The softness of his heart gave unwonted eloquence to his lips.

Mrs. Thompson did not reply, but presently turned towards the little chamber where her husband had deposited Maggie; and, pushing open the door, went quietly in. Joe did not follow; he saw that, her state had changed, and felt that it would be best to leave her alone with the child. So he went to his shop, which stood near the house, and worked until dusky evening released him from labor. A light shining through the little chamber windows was the first object that attracted Joe's attention on turning towards the house: it was a good omen. The path led him by this windows and, when opposite, he could not help pausing to look in. It was now dark enough outside to screen him from observation. Maggie lay, a little raised on the pillow with the lamp shining full upon her face. Mrs. Thompson was sitting by the bed, talking to the child; but her back was towards the window, so that her countenance was not seen. From Maggie's face, therefore, Joe must read the character of their intercourse. He saw that her eyes were intently fixed upon his wife; that now and then a few words came, as if in answers from her lips; that her expression was sad and tender; but he saw nothing of bitterness or pain. A deep-drawn breath was followed by one of relief, as a weight lifted itself from his heart.

On entering, Joe did not go immediately to the little chamber. His heavy tread about the kitchen brought his wife somewhat hurriedly from the room where she had been with Maggie. Joe thought it best not to refer to the child, nor to manifest any concern in regard to her.

"How soon will supper be ready?" he asked.

"Right soon," answered Mrs. Thompson, beginning to bustle about. There was no asperity in her voice.

After washing from his hands and face the dust and soil of work, Joe left the kitchen, and went to the little bedroom. A pair of large bright eyes looked up at him from the snowy bed; looked at him tenderly, gratefully, pleadingly. How his heart swelled in his bosom! With what a quicker motion came the heart-beats! Joe sat down, and now, for the first time, examining the thin frame carefully under the lamp light, saw that it was an attractive face, and full of a childish sweetness which suffering had not been able to obliterate.

"Your name is Maggie?" he said, as he sat down and took her soft little hand in his.

"Yes, sir." Her voice struck a chord that quivered in a low strain of music.

"Have you been sick long?"

"Yes, sir." What a sweet patience was in her tone!

"Has the doctor been to see you?"

"He used to come."

"But not lately?"

"No, sir."

"Have you any pain?"

"Sometimes, but not now."

"When had you pain?"

"This morning my side ached, and my back hurt when you carried me."

"It hurts you to be lifted or moved about?"

"Yes, sir."

"Your side doesn't ache now?"

"No, sir."

"Does it ache a great deal?"

"Yes, sir; but it hasn't ached any since I've been on this soft bed."

"The soft bed feels good."

"O, yes, sir--so good!" What a satisfaction, mingled with gratitude, was in her voice!

"Supper is ready," said Mrs. Thompson, looking into the room a little while afterwards.

Joe glanced from his wife's face to that of Maggie; she understood him, and answered,--

"She can wait until we are done; then I will bring her somethings to eat." There was an effort at indifference on the part of Mrs. Thompson, but her husband had seen her through the window, and understood that the coldness was assumed. Joe waited, after sitting down to the table, for his wife to introduce the subject uppermost in both of their thoughts; but she kept silent on that theme, for many minutes, and he maintained a like reserve. At last she said, abruptly,--

"What are you going to do with that child?"

"I thought you understood me that she was to go to the poorhouse," replied Joe, as if surprised at her question.

Mrs. Thompson looked rather strangely at her husband for sonic moments, and then dropped her eyes. The subject was not again referred to during the meal. At its close, Mrs. Thompson toasted a slice of bread, and softened, it with milk and butter; adding to this a cup of tea, she took them into Maggie, and held the small waiter, on which she had placed them, while the hungry child ate with every sign of pleasure.

"Is it good?" asked Mrs. Thompson, seeing with what a keen relish the food was taken.

The child paused with the cup in her hand, and answered with a look of gratitude that awoke to new life old human feelings which had been slumbering in her heart for half a score of years.

"We'll keep her a day or two longer; she is so weak and helpless," said Mrs. Joe Thompson, in answer to her husband's remark, at breakfast-time on the next morning, that he must step down and see the Guardians of the Poor about Maggie.

"She'll be so much in your way," said Joe.

"I sha'n't mind that for a day or two. Poor thing!"

Joe did not see the Guardians of the Poor on that day, on the next, nor on the day following. In fact, he never saw them at all on Maggie's account, for in less than a week Mrs. Joe Thompson would as soon leave thought of taking up her own abode in the almshouse as sending Maggie there.

What light and blessing did that sick and helpless child bring to the home of Joe Thompson, the poor wheelwright! It had been dark, and cold, and miserable there for a long time just because his wife had nothing to love and care for out of herself, and so became sore, irritable, ill-tempered, and self-afflicting in the desolation of her woman's nature. Now the sweetness of that sick child, looking ever to her in love, patience, and gratitude, was as honey to her soul, and she carried her in her heart as well as in her arms, a precious burden. As for Joe Thompson, there was not a man in all the neighborhood who drank daily of a more precious wine of life than he. An angel had come into his house, disguised as a sick, helpless, and miserable child, and filled all its dreary chambers with the sunshine of love.

Susan Glaspell

A JURY OF HER PEERS

When Martha Hale opened the storm-door and got a cut of the north wind, she ran back for her big woolen scarf. As she hurriedly wound that round her head her eye made a scandalized sweep of her kitchen. It was no ordinary thing that called her away--it was probably further from ordinary than anything that had ever happened in Dickson County. But what her eye took in was that her kitchen was in no shape for leaving: her bread all ready for mixing, half the flour sifted and half unsifted.

She hated to see things half done; but she had been at that when the team from town stopped to get Mr. Hale, and then the sheriff came running in to say his wife wished Mrs. Hale would come too--adding, with a grin, that he guessed she was getting scary and wanted another woman along. So she had dropped everything right where it was.

"Martha!" now came her husband's impatient voice. "Don't keep folks waiting out here in the cold."

She again opened the storm-door, and this time joined the three men and the one woman waiting for her in the big two-seated buggy.

After she had the robes tucked around her she took another look at the woman who sat beside her on the back seat. She had met Mrs. Peters the year before at the county fair, and the thing she remembered about her was that she didn't seem like a sheriff's wife. She was small and thin and didn't have a strong voice. Mrs. Gorman, sheriff's wife before Gorman went out and Peters came in, had a voice that somehow seemed to be backing up the law with every word. But if Mrs. Peters didn't look like a sheriff's wife, Peters made it up in looking like a sheriff. He was to a dot the kind of man who could get himself elected sheriff--a heavy man with a big voice, who was particularly genial with the law-abiding, as if to make it plain that he knew the difference between criminals and non-criminals. And right there it came into Mrs. Hale's mind, with a stab, that this man who was so pleasant and lively with all of them was going to the Wrights' now as a sheriff.

"The country's not very pleasant this time of year," Mrs. Peters at last ventured, as if she felt they ought to be talking as well as the men.

Mrs. Hale scarcely finished her reply, for they had gone up a little hill and could see the Wright place now, and seeing it did not make her feel like talking. It looked very lonesome this cold March morning. It had always been a lonesome-looking place. It was down in a hollow, and the poplar trees around it were lonesome-looking trees. The men were looking at it and talking about what had happened. The county attorney was bending to one side of the buggy, and kept looking steadily at the place as they drew up to it.

"I'm glad you came with me," Mrs. Peters said nervously, as the two women were about to follow the men in through the kitchen door.

Even after she had her foot on the door-step, her hand on the knob, Martha Hale had a moment of feeling she could not cross that threshold. And the reason it seemed she couldn't cross it now was simply because she hadn't crossed it before. Time and time again it had been in her mind, "I ought to go over and see Minnie Foster"--she still thought of her as Minnie Foster, though for twenty years she had been Mrs. Wright. And then there was always something to do and Minnie Foster would go from her mind. But now she could come.

The men went over to the stove. The women stood close together by the door. Young Henderson, the county attorney, turned around and said, "Come up to the fire, ladies."

Mrs. Peters took a step forward, then stopped. "I'm not--cold," she said.

And so the two women stood by the door, at first not even so much as looking around the kitchen.

The men talked for a minute about what a good thing it was the sheriff had sent his deputy out that morning to make a fire for them, and then Sheriff Peters stepped back from the stove, unbuttoned his outer coat, and leaned his hands on the kitchen table in a way that seemed to mark the beginning of official business. "Now, Mr. Hale," he said in a sort of semi-official voice, "before we move things about, you tell Mr. Henderson just what it was you saw when you came here yesterday morning."

The county attorney was looking around the kitchen.

"By the way," he said, "has anything been moved?" He turned to the sheriff. "Are things just as you left them yesterday?"

Peters looked from cupboard to sink; from that to a small worn rocker a little to one side of the kitchen table.

"It's just the same."

"Somebody should have been left here yesterday," said the county attorney.

"Oh--yesterday," returned the sheriff, with a little gesture as of yesterday having been more than he could bear to think of. "When I had to send Frank to Morris Center for that man who went crazy--let me tell you. I had my hands full yesterday. I knew you could get back from Omaha by today, George, and as long as I went over everything here myself--"

"Well, Mr. Hale," said the county attorney, in a way of letting what was past and gone go, "tell just what happened when you came here yesterday morning."

Mrs. Hale, still leaning against the door, had that sinking feeling of the mother whose child is about to speak a piece. Lewis often wandered along and got things mixed up in a story. She hoped he would tell this straight and plain, and not say unnecessary things that would just make things harder for Minnie Foster. He didn't begin at once, and she noticed that he looked queer--as if standing in that kitchen and having to tell what he had seen there yesterday morning made him almost sick.

"Yes, Mr. Hale?" the county attorney reminded.

"Harry and I had started to town with a load of potatoes," Mrs. Hale's husband began.

Harry was Mrs. Hale's oldest boy. He wasn't with them now, for the very good reason that those potatoes never got to town yesterday and he was taking them this morning, so he hadn't been home when the sheriff stopped to say he wanted Mr. Hale to come over to the Wright place and tell the county attorney his story there, where he could point it all out. With all Mrs. Hale's other emotions came the fear now that maybe Harry wasn't dressed warm enough--they hadn't any of them realized how that north wind did bite.

"We come along this road," Hale was going on, with a motion of his hand to the road over which they had just come, "and as we got in sight of the house I says to Harry, 'I'm goin' to see if I can't get John Wright to take a telephone.' You see," he explained to Henderson, "unless I can get somebody to go in with me they won't come out this branch road except for a price *I* can't pay. I'd spoke to Wright about it once before; but he put me off, saying folks talked too much anyway, and all he asked was peace and quiet--guess you know about how much he talked himself. But I thought maybe if I went to the house and talked about it before his wife, and said all the women-folks liked the telephones, and that in this lonesome stretch of road it would be a good thing--well, I said to Harry that that was what I was going to say--though I said at the same time that I didn't know as what his wife wanted made much difference to John--"

Now there he was!--saying things he didn't need to say. Mrs. Hale tried to catch her husband's eye, but fortunately the county attorney interrupted with:

"Let's talk about that a little later, Mr. Hale. I do want to talk about that but, I'm anxious now to get along to just what happened when you got here."

When he began this time, it was very deliberately and carefully:

"I didn't see or hear anything. I knocked at the door. And still it was all quiet inside. I knew they must be up--it was past eight o'clock. So I knocked again, louder, and I thought I heard somebody say, 'Come in.' I wasn't sure--I'm not sure yet. But I opened the door--this door," jerking a hand toward the door by which the two women stood. "and there, in that rocker"--pointing to it--"sat Mrs. Wright."

Everyone in the kitchen looked at the rocker. It came into Mrs. Hale's mind that that rocker didn't look in the least like Minnie Foster--the Minnie Foster of twenty years before. It was a dingy red, with wooden rungs up the back, and the middle rung was gone, and the chair sagged to one side.

"How did she--look?" the county attorney was inquiring.

"Well," said Hale, "she looked--queer."

"How do you mean--queer?"

As he asked it he took out a note-book and pencil. Mrs. Hale did not like the sight of that pencil. She kept her eye fixed on her husband, as if to keep him from saying unnecessary things that would go into that note-book and make trouble.

Hale did speak guardedly, as if the pencil had affected him too.

"Well, as if she didn't know what she was going to do next. And kind of--done up."

"How did she seem to feel about your coming?"

"Why, I don't think she minded--one way or other. She didn't pay much attention. I said, 'Ho' do, Mrs. Wright? It's cold, ain't it?' And she said. 'Is it?'--and went on pleatin' at her apron.

"Well, I was surprised. She didn't ask me to come up to the stove, or to sit down, but just set there, not even lookin' at me. And so I said: 'I want to see John.'

"And then she--laughed. I guess you would call it a laugh.

"I thought of Harry and the team outside, so I said, a little sharp, 'Can I see John?' 'No,' says she--kind of dull like. 'Ain't he home?' says I. Then she looked at me. 'Yes,' says she, 'he's home.' 'Then why can't I see him?' I asked her, out of patience with her now. 'Cause he's dead' says she, just as quiet and dull--and fell to pleatin' her apron. 'Dead?' says, I, like you do when you can't take in what you've heard.

"She just nodded her head, not getting a bit excited, but rockin' back and forth.

"'Why--where is he?' says I, not knowing *what* to say.

"She just pointed upstairs--like this"--pointing to the room above.

"I got up, with the idea of going up there myself. By this time I--didn't know what to do. I walked from there to here; then I says: 'Why, what did he die of?'

"'He died of a rope around his neck,' says she; and just went on pleatin' at her apron."

Hale stopped speaking, and stood staring at the rocker, as if he were still seeing the woman who had sat there the morning before. Nobody spoke; it was as if every one were seeing the woman who had sat there the morning before.

"And what did you do then?" the county attorney at last broke the silence.

"I went out and called Harry. I thought I might--need help. I got Harry in, and we went upstairs." His voice fell almost to a whisper. "There he was--lying over the--"

"I think I'd rather have you go into that upstairs," the county attorney interrupted, "where you can point it all out. Just go on now with the rest of the story."

"Well, my first thought was to get that rope off. It looked--"

He stopped, his face twitching.

"But Harry, he went up to him, and he said. 'No, he's dead all right, and we'd better not touch anything.' So we went downstairs.

"She was still sitting that same way. 'Has anybody been notified?' I asked. 'No, says she, unconcerned.

"'Who did this, Mrs. Wright?' said Harry. He said it businesslike, and she stopped pleatin' at her apron. 'I don't know,' she says. 'You don't *know*?' says Harry. 'Weren't you sleepin' in the bed with him?' 'Yes,' says she, 'but I was on the inside. 'Somebody slipped a rope round his neck and strangled him, and you didn't wake up?' says Harry. 'I didn't wake up,' she said after him.

"We may have looked as if we didn't see how that could be, for after a minute she said, 'I sleep sound.'

"Harry was going to ask her more questions, but I said maybe that weren't our business; maybe we ought to let her tell her story first to the coroner or the sheriff. So Harry went fast as he could over to High Road-- the Rivers' place, where there's a telephone."

"And what did she do when she knew you had gone for the coroner?" The attorney got his pencil in his hand all ready for writing.

"She moved from that chair to this one over here"--Hale pointed to a small chair in the corner--"and just sat there with her hands held together and lookin down. I got a feeling that I ought to make some conversation, so I said I had come in to see if John wanted to put in a telephone; and at that she started to laugh, and then she stopped and looked at me-- scared."

At the sound of a moving pencil the man who was telling the story looked up.

"I dunno--maybe it wasn't scared," he hastened: "I wouldn't like to say it was. Soon Harry got back, and then Dr. Lloyd came, and you, Mr. Peters, and so I guess that's all I know that you don't."

He said that last with relief, and moved a little, as if relaxing. Everyone moved a little. The county attorney walked toward the stair door.

"I guess we'll go upstairs first--then out to the barn and around there."

He paused and looked around the kitchen.

"You're convinced there was nothing important here?" he asked the sheriff. "Nothing that would--point to any motive?"

The sheriff too looked all around, as if to re-convince himself.

"Nothing here but kitchen things," he said, with a little laugh for the insignificance of kitchen things.

The county attorney was looking at the cupboard--a peculiar, ungainly structure, half closet and half cupboard, the upper part of it being built in the wall, and the lower part just the old-fashioned kitchen cupboard. As if its queerness attracted him, he got a chair and opened the upper part and looked in. After a moment he drew his hand away sticky.

"Here's a nice mess," he said resentfully.

The two women had drawn nearer, and now the sheriff's wife spoke.

"Oh--her fruit," she said, looking to Mrs. Hale for sympathetic understanding.

She turned back to the county attorney and explained: "She worried about that when it turned so cold last night. She said the fire would go out and her jars might burst."

Mrs. Peters' husband broke into a laugh.

"Well, can you beat the women! Held for murder, and worrying about her preserves!"

The young attorney set his lips.

"I guess before we're through with her she may have something more serious than preserves to worry about."

"Oh, well," said Mrs. Hale's husband, with good-natured superiority, "women are used to worrying over trifles."

The two women moved a little closer together. Neither of them spoke. The county attorney seemed suddenly to remember his manners--and think of his future.

"And yet," said he, with the gallantry of a young politician. "for all their worries, what would we do without the ladies?"

The women did not speak, did not unbend. He went to the sink and began washing his hands. He turned to wipe them on the roller towel-- whirled it for a cleaner place.

"Dirty towels! Not much of a housekeeper, would you say, ladies?"

He kicked his foot against some dirty pans under the sink.

"There's a great deal of work to be done on a farm," said Mrs. Hale stiffly.

"To be sure. And yet"--with a little bow to her--'I know there are some Dickson County farm-houses that do not have such roller towels." He gave it a pull to expose its full length again.

"Those towels get dirty awful quick. Men's hands aren't always as clean as they might be.

"Ah, loyal to your sex, I see," he laughed. He stopped and gave her a keen look, "But you and Mrs. Wright were neighbors. I suppose you were friends, too."

Martha Hale shook her head.

"I've seen little enough of her of late years. I've not been in this house-- it's more than a year."

"And why was that? You didn't like her?"

"I liked her well enough," she replied with spirit. "Farmers' wives have their hands full, Mr. Henderson. And then--" She looked around the kitchen.

"Yes?" he encouraged.

"It never seemed a very cheerful place," said she, more to herself than to him.

"No," he agreed; "I don't think anyone would call it cheerful. I shouldn't say she had the home-making instinct."

"Well, I don't know as Wright had, either," she muttered.

"You mean they didn't get on very well?" he was quick to ask.

"No; I don't mean anything," she answered, with decision. As she turned a lit- tle away from him, she added: "But I don't think a place would be any the cheerfuller for John Wright's bein' in it."

"I'd like to talk to you about that a little later, Mrs. Hale," he said. "I'm anxious to get the lay of things upstairs now."

He moved toward the stair door, followed by the two men.

"I suppose anything Mrs. Peters does'll be all right?" the sheriff inquired. "She was to take in some clothes for her, you know--and a few little things. We left in such a hurry yesterday."

The county attorney looked at the two women they were leaving alone there among the kitchen things.

"Yes--Mrs. Peters," he said, his glance resting on the woman who was not Mrs. Peters, the big farmer woman who stood behind the sheriff's wife. "Of course Mrs. Peters is one of us," he said, in a manner of entrusting responsibility. "And keep your eye out, Mrs. Peters, for anything that might be of use. No telling; you women might come upon a clue to the motive--and that's the thing we need."

Mr. Hale rubbed his face after the fashion of a showman getting ready for a pleasantry.

"But would the women know a clue if they did come upon it?" he said; and, having delivered himself of this, he followed the others through the stair door.

The women stood motionless and silent, listening to the footsteps, first upon the stairs, then in the room above them.

Then, as if releasing herself from something strange. Mrs. Hale began to arrange the dirty pans under the sink, which the county attorney's disdainful push of the foot had deranged.

"I'd hate to have men comin' into my kitchen," she said testily--"snoopin' round and criticizin'."

"Of course it's no more than their duty," said the sheriff's wife, in her manner of timid acquiescence.

"Duty's all right," replied Mrs. Hale bluffly; "but I guess that deputy sheriff that come out to make the fire might have got a little of this on." She gave the roller towel a pull. 'Wish I'd thought of that sooner! Seems mean to talk about her for not having things slicked up, when she had to come away in such a hurry."

She looked around the kitchen. Certainly it was not "slicked up." Her eye was held by a bucket of sugar on a low shelf. The cover was off the wooden bucket, and beside it was a paper bag--half full.

Mrs. Hale moved toward it.

"She was putting this in there," she said to herself--slowly.

She thought of the flour in her kitchen at home--half sifted, half not sifted. She had been interrupted, and had left things half done. What had interrupted Minnie Foster? Why had that work been left half done? She made a move as if to finish it,--unfinished things always bothered her,-- and then she glanced around and saw that Mrs. Peters was watching her-- and she didn't want Mrs. Peters to get that feeling she had got of work begun and then--for some reason--not finished.

"It's a shame about her fruit," she said, and walked toward the cupboard that the county attorney had opened, and got on the chair, murmuring: "I wonder if it's all gone."

It was a sorry enough looking sight, but "Here's one that's all right," she said at last. She held it toward the light. "This is cherries, too." She looked again. "I declare I believe that's the only one."

With a sigh, she got down from the chair, went to the sink, and wiped off the bottle.

"She'll feel awful bad, after all her hard work in the hot weather. I remember the afternoon I put up my cherries last summer.

She set the bottle on the table, and, with another sigh, started to sit down in the rocker. But she did not sit down. Something kept her from sitting down in that chair. She straightened--stepped back, and, half turned away, stood looking at it, seeing the woman who had sat there "pleatin' at her apron."

The thin voice of the sheriff's wife broke in upon her: "I must be getting those things from the front-room closet." She opened the door into the other room, started in, stepped back. "You coming with me, Mrs. Hale?" she asked nervously. "You--you could help me get them."

They were soon back--the stark coldness of that shut-up room was not a thing to linger in.

"My!" said Mrs. Peters, dropping the things on the table and hurrying to the stove.

Mrs. Hale stood examining the clothes the woman who was being detained in town had said she wanted.

"Wright was close!" she exclaimed, holding up a shabby black skirt that bore the marks of much making over. "I think maybe that's why she kept so much to herself. I s'pose she felt she couldn't do her part; and then, you don't enjoy things when you feel shabby. She used to wear pretty clothes and be lively--when she was Minnie Foster, one of the town girls, singing in the choir. But that--oh, that was twenty years ago."

With a carefulness in which there was something tender, she folded the shabby clothes and piled them at one corner of the table. She looked up at Mrs. Peters, and there was something in the other woman's look that irritated her.

"She don't care," she said to herself. "Much difference it makes to her whether Minnie Foster had pretty clothes when she was a girl."

Then she looked again, and she wasn't so sure; in fact, she hadn't at any time been perfectly sure about Mrs. Peters. She had that shrinking manner, and yet her eyes looked as if they could see a long way into things.

"This all you was to take in?" asked Mrs. Hale.

"No," said the sheriffs wife; "she said she wanted an apron. Funny thing to want, " she ventured in her nervous little way, "for there's not much to get you dirty in jail, goodness knows. But I suppose just to make her feel more natural. If you're used to wearing an apron--. She said they were in the bottom drawer of this cupboard. Yes--here they are. And then her little shawl that always hung on the stair door."

She took the small gray shawl from behind the door leading upstairs, and stood a minute looking at it.

Suddenly Mrs. Hale took a quick step toward the other woman, "Mrs. Peters!"

"Yes, Mrs. Hale?"

"Do you think she--did it?'

A frightened look blurred the other thing in Mrs. Peters' eyes.

"Oh, I don't know," she said, in a voice that seemed to shink away from the subject.

"Well, I don't think she did," affirmed Mrs. Hale stoutly. "Asking for an apron, and her little shawl. Worryin' about her fruit."

"Mr. Peters says--." Footsteps were heard in the room above; she stopped, looked up, then went on in a lowered voice: "Mr. Peters says--it looks bad for her. Mr. Henderson is awful sarcastic in a speech, and he's going to make fun of her saying she didn't--wake up."

For a moment Mrs. Hale had no answer. Then, "Well, I guess John Wright didn't wake up--when they was slippin' that rope under his neck," she muttered.

"No, it's *strange*," breathed Mrs. Peters. "They think it was such a--funny way to kill a man."

She began to laugh; at sound of the laugh, abruptly stopped.

"That's just what Mr. Hale said," said Mrs. Hale, in a resolutely natural voice. "There was a gun in the house. He says that's what he can't understand."

"Mr. Henderson said, coming out, that what was needed for the case was a motive. Something to show anger--or sudden feeling."

'Well, I don't see any signs of anger around here," said Mrs. Hale, "I don't--" She stopped. It was as if her mind tripped on something. Her eye was caught by a dish towel in the middle of the kitchen table. Slowly she moved toward the table. One half of it was wiped clean, the other half messy. Her eyes made a slow, almost unwilling turn to the bucket of sugar and the half empty bag beside it. Things begun--and not finished.

After a moment she stepped back, and said, in that manner of releasing herself:

"Wonder how they're finding things upstairs? I hope she had it a little more red up up there. You know,"--she paused, and feeling gathered,--"it seems kind of *sneaking:* locking her up in town and coming out here to get her own house to turn against her!"

"But, Mrs. Hale," said the sheriff's wife, "the law is the law."

"I s'pose 'tis," answered Mrs. Hale shortly.

She turned to the stove, saying something about that fire not being much to brag of. She worked with it a minute, and when she straightened up she said aggressively:

"The law is the law--and a bad stove is a bad stove. How'd you like to cook on this?"--pointing with the poker to the broken lining. She opened the oven door and started to express her opinion of the oven; but she was swept into her own thoughts, thinking of what it would mean, year after year, to have that stove to wrestle with. The thought of Minnie Foster trying to bake in that oven--and the thought of her never going over to see Minnie Foster--.

She was startled by hearing Mrs. Peters say: "A person gets discouraged--and loses heart."

The sheriff's wife had looked from the stove to the sink--to the pail of water which had been carried in from outside. The two women stood there silent, above them the footsteps of the men who were looking for evidence against the woman who had worked in that kitchen. That look of seeing into things, of seeing through a thing to something else, was in the eyes of the sheriff's wife now. When Mrs. Hale next spoke to her, it was gently:

"Better loosen up your things, Mrs. Peters. We'll not feel them when we go out."

Mrs. Peters went to the back of the room to hang up the fur tippet she was wearing. A moment later she exclaimed, "Why, she was piecing a quilt," and held up a large sewing basket piled high with quilt pieces.

Mrs. Hale spread some of the blocks on the table.

"It's log-cabin pattern," she said, putting several of them together, "Pretty, isn't it?"

They were so engaged with the quilt that they did not hear the footsteps on the stairs. Just as the stair door opened Mrs. Hale was saying:

"Do you suppose she was going to quilt it or just knot it?"

The sheriff threw up his hands.

"They wonder whether she was going to quilt it or just knot it!"

There was a laugh for the ways of women, a warming of hands over the stove, and then the county attorney said briskly:

"Well, let's go right out to the barn and get that cleared up."

"I don't see as there's anything so strange," Mrs. Hale said resentfully, after the outside door had closed on the three men--"our taking up our time with little things while we're waiting for them to get the evidence. I don't see as it's anything to laugh about."

"Of course they've got awful important things on their minds," said the sheriff's wife apologetically.

They returned to an inspection of the block for the quilt. Mrs. Hale was looking at the fine, even sewing, and preoccupied with thoughts of the woman who had done that sewing, when she heard the sheriff's wife say, in a queer tone:

"Why, look at this one."

She turned to take the block held out to her.

"The sewing," said Mrs. Peters, in a troubled way, "All the rest of them have been so nice and even--but--this one. Why, it looks as if she didn't know what she was about!"

Their eyes met--something flashed to life, passed between them; then, as if with an effort, they seemed to pull away from each other. A moment Mrs. Hale sat there, her hands folded over that sewing which was so unlike all the rest of the sewing. Then she had pulled a knot and drawn the threads.

"Oh, what are you doing, Mrs. Hale?" asked the sheriff's wife, startled.

"Just pulling out a stitch or two that's not sewed very good," said Mrs. Hale mildly.

"I don't think we ought to touch things," Mrs. Peters said, a little helplessly.

"I'll just finish up this end," answered Mrs. Hale, still in that mild, matter-of-fact fashion.

She threaded a needle and started to replace bad sewing with good. For a little while she sewed in silence. Then, in that thin, timid voice, she heard:

"Mrs. Hale!"

"Yes, Mrs. Peters?"

'What do you suppose she was so--nervous about?"

"Oh, I don't know," said Mrs. Hale, as if dismissing a thing not important enough to spend much time on. "I don't know as she was-- nervous. I sew awful queer sometimes when I'm just tired."

She cut a thread, and out of the corner of her eye looked up at Mrs. Peters. The small, lean face of the sheriff's wife seemed to have tightened up. Her eyes had that look of peering into something. But next moment she moved, and said in her thin, indecisive way:

'Well, I must get those clothes wrapped. They may be through sooner than we think. I wonder where I could find a piece of paper--and string."

"In that cupboard, maybe," suggested to Mrs. Hale, after a glance around.

One piece of the crazy sewing remained unripped. Mrs. Peter's back turned, Martha Hale now scrutinized that piece, compared it with the dainty, accurate sewing of the other blocks. The difference was startling. Holding this block made her feel queer, as if the distracted thoughts of the woman who had perhaps turned to it to try and quiet herself were communicating themselves to her.

Mrs. Peters' voice roused her.

"Here's a bird-cage," she said. "Did she have a bird, Mrs. Hale?"

'Why, I don't know whether she did or not." She turned to look at the cage Mrs. Peters was holding up. "I've not been here in so long." She sighed. "There was a man round last year selling canaries cheap--but I don't know as she took one. Maybe she did. She used to sing real pretty herself."

Mrs. Peters looked around the kitchen.

"Seems kind of funny to think of a bird here." She half laughed--an attempt to put up a barrier. "But she must have had one--or why would she have a cage? I wonder what happened to it."

"I suppose maybe the cat got it," suggested Mrs. Hale, resuming her sewing.

"No; she didn't have a cat. She's got that feeling some people have about cats--being afraid of them. When they brought her to our house yesterday, my cat got in the room, and she was real upset and asked me to take it out."

"My sister Bessie was like that," laughed Mrs. Hale.

The sheriff's wife did not reply. The silence made Mrs. Hale turn round. Mrs. Peters was examining the bird-cage.

"Look at this door," she said slowly. "It's broke. One hinge has been pulled apart."

Mrs. Hale came nearer.

"Looks as if someone must have been--rough with it."

Again their eyes met--startled, questioning, apprehensive. For a moment neither spoke nor stirred. Then Mrs. Hale, turning away, said brusquely:

"If they're going to find any evidence, I wish they'd be about it. I don't like this place."

"But I'm awful glad you came with me, Mrs. Hale." Mrs. Peters put the bird-cage on the table and sat down. "It would be lonesome for me--sitting here alone."

"Yes, it would, wouldn't it?" agreed Mrs. Hale, a certain determined naturalness in her voice. She had picked up the sewing, but now it dropped in her lap, and she murmured in a different voice: "But I tell you what I *do* wish, Mrs. Peters. I wish I had come over sometimes when she was here. I wish--I had."

"But of course you were awful busy, Mrs. Hale. Your house--and your children."

"I could've come," retorted Mrs. Hale shortly. "I stayed away because it weren't cheerful--and that's why I ought to have come. I"--she looked around--"I've never liked this place. Maybe because it's down in a hollow and you don't see the road. I don't know what it is, but it's a lonesome place, and always was. I wish I had come over to see Minnie Foster sometimes. I can see now--" She did not put it into words.

"Well, you mustn't reproach yourself," counseled Mrs. Peters.

"Somehow, we just don't see how it is with other folks till--something comes up."

"Not having children makes less work," mused Mrs. Hale, after a silence, "but it makes a quiet house--and Wright out to work all day--and no company when he did come in. Did you know John Wright, Mrs. Peters?"

"Not to know him. I've seen him in town. They say he was a good man."

"Yes--good," conceded John Wright's neighbor grimly. "He didn't drink, and kept his word as well as most, I guess, and paid his debts. But he was a hard man, Mrs. Peters. Just to pass the time of day with him--." She stopped, shivered a little. "Like a raw wind that gets to the bone." Her eye fell upon the cage on the table before her, and she added, almost bitterly: "I should think she would've wanted a bird!"

Suddenly she leaned forward, looking intently at the cage. "But what do you s'pose went wrong with it?"

"I don't know," returned Mrs. Peters; "unless it got sick and died."

But after she said it she reached over and swung the broken door. Both women watched it as if somehow held by it.

"You didn't know--her?" Mrs. Hale asked, a gentler note in her voice.

"Not till they brought her yesterday," said the sheriff's wife.

"She--come to think of it, she was kind of like a bird herself. Real sweet and pretty, but kind of timid and--fluttery. How--she--did--change."

That held her for a long time. Finally, as if struck with a happy thought and relieved to get back to everyday things, she exclaimed:

"Tell you what, Mrs. Peters, why don't you take the quilt in with you? It might take up her mind."

"Why, I think that's a real nice idea, Mrs. Hale," agreed the sheriff's wife, as if she too were glad to come into the atmosphere of a simple kindness. "There couldn't possibly be any objection to that, could there? Now, just what will I take? I wonder if her patches are in here--and her things?"

They turned to the sewing basket.

"Here's some red," said Mrs. Hale, bringing out a roll of cloth. Underneath that was a box. "Here, maybe her scissors are in here--and her things." She held it up. "What a pretty box! I'll warrant that was something she had a long time ago--when she was a girl."

She held it in her hand a moment; then, with a little sigh, opened it.

Instantly her hand went to her nose.

"Why--!"

Mrs. Peters drew nearer--then turned away.

"There's something wrapped up in this piece of silk," faltered Mrs. Hale.

"This isn't her scissors," said Mrs. Peters, in a shrinking voice.

Her hand not steady, Mrs. Hale raised the piece of silk. "Oh, Mrs. Peters!" she cried. "It's--"

Mrs. Peters bent closer.

"It's the bird," she whispered.

"But, Mrs. Peters!" cried Mrs. Hale. "*Look* at it! Its *neck*--look at its neck! It's all--other side *to.*"

She held the box away from her.

The sheriff's wife again bent closer.

"Somebody wrung its neck," said she, in a voice that was slow and deep.

And then again the eyes of the two women met--this time clung together in a look of dawning comprehension, of growing horror. Mrs. Peters looked from the dead bird to the broken door of the cage. Again their eyes met. And just then there was a sound at the outside door. Mrs. Hale slipped the box under the quilt pieces in the basket, and sank into the chair before it. Mrs. Peters stood holding to the table. The county attorney and the sheriff came in from outside.

"Well, ladies," said the county attorney, as one turning from serious things to little pleasantries, "have you decided whether she was going to quilt it or knot it?"

"We think," began the sheriff's wife in a flurried voice, "that she was going to--knot it."

He was too preoccupied to notice the change that came in her voice on that last.

"Well, that's very interesting, I'm sure," he said tolerantly. He caught sight of the bird-cage.

"Has the bird flown?"

"We think the cat got it," said Mrs. Hale in a voice curiously even.

He was walking up and down, as if thinking something out.

"Is there a cat?" he asked absently.

Mrs. Hale shot a look up at the sheriff's wife.

"Well, not *now*," said Mrs. Peters. "They're superstitious, you know; they leave."

She sank into her chair.

The county attorney did not heed her. "No sign at all of anyone having come in from the outside," he said to Peters, in the manner of continuing

200

an interrupted conversation. "Their own rope. Now let's go upstairs again and go over it, picee by piece. It would have to have been someone who knew just the--"

The stair door closed behind them and their voices were lost.

The two women sat motionless, not looking at each other, but as if peering into something and at the same time holding back. When they spoke now it was as if they were afraid of what they were saying, but as if they could not help saying it.

"She liked the bird," said Martha Hale, low and slowly. "She was going to bury it in that pretty box."

When I was a girl," said Mrs. Peters, under her breath, "my kitten--there was a boy took a hatchet, and before my eyes--before I could get there--" She covered her face an instant. "If they hadn't held me back I would have"--she caught herself, looked upstairs where footsteps were heard, and finished weakly--"hurt him."

Then they sat without speaking or moving.

"I wonder how it would seem," Mrs. Hale at last began, as if feeling her way over strange ground--"never to have had any children around?" Her eyes made a slow sweep of the kitchen, as if seeing what that kitchen had meant through all the years "No, Wright wouldn't like the bird," she said after that--"a thing that sang. She used to sing. He killed that too." Her voice tightened.

Mrs. Peters moved uneasily.

"Of course we don't know who killed the bird."

"I knew John Wright," was Mrs. Hale's answer.

"It was an awful thing was done in this house that night, Mrs. Hale," said the sheriff's wife. "Killing a man while he slept--slipping a thing round his neck that choked the life out of him."

Mrs. Hale's hand went out to the bird cage.

"We don't *know* who killed him," whispered Mrs. Peters wildly. "We don't *know*."

Mrs. Hale had not moved. "If there had been years and years of-- nothing, then a bird to sing to you, it would be awful--still--after the bird was still."

It was as if something within her not herself had spoken, and it found in Mrs. Peters something she did not know as herself.

"I know what stillness is," she said, in a queer, monotonous voice. "When we homesteaded in Dakota, and my first baby died--after he was two years old--and me with no other then--"

Mrs. Hale stirred.

"How soon do you suppose they'll be through looking for the evidence?"

"I know what stillness is," repeated Mrs. Peters, in just that same way. Then she too pulled back. "The law has got to punish crime, Mrs. Hale," she said in her tight little way.

"I wish you'd seen Minnie Foster," was the answer, "when she wore a white dress with blue ribbons, and stood up there in the choir and sang."

The picture of that girl, the fact that she had lived neighbor to that girl for twenty years, and had let her die for lack of life, was suddenly more than she could bear.

"Oh, I *wish* I'd come over here once in a while!" she cried. "That was a crime! Who's going to punish that?"

"We mustn't take on," said Mrs. Peters, with a frightened look toward the stairs.

"I might 'a' *known* she needed help! I tell you, it's *queer*, Mrs. Peters. We live close together, and we live far apart. We all go through the same things--it's all just a different kind of the same thing! If it weren't--why do you and I *understand*? Why do we *know*--what we know this minute?"

She dashed her hand across her eyes. Then, seeing the jar of fruit on the table she reached for it and choked out:

"If I was you I wouldn't *tell* her her fruit was gone! Tell her it *ain't*. Tell her it's all right--all of it. Here--take this in to prove it to her! She--she may never know whether it was broke or not."

She turned away.

Mrs. Peters reached out for the bottle of fruit as if she were glad to take it--as if touching a familiar thing, having something to do, could keep her from something else. She got up, looked about for something to wrap the fruit in, took a petticoat from the pile of clothes she had brought from the front room, and nervously started winding that round the bottle.

"My!" she began, in a high, false voice, "it's a good thing the men couldn't hear us! Getting all stirred up over a little thing like a--dead canary." She hurried over that. "As if that could have anything to do with--with--My, wouldn't they *laugh*?"

Footsteps were heard on the stairs.

"Maybe they would," muttered Mrs. Hale--"maybe they wouldn't."

"No, Peters," said the county attorney incisively; "it's all perfectly clear, except the reason for doing it. But you know juries when it comes to women. If there was some definite thing--something to show. Something to make a story about. A thing that would connect up with this clumsy way of doing it."

In a covert way Mrs. Hale looked at Mrs. Peters. Mrs. Peters was looking at her. Quickly they looked away from each other. The outer door opened and Mr. Hale came in.

"I've got the team round now," he said. "Pretty cold out there."

"I'm going to stay here awhile by myself," the county attorney suddenly announced. "You can send Frank out for me, can't you?" he asked the sheriff. "I want to go over everything. I'm not satisfied we can't do better."

Again, for one brief moment, the two women's eyes found one another. The sheriff came up to the table.

"Did you want to see what Mrs. Peters was going to take in?"

The county attorney picked up the apron. He laughed.

"Oh, I guess they're not very dangerous things the ladies have picked out."

Mrs. Hale's hand was on the sewing basket in which the box was concealed. She felt that she ought to take her hand off the basket. She did not seem able to. He picked up one of the quilt blocks which she had piled on to cover the box. Her eyes felt like fire. She had a feeling that if he took up the basket she would snatch it from him.

But he did not take it up. With another little laugh, he turned away, saying:

"No; Mrs. Peters doesn't need supervising. For that matter, a sheriff's wife is married to the law. Ever think of it that way, Mrs. Peters?"

Mrs. Peters was standing beside the table. Mrs. Hale shot a look up at her; but she could not see her face. Mrs. Peters had turned away. When she spoke, her voice was muffled.

"Not--just that way," she said.

"Married to the law!" chuckled Mrs. Peters' husband. He moved toward the door into the front room, and said to the county attorney:

"I just want you to come in here a minute, George. We ought to take a look at these windows."

"Oh--windows," said the county attorney scoffingly.

"We'll be right out, Mr. Hale," said the sheriff to the farmer, who was still waiting by the door.

Hale went to look after the horses. The sheriff followed the county attorney into the other room. Again--for one final moment--the two women were alone in that kitchen.

Martha Hale sprang up, her hands tight together, looking at that other woman, with whom it rested. At first she could not see her eyes, for the sheriff's wife had not turned back since she turned away at that suggestion of being married to the law. But now Mrs. Hale made her turn back. Her eyes made her turn back. Slowly, unwillingly, Mrs. Peters turned her head until her eyes met the eyes of the other woman. There was a moment when they held each other in a steady, burning look in which there was no evasion or flinching. Then Martha Hale's eyes pointed the way to the basket in which was hidden the thing that would make certain the conviction of the other woman--that woman who was not there and yet who had been there with them all through that hour.

For a moment Mrs. Peters did not move. And then she did it. With a rush forward, she threw back the quilt pieces, got the box, tried to put it in her handbag. It was too big. Desperately she opened it, started to take the bird out. But there she broke--she could not touch the bird. She stood there helpless, foolish.

There was the sound of a knob turning in the inner door. Martha Hale snatched the box from the sheriff's wife, and got it in the pocket of her big coat just as the sheriff and the county attorney came back into the kitchen.

"Well, Henry," said the county attorney facetiously, "at least we found out that she was not going to quilt it. She was going to--what is it you call it, ladies?"

Mrs. Hale's hand was against the pocket of her coat.

"We call it--knot it, Mr. Henderson."

Willa Cather

ON THE GULL'S ROAD

IT often happens that one or another of my friends stops before a red chalk drawing in my study and asks me where I ever found so lovely a creature. I have never told the story of that picture to any one, and the beautiful woman on the wall, until yesterday, in all these twenty years has spoken to no one but me. Yesterday a young painter, a countryman of mine, came to consult me on a matter of business, and upon seeing my drawing of Alexandra Ebbling, straightway forgot his errand. He examined the date upon the sketch and asked me, very earnestly, if I could tell him whether the lady were still living. When I answered him, he stepped back from the picture and said slowly:

"So long ago? She must have been very young. She was happy?"

"As to that, who can say -- about any one of us?" I replied. "Out of all that is supposed to make for happiness, she had very little."

We returned to the object of his visit, but when he bade me goodbye at the door his troubled gaze again went back to the drawing, and it was only by turning sharply about that he took his eyes away from her.

I went back to my study fire, and as the rain kept away less impetuous visitors, I had a long time in which to think of Mrs. Ebbling. I even got out the little box she gave me, which I had not opened for years, and when Mrs. Hemway brought my tea I had barely time to close the lid and defeat her disapproving gaze.

My young countryman's perplexity, as he looked at Mrs. Ebbling, had recalled to me the delight and pain she gave me when I was of his years. I sat looking at her face and trying to see it through his eyes -- freshly, as I saw it first upon the deck of the Germania, twenty years ago. Was it her loveliness, I often ask myself, or her loneliness, or her simplicity, or was it merely my own youth? Was her mystery only that of the mysterious North out of which she came? I still feel that she was very different from all the beautiful and brilliant women I have known; as the night is different from the day, or as the sea is different from the land. But this is our story, as it comes back to me.

For two years I had been studying Italian and working in the capacity of clerk to the American legation at Rome, and I was going home to secure my first consular appointment. Upon boarding my steamer at Genoa, I saw my luggage into my cabin and then started for a rapid circuit of the deck. Everything promised well. The boat was thinly peopled, even for a July crossing; the decks were roomy; the day was fine; the sea was blue; I was sure of my appointment, and, best of all, I was coming back to Italy. All these things were in my mind when I stopped sharply before a chaise longue placed sidewise near the stern. Its occupant was a woman, apparently ill, who lay with her eyes closed, and in her open arm was a chubby little red-haired girl, asleep. I can still remember that first glance at Mrs. Ebbling, and how I stopped as a wheel does when the band slips. Her splendid, vigorous body lay still and relaxed under the loose folds of her clothing, her white throat and arms and red-gold hair were drenched with sunlight. Such hair as it was: wayward as some kind of gleaming seaweed that curls and undulates with the tide. A moment gave me her face; the high cheek-bones, the thin cheeks, the gentle chin, arching back to a girlish throat, and the singular loveliness of the mouth. Even then it flashed through me that the mouth gave the whole face its peculiar beauty and distinction. It was proud and sad and tender, and strangely calm. The curve of the lips could not have been cut more cleanly with the most delicate instrument, and whatever shade of feeling passed over them seemed to partake of their exquisiteness.

But I am anticipating. While I stood stupidly staring (as if, at twenty-five, I had never before beheld a beautiful woman) the whistles broke into a hoarse scream, and the deck under us began to vibrate. The woman opened her eyes, and the little girl struggled into a sitting position, rolled out of her mother's arm, and ran to the deck rail. After putting my chair near the stern, I went forward to see the gang-plank up and did not return until we were dragging out to sea at the end of a long tow-line.

The woman in the chaise longue was still alone. She lay there all day, looking at the sea. The little girl, Carin, played noisily about the deck. Occasionally she returned and struggled up into the chair, plunged her head, round and red as a little pumpkin, against her mother's shoulder in an impetuous embrace, and then struggled down again with a lively flourishing of arms and legs. Her mother took such opportunities to pull up the child's socks or to smooth the fiery little braids; her beautiful hands, rather large and very white, played about the riotous little girl with a quieting tenderness. Carin chattered away in Italian and kept asking for her father, only to be told that he was busy.

When any of the ship's officers passed, they stopped for a word with my neighbor, and I heard the first mate address her as Mrs. Ebbling. When they spoke to her, she smiled appreciatively and answered in low, faltering Italian, but I fancied that she was glad when they passed on and left her to her fixed contemplation of the sea. Her eyes seemed to drink the color of it all day long, and after every interruption they went back to it. There was a kind of pleasure in watching her satisfaction, a kind of excitement in wondering what the water made her remember or forget. She seemed not to wish to talk to any one, but I knew I should like to hear whatever she might be thinking. One could catch some hint of her thoughts, I imagined, from the shadows that came and went across her lips, like the reflection of light clouds. She had a pile of books beside her, but she did not read, and neither could I. I gave up trying at last, and watched the sea, very conscious of her presence, almost of her thoughts. When the sun dropped low and shone in her face, I rose and asked if she would like me to move her chair. She smiled and thanked me, but said the sun was good for her. Her yellow-hazel eyes followed me for a moment and then went back to the sea.

After the first bugle sounded for dinner, a heavy man in uniform came up the deck and stood beside the chaise longue, looking down at its two occupants with a smile of satisfied possession. The breast of his trim coat was hidden by waves of soft blond beard, as long and heavy as a woman's hair, which blew about his face in glittering profusion. He wore a large turquoise ring upon the thick hand that he rubbed good-humoredly over the little girl's head. To her he spoke Italian, but he and his wife conversed in some Scandinavian tongue. He stood stroking his fine beard until the second bugle blew, then bent stiffly from his hips, like a soldier, and patted his wife's hand as it lay on the arm of her chair. He hurried down the deck, taking stock of the passengers as he went, and stopped before a thin girl with frizzed hair and a lace coat, asking her a facetious question in thick English. They began to talk about Chicago and went below. Later I saw him at the head of his table in the dining room, the befrizzed Chicago lady on his left. They must have got a famous start at luncheon, for by the end of the dinner Ebbling was peeling figs for her and presenting them on the end of a fork.

The Doctor confided to me that Ebbling was the chief engineer and the dandy of the boat; but this time he would have to behave himself, for he had brought his sick wife along for the voyage. She had a bad heart valve, he added, and was in a serious way.

After dinner Ebbling disappeared, presumably to his engines, and at ten o'clock, when the stewardess came to put Mrs. Ebbling to bed, I helped her to rise from her chair, and the second mate ran up and supported her down to her cabin. About midnight I found the engineer in the card room, playing with the Doctor, an Italian naval officer, and the commodore of a Long Island yacht club. His face was even pinker than it had been at dinner, and his fine beard was full of smoke. I thought a long while about Ebbling and his wife before I went to sleep.

The next morning we tied up at Naples to take on our cargo, and I went on shore for the day. I did not, however, entirely escape the ubiquitous engineer, whom I saw lunching with the Long Island commodore at a hotel in the Santa Lucia. When I returned to the boat in the early evening, the passengers had gone down to dinner, and I found Mrs. Ebbling quite alone upon the deserted deck. I approached her and asked whether she had had a dull day. She looked up smiling and shook her head, as if her Italian had quite failed her. I saw that she was flushed with excitement, and her yellow eyes were shining like two clear topazes.

"Dull? Oh, no! I love to watch Naples from the sea, in this white heat. She has just lain there on her hillside among the vines and laughed for me all day long. I have been able to pick out many of the places I like best."

I felt that she was really going to talk to me at last. She had turned to me frankly, as to an old acquaintance, and seemed not to be hiding from me anything of what she felt. I sat down in a glow of pleasure and excitement and asked her if she knew Naples well.

"Oh, yes! I lived there for a year after I was first married. My husband has a great many friends in Naples. But he was at sea most of the time, so I went about alone. Nothing helps one to know a city like that. I came first by sea, like this. Directly to Naples from Finmark, and I had never been South before." Mrs. Ebbling stopped and looked over my shoulder. Then, with a quick, eager glance at me, she said abruptly: "It was like a baptism of fire. Nothing has ever been quite the same since. Imagine how this bay looked to a Finmark girl. It seemed like the overture to Italy."

I laughed. "And then one goes up the country -- song by song and wine by wine."

Mrs. Ebbling sighed. "Ah, yes. It must be fine to follow it. I have never been away from the seaports myself. We live now in Genoa."

The deck steward brought her tray, and I moved forward a little and stood by the rail. When I looked back, she smiled and nodded to let me know that she was not missing anything. I could feel her intentness as keenly as if she were standing beside me.

The sun had disappeared over the high ridge behind the city, and the stone pines stood black and flat against the fires of the afterglow. The lilac haze that hung over the long, lazy slopes of Vesuvius warmed with golden light, and films of blue vapor began to float down toward Baiae. The sky, the sea, and the city between them turned a shimmering violet, fading grayer as the lights began to glow like luminous pearls along the water-front, -- the necklace of an irreclaimable queen. Behind me I heard a low exclamation; a slight, stifled sound, but it seemed the perfect vocalization of that weariness with which we at last let go of beauty, after we have held it until the senses are darkened. When I turned to her again, she seemed to have fallen asleep.

That night, as we were moving out to sea and the tail lights of Naples were winking across the widening stretch of black water, I helped Mrs. Ebbling to the foot of the stairway. She drew herself up from her chair with effort and leaned on me wearily. I could have carried her all night without fatigue.

"May I come and talk to you to-morrow?" I asked. She did not reply at once. "Like an old friend?" I added. She gave me her languid hand, and her mouth, set with the exertion of walking, softened altogether. "Grazia," she murmured.

I returned to the deck and joined a group of my countrywomen, who, primed with inexhaustible information, were discussing the baseness of Renaissance art. They were intelligent and alert, and as they leaned

forward in their deck chairs under the circle of light, their faces recalled
to me Rembrandt's picture of a clinical lecture. I heard them through,
against my will, and then went to the stern to smoke and to see the last of
the island lights. The sky had clouded over, and a soft, melancholy wind
was rushing over the sea. I could not help thinking how disappointed I
would be if rain should keep Mrs. Ebbling in her cabin to-morrow. My
mind played constantly with her image. At one moment she was very
clear and directly in front of me; the next she was far away. Whatever else
I thought about, some part of my consciousness was busy with Mrs.
Ebbling; hunting for her, finding her, losing her, then groping again.
How was it that I was so conscious of whatever she might be feeling? that
when she sat still behind me and watched the evening sky, I had had a
sense of speed and change, almost of danger; and when she was tired and
sighed, I had wished for night and loneliness.

II

Though when we are young we seldom think much about it, there is
now and again a golden day when we feel a sudden, arrogant pride in our
youth; in the lightness of our feet and the strength of our arms, in the
warm fluid that courses so surely within us; when we are conscious of
something powerful and mercurial in our breasts, which comes up wave
after wave and leaves us irresponsible and free. All the next morning I felt
this flow of life, which continually impelled me toward Mrs. Ebbling.
After the merest greeting, however, I kept away. I found it pleasant to
thwart myself, to measure myself against a current that was sure to carry
me with it in the end. I was content to let her watch the sea -- the sea that
seemed now to have come into me, warm and soft, still and strong. I
played shuffleboard with the Commodore, who was anxious to keep
down his figure, and ran about the deck with the stout legs of the little
pumpkin-colored Carin about my neck. It was not until the child was
having her afternoon nap below that I at last came up and stood beside
her mother.
"You are better to-day," I exclaimed, looking down at her white gown.
She colored unreasonably, and I laughed with a familiarity which she
must have accepted as the mere foolish noise of happiness, or it would
have seemed impertinent.
We talked at first of a hundred trivial things, and we watched the sea.
The coast of Sardinia had lain to our port for some hours and would lie
there for hours to come, now advancing in rocky promontories, now
retreating behind blue bays. It was the naked south coast of the island,

and though our course held very near the shore, not a village or habitation was visible; there was not even a goat-herd's hut hidden away among the low pinkish sand hills. Pinkish sand hills and yellow head-lands; with dull-colored scrubby bushes massed about their bases and following the dried water-courses. A narrow strip of beach glistened like white paint between the purple sea and the umber rocks, and the whole island lay gleaming in the yellow sunshine and translucent air. Not a wave broke on that fringe of white sand, not the shadow of a cloud played across the bare hills. In the air about us, there was no sound but that of a vessel moving rapidly through absolutely still water. She seemed like some great sea-animal, swimming silently, her head well up. The sea before us was so rich and heavy and opaque that it might have been lapis lazuli. It was the blue of legend, simply; the color that satisfies the soul like sleep.

And it was of the sea we talked, for it was the substance of Mrs. Ebbling's story. She seemed always to have been swept along by ocean streams, warm or cold, and to have hovered about the edge of great waters. She was born and had grown up in a little fishing town on the Arctic ocean. Her father was a doctor, a widower, who lived with his daughter and who divided his time between his books and his fishing rod. Her uncle was skipper on a coasting vessel, and with him she had made many trips along the Norwegian coast. But she was always reading and thinking about the blue seas of the South.

"There was a curious old woman in our village, Dame Ericson, who had been in Italy in her youth. She had gone to Rome to study art, and had copied a great many pictures there. She was well connected, but had little money, and as she grew older and poorer she sold her pictures one by one, until there was scarcely a well-to-do family in our district that did not own one of Dame Ericson's paintings. But she brought home many other strange things; a little orange-tree which she cherished until the day of her death, and bits of colored marble, and sea shells and pieces of coral, and a thin flask full of water from the Mediterranean. When I was a little girl she used to show me her things and tell me about the South; about the coral fishers, and the pink islands, and the smoking mountains, and the old, underground Naples. I suppose the water in her flask was like any other, but it never seemed so to me. It looked so elastic and alive, that I used to think if one unsealed the bottle something penetrating and fruitful might leap out and work an enchantment over Finmark."

Lars Ebbling, I learned, was one of her father's friends. She could remember him from the time when she was a little girl and he a dashing young man who used to come home from the sea and make a stir in the village. After he got his promotion to an Atlantic liner and went South, she did not see him until the summer she was twenty, when he came home to marry her. That was five years ago. The little girl, Carin, was three. From her talk, one might have supposed that Ebbling was proprietor of the Mediterranean and its adjacent lands, and could have kept her away at his pleasure. Her own rights in him she seemed not to consider.

But we wasted very little time on Lars Ebbling. We talked, like two very young persons, of arms and men, of the sea beneath us and the shores it washed. We were carried a little beyond ourselves, for we were in the presence of the things of youth that never change; fleeing past them. To-morrow they would be gone, and no effort of will or memory could bring them back again. All about us was the sea of great adventure, and below us, caught somewhere in its gleaming meshes, were the bones of nations and navies . . . . . nations and navies that gave youth its hope and made life something more than a hunger of the bowels. The unpeopled Sardinian coast unfolded gently before us, like something left over out of a world that was gone; a place that might well have had no later news since the corn ships brought the tidings of Actium.

"I shall never go to Sardinia," said Mrs. Ebbling. "It could not possibly be as beautiful as this."

"Neither shall I," I replied.

As I was going down to dinner that evening, I was stopped by Lars Ebbling, freshly brushed and scented, wearing a white uniform, and polished and glistening as one of his own engines. He smiled at me with his own kind of geniality. "You have been very kind to talk to my wife," he explained. "It is very bad for her this trip that she speaks no English. I am indebted to you."

I told him curtly that he was mistaken, but my acrimony made no impression upon his blandness. I felt that I should certainly strike the fellow if he stood there much longer, running his blue ring up and down his beard. I should probably have hated any man who was Mrs. Ebbling's husband, but Ebbling made me sick.

III

The next day I began my drawing of Mrs. Ebbling. She seemed pleased and a little puzzled when I asked her to sit for me. It occurred to me that she had always been among dull people who took her looks as a matter of course, and that she was not at all sure that she was really beautiful. I can see now her quick, confused look of pleasure. I thought very little about the drawing then, except that the making of it gave me an opportunity to study her face; to look as long as I pleased into her yellow eyes, at the noble lines of her mouth, at her splendid, vigorous hair.

"We have a yellow vine at home," I told her, "that is very like your hair. It seems to be growing while one looks at it, and it twines and tangles about itself and throws out little tendrils in the wind."

"Has it any name?"

"We call it love vine."

How little a thing could disconcert her!

As for me, nothing disconcerted me. I awoke every morning with a sense of speed and joy. At night I loved to hear the swish of the water rushing by. As fast as the pistons could carry us, as fast as the water could bear us, we were going forward to something delightful; to something together. When Mrs. Ebbling told me that she and her husband would be five days in the docks in New York and then return to Genoa, I was not disturbed, for I did not believe her. I came and went, and she sat still all day, watching the water. I heard an American lady say that she watched it like one who is going to die, but even that did not frighten me: I somehow felt that she had promised me to live.

All those long blue days when I sat beside her talking about Finmark and the sea, she must have known that I loved her. I sat with my hands idle on my knees and let the tide come up in me. It carried me so swiftly that, across the narrow space of deck between us, it must have swayed her, too, a little. I had no wish to disturb or distress her. If a little, a very little of it reached her, I was satisfied. If it drew her softly, but drew her, I wanted no more. Sometimes I could see that even the light pressure of my thoughts made her paler. One still evening, after a long talk, she whispered to me, "You must go and walk now, and -- don't think about me." She had been held too long and too closely in my thoughts, and she begged me to release her for a little while. I went out into the bow and put her far away, at the sky line, with the faintest star, and thought of her gently across the water. When I went back to her, she was asleep.

But even in those first days I had my hours of misery. Why, for instance, should she have been born in Finmark, and why should Lars Ebbling have been her only door of escape? Why should she be silently taking leave of the world at the age when I was just beginning it, having had nothing, nothing of whatever is worth while?

She never talked about taking leave of things, and yet I sometimes felt that she was counting the sunsets. One yellow afternoon, when we were gliding between the shores of Spain and Africa, she spoke of her illness for

the first time. I had got some magnolias at Gibraltar, and she wore a
bunch of them in her girdle and the rest lay on her lap. She held the cool
leaves against her cheek and fingered the white petals. "I can never," she
remarked, "get enough of the flowers of the South. They make me
breathless, just as they did at first. Because of them I should like to live a
long while -- almost forever."

I leaned forward and looked at her. "We could live almost forever if we
had enough courage. It's of our lives that we die. If we had the courage to
change it all, to run away to some blue coast like that over there, we
could live on and on, until we were tired."

She smiled tolerantly and looked southward through half shut eyes. "I
am afraid I should never have courage enough to go behind that
mountain, at least. Look at it, it looks as if it hid horrible things."

A sea mist, blown in from the Atlantic, began to mask the impassive
African coast, and above the fog, the grey mountain peak took on the
angry red of the sunset. It burned sullen and threatening until the dark
land drew the night about her and settled back into the sea. We watched
it sink, while under us, slowly but ever increasing, we felt the throb of the
Atlantic come and go, the thrill of the vast, untamed waters of that
lugubrious and passionate sea. I drew Mrs. Ebbling's wraps about her and
shut the magnolias under her cloak. When I left her, she slipped me one
warm, white flower.

IV

From the Straits of Gibraltar we dropped into the abyss, and by morning
we were rolling in the trough of a sea that drew us down and held us
deep, shaking us gently back and forth until the timbers creaked, and
then shooting us out on the crest of a swelling mountain. The water was
bright and blue, but so cold that the breath of it penetrated one's bones,
as if the chill of the deep under-fathoms of the sea were being loosed
upon us. There were not more than a dozen people upon the deck that
morning, and Mrs. Ebbling was sheltered behind the stern, muffled in a
sea jacket, with drops of moisture upon her long lashes and on her hair.
When a shower of icy spray beat back over the deck rail, she took it
gleefully.

"After all," she insisted, "this is my own kind of water; the kind I was
born in. This is first cousin to the Pole waters, and the sea we have left is
only a kind of fairy tale. It's like the burnt out volcanoes; its day is over.
This is the real sea now, where the doings of the world go on."

"It is not our reality, at any rate," I answered.

"Oh, yes, it is! These are the waters that carry men to their work, and they will carry you to yours."

I sat down and watched her hair grow more alive and iridescent in the moisture. "You are pleased to take an attitude," I complained.

"No, I don't love realities any more than another, but I admit them, all the same."

"And who are you and I to define the realities?"

"Our minds define them clearly enough, yours and mine, everybody's. Those are the lines we never cross, though we flee from the equator to the Pole. I have never really got out of Finmark, of course. I shall live and die in a fishing town on the Arctic ocean, and the blue seas and the pink islands are as much a dream as they ever were. All the same, I shall continue to dream them."

The Gulf Stream gave us warm blue days again, but pale, like sad memories. The water had faded, and the thin, tepid sunshine made something tighten about one's heart. The stars watched us coldly, and seemed always to be asking me what I was going to do. The advancing line on the chart, which at first had been mere foolishness, began to mean something, and the wind from the west brought disturbing fears and forebodings. I slept lightly, and all day I was restless and uncertain except when I was with Mrs. Ebbling. She quieted me as she did little Carin, and soothed me without saying anything, as she had done that evening at Naples when we watched the sunset. It seemed to me that every day her eyes grew more tender and her lips more calm. A kind of fortitude seemed to be gathering about her mouth, and I dreaded it. Yet when, in an involuntary glance, I put to her the question that tortured me, her eyes always met mine steadily, deep and gentle and full of reassurance. That I had my word at last, happened almost by accident.

On the second night out from shore there was the concert for the Sailors' Orphanage, and Mrs. Ebbling dressed and went down to dinner for the first time, and sat on her husband's right. I was not the only one who was glad to see her. Even the women were pleased. She wore a pale green gown, and she came up out of it regally white and gold. I was so proud that I blushed when any one spoke of her. After dinner she was standing by her deck-chair talking to her husband when people began to go below for the concert. She took up a long cloak and attempted to put it on. The wind blew the light thing about, and Ebbling chatted and smiled his public smile while she struggled with it. Suddenly his roving eye caught sight of the Chicago girl, who was having a similar difficulty with her draperies, and he pranced half the length of the deck to assist her. I had been watching from the rail, and when she was left alone I threw my cigar away and wrapped Mrs. Ebbling up roughly.

"Don't go down," I begged. "Stay up here. I want to talk to you."

She hesitated a moment and looked at me thoughtfully. Then, with a sigh, she sat down. Every one hurried down to the saloon, and we were absolutely alone at last, behind the shelter of the stern, with the thick darkness all about us and a warm east wind rushing over the sea. I was too sore and angry to think. I leaned toward her, holding the arm of her chair with both hands, and began anywhere.

"You remember those two blue coasts out of Gibraltar? It shall be either one you choose, if you will come with me. I have not much money, but we shall get on somehow. There has got to be an end of this. We are neither one of us cowards, and this is humiliating, intolerable."

She sat looking down at her hands, and I pulled her chair impatiently toward me.

"I felt," she said at last, "that you were going to say something like this. You are sorry for me, and I don't wish to be pitied. You think Ebbling neglects me, but you are mistaken. He has had his disappointments, too. He wants children and a gay, hospitable house, and he is tied to a sick woman who can not get on with people. He has more to complain of than I have, and yet he bears with me. I am grateful to him, and there is no more to be said."

"Oh, isn't there?" I cried, "and I?"

She laid her hand entreatingly upon my arm. "Ah, you! you! Don't ask me to talk about that. You -- " Her fingers slipped down my coat sleeve to my hand and pressed it. I caught her two hands and held them, telling her I would never let them go.

"And you meant to leave me day after tomorrow, to say goodbye to me as you will to the other people on this boat? You meant to cut me adrift like this, with my heart on fire and all my life unspent in me?"

She sighed despondently. "I am willing to suffer -- whatever I must suffer -- to have had you," she answered simply. "I was ill -- and so lonely -- and it came so quickly and quietly. Ah, don't begrudge it to me! Do not leave me in bitterness. If I have been wrong, forgive me." She bowed her head and pressed my fingers entreatingly. A warm tear splashed on my hand. It occurred to me that she bore my anger as she bore little Carin's importunities, as she bore Ebbling. What a circle of pettiness she had about her! I fell back in my chair and my hands dropped at my side. I felt like a creature with its back broken. I asked her what she wished me to do.

215

"Don't ask me," she whispered. "There is nothing that we can do. I thought you knew that. You forget that -- that I am too ill to begin my life over. Even if there were nothing else in the way, that would be enough. And that is what has made it all possible, our loving each other, I mean. If I were well, we couldn't have had even this much. Don't reproach me. Hasn't it been at all pleasant to you to find me waiting for you every morning, to feel me thinking of you when you went to sleep? Every night I have watched the sea for you, as if it were mine and I had made it, and I have listened to the water rushing by you, full of sleep and youth and hope. And everything you had done or said during the day came back to me, and when I went to sleep it was only to feel you more. You see there was never any one else; I have never thought of any one in the dark but you." She spoke pleadingly, and her voice had sunk so low that I could scarcely hear her.

"And yet you will do nothing," I groaned. "You will dare nothing. You will give me nothing."

"Don't say that. When I leave you day after tomorrow, I shall have given you all my life. I can't tell you how, but it is true. There is something in each of us that does not belong to the family or to society, not even to ourselves. Sometimes it is given in marriage, and sometimes it is given in love, but oftener it is never given at all. We have nothing to do with giving or withholding it. It is a wild thing that sings in us once and flies away and never comes back, and mine has flown to you. When one loves like that, it is enough, somehow. The other things can go if they must. That is why I can live without you, and die without you."

I caught her hands and looked into her eyes that shone warm in the darkness. She shivered and whispered in a tone so different from any I ever heard from her before or afterward: "Do you grudge it to me? You are so young and strong, and you have everything before you. I shall have only a little while to want you in -- and I could want you forever and not weary." I kissed her hair, her cheeks, her lips, until her head fell forward on my shoulder and she put my face away with her soft, trembling fingers. She took my hand and held it close to her, in both her own. We sat silent, and the moments came and went, bringing us closer and closer, and the wind and water rushed by us, obliterating our tomorrows and all our yesterdays.

The next day Mrs. Ebbling kept her cabin, and I sat stupidly by her chair until dark, with the rugged little girl to keep me company, and an occasional nod from the engineer.

I saw Mrs. Ebbling again only for a few moments, when we were coming into the New York harbor. She wore a street dress and a hat, and these alone would have made her seem far away from me. She was very pale, and looked down when she spoke to me, as if she had been guilty of a wrong toward me. I have never been able to remember that interview without heartache and shame, but then I was too desperate to care about anything. I stood like a wooden post and let her approach me, let her speak to me, let her leave me. She came up to me as if it were a hard thing to do, and held out a little package, timidly, and her gloved hand shook as if she were afraid of me.

"I want to give you something," she said. "You will not want it now, so I shall ask you to keep it until you hear from me. You gave me your address a long time ago, when you were making that drawing. Some day I shall write to you and ask you to open this. You must not come to tell me goodbye this morning, but I shall be watching you when you go ashore. Please don't forget that."

I took the little box mechanically and thanked her. I think my eyes must have filled, for she uttered an exclamation of pity, touched my sleeve quickly, and left me. It was one of those strange, low, musical exclamations which meant everything and nothing, like the one that had thrilled me that night at Naples, and it was the last sound I ever heard from her lips.

An hour later I went on shore, one of those who crowded over the gangplank the moment it was lowered. But the next afternoon I wandered back to the docks and went on board the Germania. I asked for the engineer, and he came up in his shirt sleeves from the engine room. He was red and dishevelled, angry and voluble; his bright eye had a hard glint, and I did not once see his masterful smile. When he heard my inquiry he became profane. Mrs. Ebbling had sailed for Bremen on the Hobenstauffen that morning at eleven o'clock. She had decided to return by the northern route and pay a visit to her father in Finmark. She was in no condition to travel alone, he said. He evidently smarted under her extravagance. But who, he asked, with a blow of his fist on the rail, could stand between a woman and her whim? She had always been a wilful girl, and she had a doting father behind her. When she set her head with the wind, there was no holding her; she ought to have married the Arctic Ocean. I think Ebbling was still talking when I walked away.

I spent that winter in New York. My consular appointment hung fire (indeed, I did not pursue it with much enthusiasm), and I had a good many idle hours in which to think of Mrs. Ebbling. She had never mentioned the name of her father's village, and somehow I could never quite bring myself to go to the docks when Ebbling's boat was in and ask for news of her. More than once I made up my mind definitely to go to Finmark and take my chance at finding her; the shipping people would know where Ebbling came from. But I never went. I have often wondered why. When my resolve was made and my courage high, when I could almost feel myself approaching her, suddenly everything crumbled under me, and I fell back as I had done that night when I dropped her hands, after telling her, only a moment before, that I would never let them go.

In the twilight of a wet March day, when the gutters were running black outside and the Square was liquefying under crusts of dirty snow, the housekeeper brought me a damp letter which bore a blurred foreign postmark. It was from Niels Nannestad, who wrote that it was his sad duty to inform me that his daughter, Alexandra Ebbling, had died on the second day of February, in the twenty-sixth year of her age. Complying with her request, he inclosed a letter which she had written some days before her death.

I at last brought myself to break the seal of the second letter. It read thus:
"My Friend: --
You may open now the little package I gave you. May I ask you to keep it? I gave it to you because there is no one else who would care about it in just that way. Ever since I left you I have been thinking what it would be like to live a lifetime caring and being cared for like that. It was not the life I was meant to live, and yet, in a way, I have been living it ever since I first knew you.

"Of course you understand now why I could not go with you. I would have spoiled your life for you. Besides that, I was ill -- and I was too proud to give you the shadow of myself. I had much to give you, if you had come earlier. As it was, I was ashamed. Vanity sometimes saves us when nothing else will, and mine saved you. Thank you for everything. I hold this to my heart, where I once held your hand. Alexandra."

The dusk had thickened into night long before I got up from my chair and took the little box from its place in my desk drawer. I opened it and lifted out a thick coil, cut from where her hair grew thickest and brightest. It was tied firmly at one end, and when it fell over my arm it curled and clung about my sleeve like a living thing set free. How it gleamed, how it still gleams in the firelight! It was warm and softly scented under my lips, and stirred under my breath like seaweed in the tide. This, and a withered magnolia flower, and two pink sea shells; nothing more. And it was all twenty years ago!